BOOK ONE
IRVING WISHBUTT⬤N
—— AND THE ——
QUESTING ACADEMY

Irving Wishbutton: The Questing Academy
by Brian Clopper

Printed in the United States of America
Published by Behemoth Books on July 2012

Visit https://www.brianclopper.com

BOOK ONE

IRVING WISHBUTTON

— AND THE —

QUESTING ACADEMY

a novel by
BRIAN CLOPPER

Chapter 1
DRAWING A BLANK

His ideas came to him whenever his mind could escape from his day-to-day responsibilities. In the shower, an infrequent errand trip without his two children, even on the exercise bike when he didn't have the evening news on to distract him.

Today was such a day. He let his mind wander as he raced along on his stationary bike. For him, brainstorming held a special place in the writing process.

His mind drifted far afield from the items needed on the next grocery trip or last night's dishes that awaited him in the sink. He wanted to start a new project. He wanted the protagonist to show some depth. His mind gravitated as it always did to a tale of fantasy. He knew it had to be a quest story, but one where the character discovery was more important than the fanciful settings and unearthed relics.

He pressed his mind into action, searching for the name of his main character. He found if he could conjure up a good name, everything else fell into place.

When he stepped off the exercise bike, he didn't have it.

He wasn't worried. He would continue pondering, and the name would come to him. Once he had the name, he could map out his character's ups and downs and ins and outs with confidence.

He reset the calorie count on the bike, flipped off the lights, and allowed the duties of his day to work their way back to the forefront of his mind.

* * *

I blinked into existence atop a hill.

Beside me, another materialized. For some reason, I felt interest in the other's appearance more than my own. Although, truth be told, I hadn't a clue as to my own features. This thought flitted into my head, but didn't fill me with worry.

The person next to me had the head of a dog. I wondered how I knew what a dog looked like. I had never seen one before. Black fur, cropped short, combined with an elongated muzzle, made me think it was some type of hound. It was stocky and tightly packed into its spacesuit. Its helmet was tinted a slight purple. I resisted the urge to rap on the clear plastic. I had no desire to take action, only to observe. I, again, did not know why I knew the creature was wearing a spacesuit. I just did. This did not unsettle me.

Watching what happened around me made me feel comfortable. I took measure of my surroundings rather than inspect my own self. Perhaps I was dull. Maybe that was why I had forgotten the face I exposed to the world. Maybe I had been in some horrible accident and was grappling with a fit of amnesia and apathy. How I knew what these states of mind were should've bothered me. The fact that I suffered from them should've shaken me to my core. They didn't.

Instead, I took in my surroundings.

The dog astronaut was sniffing about, growing bothered by the limitations his helmet beset on his sense of smell. The dog purposefully scouted the area, pacing about as if measuring the space would give charmed meaning to our predicament.

I gauged the land. We stood atop a gently sloping hill. Tall grass blew about, hostage to a fickle breeze. We were in a park of some sort. I saw buildings in the distance. Their rooftops peeked over the trees that wedged themselves into a tight forest around the base of the hill. I sensed where we had arrived was special. Why that would be, I hadn't a clue.

The dog, much shorter than the grass, waded through it. He was oblivious to those who approached us with much hurry in their step.

Two lanky children, a boy and a girl, raced up the incline. They were upset. Their worry was contagious. Concern washed over me. Why was I here? Where had I been before? Tears streamed down my face. I could not recall my name.

The taller of the two, the boy, reached us first. He spoke between exaggerated breaths, "Goodness, you're early. That doesn't happen much."

The girl pushed her companion aside and kneeled to greet the dog astronaut. "Never happened before. Something's definitely atwitter here."

I noticed they wore school uniforms, white button-down shirts with black pants and a plaid skirt respectively. Both were burdened with thick glasses and pale skin. Very pale skin.

"Who are you?" I asked.

The girl patted the dog on his helmet and looked up at me. "Ah, what you should be asking yourself is that very same thing. That's the puzzler, isn't it?"

I frowned. Her words ripped at me. I felt very unnerved.

Not about the astronaut dog who I had mysteriously appeared atop a hill with.

Not about the very gaunt children that had rushed to meet us.

There was now an ache in me where none had been before. It flared inside, demanding to be examined.

I felt my jaw drop. "Who am I?"

Chapter 2
SMUDGED

He cursed the shorts. Once again, while buttoning a pair of khakis, he had popped a button. It wasn't a result of a pressing gut. He was thin for his age and his shorts fit fine. He just had rushed to undo the button. He was always in a hurry to get to the next task, never spending the proper time on any current duty. His wife always told him he got a lot done quickly, but it was mostly at the expense of completing a task thoroughly. It was why the dishes were always put away quite rapidly. But if one looked in the cabinet, the sacrifice was the inefficient way he stacked them. Rather he didn't stack them. He tossed them in their alcove, always causing a ruckus.

The button landed at his feet. He tore the shorts off and grabbed the button. Marching into the closet, he placed the wounded garment on a sewing pile, knowing it would be over a year before his wife would get to it. As he placed the errant button atop its shorts, he flashed on an idea.

He raced to his dresser to retrieve his brainstorming pad. He scrawled the phrase "wish button" on the blank page.

He didn't know it yet, but his clothing malfunction was about to give him the name of his new character.

He grabbed another pair of shorts, slipped them on and raced downstairs to throw the ball with his son, who was already waiting in the backyard, glove at the ready.

* * *

They took us through the woods.

I paid little attention to our surroundings. Panic over my identity had rooted deep.

"Why don't I know who I am?" I asked.

The boy kept his eyes on the path ahead. "Don't worry. It'll come to you."

"What's that supposed to mean? Is it amnesia? Where on Earth are we?" My voice wavered.

The girl walked alongside the dog astronaut. She smiled at the hound. "So, do you know your name, little one?"

The dog waddled along the path. "I didn't at first, but it came to me when that nit was hopping about, fretting over his."

"So, what is it?" She patted his little rocket pack.

"Tiberius Booster." The dog huffed, his breath momentarily fogging his helmet.

"Very regal. You aware of anything else?" While her skin was pale, her eyes shined a ripe yellow.

"I think I'm some sort of companion." He wrinkled his lips in concentration. "I'm not altogether sure. It's a little murky in my head right now."

"So space pooch here talks and knows his name," I said. "That's just great. Why can't I figure this out?"

Our boy guide stopped. "Don't get in a tizzy. Most protagonists take a while to figure it out."

The girl's eyes lit up. She leaned toward her associate, wringing her hands with vim. "Really, he could be a top dog? I've never escorted one onto the grounds before!"

Feeling overlooked, Tiberius broke in, "Hey, what about me? Aren't I a bit special? I knew my name, and he didn't."

The girl wagged her finger at the astronaut dog. "Now, now, no reason to get all hurt. You have your place in the plot."

The boy resumed walking. The trail grew rockier as it veered upward. He motioned for them to follow. "Hurry now, almost there."

"All will be explained once we reach the grounds." She kept her voice calm and contained. "Well, as much as can be expected. It all depends how long you remain a smudge."

I looked at the girl's partner. "What does that mean, a smudge?"

"It's nothing to get bothered about. You just haven't been fleshed out yet. It'll come in time. Sometimes the real greats take a wee bit to find themselves."

"Why am I a smudge?"

"Ooh, I know," said the dog. "It's because his face is all hazy, right? Like someone took an eraser to his features and tried to wipe them away." The dog paused and eyed me up and down. "Only, it's not just his face. The rest of him is all blurry too. Except for that red—"

The pale girl cut him off. "Now, now, that's enough out of you."

I looked down at my body, suddenly aware of my appearance or lack thereof. My body indeed wavered and fluctuated. I could not decipher my garments, only that I had two arms and a pair of legs. I was at a loss as to what I was wearing, even down to my footwear. I did notice a single red button placed at the center of my chest, the only thing in focus.

"That's a red button, right?" I asked to no one specifically.

"Appears so. Wonder what happens if you push it." It was clear the dog wanted to get a closer look at the crystal clear accessory but fought the urge to jump up and plant his paws on me.

"It's not that type of button. It's sewn on." I raised my hand to touch the curious object.

The pale girl took hold of my hand and guided it back down to my side. Her touch was icy cold. "Let's not go about experimenting willy-nilly just yet, okay?"

"B-But I . . ."

"Enough nattering," our male guide said. "We're almost there." He gestured to a wall of vines blocking our path, dancing his fingers about as if he were a magician enacting a spell on a stage curtain. I half expected the vines to be tugged out of the way by some unseen force.

"Get on with it." Her gruffness revealed her disdain for his theatrics.

"I can tell you one thing, you're a modern. You knew Tiberius here was wearing a spacesuit. " He reached decisively for the curtain of vines looming ahead of us. He pushed the foliage to the side.

"What?" I said. "What are you talking about? I—" Our destination no longer lurked behind the vines. It was exposed for all to see. My eyes went wide in wonder and fear.

I now knew what the rooftops I had seen earlier sheltered. The looming sign in front of us assigned purpose to the buildings. Mounted on a stone base and stretching upward an impressive height beyond the treetops, the sign declared:

The Questing Academy
We build characters!

Chapter 3
THE QUESTING ACADEMY

He found writing sporadically suited his lifestyle. He fit in half-hour to two-hour spurts of writing between his job and family. He taught at a year-round school and having time off for a couple weeks after each nine-week session allowed him to write in concentrated bursts. While tracked in and teaching, he did very little actual writing, only jotting down ideas for new books or sketching out plot points.

He gave much respect to the saying, "One should write about what they know, about what they experience." True, all his stories were escapist fantasies, but the character moments and details all came from the everyday actions of those around him. He found small inspirations in the most ordinary task.

Take for example tonight; while he had been helping his daughter with her spelling homework, he had been stopped cold by one of her words. Not because it was difficult to spell or seemed out of place with the other third grade words. No, the word spoke to him.

Specifically, it had given him the name of his villain.

He had announced the idea to his daughter who shared his enthusiasm for writing. She had smiled in a way that served as a pat on the back and launched back into her spelling exercises.

It didn't take much to please him. His daughter's curiosity about his talents as a writer had fueled his motivation to write his first book. Her confidence in his talents had helped him ride out the endless wave of rejections that had followed until the day when an agent had finally taken a chance on him. Three books later, she was still his primary audience.

He wrote "Teardrop" in his brainstorming pad. As an afterthought, he wrote a broad statement that had stuck with him since the morning, "Modern fantasy, but with a Victorian feel." He tucked the pad in his nightstand drawer and trekked back downstairs to see if his daughter had started her reading homework.

It reminded me of a college campus. My awareness of the comparison sent chills down my spine. I had a vague recollection of what a college would look like, but I knew I had not been to one. The idea had appeared in my mind almost as if it had been placed there mere seconds before we had arrived. I counted eight prominent structures, each with at least three floors. Topped with extremely slanted rooftops showcasing the salt and pepper shingles, the buildings didn't stand straight. They leaned here and there at angles that seemed architecturally unsound. The people carrying knapsacks and cradling books like prized possessions seemed indifferent to the precarious nature of the buildings they exited and entered. A few milled about on the large expanse of lawn at the center of the campus. The numerous buildings formed a perimeter around the well-tended lawn. Sidewalks cut across the green, transforming into wide cobblestone paths under the tall trees that seemed to protectively shield each building.

The girl tugged at my sleeve, or at least at the hazy area where my sleeve should be. "Come now. Have to get you to administration to enroll. Then there's the book store and housing. Oh, and Orientation begins promptly at 11:00. Doctor Ringle would be very upset if we got you there late." She looked up pensively, preoccupied by the many details that lined up on her mental checklist.

"This is a school?" I asked doubtfully.

"The finest of its kind," said the boy guide, motioning for us to follow him toward the largest building located at the far end of the mall.

A dark-skinned boy with white hair and golden eyes walked past us, chatting with a girl whose long bangs did a poor job of hiding her antennae. Neither gave me or the astronaut dog a second look. Even though I didn't have a clear grasp of my own appearance, I knew what I saw went beyond normal.

"What kind of school is this?" I said.

The girl guide stepped in front of me and walked backward, matching my speed so she could talk to me. It was then I noticed she favored her right leg. Stepping backwards made the limp on her left more pronounced. I didn't have a chance to ask her why. She rattled off her answer. "It's normal to be in the dark. Sorry we're being so cryptic about all this, but our job is strictly to bring you in. The fine folks at the building up ahead will fill you in on your disorientation. It's only temporary for most. You'll love Doctor Ringle. He'll put you in the know!"

Tiberius asked, "The sign mentioned a quest. What does that mean?"

She clenched her teeth, accenting the crimson of her lips and the unsettling dark coloration of her gums. "What I can say and what I want to say are two different things. I'd love to spill the beans, but the mucky-mucks feel there are others better trained to do so."

"So, all you can tell us is we're about to enroll here, and that my smudgy condition will clear up?" I said.

The boy started up the steps leading to the administration building. Numerous students sat on the steps. From how tightly we had to navigate through the crowd, it was clear this was a popular gathering spot on campus. The pale boy weaved a path through them with ease. "We said it should resolve itself. There are no guarantees. But my sister and I both hope you find suitable housing." Both guides glanced disturbingly to the left at a smaller building that had clearly seen years of neglect.

"Ah, so we find out something about you finally," I said.

The girl frowned at her partner. "Guilty. Nimrod here is my brother, but that's all you're getting from us until after your orientation, alright?"

I nodded and stepped into the halls of the administration building, unaware I was going to be served up to the most sickeningly sweet denizens of the academy.

Chapter 4
OFFICE OF FINE AUNTS

He stared at the microwave door. He could never get it fingerprint free. As soon as he wiped them off, they reappeared the very next time he used it. They were eternal, unforgiving. It drove him crazy.

He looked around the kitchen for something else to clean. He felt helpless. Not because there was so much to do.

There wasn't.

He was manufacturing tasks, attempting to avoid working on the Wishbutton project.

His wife had taken the kids to a birthday party at their favorite inflatable hangout, and he had the afternoon to himself. It should've been a perfect time to flesh out the novel. Instead, he found himself seeking distractions. It wasn't out of fear of creating. He knew the ideas would come as soon as he applied himself. It was really about momentum. In the early stages of a project, he was slow to start. Only after he began on the first few chapters did he catch the bug to eat, sleep, and breathe the concept.

He stowed away the cleaning spray and headed toward the family room. He landed on the couch, avoiding his brainstorming pad, which had been left unattended for well over an hour. He forced himself to grab the pad and not the remote. He had to buckle down and get some ideas to paper.

It was time to produce a name that would unleash inspiration.

It was time to boldly walk down the rollercoaster path of creation.

He unsheathed his pen.

Of course, it was at that moment the mail carrier decided to pay a visit. He tossed the pad aside and raced out to see what had been delivered. Ever since he was a child and his parents had gotten him several comic subscriptions, he had loved getting the mail. Even bills arriving at his doorstep gave him pleasure. Their regular appearance, as well as the weekly arrival of his magazine subscriptions, offered a predictable comfort. He thumbed through the new arrivals: electric bill,

pizza flyer, credit card offer, and the new issue of his favorite
entertainment magazine all dared him to take a closer look. He resisted
the urge. The novelty of discovery spent, he tossed them in the mail bin
on the counter for later inspection.

He grabbed the pad and pinned down his imagination. It was time
to get to work.

* * *

I was unnerved by the interior of the building. We made our way down
a stark, brightly lit hallway decorated with a few generic paintings and
bulletin boards. As our guides took us deeper, I noticed occasional
offices, all with their frosted glass doors closed. Our surroundings
didn't trigger a sense of alarm that danger lurked behind the next
corner. No, the notion that I knew what an office or administrative
building looked like despite having no concrete memory of ever being in
one, disarmed me. My awareness of what an office should be felt fresh
in my mind as if it had been inserted moments before our tour was
underway.

Finally, our guides brought us into a large open office space. A
main desk manned by a large woman separated us from a tidy array of
over a dozen cubicles. Each cubicle held another woman bent over a
desk rifling through paperwork.

There was a roped-off maze leading to the main desk. No one was
in line ahead of us. Our guides hopped over two rows of rope rather
than weave through the maze. I did the same. The astronaut dog did
not. Instead, he trotted back and forth through the maze, respecting
the order the ropes suggested.

The woman at the main desk didn't look up. She was rapidly
sorting forms into several different piles. The overabundance of rings
adorning her fingers didn't slow her down. Her hair, done up in a
bouffant bundle, teetered about, swaying at the slightest movement.

Our boy guide addressed her, "Got two for you, Aunt Midge."

"Lovely, lovely. Any of the sweeties know much about themselves?
Tell me we got at least one this week that's arrived Double F." She did
not look up from her paperwork. If anything, she sorted even faster as
she talked.

The sister spoke up. "Tiberius here seems to know his name. We think he's a supporting."

She leaned over the desk to look down at the canine. Her hair bobbed slightly. "What a sweet pooch. Love the get up. Very Buck Rogers."

I asked, "Who's Buck Rogers? What's Double F? Is she your aunt?"

Midge stood up, halting her collating. I was unsure if the scene was about to get ugly.

She smiled widely and clapped her hands together with affection. "Oh, sweetie, enough with the questions. We'll get you squared away as quickly as we can." She scanned up and down my hazy frame. "I'll send you to Nance. She's partial to you smudges. Her nephew was one when he came here, you know."

The girl guide responded, her tone a little syrupy and humoring. "Really? We didn't know."

Midge added, "Oh, my, yes. I bet she's got some recent pics. So you can see what a fine upstanding character he's fleshed out to be. Be sure to ask about her Neddy."

I turned to look at our guides. I only had my back to Aunt Midge for a second.

"Please do help yourself to a cookie or three before you settle in with Nance." Out of nowhere, she produced a sheet of chocolate chip cookies. She nodded for me to take some. Her hand was noticeably covered in an oven mitt that hadn't been there a second ago.

Feeling hungry, I snatched up four of them. They were still warm. I looked about for an oven nearby but spied no such appliance.

I noticed she didn't offer her baked goods to the others. So did my astronaut companion. "Hey, what gives? No snacks for me? I can't stomach anything with chocolate."

"Oh, heavens me. I wouldn't let such a handsome canine as yourself run off without some nourishment." Aunt Midge clucked an apology and reached under her desk. She retrieved a plastic bin of colorful doggy treats. She flicked three in the air with the expectation Tiberius would catch them. The treats rebounded off the dog's helmet and landed at the girl guide's feet. She gathered them up and presented them to Tiberius. The dog knowingly whipped out his tongue, touching a row of buttons on the inside of the helmet's collar. With a puff of air, his helmet slid open. He plucked the treats from her hand and gobbled them down. His tongue darted out and punched the same buttons in reverse. His helmet closed tight again.

Aunt Midge waved as our boy guide ushered Tiberius toward a cubicle on the far left.

The girl pushed me to the right. "Thanks, Aunt Midge. See you again soon."

"Always a pleasure, Roon. You and your brother owe me a visit to my front porch one of these evenings."

"Will do, ma'am. Promise." She looked annoyed, and I guessed why with ease.

"You didn't want me to hear your name, did you?"

She rolled her eyes, which looked exceptionally bloodshot. "Just let's get you to Aunt Nance. She'll handle you with kid's gloves, which is a lot nicer than I'm feeling like treating you right now."

I looked across the maze of cubicles. I noticed all the women had coiffed beehives of high hair, surpassing Midge's already towering hairdo.

"Which one's Nance? Are all of these ladies aunts? They're not all your aunts, are they? They can't be."

"You know, you're a curious one. Trust me when I tell you that can be good and bad here." She shivered, reliving something unsettling.

"At least tell me why I'm not a Double F," I persisted. "That sounded like something good. Is it?"

She guided me through the cubicles, keeping her eyes on a very yellow head of hair that reminded me of a banana.

I stopped. "C'mon, throw me something." I knew I was pushing my luck.

Roon pulled ahead of me, and despite her slender appearance, she easily yanked me the rest of the way to Nance's cubicle, almost depositing me face first in Nance's yellow mass of hair.

As she walked off, she didn't even look back. "It means fully formed. And that isn't all it's cracked up to be either."

I turned to present myself to Aunt Nance, clamoring for answers to a million questions.

Chapter 5
ANTSY NANCE

The ideas were trickling in. He was in no hurry to start the book. After all, he had four more weeks until the quarter was over. He slid deeper into the outdoor nylon chair that was a sideline hallmark of soccer games. On his lap, his son was busy coloring an alien. He resumed watching the game.

His mind wandered as he watched his daughter execute a cutback and drive the ball away from the aggressive player who had been hounding her throughout the game. He thought of hounds. The word trumpeted the notion of giving chase. His villain, Teardrop, had to have a pack of frothy pooches. They couldn't be ordinary. He also didn't want to go the cliché route of using a hellhound. He frowned. Too tied to traditional lore for his tastes. He started throwing together other name pairs as he cheered his daughter's team on. He liked the idea of strawhounds, as their Achilles' heel was obvious. Perhaps, too obvious. One flicker of flames would be enough to do them in. This set him on the trail of another notion. Maybe fire was the answer. He could use a pack of firehounds, but that seemed too similar to the hellhound.

Right when his wife was nudging him to pay attention to the action around the opposing team's goal, he had his slobbering mob of beasties. He cheered at the goal his daughter's teammate had scored, uncertain if his enthusiasm was for the events happening around him or for the creative victory that made his mind hum in satisfaction.

There would be emberhounds unleashed in the story. He imagined their characteristics as he helped his wife deliver the halftime snack of juicy orange slices to their daughter's hungry team.

* * *

Aunt Nance was a neat freak. She kept arranging objects on her desk to line up with guidelines only she could see as she talked to me. I think she moved her stapler three different places before I got out my answer to her first question.

"So how's your day been going, honey?" she asked.

I sat on the chair she scooted my way. "I can't say. I don't have much to compare it to."

"Feeling a little blank slate, are we?" She nodded, retrieving a clipboard with a packet of forms already hanging from it. She tipped her head forward, causing the wiry spectacles resting on her forehead to fall neatly into place. She adjusted the tilt of her small desk lamp, while scooping two paperclips from her middle desk drawer.

"Yeah, I know basic stuff, but I don't have any concrete memories. And that's not even addressing why I can't make out what I look like aside from this button." I reached to touch it.

Faster than I'd give her credit, she knocked my hand away from the only distinct feature on me. "Now, now, no messing with that until you know what it does. You don't know yet, do you?"

"Um, no. It's just a button."

She frowned as she sharpened her pencil to a lethal point. Not content to do just one task, she adjusted her chair height and removed two pieces of lint from her sleeve. She was in constant motion, which would've been distracting to me if it wasn't so purposeful. "Probably not. My guess is it's magical. Hopefully not of the doomsday variety."

"What do you mean?"

She patted my knee. "Oh, I'm sorry, sweetie. Didn't mean to get you all out of sorts."

"I've been not too sorted this whole time. When can I get some answers?"

"No problems there. You just give me your name, and we can start cluing you in." She placed pencil to paper, anticipating an immediate response.

When I didn't respond, she relocated her stapler to sit next to her desk lamp and lined up the extra push pins on her bulletin board from their current perfect equilateral triangle arrangement to that of a perfect letter N in the lower right corner, the only spot not covered by memos.

My silence pushed her into further activity. She couldn't stand not being occupied with something. She moved the stapler to the other side of her lamp. She tapped her pencil on the metal clamp of the clipboard five precise times. "That's understandable, dear. You're a smudge after all. We've got time. We can just sit here until you know."

I sat.

She, however, pulled a large file box from under her desk and began filing a stack of papers in the appropriate folders. She again moved the stapler, this time closer to allow easy retrieval. I watched her staple several forms together before having them disappear into the correct folders.

"So, we just sit here until I know who I am?"

She didn't take her eyes away from the filing. "Certainly. We have rules. I can't proceed until you know your name. Don't worry, we've got time."

"What about my orientation with Doctor Wiggle, is it? Isn't that next?"

"Doctor Ringle, dear, and he'll keep. He'd rather you come with your name. No sense showing up for orientation empty-handed. You miss this morning's, there's always tomorrow."

I didn't care for the idea of being stuck here all day. "Your nephew, they said he was a smudge. Did it take him long to figure himself out?"

She put the file box down and grabbed her hand bag, placing the stapler back next to her lamp yet again. She unzipped a side compartment and produced a small accordion slipcase of photos. She displayed her nephew's photo, beaming with pride. "Ned Firebreak, the best darn dragonslayer in all of the Archrealm."

I peered closer at her nephew. Ned wore elegant armor from head to toe. He held his helmet in one hand and an imposing lance in the other. He was smiling nervously. He looked all of thirteen. The odd thing was the eye patch. I wondered how someone his age had managed to lose an eye. It was out of place.

"Real shame about the eye, but that's what happens when you face off against a horde of quill tigers all by your lonesome. He did manage to rescue that particular princess."

"Is this place the Archrealm? Does your nephew go to this school?"

"Heavens no! This place is definitely not the Archrealm."

"Is your nephew still here? Did he graduate?" I said.

"If he had, I wouldn't be here talking with you, now would I?" She said it like it was the most obvious statement in the world.

"What do all these students study? What's a questing school?"

She smiled as she put away the photos. "Ah, you certainly like fishing for info, don't you? I bet your creator made you a curious one."

"My creator? What are you talking about?"

Embarrassed, she covered her mouth. "Dear me, look at that. You managed to get me to tell you several somethings. I have to say that doesn't happen often. I'm normally very tight-lipped until the time is right."

She resumed filing with a bit more passion than before, perhaps hoping to take her mind off her little leaks.

If I had been inside Nance's head at the time, I'd have seen how conflicted she was. It was beyond her why I would cause her to ignore regulations. She was the most steadfast of all the aunts. She had to be. It was written in stone.

She shook her head, hoping to clear her thoughts.

She shifted in her seat and gave me a stern, but loving look. "Nothing more out of me, sweetie, until you know your name."

I sunk into my chair, cursing my amnesia, but knowing it was more than memory loss. It was a trickle of a thought that came to me, but one that quickly grew bold and indisputable. I didn't know how I knew what I knew. I just did.

Deep down, I knew I didn't have any memories. I knew because they hadn't been given to me yet.

And that thought chilled me to the bone.

Chapter 6
TEMPERATURE DROP

Characters needed to have flaws. If his reader met his hero and the boy was perfect, then there wouldn't be much tension. Fears were a good source of character development. He thought back to his childhood. He cringed, recalling the rock garden incident involving his young friend, Freddie. It was still something he was ashamed about. He had handled it all wrong, attempting to hide the truth. It seemed only fitting to take such a defining experience and spice up his hero with it. It was decided. He would use a weakness he had plenty of experience with, hiding the truth and lying. After all, he hadn't learned his lesson with the rock incident. It had taken many repeat performances before the proper behavior had sunk in. It was also a trait many boys in his class exhibited when they got in trouble.

He made note of this new character wrinkle in his pad, clicked off the light and played his usual cat-and-mouse game with sleep. Tonight, it only took him forty minutes to settle his mind.

* * *

The sudden drop in temperature was immediate. While the realization of my lack of memories had thrown me, it was not what had me on the receiving end of some serious chills. The one responsible strolled up behind Aunt Nance, fully aware she had everyone's complete attention.

Everyone, except Aunt Nance.

While all the other women in the room looked up from their cubicles, stopping their work in mid-stride, Nance continued to plow through her ever-present to-do list.

I found I couldn't take my eyes off the office intruder. She was gorgeous.

It could've been any of her striking features or the sum of all of them: her lively blue eyes, the fullness of her lips, or the graceful slope to her shoulders.

The temperature in the room had dropped nearly ten degrees with her arrival and from the most breathtaking part of her appearance, it was clear why.

She was made of ice.

Aunt Nance, with her back to the ice girl, didn't look up from her filing. She had not noticed or was ignoring the abrupt climate change. I had a hunch she was ignoring the girl.

The ice girl spoke, her breath chilling the air. "Nance, you simply must tell me where he's run off to now."

"More than likely, as far away as possible from you, dear." She clearly knew who she was talking to without even looking.

The icy newcomer balled up her delicate fists. I noticed her garment was the same frigid pale blue as her skin. It also looked very elegant with embroidered snowflakes rimming her skirt and fluttering pleasantly around her knees.

"He's always playing games with me. I know it's your doing. You're trying to drive him away from me, I know you are." Her nose wrinkled to my mind quite pleasingly. She was adorably miffed.

"You're doing a splendid job of keeping him away all by yourself, dear." I could tell Aunt Nance was addressing her politely, even if her comments were a bit pointed.

"Er, hello." I braved a word, two words point of fact. Neither of which left any impression on her. I wanted her to look at me.

"Hello," she replied. Ignoring me, she directed her growing annoyance at Nance. "Answer me! I'm in dire straits."

Aunt Nance clutched her stapler, attempting to maintain focus on attaching a large swath of forms.

The ice maiden leaned in between us. I could feel the air temperature drop further. "Stop wasting my time! You know what I'm capable of."

Aunt Nance, still seated, whirled around to square off with the irritated girl. "I do indeed and that is why I will not help you locate my nephew. You know it's a breach of campus code for you to associate with him and yet you continue to seek him out. I'll give our creator points for your unflinching drive, witch, but I'll not see you further burrow your claws into my darling Neddy. He's not yours yet. Wait until your graduation and see who you end up with. I'll wager, if our scribe has half his wits about him, he'll not set you upon Ned."

The ice girl's tongue flashed over her bottom lip, creating a delicate rim of frost along the edge. "I can't help myself. He has to choose me. I have to have a happy ending."

"Oh, I have faith you'll have an ending, but not one to your liking if the fates are truly looking after Neddy." Aunt Nance made eye contact with me. "Now be off, you're distracting this young fellow who's about to tell me his name, aren't you?" Her smile coaxed a response from me. "You don't want me to report to Dean Harmstrike that you interfered in another's self-discovery, do you?"

"Oh, please, this piddly smudge isn't anywhere close to knowing his name. Looks like you got yourself another clueless nobody."

Despite her harsh assessment of me, I had a hard time bearing her any ill will. I wanted to protect her.

Nance continued to badger me. "Nonsense, he's found his name, haven't you?" She leaned closer to me, abandoning her file box to the floor.

I was unsure what to do next. I didn't want to disappoint Aunt Nance, who clearly wanted me to make a move. I also felt quite giddy about the girl who had intentions, whether they be good or bad, only for Nance's nephew.

"Well, do you have it yet, smudge?" the ice princess sneered. Her contempt for me was apparent, but I knew if she just took the time to get to know me, she'd feel differently. I wanted to run off with her and let her get to know the true me. Of course, with this realization came the nagging itch I couldn't scratch. I was a smudge with a button, and a garish oversized one at that. I still had no idea who I was and why I was here.

"Uh . . ."

She waved a frigid finger at me. "See, he's paralyzed. Just another creative misfire if you ask me."

"Oh, I'm confident he knows the right thing to do here." Nance winked warmly at me.

This simple gesture broke the spell. Whatever hold the ice maiden had on me evaporated. I realized what Nance wanted. I cleared my throat, sat up straight and lied through my teeth.

"I know it now. My name is William Featherwick."

The ice maiden fumed. She did not want to give up the spotlight. For a minute, the room temperature spiked upward. When she finally spoke, the chill returned to the air. "Fine. I'll leave you with your nobody who thinks they're somebody all because they trotted out their glorious name."

"Good riddance, dear. Give my regards to Toadswump."

The ice maiden left in a huff, averting her eyes from all in the room as she stomped out. I got the impression this was her usual method of departure.

Once absent from the offices, the temperature returned to normal and my infatuation with her fled.

I shook my head.

Seeming to know what I was experiencing, Nance consoled me. "There, there, child. Pay her no heed. Your attraction to her was manipulated, magnified by her magic. As soon as she left, you came to your senses, didn't you?"

I nodded.

"Her hold can be strong. One of the reasons I try to keep her away from my nephew."

"I don't understand. What just happened?"

"Don't worry about her. She's not meant for you. She's a paltry plot twist desperately trying to win the prize." Nance grabbed the clipboard holding my blank paperwork. "But she did reveal something about you."

"Oh, that name, I made it up. That's what you wanted me to do, right?"

Nance smiled. "Of course. But that's not what I'm talking about."

"But nothing came of that. I don't know anything new about me." I weakly thumped my fist on my chair arm.

"Not true. Not true. We found out something very telling."

"I don't see."

"You fooled a sly ice princess. You, my dear, have quite the convincing knack for lying."

I looked at Aunt Nance. I could see she spoke the truth. I was good at spinning lies. It didn't fill me with glee or satisfaction. Instead, it was a realization that robbed me of my perceived innocence.

I suddenly felt ashamed of what I knew about myself. I didn't like that my author had made one of my first traits a flaw.

"Don't fret. We'll order in dinner from the dining hall. I have a feeling you and I might be pulling an all-nighter." She snapped her fingers and a dragonfly nearly two feet in length zipped over to us from points unknown in the office. She whispered to it in a strange language comprised of clicks and hisses and set the insect off on its appointed duty.

She wagged a finger at me. "Relax. We'll sort this out soon. Your name is coming. I can sense it."

Deep down, I did too. I slid back in my chair, resigned to my fate.

Chapter 7
FOR NAME'S SAKE

*He returned to his brainstorming. He needed to create a name. He knew
the story was going to be about a wishbutton, but it wasn't clear what
the button would do for the person. He knew the main character would
have to wear the button. That it was going to almost be like a uniform
for him. He thought of names that had a Victorian flavor. One of his old
favorites, Ichabod Crane, nudged aside numerous others lifted from
some of his favorite adventures. He wanted his character to have a
classical name, but wasn't so pompous that it couldn't be playful.*

*He retraced the word "wish," adding ornate serifs to the plain
letters. He smiled. Why not have the character's last name be
Wishbutton? He liked that. Now to think of a first name. He dismissed
Connor and Carson as too modern. He liked using the first names of his
students for supporting characters. Perhaps Connor or Carson might see
the light in that respect. He ran through the rest of his class list. None of
their names had an older feel to them. Ichabod spoke to him so much
because it bestowed generous fumbling and ineptness to the character.*

*Irving leaped out at him. It was perfect. It conveyed shy
incompetence with a hint of hidden strengths. He wrote the name, Irving
Wishbutton the III, scratching out the Roman numeral almost as soon
as he had written it. Irving needed to stand on his own. Underneath the
name, he identified Master Wishbutton's overt trait: way too curious.*

* * *

It happened before the dragonfly creature returned with our meals.

Nance had resumed her filing, leaving me to my own devices.
Staring at the ceiling didn't help. Spinning around in my chair only
made me dizzy. Tapping summoned Nance's annoyance. I tried to zero
in on the key to getting Nance to answer my questions. I had to have a
name. Why was I so incomplete, so half-finished? No, correct that, not

even half-started. I knew this was true. I was empty. I wanted to be filled, but lacked the ability to do it myself.

A few cubicles away, I heard a high-pitched voice warbling on and on about themselves. I tried to look over the cubicle walls to see the voice's owner, but only saw two antennae bobbing about and the stationary and distinctive high hair of another office worker. The antennae moved about frantically. The speaker was obviously energized by her own self-discovery. The tower of hair periodically nodded.

One secret after another came spilling forth.

"I like taffy. In fact, I'm pretty addicted to all things candy."

Definitely a girl's voice.

Drawing a blank about myself, I became caught up in the other's disclosures.

"My little sister is missing in action. I'm pretty sure that I'll only be able to rescue her with the help of the Mighty Slip Jenkins. He's come to our glade as a part of his quest, and I have to convince him to rescue her."

There was the mention of a quest again. Was the girl describing an adventure she had already been on or one yet to be?

"I know I talk a lot. My brother says I'm a tidal wave talker, that I sweep away everyone else in a conversation." Her thoughts zigzagged. "My hair sparkles. Oh, this is so fun. Everything's coming so quickly, unlike yesterday. I'm so glad you told me I could come back to talk with you anytime. No one at my hall wants to hear about me, can you imagine that?"

Listening to her was frustrating. Her ramblings did not make anything clearer.

Her voice dropped. I detected sadness as she gulped out her next tidbit of awareness. "My mother died when the Toadstool Terrors ransacked our treehouse." She started to cry.

After that, her voice lowered to a whisper. Rather than strain to listen, I decided to respect her privacy.

Aunt Nance remarked, "Gerty's got a live one over there, hasn't she?"

"I thought you couldn't tell me anything until I figured out my name?"

"You heard what you heard. Nothing saying you can't dig a little in that patch of soil. What do you think's going on with that one?" She nodded in the direction of the cubicle with the antenna girl.

"It sounds like she needs someone's help. She's waiting on someone to come to her aid. A Slip Jenkins."

"Good. She can't do it alone. That's important to knowing what she is. Why do you think she's figuring out so much about herself?"

I bit my lip. "I don't know! This whole place makes me feel upside down." I let slip a weak growl.

Nance stopped working and looked into my eyes. There was warmth and intention in her gaze. "You're not some half-cooked notion. It won't be easy for you, dear. You will need others, but they will need you more."

Before we could deliberate further about my eavesdropping episode, it came to me.

My name had arrived.

I stood, sending my chair crashing against the close quarters of the cubicle wall behind me.

"I'm Irving Wishbutton!"

A spark had been set off. I had no recollection of my past, but I suddenly knew my name.

And much like the antenna girl, it filled me with excitement, with unlimited potential, and one wallop of dread.

Chapter 8
FINALLY, WITH SOME ANSWERS

An online search of the writer of The Headless Horseman had turned up Washington Irving. That explained why Irving had come to him so easily. He liked happy accidents. Because he had been so taken with Ichabod Crane, it had led to a superb character name for his little well wisher.

He glanced at the clock. His family would be home soon. He needed to get down more ideas. He looked at what he had written only minutes after he'd nailed the name. He had determined an early scene in the book would have the emberhounds sent to retrieve Irving from Earth. He had debated about using the setting of the backyard or a baseball practice. The practice won out. He hated when the fantasy goings-ons happened away from the character's public life. He wanted the world to see the unreality crashing down on Irving. He was debating if the hounds should cause any injury to the other teammates to indicate the stakes of the danger, when his children came bursting through the front door.

He smiled. Reality again took center stage. He would escape to Wishbutton's world soon enough. After all, his school break was only nine days away.

* * *

I thought Aunt Nance would be more impressed that I finally knew my name. Instead, she checked its spelling and filled out the first line of the form on her clipboard.

"Any other thoughts about yourself?"

"Um, not really, no. But knowing my name, that's good, right?" I offered.

"Very much so. It frees me to tell you a little more about where you've wound up."

The dragonfly courier returned at that moment with its food delivery. Aunt Nance signed for it, winking at the insect as it buzzed off. She retrieved two food boxes from the bag, handing the larger one to me. "Be sure to eat up. I know you must be starving. I'll talk while we eat."

I opened the food box and was greeted with the rich aroma of hot dogs and beans. A small cup of fresh fruit nearly spilled out of the box as I grabbed for the hot dog and took two big bites, my stomach grumbling. I had not realized how hungry I was. The cookies handed out by Aunt Midge had apparently not been enough.

"This is a unique school. You're about to be admitted to The Questing Academy."

"I saw the sign on the way in. Is this a place where heroes are trained?"

"Yes, that's done here and more. We take care of all cast members, no matter how big or small." Nance started in on her bowl of soup. The meat and veggies caught in her spoon were bizarrely bright colored.

"Why did I arrive here without any memories?" I asked. "Not everybody comes here like that. Tiberius, the dog who showed up with me, he knew who he was."

Nance said, "And that's to be expected. More than likely, he's a supporting character. They usually arrive more fleshed out."

I finished off my hot dog and popped the top on the fruit cup. "I don't follow. Characters?"

"All of us, we're characters. The university is a place where characters go to be educated."

I felt sick to my stomach and it wasn't from the food. I stopped eating. "What? What do you mean?"

"You are a creation of a writer. Upon conception, you showed up here. As your writer puts your story to paper, you'll find out more and more about yourself. This school is here to help you along your path."

"My path? What do you mean? You're saying I'm a character from a book?" I pushed the food aside.

"Why, your path to graduation."

"Graduation from a school that teaches characters how to act in their stories?" Even without any concrete memories or experiences, I found what she was saying hard to believe and downright strange.

"Ah, we don't show you how to act. That's written for you by your creator. No, we show you how to handle the twists and turns your author tosses at you. It's exhilarating and taxing at the same time."

"So, what am I?"

She remained calm as if she had encountered my reaction many times over. She drew a finger to her lips, assessing me thoughtfully. "Well, I have a knack for sizing up newcomers. I'd have to say you're one of the big guns. We haven't had one of your stature in some time. I'm going to say a hero. A grand protagonist to be remembered for ages."

If I hadn't already been sitting, I'm sure my legs would've chosen that moment to give out on me.

Chapter 9
INTERRUPTED

He still had no idea what the button would do for his hero, but that wasn't important to him yet. His mind had latched onto the emberhounds scene and wouldn't let go.

Throughout dinner, he had listened to his children narrate their acrobatics at the inflatable party. He had joked with them about their desserts having run off while they had been out of the house. As they played a challenging game of hot and cold to find where he had hidden their coveted chocolate, he thought about Irving and his emberhound problem. Irving had to already have the wishbutton on his person. The hounds could only find him because they were tuned to its scent. He'd have to write a sequence showing the boy obtaining the wishbutton almost from the beginning. This caused a conflict. Would Irving's name start out as Wishbutton, or would it be revealed later? He opted for later. He'd need a commonplace last name to brand him with at the start of the story.

His chocolate hide-and-seek game had led his kids upstairs, heading toward the laundry room where he had sequestered their chocolate bunnies. He joked with them about using their sniffers and not their peepers to locate their quarry.

His chocolate chase dovetailed with the hounds' refined senses. Leading his family on a merry chase, his mind tinkered with a scene about an unwitting hero being pursued.

As his children sniffed out their prize, he clicked off his writing mind and returned to his role as dad. They had found their bunnies and were demanding he tell them how much of their fluffy-tailed prey they could feed on. After telling them they could eat the ears and head, he walked them back down to the kitchen, keeping their chocolate-smeared hands away from the stairwell walls.

* * *

"It's perfectly natural to feel a little anger. It shows your creator has seen fit to give you some strong internal conflict," Aunt Nance announced.

I held her stapler high. She didn't grab for it. "Stop working!"

After we had finished our meals, Nance had continued to answer my questions. She also had resumed working. The outlandishness of my situation and how low-key she acted, continuing to work as she pacified me with pat answers, had me frazzled. I responded childishly.

Here I was, standing in my chair, brandishing her coveted fastener. The other aunts in the office mustered barely a glance my way.

"Your theatrics are perfectly normal. It's a lot to take in, and you're not quite yourself yet. These things take time." She paused. "May I have my stapler back?"

Her eyes radiated calm. I let my arm drop, placing the stapler on her lap. She left it unattended. Her focus was on me.

"Once you get out and about and meet others, it'll start to feel natural. The instructors here are marvelous."

"Are you a character?" I already knew the answer, but I wanted to hear it.

"Oh, yes. Everyone is. All of us in this office are a distinctive, nurturing type of supporting character."

"Which is?"

"We're aunts. The ones our nieces and nephews go to for a kind shoulder to lean on. Our warm demeanors make us perfect to work here in this office, helping new arrivals such as you adjust." She kept a bead on me while she deposited her food trash in the wastebasket under her desk.

"So, will I have an aunt here?"

"It depends. Some adventures don't use us. You'll find others from your cast, but probably not soon. You're still early on in the creative process. I doubt your author has done much more than conjure up your name."

At that moment, a pack of creatures crashed through the only window in the office. There were seven of them. Their features were smudged like my own, but they had enough shape for me to determine they were dogs. Despite not being fully formed, I knew what they were and had a vague sense why they were here.

"Those are emberhounds, and they want my wishbutton!" I shouted.

Registering my outburst, they crouched on all fours and looked in our direction. Immediately zeroing in on me, they growled and sprang.

Chapter 10

WITH THE PUSH OF A BUTTON

After tucking in his kids and watching TV with his wife, he settled into another round of brainstorming. This time, he was sketching. He still hadn't gotten down the workings of the wishbutton. He knew he didn't want it to infinitely grant wishes. It would be too powerful and make it too easy for Irving to get out of tight spots. He'd have to let the wishbutton's properties stew a little more before tackling it.

Tonight, he wanted to map out the appearance and abilities of the emberhounds. He played with the proportions of a Doberman, liking the trim look of their torsos. He added hints of reptilian scales concentrated along their back, but abandoned the texture. He enlarged the jaws, stuffing the mouth with rows of teeth like those of a shark. He ran upstairs and found his animal encyclopedia. He wanted the animals to have a crest of hair, maybe have it run down along the back to punk up the animal. He got sidetracked looking at the quills of a porcupine.

After searching through the book and finding nothing that caught his eye, he decked out the emberhound with a ragged upright row of purple and yellow fur patches along its spine.

He went back downstairs, snagged a plate of crackers, and began jotting notes next to his completed drawing of the emberhound. He needed to figure out what about the creature related to embers.

He took fifteen minutes more with his thoughts, committing many to paper. By the time he snuck up to bed, he had fully fleshed out a pack of nasties who would no doubt engage in a wicked game of fetch with Irving.

* * *

Aunt Nance leaped into action.

For a woman of her age and size, she moved swiftly toward the hallway marked with an exit sign. Was she retreating? Even with not having known her very long, I couldn't picture her withdrawing.

Although, when I looked at what was bearing down on me, I didn't blame her.

What I found odd about the attacking beasts was their sudden defined appearance. When they crashed through the window, they had been smudges like me, indistinct and in a fog. As they had loped toward me, their features had shifted sharply into focus.

The beasts were all muscle, sleek and mean. Utterly nasty things.

I would've preferred for them to have stayed blurs.

Their fur held a black sheen, except for ridges of yellow and purple hair patches that stood on end along their spines. For a second, scales and rows of nasty quills appeared along their sides, but just as quickly disappeared. Their ears were tight against their skulls as they let loose with calculated roars. Their monstrous outbursts should've been enough to terrify me, but when I saw what was in their snapping jaws, I lost it. I had never seen so many teeth before. Granted, I was short on real-world experiences at the moment, but I was certain the multitude of pointy incisors contained in the mouths of each hound went beyond extreme.

Aunt Nance shouted at me from the hallway. "Whatever they are, they're not fully formed! See how their features are coming and going. Your author must be working on them as we speak. Don't just stand there, defend yourself, Irving!"

She hadn't left after all. She wrestled with something obscured by the doorframe. She tugged at it, propping up one leg against the wall for leverage. Embarrassment colored my face as I saw her support hose only went up to below her knees. She made for an unusual action hero. I sensed she was mounting a rescue attempt.

If she could think on her feet, I reasoned that I could too. She had said I was supposed to be some high-and-mighty hero. Even though I had my doubts about her revelation that I was some divine character from a storybook, I should at least be able to act like one.

In seconds they would be on me. I looked for something to defend myself. The scant office supplies available to me in Nance's cubicle were nowhere near lethal. What was I going to do, staple them within an inch of their lives? Even my chair was dinky and insubstantial. Despite its inadequacy as a weapon, I went with the chair. Grabbing it by its high back, I swung it around. The hound that got to me first slammed into the three-pronged metal legs of the wheeled furniture.

Rather than knocking the hound to the side, the chair melted on contact.

The hound landed on Nance's desk, its claws scrambling for purchase. Paperwork went everywhere. Surprisingly, nothing burned from the touch of its paws. A few forms fluttered to rest on the hound's muzzle. They ignited into flames.

"Their heads are hot!" Pleased with my discovery, I spared a glance at Aunt Nance, hoping she would acknowledge my observation.

She charged down the hall, returning to the office with a large red fire extinguisher in tow. It looked heavy and cumbersome, but she carried it like it weighed nothing at all. "I figured as much when you identified them as emberhounds. You might want to duck."

"What? Why?"

Aunt Nance didn't have time to answer. She hurdled over the far cubicle wall, pointed the fire extinguisher at the nearest hound and let loose a geyser of foam. The dog took it square in the face. Steam engulfed us. I cringed and covered my eyes. Thinking the dog would not be stopped so easily, I tried to exit the cubicle on all fours.

"Stay put. That seems to have done the job." Aunt Nance stood over the still form of the lead hound. It was unconscious. "I think snuffing out its head knocked it out, but I don't know for how long. Let me take care of the rest of the pack and I'll call whoever's on duty over at the Menagerie to come get them."

Before I could respond, three of the remaining hounds knocked Nance to the ground, the impact of such severity that the extinguisher flew several cubicles out of reach.

Two of the hounds had her pinned to the ground, drooping their muzzles dangerously close to her face. I could only imagine the heat coming off their heads. The remaining dogs circled around their unconscious leader, eyeing me with hatred.

She said, "Look's like it's your turn, sweetie."

I stared at her. What on Earth could I do? My pathetic chair defense had failed. I had no other weapons at my disposal. I felt out of my league. These emberhounds had such purpose in their actions. Why were they more fully formed and motivated than me? What could I do?

The circling hounds never took their eyes off me. Scratch that, it wasn't so much they were trying to stare me down; they weren't even looking me in the eyes. Their gaze never strayed from my wishbutton.

That was why they were here. I felt that quite strongly. Probably one of the first concrete feelings I had experienced since my arrival.

Their gaze told me their intentions, but it also told me something else. They were afraid of the wishbutton. Each dog coveted what I had, but they also were terrified of it.

In that instant, I knew what to do.

"You want this so badly, then let's see what happens when I. . ." I paused. I didn't know what to say to finish my thought, but I did know where I was going with my threat.

I pushed the button.

Nothing happened.

It was then, the emberhounds started snickering.

Chapter 11
POPSICLE POOCHES

He didn't want the wishbutton to work like a birthday wish. He also wanted to stay away from anything genie inspired.

He tapped his feet as he waited in line at the grocery store.

The wishbutton was a crucial element in the story. Should he have Irving only be able to use it once? Would the wishes materialize exactly as worded?

He paid for his items and wheeled the cart out of the store.

Did the wishes need a trigger? Did he have to offer up something? Eat something? Perform a task for an ancient race of fussy elder gods? Was the wishbutton stolen merchandise?

He suddenly thought of a place, Wish Haven. Would that be something that made sense in his story? Would Irving have to go to Wish Haven? Why?

He loved all the questions ricocheting through his head. There was a manic energy to the process that made him feel alert and engaged. It had him curious and motivated. When he got home, he'd write Wish Haven on his pad and try to nurture the idea. He had a hunch it would help him figure out the wish power if he spent some time fleshing out what Wish Haven would be.

He slammed shut the hatch of the van and returned his thoughts to the two other errands he had to run before picking up lunch for the family at their favorite pizza place.

* * *

The dogs started toward me. Even the two atop Aunt Nance had abandoned her and were approaching me from the right. The pack's eyes were cold and unwavering. They intended to take the wishbutton from me, and it was clear keeping me alive was not part of their plan.

I scrambled up on Nance's desk, casting glances into the other cubicles for anything with which to arm myself. Finding nothing nearby, I spied a watercooler wedged between two vending machines. Could it be that easy? Could I put a stop to these fiery intruders with a good dousing?

I awkwardly jumped toward the cooler, sailing over two cubicles before crashing into a very firm cubicle wall. The workspace was occupied by an aunt dolled up in a flower print dress that barely stretched across her wide frame. The other occupant, a giraffe-headed boy weighed down with a plunger he held like a sword, rushed to protect the aunt. Was he a hero too?

Two emberhounds landed in the cubicle. One grazed its skull against the bulletin board above me as it sought to pounce on me. The memo-swamped board and the cubicle wall holding it burst into flames as the hound's front paws came down hard on my chest.

I squirmed free of the emberhound, rolling away from the heat of the flames that were igniting the entire cubicle. The giraffe boy rushed his aunt away from our fight.

The hound's head slammed into the wishbutton. Expecting to experience an unbearable heat, I was surprised when I wasn't reduced to a molten puddle. The button even looked unaffected. Maybe it acted as a force field. I wasn't satisfied with that answer. After all, I could feel the heat coming off the emberhound. I couldn't risk any more time pondering this turn of events. The hound backed away, equally perplexed at my resistance to his hot head.

Taking advantage of this, I vaulted out of the cubicle and made haste to the watercooler. I hugged the clear plastic top and tugged. The large jug separated from its bottom half, spilling a sizeable amount of water as I attempted to turn it right side up.

The emberhounds had again regrouped and were creeping down the main walkway between the workspaces. I doubted my wishbutton could protect me if they all attacked in unison.

My plans were very immediate. I wasn't thinking two steps ahead. Was that because of my inexperience? Was being a freshly formed character the reason why I couldn't handle extensive strategizing? Or was it simply the situation? A surprise attack by a pack of smoldering dogs didn't lend itself to thinking too clearly. Was I going to pour water on them as they charged toward me? There was no way I could soak them all before they knocked my water weapon out of my hands. I pressed on the sides of the watercooler. The plastic had plenty of give.

Maybe it would burst on impact if I threw the whole thing into the middle of them.

I swung the container backward, bracing my legs for the toss. It was heavy, but I was confident I could fling it a few yards.

I hurled with all my might, letting loose with a wrenching grunt. My muscles strained as I released the water grenade toward my target.

At such close range, the emberhounds didn't have time to react. I shrunk back, raising my arms protectively.

The watercooler landed three feet in front of my vicious assailants. Water didn't spill all over the dogs.

Instead, the container took a bounce, sending it in a wide arc over the pack and rolling to a stop along the far wall. As it came to a rest, a steady stream of water chugged harmlessly from the spout, soaking the carpet.

The emberhounds bore down on me. With no escape route apparent to me, I fell to my knees and held my hands up to fend off the creatures.

Any second, their claws would rake across my forearms as they burrowed their furnace-hot faces into my tiny frame. Wishbutton or not, I wouldn't survive this onslaught.

A booming voice shouted, "Enough!"

It was not one of the aunts. The voice was very deep and decidedly male.

The emberhounds never closed the three-foot gap between us. I looked up to see the six hounds frozen in mid-air. They emitted a blue glow that hadn't been there before.

A man dressed in a suit and tie carrying a device that resembled a toaster married to a bazooka walked down the aisle, checking on the safety of each aunt as he passed them by. From the way the aunts fawned all over his noble gesture, it was clear he was a figure of authority. A lazy curl of glowing blue energy trailed from his weapon as he ducked under the popsicle pooches.

"That's enough destruction of property for one day, don't you think, smudge?" He frowned at me.

"Umm," I said.

"So much for making a good first impression, huh?"

My tongue froze.

Ignoring my mute status, he spun neatly around and talked into a walkie-talkie that had slid out from his jacket sleeve. "Harmstrike to

Menagerie." He didn't wait for a response. "Fetch a containment crew over to the Administration building. Got some nasty beasts here. Also, send to my office whoever was in charge today. I wish to have words with them over the lax protocols that resulted in this mess."

I heard the person on the other end issue a terse affirmative.

He set his weapon on a nearby desk and dusted off his hands. He extended one and smiled coldly. "Dean Harmstrike, young smudge. Welcome to my academy. After the events of today, I believe an audience with me is in order, don't you think?"

I nodded. The dean taking such a keen interest somehow frightened me more than the pack of hot-headed hounds. I felt like an even larger target as I said goodbye to Aunt Nance and followed Dean Harmstrike out of the building.

Chapter 12
SPECIAL INTEREST

They were engaged in a game of word play. He couldn't remember how they had gotten on the topic, but here they were. He had made a comment about stealing his daughter's nose. She had giggled at the idea and asked him what he was going to do with it. He hadn't intended to make a joke involving the simplistic game of "Got Your Nose," but once he brought up the nostril napping, he couldn't resist pointing out the connection. She doubled over, laughing hysterically. His wife smiled and rolled her eyes at his groan-inducing humor.

Luckily, his children were still at the age where they found him hilarious. He knew he didn't have that much time left before their funny bones grew too sophisticated and their wonder would switch to embarrassment.

The simple act of being silly with his kids caused his brain to make several leaps. It jumped into focus. He had the premise for Wish Haven. When a wish or dream is stolen or taken away from someone, it is recovered by wish agents who take the wish to Wish Haven. Once a wish is stripped from someone, it can never be reacquired. The person may pine for it, but their wish will be different if they evoke it again. It would be slightly jaded by the fact that it was a rewish.

His brain hurt. The logic of the idea bore down on his thoughts a bit too heavily. He'd have to develop it more, but he had his breakthrough.

Irving would be a wish agent. The wishbutton wasn't for his wishes. It was for wishes he had been sent to fetch. He couldn't use them for his own gain. That would break the wellwisher code.

He got up from the table, pretending to hold his daughter's nose hostage in his left hand. He dashed into the dining room. Both children took up pursuit. His son, perhaps because he was younger, threw himself into the endeavor with more commitment. His daughter played along, but he could sense she was not as impressed with his nose feat as her brother.

Regardless, he led them on a merry chase. He added one more painful pun about being on the run with her nose.

Both his daughter and wife groaned out loud at that one. He smiled and allowed himself to be caught booger-handed.

Their wrestling became a tangle of giggles and gasps.

* * *

He ushered me into his office. It was wall-to-wall bookcases. The only wall area absent from organized shelves of books lurked behind his desk. Two large windows managed a wide view of the campus. Thick red drapes hemmed the windows. Despite the windows being huge, they appeared crowded, overwhelmed by the books in the room. My escort sat down in a high back chair lording over the desk and gestured for me to take the smaller seat on the other side of the desk.

I sat on the chair edge.

"You like my office?" He waved a hand, drawing attention to the books packed into the room.

"It's nice."

"I am Dean Harmstrike." He held up a folder from his desk. "Nance sent over your file. Rather thin, but that's to be expected."

I listened.

"Irving Wishbutton. That would explain the only gaudy artifact on your person." He dismissively pointed two fingers at my chest. "You see yourself as one of the greats?"

"I'm not sure . . ."

He rose and walked to the nearest bookcase. "Everyone who's met you so far has been impressed." He paused, retrieving a book with a green spine from a shelf at eye level.

"I can't say I've done much."

"I would say too much. I detest those who draw attention to themselves so early on. Usually they're the showy, but simple ones." He waited for me to respond.

"I'm not altogether sure why I'm here. Is this place for real?"

The dean paced over to me, leaning down to peer into my eyes. He held the book open with one hand, but I couldn't see its contents. "Our academy builds characters. We are a vital part of the creative process. Your story is being written as we speak. While it is in the hands of your author, you are here, being trained in the basics of how to survive the perils of fiction."

"But how did this school get here?" I looked out the window at the sprawling campus.

He ignored my question. He snapped shut the book, waving it in my face. "This book, as well as all the others in my office, do you know what they are?"

"I don't . . ."

He slammed the book down on his desk. "They are my graduates! All of these spines are students who have come through the academy. I know the titles of their stories, all of them!" He swept his hand about possessively.

"That's good!"

"Oh, I suppose." His voice wound down. "While they're here, I make it a point to get to know everybody who sets foot on my campus."

"Uh-huh." I didn't see me cultivating a chummy relationship with him.

"I work tirelessly at being aware of the goings-on here. It is, after all, what I was created to do." He pressed the book into my hands. "Tell me the title. Go ahead. I'll tell you all about the student."

I looked at the spine. The title was written in flowing cursive. "The Deplorable Destiny of Wilson Hammerfudge."

"Wilson was a smudge like yourself when he arrived. Of course, he didn't draw much attention to himself. Very inward boy. Went to classes, gained a noble appearance after the first week. He was very involved in our clubs. Spoken highly about by his housemates. He learned how to be a hero without mucking about."

"Sounds like a perfect student."

"Yes, he was." He paused, his face momentarily revealing sadness. "Open his book."

I flipped through the pages. Every single one was blank. "There's nothing here."

"Therein lies my pain. While here, I work so hard to help them to know themselves. It's a thankless job for as you see, when they graduate, empty books appear to mark they have been published."

"They just poof into existence in your office?"

"Yes. Sounds quaint, I know, but that's one of the apparent rules of this place. Their story exists on the printed page out in reality. Here, we get a memento of their time at the academy with the title of their quest wrapped around blank pages." He retrieved the book and returned it to the shelf.

"That's horrible."

"Yes, it is." He paused, lingering at his window to look at the students populating his campus. "I get to know everyone here, even down to the random background characters that service the plot by opening a door or standing guard on a rainy tower. They all are vital to telling the story."

I gripped the arms of my chair.

Harmstrike didn't look back at me. "I take special interest in only a handful of students."

"I see."

"Some of my special projects, they're good. And some are bad."

"I don't think I'm a villain."

He turned and glared at me. "Oh, I didn't say you were. You're a hero. There's no doubt in my mind, you're a hero. I was talking about your aptitude as a student. Young Master Wishbutton, you need to be one of the good ones. You don't want to suffer from poor judgment."

Before I could answer, a boy with a noodle for a head, burst into the room. Perched on his shoulder was a brilliantly colored bird. "You desired to see me, Dean Harmstrike?"

Harmstrike rolled his eyes and shook his head. "If you are the one who was watching over the Menagerie this morning, then yes."

The new arrival sunk his head into his shoulders and raised his left hand meekly. "Guilty."

The dean's didin't look at me as he addressed me one final time. "Wishbutton, I will keep tabs on your progress. There's a fellow smudge waiting outside. She will see you to your housing. Do try to end your day much less remarkably than you began it, will you?"

I nodded and slunk out of the office, hoping I'd never have to endure a return visit.

Chapter 13
A FAIRY'S FLURRY

He was on a roll. Ever since coming up with the Wish Haven setting, ideas had come charging out of his head onto the paper with ease. With only a week to go before he tracked out, it was perfect timing. He'd start writing the book during the three-week break. He always managed to squeeze in one or two hours a day to write when he was home with his children.

Their trip to the store had taken longer than expected. He had finished shopping for groceries with his son and was waiting in the van for his wife and daughter to finish their end of the shopping. His wife took longer, mostly because she hunted down the out-of-the-ordinary items they needed to run the household. His task, the groceries, ran more on autopilot. He bought the same ingredients to create their meals each week. Heaven forbid they deviate from Taco Tuesday or the Friday sacrifice of spaghetti noodles to satisfy his daughter's number one craving.

His wife, however, sought out the more unique items, such as band-aids, vitamins, new towels, or whatever supplies the kids needed for their school projects. She also knew when they outgrew their pants, which happened more and more.

He always brought a book or his pad for times like this. While his son played with his newest action figure in the back, he let loose his creativity onto the blank page.

Irving was going to get yanked to Wish Haven too soon. Without a guide, he was going to cause quite a few incidents. When the higher-ups in charge of the wish agents finally got a hold of him, they'd lay into him about all the trouble he had caused. Irving would try to lie his way out of it.

He paused. This presented a problem. If the lying was too obnoxious, Irving would come across as bratty and spoiled. He'd have to be careful and make it a lie of necessity.

He was interrupted by his daughter rapping on his window. Startled, his pencil flew out of his hand.

He smiled and helped them load the van.

In one short week, the world of Wish Haven would open up to him and he'd make some major headway into the story of one Irving Wishbutton.

* * *

I exited the dean's office without looking back. Standing in the foyer was the antenna girl from the Office of Fine Aunts. Her antennae swayed like cattails on a summer breeze. It didn't bother me that I knew what cattails were, even though I had no recollection of roaming through pond-friendly landscapes. I chalked it up to my author embedding some basic knowledge into me. Her hair was pink and draped over her shoulders in thick tresses. A butterfly hairclip, at least I suspected it to be a stationary item of grooming and not an actual perched insect, held her hair back from her face on her left side. Translucent wings arched from her back, their emerald and black pattern resembling stained glass. They rose behind her, cresting well past her antenna. I didn't recall seeing her wings back at the administration building. Her lips were thin and readily creased into a smile. Other than that, everything else about her was smudged. Her eyes, nose, arms, torso, and legs existed in a haze, much like me. She resembled a fogged fairy.

"You're a smudge too?" I asked.

She nodded. "You're the guy who got attacked by that nasty pack of dogs." She moved about, aflutter with energy. Her wings were in constant movement. I found the breeze she produced pleasant.

"Those wings, they're new?"

She smiled, pleased I had noticed. "They are. Popped into place on my walk over to fetch you. Aren't they just charming? I knew I was meant to be skybound." She clamped her hands together. Perhaps because of their undefined nature, they didn't produce a distinct clap, only a muffled thump.

"I'm Irving Wishbutton." I extended my own blurry hand.

Her mouth drew into an oval of surprise. Her body movements grew still. Even her wings came to a halt. She looked at my hand and her own indistinct palm. I didn't know whether to withdraw my hand or not. Had I offended her?

She shrugged and slid her hand out to meet mine. We shook. The sensation was odd. It felt like we had made contact, but also that our hands had become embedded and intertwined. When we pulled back from the handshake, our uncertain fingers stuck for just a moment. Cobwebs like those left behind by tacky chewing gum stretched into nothingness between our retreating hands. It was not painful, just disturbing.

Despite her face being a smudge, I witnessed her cheeks reddening. "Kind of an unspoken rule. Smudges keep contact to a minimum. When we touch, we tend to mix together. I found that out the hard way when I hugged my roommate. Took us most of an afternoon to untangle ourselves."

"Why'd you shake hands then?"

"I thought it might be different. Guess not. It wasn't all bad. A little tingly and with much less panic."

"Made me feel like I'd dunked my hand in taffy."

"Yeah, that too." She resumed her manic actions. She performed a neat spin and angled toward the door leading away from Dean Harmstrike's office. Even though her feet were just as muddled as the rest of her, I got the impression she spent most of her waking and walking moments on her tiptoes. "Come on. Let me give you a quick look-see around campus."

"Wait, I don't know your name." I stumbled toward her.

Her hands covered her mouth playfully. "Oh, that's right. You're all obsessed about names right now. I remember a time when I was like that. All caught up in the importance of finding out my name and demanding the identity of those around me."

"Was it that long ago?"

She beamed. "Just yesterday. I thought it was so incredibly important then. That seems so far behind me now."

"Yeah, that sounds absolutely ancient." I sighed and walked out the door with her.

"It's Sarya Lorn of the Harvest Village." She flitted down the steps and flapped her wings expectantly. "Now c'mon, I wanna show you around a bit and get back to the house in time for lunch."

She led the way, and I gave pursuit. She had promised a whirlwind tour, and I was fearful that was exactly what I was going to get.

Chapter 14
TOUR DE WORSE

So much of his writing dealt with bullies. He knew the bullies from his childhood had been constants. They had popped up here and there, but he wouldn't say he defined his difficulties in life from the encounters. Two of his self-published stories had dealt with bullies. It was an interesting plot device, but he wasn't on a crusade to right the wrongs of the bullying that had been visited on him.

In his classroom, he tried to remain vigilant with any social or physical bullying, but it was sometimes hard. It mostly happened during the more unstructured times, recess and lunch. Whitney's outburst in his classroom today he had dealt with sensitively, he thought. She had been upset over Lauren and Melissa including her one minute and excluding her the next. Her frustration had come to a head in reading groups when Melissa had saved a seat for Lauren, but not for her.

The social power play between girls was sometimes brutal. Two girls together were fine. Throw in one more, and the newly formed threesome had trouble.

He glanced at his daughter doing her homework and hoped she would be spared the bullying. He knew the next few years were a minefield of possible encounters. He knew it would be hard to avoid. He also hoped she would never be on the giving end of unfairness or hostility. Did parents of bullies know of their children's wrongdoing?

He was uncertain if Irving would face a bully, but he knew Irving would be a little bullheaded about it and side with the victims.

He grabbed a post-it note from the junk drawer and jotted a character note: **Irving wouldn't turn the other cheek.**

* * *

She skipped across the wide expanse of green, stopping only when she arrived at the intersection of two diagonal walkways that crossed the large mall. She had been silent the whole time. I didn't dare try to ferret out any information, sensing her conversational floodgates were about to open.

Arriving at a spot she deemed sufficient to be our starting point, she whirled around and waved her hands about expansively. "This is the exact center of The Questing Academy. Here, on the mall, we can see most of the buildings that house our classrooms."

She took a breath and waved toward the buildings. From her more restrained wrist motions, I could tell she was indicating what lie on the outskirts of the campus. She waved only her left hand. "Beyond those classroom buildings are the larger dorms, home to supporting characters and window dressing."

"Uh, what's window dressing?" I tried to see what structures lay beyond the classroom buildings, but a line of healthy trees blocked my view. All I was awarded with were glimpses of an occasional rooftop.

"The characters in the story that perform a simple task. You know, like answering the door or milking a cow. They're strictly background, functional, but not altogether very remarkable."

"Oh. What are their buildings like?"

She thrust her hands on her hips and leaned toward me. She frowned. "Not important right now."

I smiled sheepishly. Since I was a smudge, I was uncertain whether she could read my expression. "Continue with your tour."

She skipped toward the right and fanned out her vague fingers. "Over here, past the dining halls, are Hero Row and Villainy Way. Major happenings going on there. I hear it's the place to be."

I nodded.

Irritated I was not more impressed with her opinion, she flicked her antennae toward the building across the mall from the dean's office. "That's the library."

It was the largest building on the campus. Ornate stonework around the windows and tall columns framing the entryway gave it a dignified appearance. The stone gargoyles rimming the ledge around the four turreted corners of the building imparted a sinister air to the place.

She gave me little time to inspect the architecture. Gesturing at the other end of the mall, back at the one we had exited, she reported, "We just came from those administrative buildings. The bookstore's in the lower level of the dean's building. Oh, the stadium is back that way, too. I've not been yet. No tournaments are scheduled during the weekdays."

I was about to ask her what type of tournaments when Sarya found herself at a loss for words.

This was most likely due to her being knocked to the pavement by a large troll and his companion, who was decked out in golden armor. Although my back had been turned to her and I had not seen the incident, I sensed she had been deliberately driven to the ground.

Their words confirmed it.

"Really mustn't block the walkways, smudge. Some of us have busy schedules." The golden knight, his eyes a deep blue and his blond hair flowing past his strong cheek bones, strode on by. He patted his troll companion on his upper arm. "Thanks for clearing the path, old friend."

The knight brushed against my shoulder as I reached to help Sarya up.

My fairy guide declined my aid, perhaps not wishing to repeat our handshake knot from before. She rose on her own, fluttering her wings contemptuously. She turned away from the pair.

"He just knocked you over!" I said.

"Don't worry about it. Not my first run-in with those two trolls," Sarya replied.

"Well, I think only one of them is a troll. The other looks to be a human like me."

Her head sagged. "I hope he's nothing like you. Don't tell me you aspire to be vile and full of yourself, do you?"

Perhaps inspired by her words, the desire to make things right swelled within me. I shouted the duo down. "Hey, you owe her an apology!"

The troll shot me a foul look. The knight didn't glance back.

I took two steps toward them. I cupped my hands around my mouth to better project my displeasure. "I said you owe her an apology! Get back here!"

This stopped the knight in mid-step. With grace, he spun around and walked casually back toward us.

He presented himself, holding his chin up. He looked me over. "Ah, the button boy. I've heard of you. Made quite a show at administration. Heard Harmstrike had to intervene." He leaned closer and whispered, "You know, a true hero cleans up his own mess."

"You don't knock someone over and just continue on your way. Who do you think you are?" I felt him inspecting my wishbutton.

The knight frowned. "Oh, dear, you really are poorly defined. Just a wee button is all there is to you. Not much to draw the attention of anyone."

"And yet here we stand having our little chat. You going to apologize?" I braced my legs, expecting our conflict to get physical.

The troll stepped between me and his companion. Sarya shuffled backward, saying nothing.

The troll leaned down, his upturned tusks and his rotten breath intruding on our chat. He was a full three heads taller than me and just as wide. From his green skin riddled with scars, tiny two-inch thorns sprouted forth, oozing a sickly orange substance. His savagery and stench could not be mistaken. He snorted at me.

The knight moved his troll companion aside with the wave of a black glove. "None of your berserker rage is required here, Squire Helmurk. Let's have you sit this one out, shall we?" The knight's eyes directed the troll to back away.

The troll's demeanor became immediately passive. The thorns retreated back into his skin, and he slouched back behind the knight, like a scolded child deprived of dessert.

Sarya said, "Always relying on your silver-tongue, eh, Gared?"

Gared did not turn her way, but answered her taunting comment. "When you got it, flaunt it." He wagged his tongue about. It was indeed silver.

"Yes, well, that's all you've got to force others into befriending you. Must be lonely to be you," Sarya said.

The troll had backed down abruptly at Gared's command, almost as if he were being controlled. Did Gared have some sort of commanding voice? Is that what Sarya had meant by her friend comment?

"Not nearly as desperate as being a smudge." The knight twitched his neck at the fairy.

Recovered from the fright set upon me by the troll's presence, I persisted. "What about the apology?"

Gared puffed up his chest. "Yes, yes, you would do well to not push buttons. Seems to me that's something you'd have an inkling about." He patted his empty scabbard. It was a threat even with the weapon missing. "This is your first day. I will *cut* you some slack. You smudges have enough hardships heaped on your imprecise frames."

He stepped back and bowed. "I'm sorry. Please accept my apology."

Before we could respond, he turned, beckoned the troll to follow, and they set off.

I was about to blurt out a response, when Sarya's hand covered my mouth. Her fingers passed through my jaw as our blurry parts again became momentarily tangled.

"He didn't say what he was sorry about," I said as she withdrew her hand from my mouth.

"Yes, I heard." Despite her eyes being held captive in a fog, I could tell she was weeping.

"He was feeling sorry for me being a smudge." I clawed weakly at the wishbutton.

Sarya nodded. "For both of us."

I paused. She was right. The incident affected more than just me.

Why had I thought only of myself? Was that a character trait my creator had inflicted upon me? If so, I was feeling less and less a hero. I tried to lighten the mood. "You can't tell, but I'm smiling." I pointed a smoky finger at my indistinct face.

Her smile was crystal clear. She gushed, "Oh, I can tell. It's in your voice. You carry so much weight and emotion in your words." She sighed fondly. Her mile-a-minute charm had returned.

"Thanks," I said. The silence grabbed hold for a few awkward seconds. Still fixated on sorting out our encounter with the knight and needing to change the topic of discussion, I pressed her for more. "What was up with Gared and that troll? It was like it would do whatever he ordered."

"Gared's author chose to give him a true silver tongue. With that, he has the ability to command others to do his bidding."

"Why didn't he try bossing us around? Make us do something embarrassing?"

"His talent only works on monsters. Kind of fitting, isn't it, with him being so rotten and all?" She darted down the walkway leading away from the knight's path. "C'mon, tour's over for now. Let's head to the house and hit the fridge. I'm famished."

"Gared, he's a villain, right?"

She frowned, "No, he's not."

I waited for her to pin a label to Gared.

She bit her bottom lip as if uncertain she wanted to release her response. She rushed it out, hoping speed would lessen the blow. "He's a hero, like you."

Chapter 15
NO JACKET REQUIRED

Sometimes it came down to wardrobe, he decided.

The kids were in bed, reading with his wife, and he had a little down time. Not feeling up to grading the last few writing assignments, he had stuffed them back in his pack for later, but not before drawing motivation from their work. He had given his students the task of writing a story where their main character found a magical item of clothing and they were to narrate how the magical powers complicated their character's life. Most had selected magic pants or gloves this year.

He smiled. The topic seemed wholly appropriate at the moment. It dovetailed perfectly with his brainstorming of Irving and his wishbutton. He had decided the first chapter would focus on Irving waking up to find himself garbed in the sleek jacket of a wish agent. He sketched out a jacket, adding tails to the back. He liked how it looked, slightly flashy and like a magician's getup. Not having colored pencils handy, he took color scheme notes. The jacket would be a dark blue with almost a velvet sheen. He indicated purple trim at the end of the sleeves and around the collar, emulating druidic twists and turns to give it a Nordic feel.

Lazily, he drew two buttons on the front of the garment. Reaching to erase the lower one, he hesitated. He had always assumed Irving would only have one. He homed in on a twist to the wishbutton. What if his wish jacket had arrived defective, with one button missing? When Irving got to Wish Haven he'd see the others with two buttons and wonder what happened to his. He liked the mystery behind the idea. All of the agents would be given two buttons, except Irving. He didn't have the reason why Irving was missing a button, but he knew it would be a big deal in the story. It also set up Irving to feel incomplete and separate, a key ingredient to starting him along the path to becoming a hero. He needed to show that Irving was a work in progress, and this did the trick nicely.

He designated the top one to be red, adding a sentence describing the button as ordinary, but a little larger than normal. It was not to look like a push button, but its presence definitely made all around it aware that it was more than a commonplace fastener.

Seeing his wife coming down the steps, he slid the pad to the side and made room on the couch for her. Tonight was movie night. He held out the theater candy boxes he had bought earlier that day, earning his wife's confectionary approval as he started the movie.

* * *

We arrived at Smudge Hall, at least that was what I thought the faded sign emblazoned along the rooftop read.

"I've seen this place before. When Roon and her brother were taking me to see Aunt Nance." I squinted suspiciously at the wooden steps that promised an uneven trip to the front door.

Sarya had flown up the steps, ignoring the creaking protests even her delicate footsteps produced. Smudge Hall was a rickety three-story manor that at one time might have been an impressive mansion. In its current state, it brought new meaning to the term fixer-upper. It not only looked rundown, but also run over. Its multitude of windows warped and accented with different degrees of cracks competed for the title of chief eyesore versus the peeling and cracked paint that graced the siding slapped on with crooked care. Brown grass fought a losing battle with imposing clumps of crabgrass in the yard. Scattered shrubs that resembled tumbleweeds glued onto a child's diorama of a desert clustered along the edge of the porch. A broken porch swing hung by one chain at the far end of the entryway's landing. I tested each step before reaching the porch alongside Sarya, who seemed oblivious to the home's condition. She yanked open the screen door featuring multiple puncture wounds in its rusted mesh.

"What is this place?" I stepped over the threshold into an entryway that was as equally downtrodden as the exterior.

She waltzed down a hall, avoiding several holes in the hardwood flooring. "Mind the holes. We call this hopscotch hallway. Just make your way through without snagging yourself in any of them."

"This is Smudge Hall?" I inched along against the right wall, sticking to a path that seemed relatively hole free. "Why's it in such bad shape? Don't you take care of it?"

She stopped short of entering what looked like a kitchen and replied, "Yes, this is our, your, new home. Smudge Hall is where we stay until our creator fleshes out our appearances. And it looks this trashy because . . ."

She was unsure how to finish her answer, clearly uncomfortable with confiding in me on this particular topic.

The answer came from the smudge sitting on a barstool at the counter. His body was in a fog except for his penetrating brown eyes and a finely polished cybernetic arm that hung opposite his normal dark-skinned left arm. "This place is cursed."

I stepped back, nearly dropping a foot in one of the hallway holes.

The smudge dismounted and strolled toward us. I could hear the whirring of gears as he lifted his robotic arm to shake my hand.

Expecting a similar handshake result as what had happened with Sarya, I hesitated.

He chuckled. "Yeah, don't blame you for skipping out on a proper squeeze. Kind of creeps me out with the whole passing through each other anyway." He withdrew his hand, pausing to polish a spot on his wrist that appeared to have a scuff.

"Uh . . ." Now that he had stood, I saw he was about seven feet, give or take a few fuzzy inches. He tipped his head as a substitute greeting. "Name's Valiant Forge. Call me Val."

Sarya raced to the fridge and began emptying out sandwich ingredients.

"She's quite a gal, isn't she?" Val waved for me to have a seat at the bar. As I did, I noticed two other smudges raising voices at each other as they lounged on a bench in a worn breakfast nook. Both had beards and oversized boots sharply in focus. Everything else about them was a blur. They acknowledged my arrival with a nod and resumed their arguing.

"Yes," I responded.

"Only been here two days and she's already become the house favorite. Shame she won't be around much longer."

"Why's that?" I surprised myself with how genuinely concerned I was about the fairy.

Val said, "'Cause she's nearly thought out. Look at her. Only had the hair and antennae this morning and now she comes back with a full set of wings and a winning smile."

Sarya allowed a mute snicker to escape at the compliment.

"She's not going to leave the academy? I thought you only left when your book was published," I said.

"True. No, that's not what I'm talking about. Her creator's real close to figuring her out. Once she's all gussied up with her fancy appearance, she's gotta leave Smudge Hall. That's the way of things."

"So this is only a temporary place? I won't be staying long either?" I asked, eyeing the numerous flaws in the kitchen. All the cabinet doors hung askew, with a few standing slightly open. The counter was chipped and scratched with coffee rings patterning its surface like an out-of-scale map of the planets.

"Most of us stay a few days. Sometimes it can take weeks. I hear the record is just under four hours." He shifted in his seat. The stool creaked a warning of disgust at the weight it bore. "Me, I've been here almost six days and only have this robot arm and a desire to go on some Revolutionary War time quest to show for it. I think I'm one of those historical fantasy mash-ups. At least, that's what Doctor Ringle thinks."

"Everybody likes to talk about themselves, here, huh?" I took the plate Sarya offered me. While the cabinetry that had housed the ingredients Sarya had used looked junkyard chic, the contents of my sandwich were world class. Crisp lettuce sheltered generous layers of ham and cheese. The mustard aroma was mouthwatering. I thanked her and took a whale of a bite.

"Of course. It helps us deal with what we're missing," Sarya offered, sliding onto the stool next to me and dropping a napkin in my lap. She was careful not to touch me. "This school is all about figuring yourself out and not just the surface stuff either."

Knowing so little about myself and feeling a bit tightlipped about sharing what I did know, I concentrated on my sandwich. Finishing it in record time, I returned the topic to the notion of the hall being cursed. "What did you mean about this place being cursed? Can't you just clean it up, fix all the holes and plant new grass?"

"Believe me, everyone's tried. I even fixed the darn shower leak in the upstairs water closet, but it went back to being broken the next morning." Val eyed Sarya's sandwich. She nibbled on it for a few more seconds before passing it to him. He politely tipped his head in thanks. I watched as the sandwich disappeared where his mouth should've been, wondering if that was how I had looked as well when I had wolfed down my meal. "Yesterday evening, Sarya pulled up a bunch of those scrawny bushes out front and replaced them with a lovely bunch of flowers she got at the school store. Guess what we woke up to this morning?"

"What?"

Val did in the sandwich in one gulp. "No sign of the flowers and the return of the blasted bushes, looking even worse the wear. I'm tellin' you, this house doesn't want to be fixed up. Word has it there's a curse behind it all. So, we smudges just sort of resign ourselves to living like this for the short time we're here. It's really not all that bad."

He stopped talking and stared at me. His eyes grew wide.

"What's wrong?"

"Well, aren't you a fancy Dan. Look at what you're sporting now." He jabbed a crooked steel finger at my chest.

Expecting to see my wishbutton mutated into something more embarrassingly eye-catching, I examined the area.

What appeared to be a dark blue magician's jacket was wrapped around me. The wishbutton held it together. I stood up, patting the material in awe.

"Look, you have a missing button," Sarya said.

True to her words, there was a slit for a button below the wishbutton that was missing its partner. The jacket made the red of the wishbutton stand out even more.

Val inspected my backside much to my dismay. "Looks like you got some swanky tails on that get-up too." His robotic arm grabbed hold of the loose fabric and waved one of the tails in the air.

I pulled out of reach. "Hey, watch it!"

"No wonder our little home doesn't pass muster with you. Comin' from the upper class like you do, we must look like yesterday's trash." Val didn't speak from meanness. He was merely trying to rattle me. "Don't worry, we take all comers, here."

I was overwhelmed and felt exposed. I snapped at Sarya, "Take me to my room!" I regretted my tone immediately.

Her shoulders slumped as she half-heartedly motioned for me to follow her. I left the kitchen, Val's heavy laughter mixing with the guffaws of the two bearded onlookers from the breakfast nook.

I needed to be alone to make sense of my day. I didn't want to hear anymore from Sarya and robo-arm downstairs. I followed the fairy up the steps, barely mindful of the splintered worn spots on several of them. She escorted me to the third door on the right. Grunting out thanks, I entered my room and slammed the door.

A picture frame fell off its nail and flopped onto my roommate.

A roommate, like so many other smudges I had met, who I was about to find was never at a loss for words.

A roommate who could best be described as a pile of ash with a mouth.

Chapter 16
ADDING IN SOOT TO INJURY

Car rides allowed him the best brainstorming sessions. Especially if he was by himself. Tonight, they had decided to order out for sushi, and he had volunteered to go. The ride to the restaurant had not yielded much, being spent mostly thinking about what their Saturday would entail. The ride home, however, had delivered character details about Irving he was eager to catalog in his notes.

Irving's sister would be part of the story. She was going to be abducted. He also decided on Irving's mom not being in the picture. He wasn't sure if he wanted to make Irving's dad a widow or a divorcee. He thought widow added more sympathy, but he remained indecisive.

Irving's last name would be Holland. His sister would be older, and he'd have a good relationship with her. That would make the stakes of her abduction that much more meaningful. Her name didn't present itself yet, but he did know she would have long red hair and librarian glasses. She was going to be the well-read dispenser of knowledge type, always with her nose in a book.

He parked and closed the garage door. Dropping the carry-out on the kitchen counter, he went up to help his wife finish reading to the kids. It was his night to cozy up with his daughter, who was beginning to show interest in fantasy novels. She had agreed to let him read a chapter a night of a little book about a young wizard with a scar on his forehead. He was eager to begin. He took the steps two at a time as he always did.

* * *

Being verbally attacked by a pile of ash was not what I expected. After slamming the door, all I wanted was to lie down and put my thoughts in order. A tiny dorm room with a barely big enough bed and desk with legs as spindly as a gazelle's? That should've been what greeted me. A cramped room in which to mentally regroup? That would've done the trick.

Instead, I was apologizing to a pile of ash and not getting anywhere with my apology. "I'm so sorry. I didn't know anyone else was in here."

The ash rested atop a sunken mattress on a wooden framed bed. A tattered yellow blanket covered part of the black powder. It had no mouth, but that didn't stop it from lobbing insult after insult in my direction.

"Let's not cause this sorry excuse for a residence to fall apart further, nimrod!" To my surprise, it pushed the picture frame off itself with a shrug of its soot. It lifted up into the air, swirling into the shape of a spiral. It looked like an angry swarm of bees bent on handing out a plethora of stings. "Don't tell me another one of you yahoos is infringing on my personal space again."

The ash shouted louder, directing its anger to specific persons outside of the room. "Just 'cause my digs have two beds, doesn't mean you have to keep shoving newbies in here!"

The ash paused. Its shape recoiled, snubbed by the lack of response from the outburst. It coalesced into a tightly packed sphere and floated toward me.

"Uh . . ." I said.

It sounds silly to admit to being intimidated by a cloud of dark dust, but that exact feeling took hold of me as my new roommate apprised me of how things were going to be.

"Listen up, smudge. I don't want to hear about your name. I don't want you blathering on and on about your self-discoveries; how it just dawned on you that you're a hero because of how your father treated you as a kid or how your family owns a sizeable tract of land in East Buddletuck." It drew closer. "I don't want to hear about what happened in your classes or who asked you to a picnic lunch on the mall."

With the angry cloud mere inches from my nose, I held my breath, afraid if I inhaled sharply, I'd find myself with a dusty lungful.

"Don't pry into my business. Don't ask me about my comings and goings. Don't offer to launder my sheets. And most important of all, don't snore." It reshaped itself into a fuming tornado. "I cherish my snooze time and I'm a light sleeper."

I stood, unwilling to move off my spot. The ash funneled itself back into a pile on the lone rickety desk, arching a dark tentacle upward. It latched onto a pencil from a tin can and began scribbling into a journal.

It muttered further threats as it wrote. Luckily, its words were indecipherable.

I hopped onto the other bed, drew the woefully thin sheet over my head and curled into a ball. As I struggled to calm myself, new thoughts filtered into my head. I had a sister. She was someone I looked up to. She was sort of an egghead. My author must be at work hammering out my family tree. I knew I had a dad, but was uncertain about my mother's whereabouts. Not knowing disturbed me..

It was over an hour before I feel asleep, my roommate still transcribing his disturbing thoughts.

Chapter 17
GIRL TROUBLES

It paid to dwell on the chapter titles. It was what helped him configure each scene. Most of the time he relied on word play, sometimes alliteration. He wanted the opening to show Irving waking up with his wishbutton uniform on. He wanted to also introduce the family dynamic of how Irving related to his sister and father. When Irving flopped out of bed and realized he was not wearing his normal sleepwear, he'd rush to check out what he looked like in the bathroom mirror.

It seemed a little lazy to have him look in a mirror and give a rundown of Irving's features and new wardrobe. He decided to complicate matters by having the sister in the bathroom, hidden behind an opaque shower curtain. When the newly appointed wish agent finally entered the bathroom, the steam would prove too much. As fast as he could wipe off the condensation, the mirror would fog up and he'd only get snippets of what he looked like. He'd focus on describing the character's new threads and Irving's disbelief at his transformation. He would then slowly reveal Irving's facial characteristics throughout the first few chapters in a more natural fashion. He hated lengthy paragraphs spelling out all the surface detail of the character and used them as only a last resort, mostly to introduce supporting characters.

*He grinned when the chapter title came to him: **The Clothes Wake the Man.***

* * *

I woke up with my legs tangled in my sheet. I dared a glance over to my roommate's bed. He wasn't there. I sat up and looked around the room. The ash was gone. I stood and stretched. His journal was on the desk, closed. A small note was tacked on the front: *Open this and feel the pain!*

Avoiding the journal, I opened the lone closet door, half expecting to be assaulted by a vengeful cloud of ash. Inside, two wire hangers dangled, empty. A faded pair of purple sneakers sat on the floor. A previous roommate? I doubted the ash had any use for them.

Thankful to be spared another encounter with my roommate, I exited my room and tiptoed downstairs. I heard a soft feminine voice originating from the kitchen.

Hoping to track down Sarya and apologize for last night, I hopped delicately through the hole-riddled hallway and entered. Val was whipping up pancakes in a frying pan. The two bearded smudges were gone. In their place, a young elf with suction cups lining her fingertips was pouring syrup onto a short stack of pancakes. It was her singsong voice that had lured me into the kitchen.

Favoring his robo-arm, the roughneck flipped a pancake high into the air. "Look what dragged itself out of bed, Kylene. Our newest arrival!"

The elf giggled and waved. Her face and hair were smudged along with everything below her waist. "Nice to meet you, Irving!"

"Was just telling Kylene about you. Why don't you sit down and fill 'er up. I make a mean chocolate chip pancake." He flung one across the room toward the elf. A long yellow tongue whipped out from where Kylene's mouth should have been and snatched the pancake before it had begun its downward arc. She deposited it on her plate and retracted her tongue back into her blurry face. "Crazy, isn't it? My creator getting all the specifics on my suction cups and tongue just right and neglects to write what my face is to be." She waved again. The suction cups wiggled slightly.

"Where's Sarya?" I waved away the plate of pancakes Val held up toward me.

"See you're still sportin' the fancy jacket. That's your look from here on out, huh? Not too shabby. A bit on the flowery side, but that's just me." He started cleaning the batter spilled all over the counter from the pancake prep. Almost an afterthought, he added, "Sarya's off to class. She was first out the door. In a real hurry."

I frowned. Glad, for once, no one could see my true expression under my smudged appearance.

"Don't you worry. You'll see her tonight at dinner. The whole house'll be here."

"Why's that?" I was not in the mood to meet anyone else, especially if they were anything like my roommate.

"Big dinner for you and the other smudge that arrived last night. The other came about an hour after you stormed upstairs. Real easygoing fella. In fact, he left with Sarya this morning. Wanted to get a jump on the day, he said."

The elf chugged her milk. "She'll be back later today. I'll try to talk to her if I see her first. You know, smooth things out a little bit. I'll remind her how moody new arrivals can be. She's my roommate. I'll tell her to give you a second chance." Kylene stood and handed her plate with two uneaten pancakes to Val. "Thanks, Val. Gotta dash."

Kylene bustled past me and raced out the front door.

Val slapped his thigh. "Gotta tell you, boy. You know how to chase the girls away. Never seen anyone clear out a room as fast as you."

"Ha, you should meet my roommate then." I sat at the counter. Val ignored my comment and slid a plate of pancakes under where my chin should've been.

The aroma was too hard to resist. Grabbing a fork and the syrup bottle, I set upon the breakfast. Between bites, I thanked Val. "This is so good."

"As good as your mom makes, I bet. I'm always hearin' that. Comes from the way I whisk in my special ingredient. It's cinnamon." Val hunkered down on the stool next to me and began wearing away at a stack of pancakes that would rival the Eiffel Tower.

"Uh, I don't know if I have a mom," I said.

Val gave me his attention.

"My writer must've been working on me last night. Before I went to sleep, I found out I had a dad, but I don't know about having a mom." I licked at the syrup trailing down the handle of my fork. Even without being able to see I had a mouth, it was evident I had teeth and a tongue. It was a weird sensation, eating. The forkful of food went into the fuzzy space where my mouth was, but I couldn't see anything other than a hazy cloud.

"Anything else?" he asked.

"I know I have a sister who likes to take long showers." When I said it, it sounded off. "I mean, she takes too long in the bathroom. Apparently, I get this jacket in my sleep and wake up with it on. In the scene, I barge into the bathroom to get a good look at my jacket. I guess I wanted to see it from all angles."

"Uh-huh."

I continued, "Well, I don't get to see much of it because my sister, I don't know her name yet, she steamed up the mirror a whole lot. I try to clean it off enough to see the jacket and only get to see part of it."

"Let me guess, you don't get to see what your face looks like in the process?" Val said.

"No, I don't. That's kind of weird." I finished the last pancake.

Val took my plate and his own and ran them to the sink. Rinsing them off, he added, "Don't fret. You'll learn all about your ugly mug soon enough."

"How long does it take? Didn't you say it could be a few hours?"

"That's the record. Most of us take a few days. Way I've been told, the authors, many times, get down their character name, some of the plot details and start jotting notes before they begin work on the actual chapters. That's where the real character work gets figured out. It can take days, weeks, and, in some unfortunate cases, months."

"How long have you been a smudge again?" I stretched, easing the stool back under the counter as I stepped back.

"It'll be seven days clean and simple at high noon today." Val dried his hands with a worn towel. "Look, we can stand around here in this kitchen all day jawin', but wouldn't you rather get yourself all situated and informed at Orientation? There's a session scheduled for eleven o'clock today." He peered through the bent blind slats covering the kitchen's small window over the sink. Outside threatened to be sunny and pleasant.

"What time is it now?" I asked.

"About 10:43, if I'm readin' the sun right." He released the blinds, allowing them to flutter back into their original rumpled and not very parallel positions.

"Oh, geesh, I'm gonna be late." I dashed down the hall and out the door in such haste, I registered Val talking to me but not any of the specifics.

I was flying down the steps when I realized I didn't know where I was going. I skidded to a stop and turned to go back into Smudge Hall. Val could tell me where to go.

I never got the chance to ask. Rounding the far corner of the porch, Roon, my pale guide from when I had first arrived, sauntered into view. I couldn't be sure, but I got the impression she had been waiting for me outside this whole time.

"About time you showed your face." Realizing what she had said, she wrinkled her face in dismay. "Oh, sorry. Poor choice of words."

"I'm late for Orientation," I blurted out.

"Relax, I'll get you there in one piece." She threaded her arm through mine and dragged me forward. Unlike my awkward handshake with Sarya, we didn't get tangled. She was solid, and we didn't mix or mingle in the least.

I allowed her to lead me to my next destination, my dissatisfaction at being nowhere near in control yet again gnawing at me.

Chapter 18
ESCORT WITH RETORT

When wishes fall by the wayside, he's there to collect them.

He eyed the sentence with suspicion. It sounded a bit too much like an action movie pitch. He circled it, separating it from his other jumbled story notions. Did it make Irving's job sound too much like a trash collector? Were the wishes cast off, lost, misplaced? How did a wish agent go about hunting for their quarry?

His mind was shifting into full brainstorm mode, anticipating the sudden surplus of writing time.

He was three days away from tracking out and being able to work on a chapter a day for ten straight days.

Until then, he was working on the premise behind the wishes. He liked the idea of having Irving's wishbutton be incomplete, with the second button missing. Perhaps the second button was an alarm. Stripped of his second button, Irving could do what no other wish agent could; he could access his stored wishes and use them. Unfettered by an alarm that would alert the rulers of Wish Haven to tampering with the gathered wishes, Irving could take advantage of the whims he collected. This would also give him something to lie about. He'd lie about using them.

Of course, at the beginning, he'd have no wishes.

Again, the fine line of how much lying Irving could get away with came up. Irving's motive for using the wishes had to be for the greater good. Would he be facing off with Teardrop?

He thought of his villain. With only a name, he didn't have much to go on. He liked what a teardrop symbolized. When it was shed, it could be hope or fear, joy or sadness.

He shelved his brainstorm pad in the mail cubby and returned to putting the dishes away. Before he started the chapters, he needed a breakthrough on his villain. He also really needed to figure out the status of Irving's mother.

He'd spend the weekend close to his pad, gathering stray thoughts, nursing half notions.

* * *

As Roon dragged me to Orientation, her mood was very unsettled. She wasn't happy with me, launching into a rant before Smudge Hall was even out of sight.

"Already making a splash here. A trip to the dean's office on your first day? High profile. A run-in with the biggest blowhard on campus? What were you thinking, facing down the Golden Knight? My brother thinks you're a fool." Her eyebrows, tiny and thin, wrinkled in distaste, but her appearance didn't come off as harsh. It was playful.

"So now you're all about talking. What happened to yesterday, when you couldn't reveal too much?" I remarked.

"Hey, that's what you do when you do a pick-up. Can't tell you too much or you'd overload. It's not pretty. We have far fewer newcomers suffering from shellshock these days. Harmstrike knows what he's doing most of the time." She darted through a crowd of students who were passing out flyers to some sort of party. I noticed they avoided handing me a flyer but went out of their way to place one in Roon's hands.

It was a beefy warrior troll carrying a large battle axe and a small backpack who delivered her the invite. "Roon, please do come to our little get-together. We need some *life-of-the-party* types." He snickered at his comment.

Roon scowled and snatched the invite out of his hand.

As I sailed by, the troll turned away, deliberately snubbing me.

"What was that about? He acted like I wasn't there."

She stopped and squared off with me. "And what are you going to do? Shout him down like you did The Golden Knight? Not everything is about confrontation. Is that a trait your creator burdened you with? 'Cause if it is, you're in for a rude awakening."

We resumed walking, only our pace slowed as our tempers rose. "So what if I want to take matters into my own hands? Why didn't he give me a flier?"

"That's not how things work at the academy. After you've been here a while, you'll figure out your place."

"So where's your place? Taunting newbies? Trailing behind your brother and doing whatever he says? Where is your brother, come to think of it? I got the impression you two were inseparable." At the mention of her brother, I knew I had gone too far.

She punched me hard in the gut. I bent over. Despite me looking like a gray wispy haze, she had landed a solid blow.

"Keep my brother out of this! He's not here because he thinks you're not worth the time. There's very little he and I disagree on, but there you are. I wanted to help you. He didn't. Our escort job was over the minute we dropped you off with the Fine Aunts." She took a deep breath, regaining her composure. Having ended the discussion of her family dynamic, she volunteered more details on my status. "You're a smudge. A lot of people avoid smudges. It's silly. I think it's because they fear you're contagious."

"I don't understand. What's wrong with smudges?" I stopped. She pulled me over to a stone bench. I sat reluctantly. She kneeled in front of me.

"It's not permanent. Your author will figure out your appearance soon, and you can make real progress. You can move out of that wreck of a hall and into your proper quarters." What she said next sounded hollow as if the more she said it would make it a reality. "Hero Row is a very coveted place to be. You'll like it there. Everyone who's anyone is there."

"Are you a hero? I mean, a heroine?"

"Sort of. My brother and I are a team. Since we have double billing in our stories, we live in a house just off of Hero Row called Partner Place." She frowned. Something about her brother bothered her.

I didn't like seeing her unhappy, even though moments ago, that had been the farthest thing from my mind. I tried to put our argument aside. "That's good you're together."

"It is." It felt like she wanted to say more but lacked the conviction or the trust.

"If you need—"

She rose and cut me off. "C'mon, let's get you to Orientation."

Her demeanor was all business. We took a stack of steps to a building called Narrative Sciences. She ran me through a maze of halls, delivering me to the auditorium where Orientation was already in progress. We had arrived three minutes late.

I took a seat in the back and was surprised to see Roon sit down next to me. I had thought for sure she'd have dropped me off and scurried on to some other task, eager to be free of me.

Our argument hadn't made her run off. Her brother's disapproval of me hadn't changed her view of me. Was this how friendships were formed?

Feeling still very sketchy, I was unsure. But whatever had happened made me smile. Luckily, Roon could not see it with my blurred features still operating to create a mask. Again, I was thankful being a smudge.

I leaned forward, intent on listening to every word, every clue to knowing myself and my surroundings, Doctor Ringle had to say.

Chapter 19
IT TAKES TWO TO TANGLE

Teardrop would take Irving's sister. Shortly after the failed attempt of sending the emberhounds to get Irving, she'd send some other beastie to get his sister. It would happen when Irving was visiting Wish Haven for the first time.

He paused. He hated how so many fantasies that had children being whisked away left the parents clueless. He wanted real consequences to the abduction and Irving running off to Wish Haven. Their father would not witness Irving's departure, but he would be front and center in seeing his daughter taken. In fact, he'd get injured. He'd also see what took her and be just as in the know as the kids.

What type of beast would be right for the task? Something large, able to knock through a roof maybe, leaving some impressive proof of strange happenings for the authorities.

Irving's sister remained nameless. Abby was the closest he'd gotten to a name, but also remembered that Abby Holland had been the name of the wife of a well-known comic book swamp creature.

He finished taking a few notes, deciding to sketch out some monster drawings tomorrow.

* * *

The lecture hall was huge, easily able to seat four hundred. This morning, it held nine. I sat in the back and had a clear view of the other recent newcomers.

Tiberius Booster was in the aisle, pacing back and forth. Two twin brothers dressed in tattered capes sat three rows down and to our left. Each fiddled with odd tools they kept pulling from within their cloaks. Every detail of their appearance was in sharp focus like the astronaut dog. I spotted two other fully formed characters in the row behind Tiberius. A raccoon wearing aviator goggles and a beautiful princess whispered back and forth as Dr. Ringle lectured.

Near the front, I spotted Sarya. She was with a short smudge who had two long curly horns coming from the sides of his head. He also wore a purple and black striped hat that bordered on the ridiculous. Evidently the go-getter who had left early with her. When she turned to look at me, even without distinctive eyes and a nose, I could tell she was projecting indifference. She deliberately let out a huff at seeing Roon beside me.

Dr. Ringle paused at this, noticing for the first time his audience as individuals.

"Ms. Sarya, you do know that you only need to attend one of my orientations, don't you? Didn't get enough of my sparkling wit the other day?" Doctor Ringle was, simply put, a mad scientist. He wore a lab coat whose deep pockets overflowed with piecemeal lab equipment. His hair had all but given up the fight. Two thin clumps sprouted from behind his ears, giving him the look of being in a perpetual state of shock. He had more hair under his nose than on his head. His white mustache hung so low, I was uncertain he even had an upper lip.

She spoke loudly enough for all, especially me, to hear. "No, just trying to help someone out. Lord Raggleswamp here arrived late last night, and I'm trying to get him sorted out."

Her companion's voice scraped at my eardrums. "She's been a real gem. Taking the time to make me feel at home. I can't imagine a better welcome wagon."

"Yes, well, the Academy certainly encourages extending a helping hand." Doctor Ringle glanced up at us. He shook his head in disapproval at Roon. "It looks like old home week here. Did I miss a memo? Were we all supposed to drag along someone who should be attending class this morning?"

"I wanted . . ." Roon began. She was flustered.

Ringle didn't let up. Seeing Sarya attending to a newcomer and then spying Roon also putting in an appearance, he was shifting the bulk of his irritation to Roon. "I believe you're missing Professor Gartensleef's Plot Dynamics class. You know how she is about slackers. Isn't that a class you can't really afford to miss? Your performance in that area has been a bit lacking according to her."

Sensing that no matter her answer, Ringle would lay into her further, I came to her rescue. "I'm a real mess, sir. Roon helped me to pull it together. I'm sorry I'm late. She really went out of her way to get me in the swing of things here. I mean, you should've seen how gone I

72

was yesterday. Frazzled like nobody's business. She's a wonderful guide. Escorted me to the Fine Aunts, then made sure I got to Orientation."

"Wishbutton, correct?" he asked.

"Yes."

He paced like a man concerned with doomsday. Even though he was trying to sound warm and inviting, his welcome tone seemed more designed to incite than encourage. He wanted to bring down the house on me, but something held him back. "I want you in the front row of all your classes. None of this slinking in and finding the view from the rafters suits you just fine. Understood?"

"Yes, sir."

He spun around and marched back to his podium. Without looking up from his notes, his voice more muted, he said, "Sarya and Roon, run off to your classes. I'm sure these fellows can manage an afternoon without you."

As he shuffled his notes, the girls snuck out.

Once gone from the room, he peered at Sarya's companion and squinted up at me. "Since you two find yourself in such the mindset that you need a partner, why don't we make you orientation buddies for the duration today, hurm? Mr. Wishbutton, do come down and have a seat with the horned gentleman."

I made my way down to the front.

"Raggleswamp, sir. Lord Raggleswamp of the Bone Dimension," Sarya's companion corrected Doctor Ringle.

Doctor Ringle's nose wrinkled peevishly. "Yes, cling to that title, young man. We must cherish every word, every fuzzy fact made clear, that pops into our minds. Your creators are the bridge to the real world. Any and all info gleaned from them will make your path more assured. The more you know about yourself, the better you'll do in the Academy's rigorous curriculum."

As I sat down next to Raggleswamp, I misjudged the width of his horn-framed head and knocked against one of his horns.

He grunted at me as Doctor Ringle resumed. There were no further interruptions.

Chapter 20
CAST OFF LIMITS

The villain was threatening to take over all his time. Teardrop had been on his mind all weekend. She would have ties to Irving's mother, who was still missing but with no good reason other than he needed her out of the picture. Irving's mom had to be connected with Wish Haven. Maybe something happened when Irving was born that drove her away. Did the father resent the magic she brought into his life? Did he see it as a curse? When Irving becomes a wish agent, would the father root for him to fail?

His sketch of Teardrop's large minion sent to steal away Irving's sister stared back at him on the small post-it note. Riding to the library, he'd scribbled out a rough sketch of the beast. It looked like a supercharged triceratops mounted onto a blimp of a body. It was a floating mess of tentacles resembling the dangling curlicues of a jellyfish. The sister would be stowed away in a jelly-filled chamber that would elicit disgust from its passenger.

Teardrop wanted Irving's wishjacket because of its flaw. She wanted access to the wishes of others. Why? What could wishes be changed into? Did she plan to warp them into something else? He knew she was going to be tragic and vicious.

As they pulled up to the library, he shelved thoughts of his villainess until later.

He hoisted the box of books out of the van. Over thirty this time. His kids were at a stage where they loved going to the library. It reminded him of his own childhood trips to the library and the spinner rack of tattered science fiction and fantasy novels he raced to pour over, hoping to find a book he hadn't read or discover a new author made just for him.

Maybe he'd ask them what they liked about the bad guys in their books. He held the door open as they raced to help drop their latest have-reads in the book return and dispersed outward in search of their newest must-reads.

"Before young Wishbutton arrived, I had just finished introducing myself and my background," Doctor Ringle said. "I'll spare everyone a rehash of my accomplishments and just let Irving know I teach Villainy 101, a course all here will attend tomorrow and every Thursday thereafter at nine sharp."

Even though the others had heard the announcement before, all in the audience nodded.

I found it a little hard to concentrate, as my author must've been working on my villain. I knew Teardrop was her name. She wanted the wishes in my jacket. Although, right now, I was pretty sure my jacket was empty. Would she arrive today? Would she be a smudge? Would I have to live under the same roof as her? I was saddened that my creator was spending so much time on my nemesis, but so little on my family. Why wasn't my family at this orientation? My author had thrust them into being last night.

Way too many questions jockeyed for my attention as I tried to latch onto Doctor Ringle's words.

"Looks like most of you are fully formed. Hopefully, you find your housing to your liking. We have residences for heroes, villains, supporting, window dressing, and family. Smudges have two houses, both are temporary. Once your appearance is realized by your author, you'll move on to your appropriate home. Smudges do attend regular classes, and I ask that everyone be patient with them. It takes a while to craft characters."

I was bothered by how he singled out smudges, but my equally smudged "orientation buddy" wasn't fazed. Raggleswamp hung on every word like it was spun gold.

Ringle cleared his throat, wiping his walrus-like mustache thoughtfully. "The Questing Academy is for characters caught up in adventure stories, who must complete tasks or retrieve objects. While most of you are knee-deep in fantasy, we get a few science fiction types, such as myself and the space hound, who really needs to stop pacing about."

Tiberius sat on his haunches; his tail wagged hesitantly.

"The average stay is about two years. It seems to be the length of time it takes to complete a story and see it through to publication.

Some will be here longer. Our program is designed to be completed in two years. Those here beyond that will take advanced courses and also offer up their time as tutors to you freshmen.

"Your course of study, regardless of character type, contains the same core classes in your first semester. After that, you will take more specialized courses in your character specific area.

"Dean Harmstrike is very happy to have you here and wants you to avail yourself of all the opportunities on campus. We have clubs, sports teams, social opportunities, and quite a few intriguing part-time jobs. I, personally, am looking to hire a lab assistant to help me with some of my more ambitious tinkering." He paused, almost expecting one of us to volunteer. When no takers presented themselves, he forged on. "There is one major rule with socializing. The faculty takes a firm stance on this. You are forbidden to associate with characters from your own story."

My eyes widened.

"I know that sounds unfair, but Harmstrike feels it would erode the spontaneous nature of your stories when you meet them inside your actual books. Anyone caught attempting to associate with a fellow cast member will be delivered to Dean Harmstrike, who will administer consequences that put the destructive outcome of my orbital defragmentor and world juicer to shame. You must find out about yourself without the aid of others from your narrative.

"Your next stop after this will be the book store. There, you will be given your course schedule, materials list and a dining voucher. You will also be given a small amount of credit to buy a few more furnishings that will add a little of your personality to your living quarters. Your classes begin tomorrow. Make sure to start your stay here at the Academy with your integrity on display at all times."

We sat, unsure whether to clap or stand up to leave.

Almost as an afterthought, Doctor Ringle said, "Oh, yes, any questions?"

I was the only one to raise my hand. "What's the Menagerie? You didn't mention that."

"Ah, yes. Young Wishbutton, I can see why that would weigh on you, what with your little dust-up at the Office of Fine Aunts. Heard it wasn't very pleasant, encountering beasties from your own story."

He looked out at the others, waving a hand at me. "Irving ran afoul of some creatures from the Menagerie. Not quite sure how they got loose, but then I'm not involved in campus security. Anyway, it's a zoo of sorts. Houses any of the creatures assigned to your stories who lack the ability to speak, just run-of-the-mill wild and domesticated types."

Tiberius raised a paw. Ringle pointed at him, acknowledging his question.

"So, talking animals don't go there, right?" Tiberius asked with concern.

"Correct. The Menagerie is for creatures that rely on their base instincts, having no higher intelligence such as yourself.

"Now, if there's nothing else, we can bring this to a close and send you on to the book store. I must get back in the lab and check on a delicate experiment that's got me quite vexed. Who'd have thought weaponizing toast would prove so difficult?"

Doctor Ringle exited the auditorium, as we meandered out. Lord Raggleswamp led the way, declaring how he had scoped out the store's location before arriving at Orientation. He was prattling on about life being some such percent preparedness as we marched down the steps of the Narrative Sciences building.

I didn't know how a villain could come across as such a syrupy boy scout, but Raggleswamp was more than proving it possible.

I followed at the back of the pack.

Chapter 21
THE HUNT IS ON

It was so close. Tomorrow morning would be the first day he could work on actual chapter writing. He glanced at the clock. It was 11:38, almost midnight, and he was still wide awake. His wife lay fast asleep next to him. He took care not to rustle his papers when he reached down to retrieve the pad when an idea came his way. Irving would find out that the wishjacket and pants couldn't be taken off. He'd have to go to school in them. He sketched out loose-fitting pants with two extra side pouch pockets. The pants would be black with the stitching a rich purple thread that would glow neon when the wishbutton was used.

Of course, he'd slated Irving to be at baseball practice when the emberhounds attacked. How was he going to get the coach to let Irving practice in such a ridiculous outfit? Warm-up pants and a hoodie would cover everything up nicely. It would be a little bulky, but Irving would just have to suffer. Irving would tell the coach he had a skin reaction that was aggravated by the sun and that was why he had to be covered from head to toe.

Instead of sketching Irving in the bulky disguise, he took a series of bulleted notes.

He put the pad down and curled up, bunching up more than his share of the spread under his chin. He shut his eyes tight. He didn't want to be up past midnight. He scolded his brain for being so lively. Squelching any further ideas as best he could, he tried to fall sleep. More ideas fluttered through his mind, but he refrained from writing them down. If they were truly worthwhile, he'd remember them in the morning.

* * *

Suddenly, I had pants.

We were entering the school store when the garment appeared. I searched the pockets for anything extra, finding them empty. Sadly, my feet were still blurry.

At that exact moment, I noticed a sign on the glass door leading from the foyer into the store proper. It read: *No Shirt, No Shoes, No Service.*

In smaller type below: *Except for smudges.*

Lord Raggleswamp commented on the sign, "Makes sense. Good thing, too. If they tried to keep me out, they'd find a world of hurt from my killer tail."

He swished a long muscular tail twice as long as his short frame up to my eye level, whipping it like a towel.

"Hey, you didn't have that on the walk over," I remarked.

"Nope. Appeared right around the time you were granted pants. Bit more practical, if you ask me. I'd rather have this intimidator than frumpy coverings for my lower half." He swiveled his head about, seeking attention for his impressive set of horns.

The book store was vast. At the front, rows of textbooks stood, occupying over a dozen tall aisles of wooden shelves. Beyond, I could see a small grocery section and then what looked like a large area of home furnishings. A wide set of stairs at the opposite end threatened another level of consumer wants and needs.

A gargoyle flew up to our group and asked our names. He fished through a folder of papers, producing a packet for each of us except for the cloaked brothers. Urging the paperless pair to follow him, the gargoyle retreated to an office to search for their packets.

The princess and raccoon politely excused themselves and set forth in the large textbook section to our left.

Tiberius stayed with us, a gesture I appreciated. We opted to start with textbooks as well.

"I'm a terrible villain," Raggleswamp remarked. Realizing how it sounded, he amended his declaration. "I mean, I'm terrible as in rotten and dastardly, not that I'm terrible at being a villain."

He continued, taking our silence as a request for further information, "It's because I really think everything through. I'm a planner. I love commissioning blueprints and elaborate maps of my respective devices and schemes. I'm going to be introduced in the third or fourth chapter. I'm a smudge right now because my creator is still brainstorming."

Ignoring Raggleswamp, I scanned my packet. "What classes do you have?" I looked at the astronaut dog.

Tiberius said, "Villainy 101, Heroic Deeds and Misdeeds, Intro to Narrative Sciences, Tournament Basics, and Soul Searching Studies. How about you?"

We compared schedules. I kneeled to look at Tiberius's list. They were identical, except for two of our classes; Soul Searching and Narrative Sciences were offered at different times.

"We've got three classes together," said Tiberius.

Surprisingly, it felt good to know he would be in those classes.

Raggleswamp was hopping up and down behind me, attempting to discern my classes. Even crouching, I was still a foot taller than him. What type of villain is so short? Was the hero his author would pit him against even smaller?

The villain said, "Hey, it appears we will have all our classes together. We're identical, Wishbutton! That's excellent. Clearly, you're a hero of some stature. Examining the classes from your perspective as well as my own villainous viewpoint will provide me multiple ways to take in the scholarly knowledge."

I was about to issue a sarcastic "Yippee," but was prevented by the return of the winged gargoyle. "Name's Finn. You dirtnips need any help minding the stacks?" He nodded a horned eyebrow at the aisles of shelves stacked high with books.

"What an odd choice of a name. You would think the creative who penned you would go with Wing or Flap over Fin. What does a gargoyle have to do with aquatic anatomy?" Lord Raggleswamp examined the gargoyle with dismay. "Unless your author is all about bizarre combos. Are you perhaps a gargoyle who is of the seafaring nature? Maybe an aerial and aquatic pirate beast?"

"It's F-I-N-N and I've nothing to do with water or fish parts. My writer just liked the double Ns." The gargoyle folded his arms and flapped his wings in a more pressing manner. "Do any of you need my help?"

Tiberius leaped into action, using his helmet to push me down an aisle. He called back to the gargoyle, "Irving and I will find our way, but this base villain needs much of your guidance. Please do let him take up your time."

Raggleswamp was about to protest, "Well, I really think we—"

Tiberius bellowed, "Lord Raggleswamp, think of how much more efficiently you could retrieve your books with a guide. Why, I bet you could even beat Irving and me. Why don't we make it a friendly competition? See who makes it to the checkout first?"

If Lord Raggleswamp's eyes could be seen, they would have gleamed with excitement. Instead, the only indication that the evil smudge's craving for competition was piqued could be seen in his hunched posture and the crafty manner in which he wrung his hazy hands. "Yes, what wonderful sport. To me, my aide." Raggleswamp snagged Finn by his tail and dragged him down another aisle.

"That was genius!" I spouted to the dog.

Tiberius scanned the shelves. "I know, but also a bit of truth behind it."

"What do you mean?"

"My author really gave me quite a competitive streak." He smiled and let his tongue loll playfully. "C'mon, I want to beat the pants off him!"

"Hey!" I batted at the dog.

He ducked my attack. "I couldn't resist. Those are some fine trousers you're sporting, Wishbutton."

With that, the hunt was on. I put my chances at above average. After all, I had a dog on my side, a devious dog at that.

Chapter 22
DECOR DENIED

It was the first official day of their track out, and his kids had finished cleaning up breakfast. His daughter had opened up a bin of beads and was making a pizza with choice orange and yellow ones. His son had roped him into playing with the walkie-talkies. In the afternoon, he'd have them watch a few shows while he worked on his first chapter. He'd try to squeeze two hours out of it, but it would depend on if they could play together without him for a while.

Before joining his son in the play room, he wrote a name, Tyler Holland, on his brainstorming pad. That was to be the name of Irving's sister. She would be in eighth grade, while her brother would just be starting into middle school. Both details had been stirred to life before going to sleep. They had weathered the memory drain of a decent night's rest and lasted through their morning routine. Now, beckoning to be committed to paper, he set them to print.

Putting the pad down, he grabbed a walkie-talkie and reported for duty as Agent D, specialist in covert operations.

His son raced upstairs, bragging through his walkie-talkie how he'd never be tracked down. He gave pursuit, hopping over the couch with style.

* * *

Despite having a hound, who you would think to be an excellent tracker, we lost to Raggleswamp. He snatched up all his books and was through the checkout when we arrived.

Our textbook expedition had gone smoothly up until we had been looking for the Soul Searching texts. Tiberius had knocked over a precarious stack of thick hardbacks with his tail and a very librarian-like clerk forced us to reconstruct the display exactly as it had been before.

Upon arriving at the checkout, we were both surprised to see Raggleswamp was a smudge no longer. He was still short, but all his features and villainous accessories were on display.

He spun around, showing off his completed look to the cashier. His horns and tail were the same. He wore a tiny suit of black armor that spread over his torso and down to midthigh. Brown boots with marginal heels and silver designs playing across his ankles gave his appearance a regal air. A short amber cape trailed to just above his tail. Black leather gloves cloaked his spindly four-fingered hands. His face was a black mask of fur with a bright orange muzzle jutting out and topped with deeply slit nostrils.

Raggleswamp proclaimed, "I was in seek-and-destroy mode, boys. It was a thing of beauty. Rooted out all my books in under seven minutes. Real shame you two couldn't keep up."

"You're not a smudge anymore?" I said.

"Nope, check me out! All kinds of cool, aren't I?"

"Where's your help?" I asked. The gargoyle clerk was nowhere to be found.

"I gave him leave. He was slowing me down, truthfully. Decent fellow, but really bad sense of direction." Lord Raggleswamp grabbed the two heavy canvas bags loaded down with his texts. He hung one on each horn and waddled toward the home furnishings section.

I highly doubted Raggleswamp had dismissed Finn. Rather, the gargoyle's patience had probably been stretched too thin with the uppity villain, and he had abandoned the smudge. I couldn't blame him in the least.

Raggleswamp said, "Well, hurry now. Let's be off. Much merchandise to snag to outfit our dwellings in striking fashion. Get your credit voucher from the clerk and have at it with me. There's a deeply comfortable recliner with my name on it, and I aim to be relaxing in it before the dinner festivities are in full swing."

The clerk waved him back and handed him a card. "You'll need this if you want to buy in Home Furnishings."

After accepting an overly sincere thank you from Raggleswamp, the clerk rang up Tiberius. I didn't see the total, but overheard the checkout girl, a tall blue-skinned elf, inform Tiberius that his account easily covered the cost. She handed him a wafer-sized card with the letters HF emblazoned on it in a jazzy font. "Go right on over to Home Furnishings, honey. Pick yourself something nice for your room. Don't go over 500, though." She tucked his bagged books in an alcove at the end of her checkout. "You can come back for your books after you finish shopping."

Tiberius stepped to the side and sat. He looked up at me expectantly.

"You go on ahead with Raggleswamp." I shooed him away.

"No, it's only polite I wait for you. So we can endure his company together." Tiberius yawned, briefly fogging his helmet.

The cashier finished ringing me up and dropped my books into two bags. Much like she had said to Tiberius, she announced I had enough credit in my account. However, she closed out my transaction by wishing me well. She did not hand me a Home Furnishings card.

"Um, excuse me, miss?" I asked.

She was already ringing up the books of the patron behind us, a tortoise with a rocket pack, and seemed irritated by my inquiry. "Yes?" she said sharply.

"Do I get a card, too? For Home Furnishings?" I said.

Tiberius held up his card with the expectation that my missing card was an oversight apparent on his face.

"No, you don't get one, sorry." She resumed chatting with the tortoise as she rung him up.

"Um, but why not? I mean, you gave one to both of my companions."

"Sweetie, you're a smudge. Now don't go feeling all embarrassed. It happens. Store policy is to not issue smudges furnishing privileges. When you sort yourself out, get your looks all in place, come back and I can give you a card." She flashed a belittling smile.

"But . . ."

"It's easier for you smudges this way. You don't want to buy a bunch of stuff and then have to move it to your more permanent residence once you're fully formed, do you? Besides, I hear both Smudge Halls are furnished with oodles of charm. Now scoot along, I have other characters to ring up." She shooed me away with both hands.

I wanted to protest but didn't. I felt like such a second-class citizen.

I accompanied Tiberius to Home Furnishings to select his purchases. We successfully avoided Raggleswamp, but that did little to lift my spirits. Being a smudge felt like banishment. I was not at all eager to return to Smudge Hall, my angry ash roommate, and the impending dinner party.

Tiberius walked me home. He wished me well and promised to save me a seat in Dr. Ringle's class. He boasted that he would be there ahead of the masses, as his creator had just penned the advantageous character trait of being an early riser. I smiled and issued a half wave before carefully walking up the steps and into my temporary, but somehow permanent-feeling, house of exile.

Chapter 23
LAST IN, FIRST TO LEAVE

Chapter One was off to a solid start. He had gotten Irving out of bed, incorporated some description of his room into the action, thus smoothly indicating some of the lead's interests. Above his bed would hang a poster of the most current hot video game. Decorating the space around Irving's desk would be mini-posters of his favorite band, Cooking with Zombies. It was a fictitious band, but it seemed to ring true. Plus, he loved working in any references to the walking dead.

As he typed, he had Irving attempting to burst into the locked bathroom. Irving was eager to give his change of dress a once over. As he was writing the exchange between his sister and Irving through the closed door, the door of his own studio was under assault.

His two children were arguing over how to decorate a paper bag puppet they had been working on downstairs. Both barreled in, nearly knocking over his plate of munchies teetering on the edge of the desk. He saved his progress and exited the studio. He would resume work on the scene after lunch.

As he walked down the steps, he ended the argument and refocused his children into working as a team.

* * *

It came as no surprise that what I heard upon entering Smudge Hall was the proud declarations of Lord Raggleswamp. He was holding court in the kitchen, and everyone huddled around him at the breakfast nook, listening with rapt attention.

Sarya sat on the bench with the now fully-formed villain. She looked at me and then just as quickly glanced away. Val was again cooking, the smell of bacon frying, mixed with other equally appealing aromas, kicking me square in the appetite.

There were at least seven other smudges crowded around, all ranging in their degree of fuzziness. The most distinct of the bunch appeared to be a bigfoot with a halo. His only facial feature in sharp focus was the vicious teeth lining his mouth. He smiled carnivorously in my direction before being sucked back into Raggleswamp's overbearing delivery of his newfound status.

"As you can tell from my refined appearance, I've really been fleshed out. Yep, I'm moving up in the world. My creator completed four chapters this afternoon, and two dealt exclusively with my background and motivation. I know why I'm such a bad guy!" he gloated.

"Tell us," pleaded Sarya.

Raggleswamp's eyes narrowed. Half his mouth snagged upward, sneering with glee. It was disturbing, seeing his features in contrast to the very threadbare or nonexistent expressions on his audience's faces. Like the others, I was drawn to the animation and detail sweeping over his face with every second that passed. As obnoxious as he was, a certain pride fell over me that one of my own was going on to something bigger.

"I really would love to go into all the details, but being of such gore and guile, I think it not appropriate to discuss with a lady present." He tickled Sarya, then added, "While I may be devilish, prone to torture and mayhem, I've been given to flights of nobleness here and there. I'm afraid that will be my downfall. My writer's a bit heavy-handed with the foreshadowing."

"What are you talking about? Foreshadowing?" I felt I should know this.

Sarya interjected, "It's a narrative tool. I was telling Raggles about it on the way back from Orientation. It was something we were talking about in Narrative Science today."

"They're hints at what's to come, little tidbits that pave the path for bigger plot twists, if I understood this beauteous creature correctly." Raggleswamp put his arm around Sarya, who was happy for the attention.

Raggleswamp's demeanor unsettled me. His words were polished, but underneath his foul nature held sway. Couldn't the others see he was toying with Sarya? That he didn't care about her? He was, after all, cast to be a villain.

My fascination with his resolved appearance evaporated. The spell broken, I looked at the others for any signs they were seeing the villain for what he was. They all still hung around him, waiting on every word.

"So, what next?" I asked.

"If I understand the way things are done around here, I'm off to Villain Way. Already had my purchases from the store sent over." He stood up. "Say, my time as a smudge, did it set any records?"

"Nope," Val remarked. He looked up from the pot he was stirring. I noticed a small flock of winged smudges no taller than salt shakers flying about, assisting him with the dinner preparation. They had long ears and slender limbs, the only aspect yet to be described was their faces. The largest, a chubby little devil, delivered a rack of several spices to Val. He thanked his help with a nod. "You got yourself together quickly, I'll give you that, but it's no record. You'd have to beat a little under four hours."

"Shame. Felt like a record." He flung up his hands. "Anyway, I guess I should be on my way. I hope you all find yourselves fully formed very, very soon. Please feel free to drop by my place any time." He started to exit the kitchen.

"Wait, you must stay for our dinner. After all, it's to celebrate the arrival of you new smudges this week, you and Irving. Just because you were a smudge for such a short time, doesn't mean you shouldn't attend. I'm sure Irving would want you to stay, right?" Sarya looked my way, holding her gaze.

I fumbled with my answer. "Oh, sure. Yes, that would . . . be . . . quite good. Please stay."

Raggleswamp let the silence linger, drawing even more attention to my awkward and insincere response.

Sarya said, "No reason to be that way, Irving. Even though we can't see it, your jealousy is written all over your face."

It was clear she was still hurting from last night's outburst.

"I . . . I didn't mean to . . ." I stammered.

"Save it." She slid out of the breakfast nook and took Raggleswamp's hand. Leading him toward double doors off to the far left I had not noticed before, she said, "There's just enough time before dinner. Every smudge has to check this out before they leave. It's kind of a rite of passage."

"Well, certainly," Raggleswamp said. "If it means more time in your company, then let's be off. What is it exactly you are showing me?" He puffed out his chest.

She grabbed hold of the right doorknob and tugged the door open, its hinges emitting a faint creak. From my angle, I could see very little of the room's interior. It looked very dark and very empty. The light from the kitchen that found its way into the room revealed a thick rug resting on a well-worn wooden floor. "Oh, I'd love to go with you, but smudges aren't allowed in. It's a privilege of those who get their acts together. Only when we leave can we enter."

"Positively mysterious, my dear. You've ratcheted up my curiosity a thousandfold." Raggleswamp entered the room with ease.

Sarya closed the door behind him, being careful not to catch hold of the villain's cape. "Take your time and come out when you're ready. Dinner will wait for you."

The door clicked shut.

Everyone in the room scrambled about, assisting Val in various ways. With an oven mitt covering his robot hand, he tipped a pot lid my way. "Why don't you catch some rest up in your room. We'll call you down, when it's mealtime."

"Can't I help?"

Sarya walked past me. "You've done more than enough. Just wait upstairs. I mean, all you talked about last night was getting off away by yourself, right?" She retrieved a large knife from a nearby drawer and began chopping up a head of lettuce placed moments ago on a cutting board by three of the flying smudges that buzzed around with even more bluster now that the kitchen had grown crowded with help.

Wanting to say something in response, I exhaled then spoke, "Hey, I didn't . . ."

Val dropped the lid down on a large pot with a clatter. "Go on, kid, git. It's hot enough already in this kitchen." The smudge wiped his robot arm across where his sweaty brow should be.

I retreated to my room, hoping my roommate was still missing in action.

Chapter 24
ASH AND YOU SHALL DECEIVE

It was a good start.

He read over the chapter. It held together well. Irving's sister came off as sympathetic and a comfort to him while still being a bit nagging as older sisters should be. She would keep him from being too lazy. He had her deliver several very telling lines indicating her wide ranging knowledge of mythology, her role as a surrogate mother figure, and her growing anxiety at high school being around the corner. The paragraph of her appearance clearly established her insecurity over her looks. He also had her talk with an enthusiasm that ebbed and flowed on a whim.

For Irving, he nailed the look of the jacket and the pants. He even loved how the boots appeared as an afterthought in a flamboyant puff of smoke. Irving's frantic dance to extinguish a non-existent fire raging on his feet was a nice touch.

Having Irving tell his Dad the uniform was a costume he had to wear for a psychology social experiment for school felt right. Did middle schoolers have psychology classes? Probably not. Maybe Irving's teacher could be a bit of a rogue and inject his history class with some random stunt lessons on the human condition. The author fondly remembered how the world opened up to him when reverse psychology was revealed to him by one of his own high school teachers.

His mind wandered from the manuscript. Maybe Irving had a close relationship with the teacher. Could he be the adult anchor Irving would confide in? Would he avoid telling his dad about his adventures and instead go to the teacher? If Irving's father had connections with Wish Haven through Irving's missing mother, wouldn't he recognize the wishjacket for what it was? He would. Good thing he thought of this detail before beginning the next chapter. He found it comforting how the chapters ushered in story points for the next one. It made his writing feel second nature, like he was specifically attuned to the wants and needs of the plot.

He jotted notes in the margin.

Looking up, he saw the kitchen was a full-scale Playdoh disaster zone. Both his son and daughter were busy making rainbow meals out of the clay. He set the chapter aside and assisted in fashioning several purple and yellow meatballs to set atop their mountain of orange spaghetti.

* * *

My roommate, the off-putting ash, was back.

Even worse, it was on my bed. It had coiled a segment of itself into a circular loop that floated in front of it. The main mass was still a large pile of ash connected very thinly. The airborne portion acted like a television screen. From my vantage point, I could make out images of two figures arguing with a volcano erupting in the background. My ashen roommate was engrossed in the scene.

I inched the door open further to get a better view of the floating picture portal. I knew what I witnessed was only for my roommate's eyes, but I couldn't help myself. I was curious about everything and everyone at the Academy, even Raggleswamp to some extent. I risked a step into the room.

I wish I could say I was caught peeping because of a noisy floorboard or the creaking of a fussy hinge, but I was squarely to blame for further eroding my already poor relationship with my roommate. The sudden appearance of my footwear in a puff of dramatic smoke produced a weak shriek of concern from me.

The ash, alerted to my presence, collapsed the portal back into itself and shot through the air to hover over me. "Hey, what did you see?"

"N-nothing," I sputtered, backing out of the room a few inches.

The ash swirled about, clearly fuming. It could see through my lie. It abruptly retreated to its bed, saying nothing.

I sidled over to my own bed and dumped my textbooks out. Looking around for a wastebasket to toss the bags in, I saw the journal on the solitary desk was open. I reached for it to hand to my roommate as a peace offering.

My hand was swatted away by a thick tendril of ash. It stung.

"Hands off!" it thundered.

"I was just going to close it and hand it to you. I wanted to show you I respect your privacy." My words felt like I was backpedalling. Even I didn't believe my intentions. "I didn't see anything."

"Stay away from me!" The ash wrapped itself around the journal.

"How can I? This is my room too! I'm not going to be driven out of here by a . . ."

It streaked through the air, coiling into the shape of a snake perched to strike. Again, it was only inches from my alleged face. "By a what?"

"For someone who gripes about their space, you certainly like getting up way close!" I barked. Why was I aggravating it so? Just back down. Had my writer embedded a stubborn streak in me? I knew much more about my sister thanks to him writing chapter one. Other than my new boots and a more refined appearance to my wishjacket and pants, he hadn't really pushed building me to the forefront. Was it possible to develop a personality outside of what he wrote for me?

The ash glowered. Still holding the journal tight, it curled in on itself and winked into nothingness.

I knew it hadn't disintegrated. I had a sneaky suspicion it teleported away. To where? And when would it come back? Should I tell anyone about my foul-tempered roommate? Should I ask for another room? Yes, that was it. I'd demand another room. I'd tell them I didn't want to be cooped up with a pile of ash who was unbearable.

I exited my room, intent on never having to deal with my roommate again.

Even though I had told him I hadn't looked in the journal, I had lied. I had glimpsed the most recent entry. It would've been hard not to see it, being written in such bold capital letters and taking up nearly half the page.

The angry ash had written: *HARMSTRIKE MUST DIE!*

Chapter 25

HALLWAY HUFF

He was so thankful for his wife. She was his sounding board, the person he could gush to about his writing plans and ambitions. She helped him talk out his scenes. She listened as he rambled on about doomsday devices and portals to other worlds, when her own tastes leaned toward more realistic fiction.

Tonight, he wanted to tell her about his first writing session with Irving.

He carefully put away the dishes and wiped down the counter. Calling his daughter over, he stuck close as she began her homework. She rarely needed their help anymore, but he liked to keep tabs on her. She was working on a pirate research project due when they tracked back in. She did not procrastinate, deciding on their first day out to start writing a plan for her research. He admired her organization and enthusiasm for creating lists.

He listened as she narrated what she had written.

* * *

I felt too closed in. Having read my roommate's journal, I didn't want to stay in the room a second longer. I retreated to the upstairs hallway. Not wanting to draw attention from those downstairs, I closed my door with care. Keeping my hand on the knob, I slid my forehead against the door and panted slightly. What was going on? Was I in any danger from a pile of ash? The dean was not one of my favorites, but it didn't make any sense that someone would want to kill him.

My frantic thoughts were quieted by a voice from behind me.

"Who were you shouting at in there?"

I turned to see Sarya sticking her head out of a doorway farther down the hall.

"What do you mean?" I said.

She stepped into the hall and closed her door. She fluttered her wings and hovered closer. "I guess the way you bark at people, it takes lots of practice. That what you were doing, right? Warming up to tear into someone at dinner? Maybe Raggleswamp? I bet you're not too happy he found his face before you."

"Look, my roommate, he's crazy!"

"What are you talking about? We set you up with a room all by yourself. You don't have a roommate," she said.

"What?" My hand fell away from the doorknob.

Sarya brushed me aside, not caring if we mixed together. She pushed open my door and entered. She inspected her surroundings. "There's nobody here, Irving. What's wrong with you?"

I reentered. "He was just here. He's a pile of talking ash. He threatened me and then teleported away." My voice dropped as uncertainty crept in. "I don't understand."

"This room was vacant before it was assigned to you. Val's in charge of the rooms and he's very particular." She began to exit.

My arm shot out, loosely grabbing her indistinct forearm. It tingled as I tried to tug her back. "But there are two beds. You see two beds, don't you?"

She sat on my roommate's mattress, bouncing up and down on it. I expected the ash to reappear and scold her. It didn't. "This room is set up for two occupants, but there's only you here."

"It left! I told you that. It floated in the air, then wrapped in around itself and disappeared."

"And does this roommate made of ash have a name?" Her tone was syrupy. She was humoring me.

"Uh, no, he told me I didn't need to know his name. It was none of my business is how he put it. At least I think it was a he," I said.

She strolled to the door. "Look, just go to dinner. Leave all your craziness up here and come down to a peaceful meal. You start classes tomorrow and you really ought to get a good night's rest. You have this room to yourself. You're one of the few here with your own room. Enjoy it."

"It was here! It's a grumpy thing! And I think it wants to hurt people."

Sarya raised her voice, something that felt at odds with her plucky nature. "So your imaginary roommate wants to hurt someone here at the academy? Who?"

I replied, my voice barely a whisper, "Um, Harmstrike."

She paused. Her lips crinkled. "Look, I know your meeting with the dean didn't go that great. I was there, outside his office. I heard a little of what he said to you."

"You eavesdropped?"

"Well, my creator did brand me with a healthy curiosity. I couldn't help myself." She refocused her attack. "Is it any wonder the dean is a little sour on you? You made a mess of the Fine Aunts Office."

"That wasn't my fault. How was I to know I'd be attacked?" I said.

She tore into me. "So when you say you have an imaginary roommate who wants to harm the dean, you'll have to excuse me if it doesn't seem a little like someone projecting their feelings so they don't have to be held accountable!" She crossed her arms, pleased with her analysis.

"I can prove it! He wrote it in his journal. He wants to kill Harmstrike!" I scrambled to retrieve the journal from the desk. I stopped, remembering where the journal had gone. I turned around to face Sarya. "He took it with him."

"Isn't that convenient," Sarya said.

"But it's true! He wrote the threat in his journal! I think he realized I looked at it and took it away with him," I said.

Sarya shook her head. "Irving, you're making a mess of things. There's no roommate!" She lingered in the doorway. "Take a little time to pull yourself together and come down to dinner. Don't mention this murder-minded pile of ash to anyone else. Don't hassle Raggleswamp. Don't stir up any trouble whatsoever. You already have a rep as a bit of a flake. No sense making it worse."

I didn't know what to say.

Her voice softened, "I want to be your friend. I think there's something good about you that I need in my time here, but not if it means putting up with more craziness. Go to classes, wait for your author to rein in your appearance, and be happy. We're only here for a little while. Make the most of it."

She closed my door and left me to myself. My roommate, real or imaginary, did not return.

After a few minutes, I went downstairs to dinner.

Chapter 26
A HOT MEAL AND HOUNDED

Tonight, his mind was buzzing with ideas. Tomorrow brought another chance to write a chapter. He had reread Chapter One just before going to bed. While he had intended the emberhounds to attack at a baseball practice, it was forcing it a bit to have Irving comically create an excuse to his coach as to why he was wearing such a flashy item of clothing to practice. It would be better to have the hounds attack at recess. The whole school would be witness to it, and Irving's dad would be called to the school over the matter. If the local authorities kept them afterschool for a while, this would leave Tyler home alone and fair game to be snatched away. Teardrop would send her big bruiser of a hunter and leave behind a gaping hole in the Holland roof.

He jotted down the revisions before clicking off his reading light, thankful he would be spared writing the scene with Irving dressed in a hoodie over his wishjacket.

Chapter Two was going to deliver action. He would definitely utilize the playground equipment to full effect.

* * *

Even as I walked down the stairs, I could hear Raggleswamp blathering on about his villainous abilities in the dining room off the kitchen. I entered and tried to ignore his bluster, choosing to focus on the decor and the other partygoers instead of giving him any of my attention. A dusty chandelier dangled at an odd angle, threatening to crash into the sweeping spread of food laid out before the dinner guests. Spotting only one open chair, it was clear I was the last to arrive. Even Sarya, who had been upstairs making me thoroughly doubt the existence of my roommate minutes earlier, had already found her seat. Naturally, it was next to Raggleswamp, and, naturally, that didn't sit well with me.

Val directed me to a chair next to him. I sat and discovered it was gifted with a nasty wobble. I noted Raggleswamp's chair, high-backed and stable, suffered no defects.

Raggleswamp offered up a grace that was too long and peppered with self-congratulation on his newfound fully formed status.

After the blessing, everyone filled their plates and just as quickly began emptying them. I sat across from the bearded smudges who enjoyed putting food in their nonexistent mouths almost as much as in their facial hair. The angelic bigfoot sat on Val's other side. The winged smudges who had helped Val concoct the meal, sat cross-legged on the mantle of a fireplace that was blackened from use. They tittered and pointed at Val, not even trying to hide their affection for their head chef. Four smudges I had not met sat next to Sarya. Two had wings, one pair leathery, the other feathered. A decidedly gaunt fellow, a crimson skeleton with a hood that covered his smudged face, employed a curly straw to slurp the pungent contents of a gigantic brown egg. On the opposite end of the table from Raggleswamp perched a flame-headed birdman whose eyes and lower body were undefined. His sharp beak tore into a rare cut of steak, causing my stomach to lurch.

Thankfully, there was more than undercooked meat and sour giant eggs to choose from. What I picked proved delicious. I helped myself to a mound of potatoes, two spoonfuls of green beans, and several helpings of chicken wings Val assured me were not too spicy. I focused on my food, not wishing to enter the conversation. The other honoree of the dinner had enough gab in him to make up for my silence.

Raggleswamp droned on and on about the proper aspects of secret lair design and just how many warning systems the modern security-minded villain should have. I wondered how he was so concrete on so many points. How fleshed out had his writer made his role in the plot in only four chapters? I wanted to ask, to shoot holes in his cockiness, but something held me back.

Raggleswamp had no such qualms. He laid into me before he'd even finished his spring salad. "Wishbutton, what about your author? What's he transcribed of your life so far?"

So he wanted to play that game. Comparing how far down the creative path I was? Probably would interject with his revelations. How fiendish of him.

"Well, he's written one chapter, but he's taken lots of plot notes so far, especially about my villain." I added, "I guess that part comes easy."

Raggleswamp abandoned his salad and attacked the rack of ribs burdening his plate. Now with savory sauce smeared across his orange muzzle, he said, "An early obsession with your villain? Interesting how authors dive right in with the motivations and appearance of their wicked characters, isn't it?"

"Her name is Teardrop, and she wants my jacket." I shoved potatoes into my mouth, concentrating on chewing and not talking.

Raggleswamp tore deep gashes in the ribs, slurping the meat down his gullet as he plowed forward in the conversation. "A villainess? How delicate and devious. What does she want with your gaudy costume?"

I finished my potatoes. Looking to buy myself more time out of what was feeling more and more like an interrogation, I scanned the smorgasbord for any food to occupy my mouth. I zeroed in on an appetizing three-bean salad. I reached for it. Unfortunately, the bigfoot commandeered it, sweeping it up in his meaty hands and preventing me from restocking my now empty plate. Without any food to curtail the conversation, I supplied an answer, "I'm not sure. I think it has a defect she wants to exploit."

"So, you don't know what it does?" He pointed to my jacket, wagging his finger about dismissively.

"Well, it's supposed to hold the wishes I gather up," I said, watching the bigfoot empty the salad onto his plate. I grabbed a basket of buns left unattended and buttered two of them. Their doughy goodness might offer up enough shielding from the interrogation. I was growing tired of playing Raggleswamp's game. Conversation drained me, and I wanted to retreat to my room, ash or no ash.

"You steal wishes from folks?" Sarya seemed hurt at the notion.

"That sounds a bit shady. Are you a ruthless anti-hero? Those fellows are quite slippery and uneven. Tend to cause a lot of damage to those around them in their pursuit of doing good." Raggleswamp patted Sarya on the shoulder.

I spit out the roll and defended myself. I didn't want her to think less of me. "No, it's not like that. The wish agents retrieve lost and stolen wishes and bring them back to Wish Haven. The jacket is what holds the wishes. The jackets have two buttons. One is used to gather up the wish and release it, and the other button isn't a button at all."

"What is it? Is that the button you're missing?" Raggleswamp abandoned the ribs and leaned forward. "Why does this Teardrop want your *flawed* wardrobe?"

"The second button, the one I'm missing." I played with a loose thread where the absent button should've been. "It's a failsafe feature. It prevents the wish agent from using their gathered wishes for their own benefit."

Raggleswamp smiled. "You mean your jacket can be exploited? You could use any of the wishes gathered up in its fine folds?" Raggleswamp's attitude toward the wishjacket had precipitously shifted. He regarded it, not me, with more import. "That's why she wants it! Your villainess could hijack the desires of others, couldn't she?"

"I think. My writer still has to fine tune her motivation."

"I wonder if the wishes would work here at the Academy? Would one be able to evoke such power here?" Raggleswamp was caught in his own back and forth. "I would imagine so. If one's writer gave you ice breath, then it would have to work here. I mean, those little gnatty smudges over there," he said, gesturing to the fireplace mantle and its tiny inhabitants, "they fly because of the power of their writer's description."

Raggleswamp teetered on the brink of dangerous territory. He seemed a little too excited about the power my wishjacket might hold within. I suddenly feared he might try to steal it from me and use it for his own vile purposes.

I had to shut down his line of thinking. "But the wishjacket is useless right now."

"How so? It holds the ability to make wishes reality. Is that not grand?" Raggleswamp swayed, his eyes focused only on my garb of enormous potential.

"My writer hasn't filled it with any wishes yet." I was again thankful for being so early on in my narrative.

Raggleswamp's voice sank, the tremble of enthusiasm evaporated. "Nothing's there? It's devoid of wishes?"

"Uh, yeah, I've only just come across it in chapter one. It isn't loaded with wishes yet, at least according to his notes so far. Everything's fine. Nothing extraordinary has happened."

Val cut in, "Except you've been attacked by creatures from your own narrative. That's alarming." He crossed his arms, resting his robot arm on top.

I said, "What? The emberhounds? They broke out of the Menagerie and found their way to me. Dean Harmstrike took care of them. That won't happen again. He wants my stay here to be normal."

"But you have to know something, Irving." Val inhaled slowly. "I did some snooping around, chatted up a few of the upperclassmen. No one's ever been attacked by their own beasts because nothing has ever escaped from the Menagerie. That place is locked tight. I went up there. Getting in and out is a tremendous ordeal. All sorts of permissions, forms, and quite advanced security systems."

Sarya piped in, dealing a chilling blow. "They didn't break free on their own. I didn't want to say it, but it's going to get out. Someone let them loose, Irving. Someone found a way to get into the Menagerie and sic those things on you."

Chapter 27
HOME INVASION

The scene was coming together well. He stopped typing to listen in on his children down in the kitchen. They were painting together at the counter, creating works of art with their fingers. Everything sounded peaceful.

He returned to the opening half of chapter two.

Mounting a defense from the turret of a curly slide had loads of appeal. As he wrote, he found the battle on the playground evolved very swiftly. The hounds had descended on the school grounds from a nearby field, lighting the tall grasses on fire as they wove toward the school with menace on their minds. The children on the soccer field scattered as the hounds caught the soccer nets on fire with their smoldering heads. Irving had been playing on the monkey bars when the disturbance occurred. Scaling to the top of the equipment, he watched the emberhounds racing toward his location. Even from a distance, he knew their eyes were on him, specifically the jacket he had been traipsing around in all morning.

He was about to have the first hound leap onto the roofed turret of the curly slide, Irving's vantage point, when the phone rang. He answered it, quickly arranging a play date with his children's cousins for after lunch. As he put the phone back in its cradle, he tried to reengage his mind in the mayhem of the scene.

Unfortunately, that proved difficult. Mayhem on a much smaller scale had erupted downstairs. His daughter was hoarding the paints, and he heard the early rumblings of his son about to lash out with a fist or foot.

He raced downstairs to put out the fire. It was time for a snack and perhaps some family drawing time. He'd play with them until after their visit with the cousins and return to his chapter later. He knew it would be easy to reignite his imagination. The scene presented so many playful possibilities.

After dinner, Raggleswamp prepared to leave Smudge Hall. He managed to make a big deal about it as he paraded out the front door with Sarya and myself at his side. I should've slipped upstairs after dinner, but really didn't like the idea of leaving the fairy alone with the villain. The appearance of a quartet of fellow evildoers from Villain Way made his exit even more theatrical. They'd arrived on the porch almost as if they knew Raggleswamp had been on the move. The despicable characters—a loud troll with antler-like horns, a robed wizard with much too expressive eyebrows, a creature made of shadow that constantly tinkered with the gadgets mounted on his enormous gauntlets, and a ghostly groom brandishing a rather long wooden staff that glowed—were all bear-hugs and back-patting as they welcomed Raggleswamp into their fold.

The five villains immediately engaged in a lively conversation about who was the most insidious and which among them had more ounces of wickedness flowing through their veins. They carried on about their misdeeds for quite some time.

I didn't stay long, preferring to retreat back to my room, regardless of whether I was tempting a run-in with my ashen roommate. Sadly, as I mounted the steps, I witnessed Raggleswamp a bit too affectionate with Sarya, hugging her a little longer than necessary. I knew it had been an act meant for me to see.

Once back in my room, I was relieved to be away from the rowdy porch celebration. My roommate hadn't returned.

I kicked off my boots, marveling at the footwear and how worn and well used they appeared despite being summoned into existence less than a day earlier.

I flicked off the light and lay staring at the ceiling. The hubbub downstairs died down a full half hour later when Raggleswamp finally left with his newfound comrades. I wondered briefly what their housing might look like, imagining dorms laid out in a mad scientist theme, before falling asleep.

I eventually fell asleep.

* * *

The sound of my window being pushed open startled me awake. Someone slid into my room from the porch roof outside.

I rubbed my eyes, willing myself to alertness. The intruder stood with his back to the dim moonlight allowed in by the shoddy blinds he had displaced in order to gain entry. He was large and had a distinctive golden hue.

His voice, drenched in malice, cut through the night air. "Wakey, wakey, Wishbutton. Time to take a little journey!"

Before I could slip out from under my covers, I was dealt a blow to my head. Reeling from the brutal impact, I caught a glimpse of another through my window. My intruder had an accomplice. Out on the rooftop leading to my room, a brutish troll snorted in excitement, his breath crystallizing in the chill night air.

I recognized my attackers. Flush with panic, I fought to stay conscious.

Seeing I hadn't crumpled to the ground did not sit well with my unruly houseguest. I was dealt another more severe wallop.

A loud, sickly crack preceded and then the lights truly went out.

Chapter 28
BRING ON THE WATERWORKS

The action and bluster of chapter two had gone well, supercharging his desire to write more. He had reviewed the scene last night before going to bed and made notes increasing the description of the destruction left behind by the hounds.

Irving had seen how the hounds were firestarters and had led them to a pond located on the far corner of the field. It was a small manmade pond that caught the run-off from the sloping school grounds. He had based it on the meander and pond at the school where he taught, even down to the dense population of cattails that stood guard in the murky water. Irving had successfully gotten his attackers to extinguish themselves in the pond. While it had not stopped the pack of dogs entirely, it had delayed them long enough for the police and fire departments to arrive. Overwhelmed by the sirens and the large throng of law enforcement heading toward them, the emberhounds had beaten a retreat through a floating portal. Irving had been the only one to see the portal.

Besides depicting Irving as having heroic, if a little bumbling, leanings, the pond sequence had also given Irving something new. At the water's edge, his wishjacket had detected a misplaced wish and retrieved it. Irving now had a wish stored in his clothing, but no idea what it was and what to do with it.

This morning, he was putting the finishing touches on chapter three. He was pleased with the real world consequences of the otherworldly attack on the school grounds. Police and government investigators were swarming all over the place in chapter three, giving Irving and his family barely a chance to breathe. So far, prying eyes were not targeting him. That would change with the abduction of his sister in the next chapter. He had a particularly wicked twist planned for the sister that would involve some magic gone awry, causing Teardrop's plan to be successful but in a way that thoroughly complicated matters for all.

He paid special attention to how Irving's father reacted, making sure the son noticed his father's behavior. Mr. Holland tried to act shocked over the whole debacle, but both his sister and Irving detected their father knew more about what had happened than he let on when interviewed by a very friendly detective.

The chapter closed with Mr. Holland rushing his children off and attempting to talk about anything other than what had occurred. With suspicions raised, the scene ended. Next chapter, Irving would confide in his sister. She would not respond with hysterics, but with support.

Of course, that would make it the perfect time to turn Irving's world on end and snatch his only support out from under him.

He saved the document and headed downstairs.

Today was library day. The children piled into the van with relish, and they took off to their second favorite spot in the world.

* * *

The blast of cold water to my face brought me wide awake. I was upside down, hanging from a wooden support beam by thick rope tied around my lower legs. My hands were tucked behind me, also secured by rope. Despite lacking a suitable nose, I sneezed, expelling the water that had just soaked my face.

"Look at that, Helmurk, you were right. Smudges must breathe regular. It sneezed," said a three-foot-tall red dragon that flew around me on tiny wings. The tip of its tail was a nest of nasty spikes. At several points in the creature's flight path, the tail swerved dangerously close to my head, intentionally. "Fling another bucket at it."

The troll, the same one from outside my window, came racing into the room. He held up a full bucket of water. "Let's see if we can get a good sputter out of the sap, Singe. Won't that be music to your ears?"

"Certainly. As long as you can keep him upset, it suits me just fine." The dragon landed atop the back of an ornately carved reading chair. I couldn't escape the feeling that the beast was awash in stolen courage.

The troll swept the bucket back, preparing to douse me again.

I fished for information. "Hey, I'm awake already. You don't need to do that again. What would your shiny golden boss think?" I said.

The troll said, "What do you mean? Gared, he told me to wake you and not to be nice about it."

I now knew my abductors; they had been the ones who rudely interrupted Roon's tour of the campus. The two from whom I had demanded apology for knocking her over apparently held a grudge. And they were supposed to be heroes? I looked around. Was I in a house on Hero Row?

I glanced down at the carpet mere feet from my head. The rug looked very expensive and formal. In fact, the entire room had the appearance of a reading room, from the shelves of books that lined the wall opposite the fireplace, to the two carefully placed chairs situated to receive just the right light from the lazy fire nestled in the stone hearth. It must've been all the blood rushing to my head, but it took being held upside down to finally get me to think on my feet.

I decided I wanted some answers. "So he asked you to truss me up like this? Let me guess, this is the only place in the house with a beam to tie a rope to, huh?"

The dragon looked deflated. His shoulders slumped. "Hey, he's not altogether worked up. You said you could get him really in panic mode. Hit him again with the water, Helmurk."

The troll froze. His brow furrowed. He didn't know where I was going with my questions. "Yeah, it's also far enough away from the festivities. He didn't want anybody stumbling onto you like this. He has a rep to uphold as a fine hero after all." His words emboldened him. He again prepared to let loose with the bucket's contents.

"And he told you to wake me up so he could have a little fireside chat with me, did he?"

"Yeah, so?" The troll held the water high, delaying its downward arc.

"And he left it up to you to figure out the best way to wake me?" I rubbed my wrists against the ropes. They were snug.

The troll nodded.

The dragon again badgered him. "C'mon, I haven't got all day. You promised you'd get him all riled up. How am I supposed to get anything out of him if you can't?"

I wasn't sure what the dragon was talking about but felt it was the least of my problems. I had the troll doubting his actions. If I worked it right, I might even get the dim-witted brute to untie me. That was a big if.

"So hitting me with water was all your idea?"

He again nodded, this time slower.

"Don't you think a slap to the cheek would've done the job a bit better? Saves you the mess. I mean, now you've gone and soaked a fine looking rug in the process." I rolled my eyes in the direction of the water still dripping from my head.

The large wet spot on the rug caught the troll's full attention. His eyes widened. The troll's large lips quivered slightly as his lower eyelids curled upward.

The dragon again glowed with bravado. "Hey, well it's not a total loss. Your misery is just as good as his. Give me some of the good stuff." It puffed out its chest and basked in some invisible energy radiating from Helmurk.

"Gared's not going to be happy," I said and let the observation hang in the air.

The troll lowered the bucket, placing it on a small end table next to the fireplace. "No, he's not. What was I thinking?" Tears escaped, meandering down his pockmarked cheeks.

"Gotta say, I feel your pain, Helmurk," the dragon said as he hopped closer to the troll.

"So," I said, "what's he going to do when he sees what you did to this rug? This place isn't special to him, is it?"

"It's where he goes to plan, to hatch his schemes." The troll fell back into the larger of the two reading chairs, landing hard on a book left abandoned on the seat cushion.

"Why does he need to scheme? Isn't he a hero?" Something wasn't adding up with the Golden Knight, and his lackey was filling me in.

"You've said enough, Helmurk," growled someone behind me. I decided against twisting around to see who had entered the room. I already knew from the troll's reaction.

Helmurk bolted out of the chair, knocking into the end table holding the bucket of water. It fell to the hearth, dousing the fire.

The room went dark.

Light returned, but from an unexpected source.

"Singe, light up," barked the new arrival.

The dragon's entire body glowed a bright orange, casting ample light onto the golden armor of Gared, Helmurk's boss.

Gared took to one knee, bringing his face in line with my own.

"You've managed to unhinge one of mine, Irving. That doesn't sit well with me." His eyes narrowed. "Not at all."

I said nothing.

"Cut him down and untie him, Helmurk. Bring me some candles, then leave us."

The dragon flew closer. "Do you need me to stay, master?" His voice wavered as he spoke.

"I don't even know who invited you, foul misery mite. I would have none of you drainers in this house." Gared did not take his eyes off me.

The dragon's nostrils flared in irritation. "Oh, but you'll drag me out of my quarters to do your dirty work, won't you? You can't play both sides, Gared. One of these days, it's going to get the best of you. Your silver tongue only works on half of those you have dealings with. You won't always be able to talk your way out of all your ambitions."

"Yes, well, you let me worry about that, won't you?" Gared's voice took on a singsong quality.

Singe's eyes glazed over and his voice rolled out in monotone. "I will let you worry."

Helmurk returned with a candelabra housing six long candles. He quickly lit them. No sooner were they lit than Singe flew out of view, still glowing.

Gared yelled, "And use the back door! Don't want my guests to see the likes of you here. It would spoil their fun."

Helmurk cut me down, allowing me to fall to the ground with my hands still tied. I landed hard on my right shoulder, but had enough sense to roll and lessen the impact.

The troll fidgeted with my bonds, scratching my wrists with his rough nails several times as he dug into the numerous knots he had manufactured in the first place.

Finally, he had the rope loose enough for me to free my hands. I rubbed at them briefly, still disturbed how solid they felt despite being smudged.

Gared occupied the larger seat. He gestured for me to take the other. I sat.

He wagged an index finger lazily through several of the candle flames. "Now, let's have a civilized conversation, Wishbutton. I fear I need to inform you of the rules of this place, so you don't go making a fool of yourself. After all, us heroes, we simply must stick together."

"What makes you think I want to hear anything from you?"

"Did I fail to mention who's in attendance at my little get-together downstairs?" He leaned in and whispered, "Roon came. Your little pale girlfriend. It took a little convincing, but she's down there, unliving the good life. You wouldn't want anything bad to happen to her, would you?"

I said nothing.

"I figured as much."

He extinguished one of the candles with his thumb and index finger and began.

Chapter 29
GARED'S SPIN

Chapter three fell into place with little effort. He had intended to end the scene with Teardrop's next creature ripping their roof off but decided against it. It was a quiet moment between Irving and his sister, despite the panic pervading their conversation.

It had turned out to be a scene revealing their relationship, the give and take between them that was equal parts nagging and nurturing. They discussed how much their father seemed to know about Irving's new outfit. Irving had Tyler help him try to take off the jacket. It didn't want to let go of him.

Adding to their anxiety over his new garment, he related how the jacket had reacted strangely at the pond. It felt like it had gathered up something. What it had taken, Irving was uncertain.

He almost had their father listening in on them from out in the hallway, but decided it was too obvious. Instead, he jotted a few notes about the next chapter. He needed a villainous interlude, a chance to show what was going on in Teardrop's lair. Chapter four would be very dark and set up the appearance of the roof-ripping beast for the next scene.

Lured away by the sound of his children stirring, he flicked off the computer and went to investigate. These early morning writing sessions only happened when he found his mind couldn't calm down. He did not like getting up at five in the morning, but once or twice a month didn't mess up his rhythm too much. It might mean two chapters would get written today. He'd have to see.

He ran into his daughter stumbling to the bathroom in her robe. He smiled and reminded her to be quiet and not wake her brother. She whispered excitedly, requesting to make pancakes. He agreed and waited patiently for her to finish in the bathroom. After washing her hands, they tiptoed downstairs to build their trademark tower of flapjacks.

Gared didn't like me. He pretended to enlighten me as to how things worked at the academy, but it was apparent he just wanted me to know his standing on campus.

He took a deep breath and began my education. "This school is something special. It produces unique graduates. There's no other school like it. Other places of higher learning churn out doctors, business majors, and lawyers. Here, heroes and villains are cast out into the world. Can you imagine anything nobler?" Gared's eyes danced. The candlelight made his wide smile even more striking.

"But we're not really alive. We're characters. When we leave, we are bound in the pages of a book," I said.

The Golden Knight clawed at his armrests. "A limited perspective. What I'd expect of a smudge."

"Yeah, let's get past that. What's with everybody so down on us? Seems like this place should be a bit more welcoming of all types. Smudges do become real characters."

"Oh, believe me, smudges have a place here. They do. Some go on to stand tall in stories of significant weight." Gared paused for effect. "But that's not often."

He was toying with me, attempting to knock me down. I wish I could say I didn't play into his little game, but apparently I wasn't written to resist. I took the bait. "How do you figure?"

"The graduation rate for smudges, well, it's a little low." He stretched, flexing his fingers casually.

"What does that mean?"

He leaned in, his voice dropping to a plotting whisper. "Here's how I've heard it. Smudges don't get published very often because their authors lose their inspiration. Smudges don't get to see the printed page because their creators are fickle. They lose steam. It's that they maybe encounter too many rejections of their manuscripts. Entering the academy without being properly fleshed out is a sure sign of an amateur author, of someone who might not see their creation through to the end. I've heard one professor put it that way."

My dismay was written all over my face.

Gared plowed ahead, relishing my shock. "I know it sounds a bit cold, but most here don't give the proper respect to a smudge because they probably haven't earned it."

"So, a lot of smudges never leave here? I mean, the only way to be done with this place is to get published, right?"

Gared stood and walked over to the fire, pretending to warm his gloved hands. "Well, there is another exit, another way to end your stay."

I waited for him to continue.

"A lot of smudges get revised."

"What are you talking about?" I said.

Gared replied, "Rewritten. Stripped down and recast with totally different personalities, motivations and storylines. Revision Ravine is where they go. It is not a pretty place. Filled with characters stretched every which way. It's a place of creative doubt."

"So just smudges go to this ravine to be reworked?"

"Quite a few do, but some regular characters wind up there, too." He tried to sound sympathetic, but it was a weak effort. "Even I could end up there. Despite being fleshed out with such lavish backstory and magnificent motivations, I too could fall prey to revision."

I protested, "But you're not even a nice hero. Isn't that going to make it likely your creator could get frustrated with you and toss you aside?"

Gared tipped back his chair, inspecting it for flaws. "Actually, no. You see, any story worth its ink has a hero that starts out flawed. My tale, it's quite delicious. My brother, he and I, well, one of us is destined to be the villain. Our author, he's playing it back and forth as to which of us ends up filled with virtue in the end. He's far enough along that I can safely say it looks like he's chosen me to rise above my shortcomings."

"But you're quite nasty!" I cried.

"I am, but the narrative is moving me down a path where I redeem myself. I'm a bit of an antihero, and those are quite coveted these days. At least, that's what my professors tell me. It's very doubtful I'll be revised."

I caught myself holding my breath. I gulped up a patch of air before responding. "That's not going to happen to me."

"Good for you. Maintain that attitude up until the end, no matter what shape it takes." The Golden Knight saluted me smugly.

I didn't know what to say next. I felt exposed, defenseless.

Gared stepped toward the hall. He turned at the carpet's edge. "You can leave now. And when you do, please put out the candles. Safety first with open flames and all that. Be sure to use the back stairs. After all, you weren't invited, and your classmates downstairs don't take kindly to crashers." He stood up straighter and flexed his arms. "Now, if you'll excuse me, I have an entrance to make. Don't want to be a no-show at my own party. What would everyone think? I'll be sure to send Roon your best. She's so easily impressed by the littlest of things."

He departed, leaving me alone in a room lined with books. Their spines taunted me as I blew out the candles and left. My abduction had robbed me of many things tonight, chief among them, my resolve.

Chapter 30
TOOTH BE TOLD

Someone in Teardrop's camp wasn't playing nice. The spell summoning the bagbeast, the name he had given the giant squid rhino, had been altered slightly by one of her underlings. The minor spellweaver was operating on a separate agenda and his meddling was going to have huge consequences.

He was uncertain why the spellweaver was working against his mistress, but he was sure it would fall into place.

The latter half of the chapter was spent describing the summoning of the creature by Teardrop. He felt it important that the magical rituals in the book take on such depth that they became part of the setting. He did a quick check on rune magic and decided the villainess would derive much of her power from stone. The cold aspect of her power source suited the villainess.

He ended the chapter with the minor weaver altering the spell. He left it up to the reader's imagination as to how the spell was changed. Later it would become very apparent.

He saved the file and left to play with his children. An afternoon at the pool helped break up the long summer days. After three days of track out, he had four chapters to show for his labors. He was ahead of schedule. Maybe tomorrow, he'd skip a day of writing. He raced down the steps, challenging his kids to slap on their sunscreen in record speed.

* * *

I left Smudge Hall without breakfast and without witnessing the return of my alleged roommate. Sorting out if the pile of angry ash actually existed was not a high priority.

My mind still reeled from the confrontation with Gared. I had returned to my room quite late. Navigating the campus at night from Hero Row had been quite an ordeal. Only the helpful guidance of a talking lamppost had saved me from wandering into Villain Way. While the light fixture had been a bit dramatic about what would've happened if he had not intervened on my behalf, I suspect he had mostly helped me out of boredom. Either way, I was thankful. At least somebody was looking out for me, even if that somebody was a public utility and rooted to a slab of concrete.

At least my daytime trek to my first class had gone easier. I was actually a few minutes early. Doctor Ringle's class was packed. I saw Sarya sitting up in the front row with Lord Raggleswamp nudging her and pointing in my direction. She waved at me coolly. Raggleswamp smirked and turned away.

I spotted Roon in the back row. Her brother was nowhere to be seen. I made my way in her direction. Halfway there, she spotted me. She looked away. I still went through the motions, arriving at the seat next to her after squirming by an entire row of rather lumpy beasts in battle armor. Their cursing did little to lift my spirits. Roon's tight lip further eroded my confidence. I sat down, dropping my books onto the attached desk with a pronounced clatter.

I looked down at Doctor Ringle, who was writing the topic of today's lesson on the chalkboard. Roon opened her notes and wrote it as well.

Attempting to draw her into a conversation, I said, "I found out my jacket has a wish in it. My author wrote a chapter about me getting a wish from a pond. I don't know what it is exactly or how to use it, but I bet I'll learn soon."

She tapped her pencil on the spine of her text.

"In my last chapter, I had a good talk with my sister. She's actually really cool. I wonder if she's in this class?" I scanned the students in attendance. "I don't think she's a smudge. I mean, she hasn't shown up at Smudge Hall."

A few stragglers raced to their seats as Doctor Ringle cleared his throat and flung up his arms like an orchestra conductor.

"Shush, he's about to begin," Roon said as she bit her lip.

"How's your brother? Is he in this class?"

She swiveled her head slowly in my direction. Her eyes narrowed. "I would really like to take notes properly today, Irving. Maybe you should've gotten your need to chew my ear off out of the way last night when you crashed Gared's party." She shook her head, pulling her pencil eraser pensively to her upper lip. "Oh, wait, that's right. You came, but didn't have the decency to look me up."

"What?" I shouted.

Several rows in front and behind us shot simmering looks my direction. I sank into my seat.

"What do you mean?"

"I saw you sneak out the back when I was in the kitchen refilling a snack bowl. Gared came sweeping in and tried to cover for you. He said you had come to make amends for your poor conduct with him. He had asked you to stay, he said, even mentioning to you how I was there. He explained how that news spooked you the most and made you head for the hills. Is that true?"

Doctor Ringle had begun his lecture, but not before bestowing upon the two of us an icy glare.

I whispered, "He would put it like that. That guy is all wrong. I didn't duck out because of you. I didn't even go to the party."

She waited for me to continue.

"Roon, I was dragged to that house against my will! I didn't want to go!" I tried to keep my voice low but found it difficult. Luckily, Ringle was looking off in the other direction.

"Wow, that makes me feel even better." She crossed her arms.

"No, that's not what I meant. Gared and his troll sidekick broke into my room, knocked me out, and kidnapped me. I was upstairs tied to a rafter the whole time."

"Gared's a hero. You're saying he engaged in foul play? Why? Just to get back at you?" she questioned.

"Roon, I think you and I both know Gared is not much of a hero. He's rotten."

Doctor Ringle bellowed, "Mr. Wishbutton and Roon Umberdare, you are disturbing the class! If your little conversation is that important, please take it outside." He looked at us expectantly.

All eyes were on us. I felt the urge to slide further into my seat.

"Okay, we will," I said.

Several people gasped. One birdlike girl two rows up squawked.

"We'll try to be quick, sir." Rising on wobbly legs, I grabbed Roon by her wrists and pulled her up.

She didn't resist but did protest. "What are you doing? He wanted you to stop and let him continue."

"Oh, I didn't see it that way. I thought he wanted us to really leave and get this squared away." Too late to turn back, I rushed out of the lecture hall with Roon in tow, closing the double doors with deliberate slowness. I glanced at Ringle's face as the doors shut. He looked annoyed.

I slid against the far wall, still holding tight to Roon's wrists. It was then I noticed how cold her skin felt.

The hall was quiet. We both held our breath. After twenty seconds, Doctor Ringle returned to his lecture.

Roon twisted out of my grasp as I exhaled sharply. "Irving, you're an idiot!" She moved toward the double doors.

"Don't go. Let me explain. Let's slow down, and I'll tell you," I said.

Her hands went to her hips. "Go on."

"Gared grabbed me and took me to his house. I didn't even know there was a party. I didn't even know you were there until he told me. He threatened to hurt you if I didn't humor him. He lied to you. His goon, Helmutt, or whatever,—"

"Helmurk. He's a troll," she corrected me.

"Yeah, he woke me up with a bucket of water. Gared came in and basically told me smudges don't amount to much. He dragged me there to put me in my place. He doesn't like me, Roon. Why? What did I ever do to him?"

She rolled her eyes. "Irving, from the moment you arrived, nothing has been normal about your admission to the academy. You come in as a smudge. That's a strike against you. Smudges just aren't given that much status."

"But, you—"

She held up a hand to silence me. "No, I don't feel that way, but a lot of people do. My brother's one of them." She got a faraway look, then continued. "Anyway, Gared's a big boy. He thinks the universe revolves around him. He's a hero, but obviously his author needs to teach him a thing or two about humility. A lot of heroes have some growing to do. It's common knowledge that heroes have flaws."

"That's what Gared told me," I said.

"He doesn't like you because you shouldn't matter, but you do. You're the only smudge that I know of to be taken to the dean's office on the first day. Being attacked by creatures from your own story, that draws all sorts attention. Did you know people are whispering about how the Menagerie has never had escapees before your emberhounds got loose?"

"I've heard," I replied.

"Well, all those things, they set you apart. Gared's used to everyone knowing their place, and you don't."

"But how should I know my place? My author hasn't figured me out yet. How am I to blame for this?"

"Look, I'm sure you won't remain a smudge for long. Just try to keep it low key until you hit full hero status. Then, nobody here is going to care much what you do." She walked toward the classroom.

I grabbed her arm again. "Roon, wait."

She spun around and opened her mouth, hissing at me. She clamped her hands over her mouth as shame washed over her face but not before I saw what she had tried to hide. "I didn't mean to react like. . ." Her voice wavered.

"What's wrong, Roon?"

She turned away from me and reached for the door to the classroom. She sobbed, "I'm going through some changes. I can't really do anything about it. Just leave things alone. Don't stir anything up."

With that, she retreated back inside Doctor Ringle's class.

I stood in the hallway a long time, spooked by what I had seen. There was something new about Roon. Something she hadn't had before today.

She now had fangs.

What was happening to her? What was she? And why did I have an even worse feeling about her brother's fate?

Chapter 31
ROLE TO PLAY

His daughter made him do it. He had intended to skip a day of writing, but she didn't want him to. So much so, she sat at the older computer working on her own story about a dragon seeking out an apartment, while keeping one eye on him to make sure he was also typing away on a new chapter.

He had the title for the chapter, Wishful Thinking. Irving was going to discover what his jacket could do. The wish it had scooped up at the pond was going to be put to use. Of course, it was going to create more problems than it would solve. He wanted Irving's relationship with his jacket to be a bit topsy-turvy. Not being trained on how the jacket worked, he was going to trigger wishes without knowing what they did.

He knew what the wish was going to be, he just didn't know where and how it would affect Irving's life.

What if Irving returned to the scene of the crime, the place where the wish had been absorbed? Maybe he was trying to see if the jacket would do anything again. Maybe Irving was testing the theory that the location was important to getting the jacket to work.

He started in on the chapter. The ideas felt slippery. The scene was the most uncertain to date. When that happened, he usually procrastinated, waited a day to write. He looked over at his daughter. She smiled and chatted about her ideas.

He knew she wanted him to write with her. Maybe he could wheel his chair over and see what she was doing? As he did this, she waved him away, laying on a helping of guilt to get him back on track with his writing. She was one tough story cop. He was glad to have her on patrol.

He sat up straight and let the chapter unfold, gaining courage with his daughter at his back to tackle the plot uncertainties he faced.

* * *

I returned to Ringle's class a few minutes after Roon. I sat at the first seat I came to, avoiding looking at Roon who had returned to her original spot. Doctor Ringle spared a glance my way but did not pause in his lecture.

". . . motivation may not be obvious to you. Depending on the villain's writer, you may find they spill their plans quite recklessly. That's one approach." Doctor Ringle cupped his hands. "True geniuses, they keep the hero guessing."

He swept his hands outward as if readying to embrace the class. "Look around you. Among your classmates, even maybe within yourself, there may lurk a vile evildoer that is remarkably devious, infernally sly."

I saw Raggleswamp coyly smile. He fluttered his eyelids at Sarya and whispered to her. I imagined what he said was little more than bragging. He probably thought he was one of the greats.

"Motivation is major plot magic. If you have the right kind, it will transport your story to grand heights. If your writer lacks imagination, you will have to be happy with predictable plotting and simple schemes. Does anyone have any questions?"

Two rows away from me, A hand shot up wrapped in distinctive golden armor. Gared was in my class. Wonderful, two classmates who had it in for me were in my first class. What were the odds?

A throng of monsters surrounded him and hung on every word from his magical silver tongue. Gared could order them to do whatever he wanted. I wondered just how his creator thought his talent to be noble and heroic. It was shady.

He shouted his question, "Would motivation based on family clashes make the story have more substance? Does it make the reader care more about the character who is searching to find themselves?"

Wow, his question, it made him sound insecure. I had not seen that side of him yet.

Doctor Ringle replied, "Family members facing off is certainly one way to raise the stakes. Yes, I would definitely say it makes the story more appealing. It creates tension almost anyone can relate to."

Gared smiled. The answer had inflated his standing. Probably the reason he asked it.

I shouldn't have, but I did. I wanted to take Gared down, embarrass him as payback for kidnapping me last night. "Doctor Ringle, is it possible for a writer to start their story intending to make a character a hero, but write their story in such a way that the character's actions change the author's intentions to the point where they decide to make their hero a villain?"

I didn't look at Gared, but knew he was furious. I could hear it in the unsettled nature of his bestial followers. They growled and grunted at my attack.

Doctor Ringle, perhaps because he was villainous himself, didn't hesitate to deliver an answer that would aggravate. "The writing process is fluid. It can take on a life of its own. Sometimes, yes. Sometimes, it can redefine a character. Worthy writers allow their characters some freedom in forming themselves."

While I had only wanted his answer to upset Gared, it unearthed even more of my curiosity. "So this school, we're students here until our books are finished and published?"

"Yes, that was covered at your orientation." Doctor Ringle was unimpressed with my question.

I added, "A writer doesn't define every aspect. Some of the details and actions are left to the characters themselves, right?"

Doctor Ringle nodded. "And to the readers. Mr. Wishbutton, do you have a point?"

I did. "We can think for ourselves here, do what we want?"

"Within the rules of this academy, yes." He was again interested in my line of inquiry. "But once your book exists, you are bound by the written word. You leave this place and your freedom is only given when someone opens your book and lets you into their imagination."

"But here, even if our writer dictates we are heroes or villains or supporting characters, does that mean we have to serve that role here?" I asked.

Doctor Ringle's pause told me his real answer. He placed a serious expression on his face. "Wishbutton, the Academy expects you to conduct yourself the way your writer would want you to act. There is some wiggle room, but we can't have heroes going about being villains, or supporting characters thinking they're in charge."

Gared added, "Or smudges thinking they're somebodies." His entourage cackled at his insult.

Ringle said, "What you're suggesting is chaos and not at all how this fine institution should be run. While I personally salute your devious thinking, my role as your professor must express to you that Dean Harmstrike desires you see the Academy as a place to further your understanding of your character, not to rewrite your stories and motivations."

The lecture hall grew quiet.

Doctor Ringle cleared his throat and redirected the class. "I have assigned you study buddies. The pairs are posted on the doors. The expectation is that you get together once a week and work on that week's topic." He looked squarely at me. "You may not switch partners."

As the class moved to check who they had been assigned, I remained in my seat. Gared and his troops waded past me. I expected a shove but received only foul looks. When only a few students remained, I moved toward the exit. Sarya and Raggleswamp still huddled together in their seats, engaged in conversation. It was hard to tell with her smudged features, but I was certain she looked my way as I left.

I approached the list, dreading who I had been assigned. I knew from Ringle's harsh stare he had not put me with Roon.

I scanned down the list. Not finding my name on the first sheet, I started in on the second. I found my name halfway down.

I was not at all happy with Doctor Ringle's cruel selection. I left the hall and raced back to Smudge Hall, my reluctant haven.

Chapter 32
DEARLY DEPARTED

In the middle of writing the chapter, he had gotten sidetracked. His mind had turned to how Wish Haven was run. Out of nowhere, he decided to have a second place that was talked about cryptically, spoken about in hushed tones. Wish Haven would be secure, but their second outpost, a place where smaller wishes had been housed, was going to have been overrun.

Whimville came to mind. It would've been a smaller stronghold, guarding the wilder, less structured wishes. Whims were fickle dreams, easily discarded and sometimes random and outlandish. They wouldn't contain as much energy as full-blown wishes, so they wouldn't have been as well protected. Whimville would be mentioned as a place in ruins. The wish agents would haul it out as a failure.

As quickly as the thoughts tumbled forth, he jotted them down on his pad. His daughter scolded him for not writing his chapter, but he expressed to her the brainstorm he was having would help him in future chapters. Satisfied he was still technically working on his writing, she returned to her apartment-seeking dragon.

Irving's father and his past association with Wish Haven fell neatly into place with Whimville. It was a natural fit. Irving's father had not been a wish agent, but a whim wrangler. He had been there to see the fall of Whimville to unspeakable forces. The father's secret of what had happened at Whimville would tie in nicely with Teardrop and Irving's mother. He wasn't sure how, but he knew there was a rich back story waiting in the shattered remains of Whimville. He recorded all his thoughts with delight. Back story had never presented a problem in his previous books. He had always been able to nurse it naturally from his initial round of ideas. For Wishbutton's tale, it was bubbling forth easily once again. He cherished moments like these.

He wondered if his daughter experienced the same when she wrote. After he exhausted the flow of ideas churning forth about Whimville,

*he'd ask her to share what fine details she'd created for her dragon. He
knew she'd have plenty and that made him proud.*

* * *

I needed a fortress to hold back the world. Instead, I got a barely
furnished room with a roommate that may or may not be a figment of
my imagination. I wondered briefly how the ash could be imaginary if I
myself were not actual flesh and bone. Could a character dream up
their own creation? If I wrote somebody into being, would they show up
at the Academy?

My rambling thoughts were interrupted by an eager knock at my
door.

Before I could invite my guest in, she swept open the door and
stepped into my room in a frenzy. That's only partially correct. Sarya
entered in a supercharged fashion, but minus her feet touching the
floor. She flew in using her wings. This was the first time I had seen
her airborne, and it secretly thrilled me. I knew she was a magical
creature, but to actually see her ignoring gravity was spellbinding.

"I'm finished!" she proclaimed.

I knew instantly what she meant. Her face was no longer hidden.
Her eyes were gems, large opals that danced about with boundless
energy. Her nose was tiny as I imagined it would be. Her ears, long and
slender, would surely give any bunny pause. Her arms and legs were
trim and outfitted with numerous bracelets and anklets. She wore a
simple tunic that was dyed pink to match her hair. She was a smudge
no more.

"You are!" I said, feeling suddenly upbeat.

She launched toward me, arms outstretched. Remembering how
our last physical encounter had ended with mixing together, I cringed.

She scolded me as she wrapped her arms around me. Not a single
body part sunk into my hazy features. In fact, the sloppy kiss she
planted on the approximate location of where my right cheek would one
day be, felt real and alarmingly pleasant.

"Silly, I can touch you now. Only if I were still a smudge like you
would we get all jumbled." She squeezed tighter.

"This is good news, Sarya."

"Good news? No, Irving, this is great news!" She released me and flew to the ceiling, halting inches away but not before her antennae bent humorously downward. "It means my writer is working on me. My part of the story is happening as we speak."

"How's it feel?"

"Crazy. So many details about who I am are popping into my head. I know tons about my village and my place in it. A lot of it is good and some of it is bad. My cousin, Sareesha, she tries to discourage the hero who happens upon our home. I help him get his quest back on track."

"Isn't it weird having memories planted into your head?" I recalled the fresh details of my father's cryptic history with Whimville, it being the most recent detail to land in my mind.

"It's exciting, but also it makes me a little mad," she confessed. Her mood changed as she grounded herself.

"What do you mean?"

She shrugged. "I feel programmed. Like my life is run by somebody else. My author's out there putting his thoughts down, playing with my fate. What if my story is a tragedy?"

She had a point. It was a topic I tried not to think about. "But at the Academy, we have a little freedom. Didn't you hear what Doctor Ringle said? It's like our writer starts the process, and we affect how we turn out."

She rubbed her forehead. "But only here. Once we leave, we are stuck in our stories, repeating actions written on the page."

"Well, for right now, focus on your time here. No one knows what it's like when we leave. Nobody's returned, right?"

"I guess." She sat next to me on my bed.

I didn't fully understand how she could be so giddy one minute and so beaten down the next. I wanted her to feel better about her situation. "Look at it this way; nobody made you come up to my room. You did that on your own."

She looked at me, her large eyes imploring me to continue.

I said, "That's a decision you made. Your author doesn't know I exist. They didn't write you this scene."

She blushed.

"You're no longer a smudge. That's gotta feel good." It was the wrong thing to say.

Tears welled up in her newborn eyes. "I can't stay here, Irving."

"I know. You get to go to the supporting characters' dorm. You'll meet a lot of new people. Besides, we'll see you in class. Heck, my smudge days might be over tomorrow, and I can join you." Why was she getting so worked up about Smudge Hall? It was a pit.

"I don't want to go." She placed her hand on my knee. "I was just starting to make friends. And you, I wanted us to be better. We started off wrong. The first real hero who walks into my life, and I push him away. What does that say about me?"

"It says you're a good judge of character, sister," said a voice from outside my window.

Hovering at eye level was my roommate. It was clear Sarya saw him too. Her mouth formed a surprised oval.

"Don't just stand there. One of you yahoos open up. Rain's threatening, and water and me don't mix in case you haven't figured." Extending an ashen tentacle, it tapped on the window with his journal.

Sarya chose that moment to scream.

Chapter 33
BRASH ASH

The pond chapter was slow to start. Having Irving sneak out near dark to return to the scene of the crime, added a real rush. Irving surveying the cattails swaying in the nighttime breeze was certainly a memorable image. His character was waiting for something to happen. Much like his character, he was uncertain what would happen next.

His mind circled back to Whimville and Irving's dad. In a flash, it came to him. Something lurked in the cattails. That something would talk to Irving, telling him secrets about his father. He'd never fully reveal what was there. Just enough description to make it clear to Irving and to the reader that what was in the water was not native to the pond, despite being obviously aquatic.

The creature would be quite a talker. He toyed with its revelations being cast out in rhyme, but found it awkward and forced. It would be cryptic. It would tempt Irving with more secrets than it actually revealed. The unknown informant would tell Irving to ask his dad how to work the wishjacket, adding that the father would most surely know.

Perhaps the most chilling tidbit it would reveal would concern Irving's mother. In no uncertain terms, it would relate to Irving that it knew of his mother's whereabouts. That would send his hero scampering home with the tails of his wishjacket between his legs.

* * *

No sooner had I lifted the window, permitting the cloud of ash to enter, than a downpour began.

"Least I ended up on the roof. Could've been worse. Still getting the hang of my teleportin'." It settled into a heap on its pillow, its journal tucked behind it for safekeeping.

Sarya slid up against the wall. She crouched on my bed, ready at any moment to take flight. She had stopped screaming when I opened the window.

I heard someone heavy run up the steps. My door burst open and Val barged in, leading with his menacing cybernetic arm. "What's going on?"

Sarya looked at me. We both slid our eyes over to my roommate who I was about to point out to Val, when Sarya spoke up. "It was nothing. I was screaming in excitement."

Val sized me up, looking at me now as a threat. "He didn't hurt you? It sure sounded like you let loose with a bloodcurdling shriek."

Sarya gushed, "Nope. Just took my squeal a bit too far. Fairy screams are a bit hard to figure so I understand your confusion. Just go back to the kitchen and finish fixing dinner, okay? We'll be down soon. Promise."

Val backed out of my room, never taking his eyes off me. "She's special, Wishbutton. She's got it in her fool head that you matter. She might be right, but don't mess things up, got it?"

I nodded. With his attention on me, he had yet to spy my roommate. I was hoping he wouldn't.

Before he could close the door, Sarya flew over and gently eased it shut. She positioned her body to block Val from seeing my roommate. Wrinkling her nose playfully at Val, she whispered loud enough for me to hear, "It's nice having so many protectors. Thanks for looking out for me."

Val nodded and clomped back downstairs as Sarya clicked the door shut.

She frowned. "That was close." She wiped her brow dramatically. I found her expressions engaging. "At least he didn't see it." She nodded to the ash.

"Why'd you do that? A second ago, you were frightened of it, now you're hiding it from Val."

"I was in shock. Your roommate being real, it's a lot to handle. But when it entered the room, I suddenly knew it wouldn't hurt me." She looked at the ash, expectantly.

"I'm not so sure of that. All it's ever done is fire off threats," I said.

The ash sprang into the air, aping a coiled snake. Its head stabbed at me, stopping short of my smudged features by mere inches. "And you know me so well 'cause we've spent oh so much quality time together up to this point, right?"

"It's insane!" I shouted. Realizing my raised voice might tempt a return visit by Val, I lowered my voice. "It's dangerous."

"I kept it hidden because . . ." Sarya grimaced. She was flustered. "I just did."

My roommate collapsed into a fluffy cloud and eased over toward Sarya. "I appreciate your concern, young fairy, but no one sees me unless I want them to. Mister Mighty and Metal wouldn't have seen a thing even if you hadn't blocked his view."

"So you wanted her to see you?" I asked.

The ash ignored me, but answered my question while looking at Sarya. "I did. She needs to see me. She's a part of this now."

"What is *this*? What do you mean? Last I heard, you wanted nothing to do with me." I crossed my arms.

The ash chuckled, a disturbing sound. "Irving, I was playing a game. It's in my nature. I like to ruffle feathers. Plus, it is true; I'm not much of a people person. At least not your type of people."

"What? Smudges? You don't want to associate with smudges?" My hazy hands tightened into fists, not that anyone could see my aggressive action.

"No, no. Nothing of the sort."

"Then what did you mean?" Sarya bit her bottom lip.

"You characters," it said.

I was furious. "What? You're not from any book? You're saying you're not a fictional creation?"

The ash again chuckled. "Not exactly. I'm so much more."

The air filled with the electricity of anticipation as Sarya and I waited for its explanation.

Chapter 34
IN CAHOOTS

He had spent the evening talking with his wife as they watched a few of their favorite shows. An innocent topic had given him inspiration and momentum for the next chapter. Their nephew was going through the stage of always running off, and it was getting harder and harder to keep track of his bold expeditions. The image of his brother-in-law wedged under a large hay wagon as he removed his wayward son, who squealed in delight at being chased and found, was a pleasant memory from their recent strawberry patch trip. It had really hammered home the idea that their nephew was a restless soul, never wanting or willing to "stay put."

When his sister-in-law had used that particular phrase in frustration over her son's wanderings and what she wanted him to do, his mind had flashed to Irving's first trip to Wish Haven. He saw Irving being told to stay put while his guide went off to take care of some distracting problem. Of course, Irving wouldn't. What person would when faced with a mysterious new realm to explore?

He told his wife how the chapter title would be called: Stay Put. She smiled and resumed work on her Sudoku puzzle.

Tomorrow, he'd whip up a chapter really delving into Irving's first foray into Wish Haven. In his head, he criticized himself over having the next chapter not deal with Tyler's abduction. It was critical to the story and already very well mapped out in his head. It would have to wait until after Irving's Wish Haven trip. He wasn't avoiding the scene; it was just a case of the story dictating what happens when. He found with many of his books he started with signpost scenes, events that came to him early on and served as key plot points. As he wrote, other scenes fell into place, sometimes pushing the signposts further down the path and sometimes negating them entirely.

The Wish Haven trip would not cancel out the abduction. It would increase the emotional intensity of Tyler's kidnapping. He quickly decided Irving would take Tyler with him to Wish Haven. It would give the reader a chance to see their connection to each other and empathize with her eventual disappearance.

All his thoughts collapsed into a special reserved corner of his mind as their show resumed. Most nights, they fast forwarded the commercials, but when they got to talking, they held conversations during the breaks. It also allowed him to read or think about his writing.

He wondered if his mind would uncover any other story details when the next ad segment intruded on their viewing. He secretly hoped it would.

* * *

My roommate gathered itself together to form a floating question mark. It held the shape only seconds before collapsing into a pile on its bed. I waited for it to continue.

Sarya didn't. She lobbed a question at it. "Explain. If you're not like us, then what are you?"

"That will be shown much later. What I am is important, but the reveal must happen at the right time. Don't worry, the two of you will be the first to know." It sounded smug, but also immovable about the subject. It wasn't going to tell us.

Sarya didn't accept its unwavering demeanor. "That's not fair. You don't get to do that. You show up, you give us answers."

I expected it to respond harshly to her.

"These things have to be uncovered at the proper moments. Being characters, you should appreciate the grace and beauty behind letting a mystery brew to its proper point of release." The ash sounded theatrical.

"Why bother with me now?" I said, "Last time, you were pretty clear you wanted me to stay out of your way."

The ash replied, "My role is not an easy one. You didn't need a tender roommate to hold your hand. I supplied suitable turmoil for you. Now, I'm here to usher you into your next endeavor, your next quest if I may be so clever."

"You're pretty caught up in delivering the right part at the right time. Are you in Professor Darklay's Plot Dynamics class? Why haven't

I seen you there? It's a small class. I'd know if you were there." Sarya stepped toward the ash, unafraid.

"I'm familiar with his ramblings. He makes some good points, but his perspective on story structure is a bit biased. It looks at the plot from the character perspective."

"And you would look at it from what perspective?" Sarya's wings fluttered. She was agitated.

The ash thumped a portion of its body against its journal. "The reader, the writer, the candlestick maker," it said in singsong fashion.

Sarya wrinkled her nose. "You make little sense."

"Because you are seeing one piece of a vast puzzle, young fairy. Just know that I am an ally. That we three must band together against a common foe."

"What are you getting at?" I feared I knew exactly what he was getting at.

The ash held up its journal. "Come now, Irving. We both know who you saw in my journal. I let you, after all. It was the right time for you to see the name of the evil here at the academy."

Sarya pointed at my roommate, trying to imbue her slender finger with more threat than grace. She failed. "I didn't believe Irving when he told me about you. I thought he was crazy, but here you are. He told me what you wrote. Your threat, it's true?"

"Yes, your dean must die." The ash paused. "When said aloud, without understanding Harmstrike's foul deeds, it sounds a bit much, I must say."

"He runs this school. He helps us find out about our characters." Sarya was defensive. Perhaps due to her emergence from smudgehood, she felt more allegiance to the school.

"So what are the evil things he's done?" I said.

"Irving, Irving, having me tell you and having the two of you discover for yourselves are two different things. You must mount a search and in doing so must experience tragedy to obtain commitment," it said.

Sarya flew toward the door. She looked back at my roommate, her face flustered. "You appear, telling us it's time to do something, asking us to band together with you. Then you proceed to claim you won't do anything. You're just another person who wants to feel important by getting others up in arms. I know your kind. My sister, you and she would get along quite nicely."

She slammed the door behind her. I expected to hear her stomp down the stairs. Instead, she flew down the steps, the buzzing of her wings fading quickly.

I turned to face my roommate. I glared at it. I so wanted to fling an angry comeback at it.

"She'll come around. You need her and another. We'll talk about the entire band of merry folks you'll need to accomplish our task at a later date. Right now, know that I will return to move you along in due time." The ash spun tornado-like into the air.

"Wait, at least tell me your name."

As the ash teleported away, its answer echoed through my room. "Simon."

Simon disappeared. I glanced over at his bed to see he had left me a gift. His journal lay closed. A single page had been ripped out and placed atop the notebook. Written in precise cursive was a message: *Read, then gather your clues within.*

I sat down to read.

Chapter 35
JOURNAL TURMOIL

Tyler's addition made the Wish Haven trip more exciting. He looked back over the chapter, tweaking and revising. Tyler was useful. She supplied more reaction to the unique architecture of Wish Haven. As he reread the scene where Irving meets his guide, the author was pleased with the guide's personality. He was obviously held in low regard by the other wish agents. From his comments, it was clear he was a junior member and Irving was his first rookie. The guide, an amphibian boy from another dimension, was new to showing somebody else the ropes. His name was Tig Krinkster and he took his job seriously. He approached it with too much enthusiasm. The author liked how the guide tried too hard.

He added a line revealing Tig saddened to see Irving's jacket was missing its second button. He made sure Tig fretted enough about it that Irving and Tyler would realize the jacket was defective, but kept it vague enough so they still didn't know what a missing button would do for its wearer.

He decided the final scene needed work. The guide needed to be called away, and he was unhappy with the offstage problem that forced Tig to leave Irving and his sister unattended. He'd have to work on it.

Next chapter, Irving and Tyler would ignore the order to stay put, getting themselves in trouble. It would also reveal which of the siblings was more apt to barrel into the mix and which would hold back.

He saved the file and set to work finding his grocery list. Tomorrow's chapter needed to relay key details about Irving and Tyler. He wondered how much of his own relationship with his sister would make it onto the page.

* * *

The journal was a quick read. It contained only four entries. The entries were not dated but were consecutively numbered. The first was

134

many pages long and featured letters of the alphabet being written over and over again as if someone were practicing handwriting. The letters were wobbly and uncertain on the first few pages but quickly became more polished as the author gained more control.

The second entry was harshly scratched onto the page as if Simon had been upset.

Entry 2

After four days of practice, I felt confident enough to record my observations.

I arrived in a basement room. Another was here. He tried to calm me down, but he was also fearful of another. He begged me to leave and take him with me. It was clear we were confined. I was about to ask him how I was supposed to escape with him, when the lock on the door jingled. This made him more frantic. He told me to hide in the shadows. He held a crumpled piece of paper in his hands, stashing it inside his dirty shirt like it was precious treasure. Dean Harmstrike, I learned his name later, entered. He spied me immediately and grimaced. He ignored me and extended a hand to my cellmate.

The frightened man tendered his paper to Harmstrike who ripped it out of his shaking hands. What he read on the page made him frown. He tossed the paper to the ground and growled at me. In his hands was some sort of futuristic weapon. I didn't see it there when he had entered. He pointed it at the paper. He fired once. The paper didn't disintegrate. He muttered something about not being able to destroy the source material then eyed me up and down. I knew what would come next. The man who summoned me here screamed at me to teleport. I looked at him as if he asked me to grow a second head. His eyes displayed his sincerity. He believed what he said. I closed my eyes and thought of someplace else. Harmstrike fired a blast at me. I melted away. I was uncertain if he destroyed me or my sudden evaporation was my own doing. I awakened in a room with two beds. Only I was not myself. I was much less. Much, much less.

Simon's arrival was nothing like my own. Dean Harmstrike came to my rescue. Who was the strange man jailed in the basement? Where was he being kept? Was he a character or, like Simon, something else entirely?

The next entry almost mirrored my own questions.

Entry 3

Who built the Academy?

Where do all the buildings, books, and food come from?

Who is the prisoner and where is he being held on campus?

Why did he summon me?

What was on that scrap of paper?

Why did Simon want me to read this? The journal didn't help any. I was more confused than before.

The next entry I had seen before. Knowing of it didn't make it any less shocking.

Entry 4

HARMSTRIKE MUST DIE!

I was interrupted by a knock at the door. Sarya stuck her head in.

"He's gone," I said, closing the journal and sliding it under my pillow. This did not go unnoticed by her.

"He gave you his journal? What's it say?" She shut her eyes and bit her lip. "Forget it. I don't want to know."

"What did you need?" My voice was soft, not threatening. I didn't want to upset her further.

She produced a weak smile. "Your study buddy is here. You were supposed to meet him at the library an hour ago. He came to fetch you. Irving, he's not at all happy."

"Oh no, I forgot." I grabbed my books and stuffed them in my backpack. I raced past her, my shoulder brushing against her cheek. "I missed your farewell dinner, didn't I?"

She nodded.

I took the steps two at a time, shouting back at her as I descended. "I'll make it up to you. How about we meet for lunch tomorrow? After Narrative Science class?"

I looked up to see her smiling and nodding. "Let's meet outside of the main dining hall over by Narrative Sciences, okay?"

"Great, see you then," I said quickly. I turned my attention to my study buddy who sat on the top porch step, rambling about punctuality to Val.

I was not at all happy to see him. He was even less pleased.

I apologized for not meeting him at the correct time. He snorted and jumped off the porch in one bound.

Lord Raggleswamp turned and replied, "Doctor Ringle has a wicked sense of humor. Come along, Wishbutton. If we are to be shackled to each other for the evening, I will need liquid encouragement."

I followed Raggleswamp, reluctantly.

Chapter 36
STUDY BUDDY

Because of the morning dental appointments, he didn't start on chapter seven until Monday afternoon. He had Irving and his sister striking out without their guide in Wish Haven. Tig was occupied with helping a squad of other agents rope a renegade wishing well that had mounted an escape. He had Irving see the rampaging wishing well stomping down an alley on giant bird legs. Perched atop the legs, the well teetered about flinging a loose shingle or two from its quaint roof to the ground as it tried to escape its captors.

He flashed to the wish in Irving's jacket. The story was due for some action. The siblings would get in over their heads as they toured Wish Haven minus Tig. Irving would summon the wish held in his garment to rescue them.

He squeezed in a sizeable chunk of setting description. Wish Haven would have a Victorian feel, with buildings slender and capped with rooftops that almost ran to the ground. Maybe the steep slopes of the roofs could be used as an interesting obstacle. As he detailed the setting on paper, he also tried to conjure up the danger they would face.

Tyler, entranced by a ghostly figure darting in and out of their vision ahead of them, would be the one to catch the spirit. What could the ghost be? A whim wraith? He liked the sound of that. Why was it loose in Wish Haven? It had to be tied to Teardrop in some way, but he was uncertain how just yet.

He closed the chapter with Tyler grabbing hold of the wraith. Upon touching it, the beast tripled in size, knocking over several nearby buildings in the process.

In a panic, Irving acted on instinct and triggered the mysterious wish held in his jacket. The chapter closed with Irving transformed by the wish. As Irving collapsed to the ground unable to breathe and clutching at his throat, Tyler reacted to what the wish had done to her brother. Her shocked declaration would also clue the reader.

Irving suddenly had gills.

Proud of his cliffhanger, he stopped. Ending with such suspense always kept him thinking about what was to happen next. He would spin the chapter around in his head, unraveling and coaxing out a strong wrap-up to the double jeopardy his characters now faced.

* * *

I stroked my neck, aware of what my writer had done. I now knew the wish I sheltered in my jacket would grant me gills. I also knew not to trigger it away from any large bodies of water. I was not happy that my writer chose to put me in such peril. Of course, the threats he wrote for me felt distant, like echoes.

The real threat sat across from me sipping a fruit smoothie and gloating about his choice of study spot.

Lord Raggleswamp said, "Isn't this nicer than the other room they reserved for us upstairs?" He swept a hand around.

Upon arriving at the library, the desk clerk, a fairy boy, a near identical twin to Sarya except for a missing left eye covered by a light blue eye patch, had checked the study schedule and escorted us to a well lit room on the second floor. It had contained a large round table with six chairs stacked off to the side. As the clerk had begun unpacking the chairs, Raggleswamp had complained that the stark room had no personality.

He had dismissed the clerk and then set upon securing us a room with more pizzazz. Raggleswamp had proclaimed the room most suited to us must be in the lower levels. After finding and descending a flight of stairs, we had wound through a labyrinth of dark and musty halls. Finally, he had settled on this room.

A floor lamp held back the shadows just barely. The walls were stacked stone, betraying the ancient foundation of the building. With each of the seven crossbeams that supported the floor above us thoroughly rotted, the ceiling sagged. Water dripped from at least three spots. Thankfully, none fell on our rickety table, which an oval beast whose legs were carved to resemble elongated gargoyles. A plate with the crusts from a sandwich sat in the center, proof that the room had long ago been host to another.

"This has the right vibe, am I right, Irving?" He knocked solidly on the table, flicking a splintered shard he had dislodged onto the floor.

I clawed weakly at my face, still feeling the remnants of the cobwebs that had wrapped around it numerous times on our reckless trek through the dank hallways under the library.

Raggleswamp noticed. "The webs were simply glorious, weren't they? Shame we never saw the noble arachnids that spun them. I bet they're oversized buggers."

I said, "Why down here? We aren't even supposed to be here. Didn't you notice the door you shoved open said No Admittance?"

"That only makes what's behind it more desirable. I simply had to uncover what lay beneath. It's in my nature to seek out dark, festering, and illegal places. You haven't forgotten I'm a bad fellow, have you?"

I grunted. Opening my text, I changed the subject. "We need to review the chapters he assigned. You read them yet?"

"Hardly. I was hoping you had," he said, standing up and running a finger along a sizeable rock in the wall that looked loose.

I flipped to the first chapter and tilted my head toward the door. "Could we at least close that? The constant wind whistling through the corridor is a little distracting."

"I find it soothing." He sat back down, propping his feet on the table. The wood creaked, threatening to collapse under the weight of his oversized boots.

"I get it. We're opposites. You like the dark, creaks and bone chilling breezes."

"We're not opposite in every sense, Wishbutton. We have one thing in common." He sneered.

He waited for me to ask what. I resisted.

Disappointed I had not taken the bait, he shared, "We both have our eye on a fetching young fairy. Now that she's no longer a smudge, it looks like my chances with her just improved."

I was about to ask him what he meant by the smudge comment, when I froze.

"Did you hear that?" I said.

He looked casually disturbed. Humoring me, he asked, "Hear what? I hear nothing other than your labored wheezing."

I looked at the open door behind me. "The wind—it's gone. I don't hear it anymore. Why do you think that is?"

Raggleswamp bolted out of his chair. With a swiftness and stealth not matching his stubby frame, he extinguished the light and crouched under the table. He hissed at me. "Someone's coming. Their body in the narrow corridor must be blocking the otherwise steady breeze. We must be still and remain undetected. Probably just the uptight clerk."

Or the giant spiders that had discharged so many webs throughout the hallways, I thought.

I could see Raggleswamp's eyes glowing in the near dark. He didn't miss the chance to have a little fun with me. "Or those spiders coming to fetch themselves a meal."

How had he done that? I didn't think he could read minds. Probably just a coincidence. Plus, I had made it pretty obvious how much the webbing had bothered me earlier. He was just good at reading my unease. I held my breath and listened. I detected the footfalls of the approaching person before Raggleswamp. "Here they come."

Raggleswamp gestured for me to be silent. Even in silhouette, I could see a clawed finger touching his closed lips.

Whoever was coming carried a light source. The hallway grew in brilliance as the footsteps drew closer. It didn't sound like an eight-legged beast.

The intruder walked by our room. The candle he held aloft gave just enough light to reveal his identity.

It was Dean Harmstrike.

Harmstrike passed by our room, oblivious to us. His eyes were trained forward, focused and determined. Where was he going?

As the dean's footsteps receded, I exhaled in relief.

Raggleswamp clamped a hand over my mouth and whispered, "Not out of the woods yet. Someone else is following our esteemed dean."

I slid away from him, slipping free of his beefy paw.

The footsteps approaching were fainter as if from someone of much less stature. They carried no light, but my eyes had adjusted enough that as they passed by I knew instantly who was traipsing around in the dark.

I waited until the second hallway shadow had safely passed us by.

Raggleswamp quietly closed the door and flicked on the lamp.

He said, "Did you see who that was? The first one was Harmstrike, but my eyes aren't so good. I couldn't make out much more than the fact that the second one was a girl."

"It was Roon," I announced.

Raggleswamp chuckled. "Goodness, me, Irving. What peculiar misdeeds have we witnessed? Your taste in companions borders on the seedy and sly. Perhaps another thing we have in common, no?"

What on earth was Roon doing under the library chasing after Harmstrike? I had to find out.

I surprised myself and my study buddy by heading toward the door.

"Where are you going?" he asked.

I turned and spoke with much more conviction than I had. "Something's up, and I aim to get to the bottom of it."

"Ah, the game is afoot. How lovely!" he uttered, scampering after me.

Chapter 37
LIBRARY LEADS

The sister saving the day was a plot twist he liked. He reviewed the scene he had just written, pleased with how tight and freewheeling he had kept the action.

Irving's sister had come to his rescue. After antagonizing the whim wraith enough, she had gotten free of his grip when the wraith had slammed her against a fallen building. Being tossed around high above had given her a brief glimpse of their surroundings. She had run to Irving's side, ready with her game plan. Taking only a split second to assess that he indeed had gills, she had dragged him down a nearby alley as several wish agents streamed in, their attention on the enormous whim wraith.

She had brought Irving to another open plaza area and towed him to its centerpiece, which she had seen earlier from above.

Ignoring Tig, who had reappeared and was scolding them for running off without him, she had slipped her brother into the basin of the large fountain.

The chapter closed with Irving describing what it was like breathing with gills as Tig informed them they had broken a very critical rule and would need to go immediately. The author chuckled at the guide's final comment. They would have to wait until Irving's gills disappeared. Tig let them know that could be hours.

As he reread the scene a third time, the chapter title presented itself: **Wet Behind the Ears.**

He loved the double meaning of it. He saved the file after checking for any stray homophone mistakes and went downstairs to build a ramp for his kids. He wanted to rekindle their interest in bicycling, and a small ramp constructed from scrap wood and a two by four was just the answer.

* * *

We crept down the hallway in silence. Raggleswamp allowed me to be in front, I suspect more from his poor eyesight in the dark than from any vote of confidence in my ability to lead. What little light there was came from patches of luminescent lichen that had colonized the cracks between the stacked rocks of the corridor walls. The pale green glow was just enough to see a few feet ahead of me.

Raggleswamp whispered, "Can you still hear if she's ahead of us?"

"Yes. I'm trying to catch up to her, but she's moving at a pretty good pace," I replied.

"What do you think she's doing down here?"

"I don't know. I think the bigger question is why Harmstrike is down here."

As we proceeded, the floor started sloping noticeably downward. Combined with the growing moisture on the stones under our feet, we had no choice but to slow down or risk slipping.

"Well she's obviously on a case," said Raggleswamp.

I kept moving forward, planting my hands on either wall to further safeguard my descent.

"What are you talking about?" I barked.

"Oh my, you don't know too much about your friends, do you? Roon's a detective." Raggleswamp inhaled sharply. "Actually, she's a bit more than that. Her and her brother are zombie detectives."

I paused. That explained a lot. Her pale features, the cold skin. What it didn't explain was her fangs. Not willing to appear completely in the dark, I offered up my own findings. "That makes sense. Although, she did confide she's going through some changes. I think her author is tweaking her."

He remained unimpressed. Raggleswamp said, "Tsk-tsk. Her case must involve our good dean. How intriguing. Wonder what dirt she has on him?" He paused. "Why's her brother not by her side? Come to think of it, I haven't seen them together since my first day when they picked me up and brought me in. From that, I gathered they were quite inseparable."

Roon's footsteps stopped. Our discussion ground to a halt.

I swept my hand out and back to stop Raggleswamp. "I think she's just ahead of us, around that bend." I pointed ahead, aware he couldn't see how the wall rounded.

"Well, let's take the plunge." Raggleswamp started past me.

I wiggled ahead of him, brushing against a large rock that jutted outward at knee level. "Let me do it. I don't want to barge in on her and Harmstrike."

Raggleswamp allowed me to again take the lead. I hunched over, making myself a smaller target as I rounded the corner.

A few yards ahead, Harmstrike was searching though his pocket for something. His candle was perched precariously on a crude shelf mounted on the door. The flames licked dangerously close to the wooden door.

Finally, he pulled out a key, long and black, and slid it into the lock. With a pronounced click, and the twist of the doorknob, it opened inward. Harmstrike retrieved his light source before entering and closing the door behind him.

I retreated, plowing into Raggleswamp and driving him backwards as well. "What did you see?" he said.

"Harmstrike went into a locked room. I didn't see Roon anywhere," I replied.

Before he could pester me further, we were attacked from above by a large bat.

Worse than the cobwebs, the bat swooped down on us, its claws raking horribly close to our faces before it landed on one of Raggleswamp's horns. As it sat there, it made no sound. I half expected it to emit a ghastly screech before resuming its attack. Instead, it inspected us almost as much as we were sizing it up. Large ears overwhelmed its head. The leathery wings stretched almost as far as the corridor width. Its snout was blunt and its mouth sealed shut, sparing us the displeasure of seeing the rows of tiny puncturing teeth we knew were there.

The bat shot me a lively look and then it transformed. As it changed, it hopped off Raggleswamp onto solid ground. When we saw what it became, we understood why the horn would've made for an unsound perch.

I gasped.

Raggleswamp tittered and huffed, "Delightful."

Chapter 38
BROTHER'S NOT A KEEPER

He sat in the vet waiting room with his two children. They were doing a good job of keeping their dog calm. With so much petting and cooing, all the two-legged and four-legged members of his family were occupied and not in any immediate danger of escape. His mind spiraled back to the chapter he would work on in the afternoon.

Chapter nine needed to comfortably explain the back story of Wish Haven. Irving and his sister would be brought to the person in charge who would give them a history of the wish agents. He would also comment on several responsibilities of being an agent and how Irving had broken a cardinal rule of using a wish for his own gain.

Tyler would notice something that related to their missing mother and the chapter would end with that revelation.

As the retriever grew restless, he tabled his brainstorming. He went to one knee and joined in with calming their hyper puppy.

* * *

The bat was gone. In its place, Roon crouched, her body still twitching from the change. As the spasms subsided, she rose. Her legs wobbled at the effort. Raggleswamp slid forward, offering a shoulder as he grabbed her elbow in an attempt to steady her.

Embarrassed I hadn't rushed to help, I offered words of concern. They came out forced. "You okay? What just happened?"

Raggleswamp convinced her to sit down. She slumped against the wall, safely out of view from where Harmstrike had disappeared.

She took deep gulps of air. Her eyelids drooped as her head slowly rolled up to look at me. "How did you two get here? Have you been following me?"

Raggleswamp explained how we had sought out a more subterranean place to study. When Harmstrike and she had passed by, he told her how we gave chase.

She relaxed slightly. "I didn't know Harmstrike was down here this time."

"What do you mean? Roon, what's going on? Why were you a bat? Zombies can't do that."

She scratched behind her ears. "You found out I used to be a zombie? Knew I couldn't hide it from you forever." Her eyes went more distant. "My writer, she's making some changes."

"The fangs. The bat change." I knew what she had become. "You're a vampire."

She held up her hands. "Guilty."

"Still a detective, I see. Still sniffing around in some rather odd locales," said Raggleswamp. "Why are you chasing down Harmstrike in such a place as this?"

"I really wasn't tailing him. I came down here thinking he was back at his office." She stood, this time with more certainty.

Raggleswamp circled back to something she had said earlier. "You said 'this time.' Does that mean you've followed him down here other times?"

She sized us up. "You have to keep this to yourselves."

We nodded.

"Not a word to anyone else," she said.

"You have my word," replied Raggleswamp.

"I promise," I offered.

"I am on a case. About two weeks ago, my brother and I stumbled on Harmstrike sneaking his way below the library. It was pure luck that we had been in the lower stacks.

"Our writer, she gave us an unswerving curiosity, especially my brother. We had to investigate." She pointed down the corridor. "He always goes into that locked room and spends an hour or so in there. Harmstrike visits at least four times a week. Last time we followed him, my brother went right up to the door and listened. He heard the dean talking to someone."

I thought of what Simon had said. My roommate had described Harmstrike keeping a prisoner. Could this be the same room? The same person?

She continued, "Last week, we came down here, determined to open the door and see who was there. The lock must be magically shielded because we couldn't jimmy it. My brother has incredible skills with a lock and even he couldn't undo it."

"So you came down here today to try yourself?" I said.

Roon explained, "I came down here thinking I was alone. I almost walked right into Harmstrike opening the door. He didn't see me. I was about to run out when I heard you two behind me. Only, I didn't know it was you. I transformed into a bat and waited for whomever to pass by. That's when you came bumbling onto the scene."

"Why did you come down here without your brother? What made you think you could break in when he couldn't?" Raggleswamp inquired.

She avoided answering the first question. "My creator, when she rewrote me as a vampire, she also gave me a magical tool. I mean, besides me being able to change into a bat." She pulled a large key out of a side pouch attached to her belt. She held it up.

It looked like an oversized key, its teeth jagged. The only telling difference was that it appeared to be made of bone.

"It's a skeleton key. My writer gave it the ability to open any door. Comes in pretty handy with detective work," Roon said.

"Very cool," I said.

"I guess." She again went distant. "But it came at a price," she said, averting her eyes. Her shoulders slumped ever so slightly.

"What's wrong?" Raggleswamp touched her shoulder.

"My creator gave me this key and turned me into a vampire. Sure, that's actually a step up. I don't have to worry about rotting flesh or slurping on brains."

"Just blood," I said. Instantly, I felt I had misspoken.

Roon sent me a wounded look. "Characters get changed all the time. Only this time, my writer did quite an overhaul."

"What?" we said in unison.

"She wrote my brother out of the story. He's gone! He's been revised!" Her eyes flared hysterically as she began sobbing.

Before either of us could move to comfort her, the door Harmstrike had entered creaked open. We heard the dean shout an angry goodbye to whoever was in there. We froze as we listened to him secure the lock and stride toward us.

Chapter 39
CONVENIENT TRUTH

At lunch, his attention wandered. He was bombarded with chapter titles playing off a wishing theme. Sometimes, creating the titles first steered his stories into fresher directions. He knew not all would be used, but the process of playing with words was a mental exercise he always craved. The first title, a result of the steam from the boiling water stinging his eyes, set him on a merry chase. Wishy Eyed, it could be about a wish that causes a tragedy. Wish Mountain appealed to him because it presented another setting possibility. He considered A Wish Served Cold, but found it too unapproachable.

He loved snatching ideas from out of the ether. It was a ritual he always tried to teach his students to appreciate.

Wish List was a keeper, but it didn't bring to mind any actions or events with it. Wish Upon a Tar, he eliminated as soon as he flashed on it. Too obvious and the tar part was forced. The Wishing Hour and Tree Wishes were the final ideas before he snapped back to reality and finished preparing their lunch.

After adding the flavor packet to the steaming noodles, he jotted down the titles on his idea pad.

* * *

Roon transformed into a bat again and wedged her small body into a narrow crack near the ceiling. Raggleswamp and I scrambled backward, hoping to evade the Dean. As we raced away, we tried to remain undetected. Unfortunately, our feet scrambling across the floor produced enough noise to be noticed.

Dean Harmstrike's voice cut through the air. "Who's there? Show yourself!"

Raggleswamp spun about and took hold of my collar. He whispered, "Play along with me, got it?"

I nodded, being careful to prevent my clouded features from drifting into his clearly resolved face.

Raggleswamp strode toward the dean. His voice inching toward demanding, he said, "Who, sir, is speaking to us? Pray you are not some foul beast with vile intentions toward me and my comrade."

Dean Harmstrike rounded the corner. He stood below Roon's hiding place, unaware of her presence. His expression shifted from alarm to recognition. "Young Wishbutton and Lord Raggleswamp, what are you doing down here?"

Raggleswamp exhaled, acting relieved. "Oh, it's you, sir. We thought we'd stumbled onto some horrid creature's den."

Harmstrike came closer. "Explain yourself. Why are you here?"

Raggleswamp replied, "Irving and I have been assigned to study together. Not my first choice in partners, mind you. Anyway, he, being the goody two-shoes, wanted us to study upstairs in the harshly lit study area we were assigned."

I couldn't believe it. Raggleswamp was telling the truth. How was that going to help us?

"I, being positively villainous, wanted nothing to do with a gloomy place such as a well-lit room. I dragged him down here and found us a more suitable area. It's right this way." He turned and gestured for us to follow. "Loads of atmosphere to it."

Dean followed, his posture stiff, doubt dictating his unflinching glare.

Raggleswamp trekked back to our study room. Entering, he patted the textbook he had left on the table. "We were just beginning to study when we heard something rustling around in the hall. We investigated. I led the way, while Wishbutton trailed behind me, sniveling about boundaries and whatnot."

The dean looked at me for confirmation. Resisting the urge to protest Raggleswamp depicting me as meek, I played the part. I nodded. "We shouldn't have come down here."

My partner continued, "I thought something lurked below, something with dark intentions toward the Academy. I have a nose for these things. Imagine my surprise when we uncovered you, sir, instead of some malevolent force."

The dean studied a page in Raggleswamp's book. He pinched the wick of our extinguished candle with a thumb and forefinger, testing for warmth long absent. "This lower level is off limits to students."

"We knew, sir, b-but—" Raggleswamp stammered a little too much.

Harmstrike held up a hand to silence him. His lips tightened before he continued. "Poor judgment I can excuse from someone written as foul as you are, Raggleswamp." He turned away from the villain. Facing me, he put his arms behind him. "But, Irving, breaking rules, floundering about in dark places, it does not suit one of heroic import."

"No, sir."

"See me in my office early tomorrow morning. Another chat is in order." He closed my text and handed it to me. "Study time is over. Back to Smudge Hall."

"Dean, sir, you never told us why you were down here." Raggleswamp smiled nervously as he pressed on in his inquiry. "Is there a vault of rare books down here only accessible to faculty?"

"Little man, I shall not explain my actions. All corridors of this institution are open to me. My comings and goings are none of your concern." He walked to the door and gestured for us to exit with him.

As we returned to the light of day with the dean at our heels, I wondered if Roon had escaped undetected. I decided I would seek her out tomorrow, after my second meeting with Harmstrike.

Chapter 40
ICY RECEPTION TWICE OVER

A chapter that was supposed to be weighed down with back story turned out to overflow with action. Well, at least the ending.

He reviewed the recent chapter as he pedaled casually on his stationary bike. He had Irving and his sister taken to the Wellwishers, the mysterious quartet overseeing Wish Haven. The Wellwishers had explained the premise of the wish agents, how they were charged with gathering up forgotten and discarded wishes. The wishes were rounded up and brought back to Wish Haven.

It had been a delicate balance, but he was happy with his portrayal of the Wellwishers. He wanted them to be open with certain information and hostile and guarded about other details. It painted the picture that their intentions were questionable.

They had given Irving a hard time about using a stored wish, claiming it was against the rules for agents to use what they gathered. Irving had pleaded ignorance, which they reluctantly accepted. After their blow up over his wish use, they had tried to appear as gracious and mindful as they could, but Irving's sister didn't trust them. She had made this clear to Irving as Tig shuffled them off to their new quarters. The Wellwishers had been unclear if Irving was to join the ranks as a full-blown agent. They expressed concern about his wishjacket and its missing button. This led the reader to the conclusion that there was more to Irving's jacket.

He found his pedaling increasing as he reread the action sequence. Irving and his sister were being taken aboard a tube rocket. An over-the-top alien arrived on the scene astride a hoverboard. Tig had tried to fend him off, but was given the boot. The mysterious and reckless arrival hijacked the tube rocket, taking Irving and his sister to parts unknown.

He'd have to think about where this new character would take his story. He sensed Irving needed a jolt, and this new addition was just the one to do it.

Upon returning to Smudge Hall, I fished around in the refrigerator. Finding several sandwiches left over from Sarya's farewell dinner, I grabbed two and retreated to my room where my roommate was nowhere to be found.

A note on my bed from Sarya told me she had left. She included the hall and room number of her new housing and ended the note with a reminder to meet her for lunch.

It was a little past ten. I knew Val was still up, having walked past him in the kitchen. For someone who was part robot, he certainly liked to be around food. Not feeling up to talking, I spent the evening reading the assigned chapters for Ringle's class then looked over my schedule for tomorrow.

I had to be at the dean's office by 8:00. My first class, Intro to Narrative Sciences, was at 11:00. I didn't have another class, Soul Searching Studies, until 1:30. I also decided I'd seek out Roon after that, if I didn't see her in any of my classes. I was unsure where she might be staying with her brother no longer with her. I thought she had said they were staying at a place where partners lived, but couldn't recall for sure. Aunt Nance would probably be able to tell me. If I didn't know where Roon was by lunchtime, I'd pay Nance a visit at the Office of Fine Aunts and ask her.

Pleased to finally have a game plan, I turned off the lights and went to bed.

No one barged into my room to scream at me nor knocked at my window to abduct me.

It was peaceful.

Very conducive to sleep.

I hated it.

Eventually, I drifted off.

* * *

The next morning, I was in Harmstrike's waiting room a full half hour early. I was not the only one there to see the dean. The ice princess from the Office of Fine Aunts stood, tapping her chin impatiently with a slender index finger as she gazed out the long double windows. The room was cold, even my breath clouded over as I exhaled a not-so-warm greeting.

She rolled her eyes in my direction, shifting her chin toward me slightly. Her air of superiority was just as present as her temperature-dropping talents. Why had I found her so attractive upon our first meeting?

"Oh, it's you," she chimed.

Even though what she said to me was dismissive, her voice sent shivers down my spine. Aunt Nance had warned me her powers of attraction were strong. It had to be in her voice. Its richness captivated me.

I responded, "Nice to see you again."

"I'm sure it is. You were that smudge who kept dear Aunt Nance from helping me. What was your name again? Featherrot?" She resumed looking out the window.

I remembered my lie. Aunt Nance had coached me to spit out a name to get her to leave. I felt bad for misleading her. I wanted to tell the truth. Maybe then, she'd want to spend time with me. "Um, about that. My name's not Featherwick."

I found myself angling to meet her gaze. Foolishly, I stepped between her and the windows.

The room temperature dropped even more as she grimaced. "You're in my way. Remove yourself before I decide to see if I can make my first smudgecicle." She snickered at her threat.

I drew back, clearing my throat.

She said nothing for almost a full minute. I should've been angry at her treatment. I should've spent that time fuming. Instead, I cataloged her beauty, drinking in her perfection. Her hair ringlets framed her face, vying for attention alongside icicle earrings that nearly reached to her collarbone. Her skin, a pale blue, glistened and sparkled. I wondered if I reached out to her, would she be hard or soft? Her eyelashes fluttered, long and amply curled. I knew it was her magic at work, but I couldn't fight it. Her allure was too strong.

She broke the silence. "I knew you lied to me. I knew Nance put you up to blurting out a name when you hadn't figured yourself out yet."

"You did?" My voice cracked. I felt shame at deceiving her.

She stepped closer to the windows. "Nance wasn't going to do anything for me that day. She never does. Your lie actually was quite helpful."

"How so?"

"My writer, she saw fit to give me quite a dramatic streak. I simply love entering and leaving a scene with the utmost upheaval in mind. We had reached a dead end in our conversation. I like to be remembered whether I'm coming or going. Thanks to you, my exit was high drama."

"Oh." I was crestfallen to be used in such a way.

"Don't fret. It won't be the last time someone uses you. You seem like quite the doormat."

I desperately wanted her to keep talking to me. Even though she said such horrible things, her voice made my heart beat faster. I said, "It's Irving. My real name's Irving Wishbutton."

"Oh, I've heard of you." She looked right at me, flush with interest.

I was so pleased to see her paying me heed. I shrugged. "I've been hearing that a lot lately."

"Mighty foolish of you to pick a fight with Gared." She slid closer.

"Oh, you heard about that?" I said.

"And Doctor Ringle." She gestured to the room we stood in. "And, it looks like Dean Harmstrike, too. My, you've been busy."

"You're here, too. You must've done something to draw attention to yourself," I stammered.

"Of course, it's what I do." She dropped into one of the two high back chairs by the window, the thick cushion barely registering her weight. She gestured for me to sit in the other next to her. I scampered over like a lost puppy overjoyed at being reunited with their owner.

"I'm Princess Stacia of the Howling Lands." She bowed slightly. "It's a pleasure to meet another who likes to be so messy." She looked me up and down, wrinkling her nose at my smudged features. "Although, I'm sure your escapades so far have been more a result of knocking over the scenery than from any graceful sense of how to draw attention to yourself."

She crossed her legs, positioning her elbows atop her knees. Her hands cradled her chin quite pleasingly as she leaned closer. Her breath smelled of pine needles and frost.

I wanted to tell her all my thoughts, all my feelings. I also knew that would scare her off and I didn't want that. I wanted to draw her closer, but I didn't know how. "I . . . this place . . . it's so overwhelming."

She fled, slipping back into her chair, looking bored again. "Dear me, you're quite the simpleton. How on earth did you get under my boyfriend's skin? Someone like you, you're beneath notice."

From her conversation with Aunt Nance, I remembered she was on the prowl for Nance's nephew, Ned Firebreak. I thought sharing I knew her boyfriend's name would impress her. "You mean Ned, right? He's quite important in the Archrealms." Adding that I knew their story's setting would surely earn me points.

She laughed. It was laced with resentment. The rhythm of her glee was off, ugly and wallowing. Her amusement broke my attraction to her for just a moment. As soon as she spoke again, my affection for her returned.

"Ned is one of my boys. While he's not my boyfriend yet, I had to have someone to call my own here at the Academy." She stroked her forearms. "And, of course, he had to be a mover and a shaker like me."

"Who?" I uttered.

"Why, the dreamboat you tangled with earlier, Gared. Isn't he just a handful?" She settled into a knowing grin. "He told me all about you."

"What?"

"So few words. To hear the buzz on campus, you'd think you wouldn't be such a letdown."

"Gared's your boyfriend?" I said.

"At the moment. Until something better comes along." She winked.

The doors to Harmstrike's office opened, and the dean entered. He gave me a stern glance, and then addressed Stacia. "Let's deal with your little fixation, young lady. I'm quite taken aback at how stubborn you are about this whole affair. Really, sneaking into a fellow cast member's room in the middle of the night. What were you thinking? You violated your probation yet again, and I'm afraid my punishment will be quite severe."

Stacia stood, and swept the back of her hand across her forehead. She teetered back, her feet unsteady as her eyelids fluttered precipitously. The dean did not rush to assist her. I soon saw her fainting spell was an act. With no one reaching for her, she ceased her drama and waltzed coldly past me toward the dean's office.

Harmstrike turned to me. "I will be with you in a moment, Wishbutton. Do try to keep yourself contained."

As the ice princess left, her hold on me dissipated. Being around her, I felt out of control. She made me feel slippery and unfulfilled. Those feelings dried up upon her exit.

Reason replaced manufactured passion. I thought of her and Gared. She had the wiles to snare any boy with her charmed tone. Gared's silver tongue allowed him sway over any monsters at hand. They were a cruelly perfect match. Interesting how two different writers had branded magic to the spoken word.

I waited for my audience with the dean, my desires and curiosities once again my own.

Chapter 41
DRAWING COMPARISONS

Trying to fix dinner and look over chapter nine had resulted in spaghetti sauce spattering on the scene where Irving fell from the tube rocket. Removing most of the red sauce with a paper towel, he deposited the unread pages on the end table. During the commercials as they watched their shows that night, he'd pore over the rest of the chapter.

The fish sticks heating up in the oven, for his picky eater of a son, were looking thoughtfully toasted.

As he drained the noodles in the colander and put the finishing touches on their Friday night spaghetti fest, he kept coming back to how neatly the events of the recent chapter had unfolded.

Their kidnapper, Sonalto the Undaunted, had been a veritable flood of information on their tube rocket ride out of Wish Haven and into the reaches of the Fringe. Sonalto rambled on about his employment as a whim wrangler's assistant; even revealing he had worked indirectly with their dad on occasion. This revelation gnawed at the sibling's thoughts. Their dad was connected to the magic suddenly invading their lives. Sonalto hinted at dark times, describing how corruption and greed had overtaken the Wellwishers leading to a battle that laid waste to Whimville. He confessed he did not know how crooked the Wellwishers were currently, but he indicated that Irving's wishjacket, with its missing button, was a prize the Wellwishers had stripped from others. He told them Irving should not let it be taken from him.

The drama of the back story was eclipsed by the sudden attack of a woman leading a flock of winged worms made of stardust. Sonalto recognized their assailant and gave her a hearty shout out. Irving and Tyler were face to face with Teardrop, their villainess. In the next breath, as they fell from their rocket mount toward a blackened ravine filled with shattered rocks, Sonalto pointed out Teardrop's connection to the children; she was their mother.

As the oven timer went off indicating the fish sticks were done, he returned to reality. Calling his son and daughter to dinner, they sat down and slurped up their noodles with gusto. He likened the noodles to the star worms accompanying Teardrop in her attack.

With the chapter ending on a cliffhanger and a revelation, his mind would be working doubly hard tonight linking together ideas for the next chapter.

* * *

As I waited, a wave of confusion and anxiety swept over me. My author had made a pivotal addition to my story. Teardrop, the villainess of my story, was my mother. The details were sketchy as the revelation had ended a chapter. I didn't like the idea of one of my parents being evil.

After Stacia stormed out of the dean's office, a feat absurdly captivating, I braced myself for my own comeuppance. Pushing thoughts of a treacherous mom I barely knew deep into a mental corner, I didn't wait for Harmstrike to invite me in. I entered without being summoned.

Harmstrike sat at his desk, writing furiously in a tattered journal.

He didn't look up. "Please have a seat. I will be with you in a moment."

As I waited for him to finish, I saw his inbox had two books stacked in it. One had a green spine with yellow cursive. The other, a black spine with red chunky letters delineating the title, was twice as thick as the book it rested on. *Gideon Thump in Mother May I Mayhem* was the title of the larger book. The letters on *A Passage Through Faerie* almost glowed.

Noticing my attention to the contents of his inbox, Harmstrike snatched up the larger book and tossed it toward me. The weighty tome landed in my lap with a thud. "New arrivals to our collection. Two casts of characters left us for the printed world last night. Go ahead; tell me what you know of that graduate."

Remembering from my last visit that the books were blank inside, I concentrated my inspection on the front and back cover. A large orange monster dressed in a black t-shirt and what looked like swim trunks covered in a quirky shark silhouette pattern waded through a throng of tentacled beasties. He was holding a girl safely out of reach of the questing tentacles of the mob. In the background, three grey-haired men in lab coats rode toward the action on floating skateboards.

"What's this have to do with you calling me here?" I protested.

He didn't look up from his journal, but his brow furrowed. "Just tell me what you can figure out."

"It looks like the monster is the hero, and he's fighting other creatures. They want the girl. I can't figure out if the scientists approaching him are there to help or not." I noticed the panic-stricken look the girl gave the scientists. "Wait, I think they might be bad guys."

"You're saying a monster can do good deeds? Something that looks foul can defeat evil and win the day?" the dean offered.

"Uh, sure."

Harmstrike rose and walked over to me. He snatched the book out of my hand and slid it onto a lower shelf. "So appearances can be misleading?" He didn't wait for me to answer. He chuckled at his approaching notion. "Pardon me for trotting out something so tired and worn, but you would say you can't judge a book by its cover?"

"I think so. What does—"

He wagged a finger at me. "Now, let me finish." He scooped the other book out of the inbox and held it up. "These characters, I barely knew. They worked hard while here, going about their business, toeing the line. Never heard a peep from them." He shelved the fairy book on a high shelf.

He glided over to the larger book. "Gideon Thump and his cast, they will not be forgotten. I must say, when they arrived, Gideon was quite scrawny and a wee bit pathetic." His eyes fell on me briefly. "When his author gave him the power to switch bodies with a nether creature, he grew interesting. Imagine, the might of a dark beast in the hands of a naive thirteen-year-old."

"So Gideon is really a boy in a monster's body?"

"Yes, but the author wasn't about to make his life easy. Switching the boy's soul into the beast wasn't without a price. Gideon had to wrestle with lingering dark thoughts. He had to fight back the urge to do evil."

I grimaced. I was uncertain what the dean's rant had to do with me.

Sensing I was lost, Harmstrike raced to his point. "Even with all that turmoil going on as he was being written, he conducted himself with honor. He made the best of everything he took on here, scoring at the top of his class, smoothing over the social wrinkles presented.

"He distinguished himself and his cast by being the best he could be." The dean strolled over to his desk and looked out his window, his back to me. "He will be missed."

I knew he was going to bring this back to me.

Harmstrike swiveled, bringing me into his full attention. "You are a hero. An overly curious one. We get those a lot. It's par for the course. But, and I've only said this one other time, there's something off about you. I can't escape the feeling that you could bring an end to all my work here at the Academy."

"I don't understand. It wasn't even my idea to go to the basement of the library. I didn't pick the fight with the Golden Knight. Those ember hounds, I didn't ask them to attack me. I'm just trying to figure this place out," I said.

He wrinkled his lips as if he had just gorged on a lime. "See, that's what's not quite right with you. You should've said you're here to figure yourself out." He paused, then continued, his voice now deeper. "The Academy is already what it is. You don't need to figure it out. You need to be concentrating on you. You need to listen to your writer, find out where you're heading."

Dean Harmstrike eased back into his chair and turned it slightly away. He did not take his eyes off of me. "I cannot send you away until your author is done with you, but I can make your stay here most unpleasant."

"Now, off with you. You've got Narrative Sciences and Soul Searching today, if I'm not mistaken."

I nodded as I stood slowly.

"Both classes will help you. I think you'll find Professor Warhinder's class to be just what you need. Look inward, Irving. That's the safest place for you to be inspecting." His lips curled upward, delivering a captured smile.

I left in a hurry, eager to be away from a gaze that looked very hungry.

Chapter 42
ENTRANCE EXAM

The sudden reveal of Irving's mom being Teardrop felt too rushed in the chapter. He would spend the day reworking the ending of chapter nine, delaying the debut of Irving's mom for later when the stakes were higher. He also felt the backstory needed more fine tuning. Why were the Wellwishers no longer good?

Plus, he had not given a concrete description of Sonalto's appearance other than him being an alien with massive muscles. On a whim, he had searched for sonata, thinking to change Sonalto's name to the musical term. Finding definitions of the word to be difficult to pin down, he had stumbled across allegro, meaning quick, lively or cheerful. Allegro was now his name and it was a better fit. He wanted Allegro the Undaunted to be of singular upbeat focus.

He added several lines describing his appearance. Large antlers weighed him down but didn't stop him from barreling into a situation. His face would be bordered by tattoos and his eyes would rest in shadow no matter the time of day due to his heavy brow. He'd have a stub for a tail and his feet would have three toes, two in front and one jutting backward from his heel. He'd be barrel-chested with squat legs that made him look perpetually off-balance.

Satisfied with the reworked chapter, he saved the file and went downstairs to play card games with his children.

Tomorrow would bring a tricky chapter where he'd have to silence Allegro before he blurted out their female attacker's identity. He already had a few comical ideas how to remove the fast-talking alien from the conversation, all involving losing consciousness by a variety of blows to his noggin.

* * *

I arrived at my 11:00 class early. Picking a row in the middle, I sat and scanned the room, searching for Roon. I saw Raggleswamp enter. He glanced my way. I waved. He nodded and proceeded down to the first row. He took his seat quietly, obviously feeling no pressure to seek me out.

I knew I didn't have to look for my space dog friend. Tiberius was not in either of my classes today. That much I recalled from comparing our classes back at the book store.

I needed to talk to Roon. My author had delivered the idea that my villainess, Teardrop, had been my mother. In a fit of reworking, he had taken that fact away, deciding to reveal her identity later in the story. Oddly, I still had memories of the story development. Why was that? Knowing that Roon had been recently revised as well, I wanted to ask her about it.

As students filtered in, they eyed the lecture stage with apprehension. A few looked up at the ceiling, scanning the many rafters that crisscrossed the auditorium. Anticipation colored with fear filled the air. This emotional undertow pulled my attentions away from looking for Roon. Why were they so upset? Was the professor that scary?

Abruptly, my first lesson in narrative science began.

Despite the daylight streaming in from the row of large windows that rimmed the upper section of the domed room, the class was plunged into complete darkness.

A few students gasped. The girl two seats to my right whimpered and whispered to no one in particular, "Too over the top. Too over the top even for him."

A ball of white light appeared on the lecture stage, floating several feet above the rich wooden flooring. It pulsed three times. With each pulse, its size and intensity increased until it was the size of a small truck.

It remained as a sphere for a few seconds longer. It was waiting. The sharp keys of a piano echoed through the room. The tune, very dramatic and eerie.

The light from the ball allowed me to see my neighbor cowering behind raised hands. She never took her eyes off the ball as she looked through her interlaced fingers, not wanting to subject herself to a complete shot of whatever was about to occur.

I leaned toward her. "What's this all about?"

She hissed at me, "Shhh! He doesn't permit talking! Don't draw attention to yourself, smudge!" She labeled me only after a momentary pause.

The ball of light shuddered and twisted about, assuming a roughly human shape. Large leathery wings sprouted from its back. The music increased in intensity as the light dimmed, escaping into the figure. As it did so, the light from outside slowly reentered the classroom. The instructor's features sprang into focus.

"It's a big bat!" I said, keeping my voice low.

What he chose to wear looked appropriate for the setting. He had on a brown sports coat over a pale yellow dress shirt. His pants, a darker brown, continued the trend of what an average academic type might look like. If, and this was a big if, if you could look past the immense bat ears that crowned his head and the compacted rodent features that presented themselves as his face. Tiny glasses nested atop his upturned nose. Mucus trailed from his large nostrils. He didn't wear shoes. Seeing the size of his taloned feet, it was understandable. They were long and slender, each joint knobbed and sprinkled with coarse hairs. Mirroring his open wings, his arms were outstretched at the exact same angle.

His voice rang out, deep and raspy. "Today, our subject, can you guess?"

A brave onlooker from the front row raised his hand.

The instructor nodded at him.

The boy who answered wore pajamas and carried a quiver full of arrows at his side. He fidgeted with a small bow as he responded, "Making a splash! Arriving in style!" With each word, his enthusiasm for his answer escalated. "You wanted us to—"

The instructor snapped his wings closed abruptly. The displaced air buffeted the boy, silencing his eagerness. He sat back down, drawing his tiny bow across his chest. "Making an entrance! Always with style, especially if the newcomer is of villainous intent." His eyes twinkled at his last comment.

Was all my schooling going to be orchestrated by evildoers? First, Doctor Ringle and now this bat creature. Come to think of it, Dean Harmstrike didn't fill me with the warm fuzzies either.

"I was going to present more about the plot point of the double-cross today. You had so many questions last week about the topic." His eyes scanned the class. They stopped when he caught sight of me. "But someone here today for the first time inspired me to go a different direction."

Was he talking about me? I willed him to keep inspecting the room. He hadn't looked at anyone in the balcony level. *Try up there. Your inspiration for this lesson must be up there.* I tried to press my thoughts outward.

His tiny eyes did not veer away.

I slipped lower in my seat. The girl next to me moved three seats farther away, fearful of being associated with me.

"Up! Present yourself, young hero! Hesitation breeds anticipation, but too much and your audience's focus wanes." He snorted, expelling mucus in a generous swath.

I fidgeted with my notebook, flipping through the blank pages with no destination in mind.

The bat instructor launched into the air, clearly aggravated at my inaction. He careened toward the rafter directly above me. His clawed feet pierced the wood as his wings wrapped around him like a cloak. He craned his neck at me. "All eyes are on you, Wishbutton. You of all types should not be one to ignore a grand entrance. After all, that's how you showed up here at this academy, isn't it?"

I eyed his nostrils with apprehension. The mucus flowing from his nose was ignoring gravity for the moment, but I had no desire to be underfoot when it rained down.

I stood and slid three seats to my right. The girl who had tried to put more distance between us huffed at me. The upside down instructor twisted in corkscrew fashion to watch me retreat. I hoped he had not guessed my reason why. I had no desire to explain my fear of receiving a shower of nasal discharge.

"Come, come, Irving. You're not helping me here. It's not often I involve others in my lessons." He tapped a solitary bony finger on the edge of his wing.

"I don't know what you want me to say?"

He shook his head. "I was giving you the opportunity to make an entrance, to bring all eyes in the room to you." He smiled, revealing pointy teeth.

I surveyed the class, thoughts of finding Roon a far-off priority. If being a hero meant receiving so much attention, I wasn't sure I was cut out for it.

As if the instructor had read my mind, he offered, "For a hero, making an appearance, demanding the spotlight, it doesn't come naturally. Whereas a villain, it's second nature."

In one fluid movement, he executed a back flip and dropped to the ground, landing smoothly beside me. A small trickle of mucus landed at my feet. He put one arm around me and yanked me closer. "Young Irving needs to understand that an entrance matters. It conveys so much. Who here can tell me how this young hero has wasted an opportunity?"

No one answered.

The instructor bellowed, "Come now, I'm giving you the chance to make your own entrance! Surely you're not all meek. No one here will stand up and make an impression?"

"I'll do it!" someone shouted from the far end of the auditorium. My head sagged when I saw who raced toward us. "Not all of us are so queasy about being center stage!"

Jogging up an aisle, his bulky frame accented by his golden armor, it was no surprise who came to my rescue. Although, he was not out to save me as much as shame me. Gared, the silver-tongued thorn in my side, again shoved himself into my life.

Gared threaded through our narrow row to arrive beside us in a matter of seconds. If he was winded, he didn't show it. He held up his hands and shouted, "I am the Golden Knight, master of monsters and fine company to the ladies who cross my adventurous path!" He wagged his silver tongue in the air. "Rise, beasts, and recognize your better!"

The students of monstrous descent were out of their seats and cheering him on. Caught up in his magic, they did as he requested. A few even chanted his name.

Gared smirked and quipped to me, "See how easy it is."

The monstrous display of devotion was cut short by the instructor. "Silence!"

Even without a silver tongue, his request held weight. The monsters fell back into their seats, their uproar immediately extinguished.

"A suitable entrance, knight. But did you think of your purpose?"

"What do you mean? I don't understand. You asked for a volunteer, Professor Snitpick," Gared said.

"And you leaped at the chance, didn't you?" Snitpick's eyes narrowed. "You were so quick to deliver, you failed as a hero.

"An entrance by a hero only approaches honor when one is rushing into the fray, charging to the rescue. Then, the arrival conveys appropriate nobility." The professor pulled away from me but still kept the pressure on by dismissively waving in my direction. "Irving handled this correctly. There was no damsel in distress, no evil afoot to stomp out. Only the pressing jealousy of an instructor trying to embarrass a new student."

"I don't—" Gared said.

Snitpick continued, "I was testing Wishbutton. I've heard so much about him, I wanted to see what sort of character he was. Many times, the rookies fall into the trap of thinking they are more important than their story." He looked at Gared. "I was imagining a blowhard, someone who needed all eyes on them. As I've said, these are not the proper traits of a hero."

His wings opened again, and he flew back down to the stage. He bowed in my direction. "Young Wishbutton, you do need to find your spirit. Not making a splash was the desired outcome today, but once thrust into the spotlight, you can't shrink from it."

"Yeah, you really looked bad," Gared said before scampering back to his seat.

Snitpick chuckled then said, "And Gared, you and your brother, your narrative leaves it up in the air as to which of you will wind up the villain." He presented it more as a statement than a question.

"Uh, yeah," responded Gared as he arrived at his seat.

"I'm thinking deep down, you already know the role you play." Snitpick took his eyes off Gared and stared out at his audience. "Now, let's talk about the numerous ways to make an entrance, shall we?"

Snitpick droned on for over an hour. After hearing so many ways to arrive on the scene, I was relieved when he dismissed us, and we were all finally able to make our exit.

As I trudged down the steps, I was set upon for the second time that day by a leathery winged creature. This one landed on my face and wouldn't let go.

I tumbled to the ground, rolling down the few remaining steps as I tried to dislodge my attacker.

Chapter 43
FACE TO FACE

It was the final day of track out. This would be the last chapter he would write on a daily basis. Once the work week started, he'd scrape together enough time to write a chapter a week. It slowed down his enthusiasm a bit, but he also knew the next track out was only nine weeks away.

Today, his wife was off and had taken the kids clothes shopping. He had a good three hours before they would return. He finished emptying the dishwasher and bounded up the steps to his studio.

He set upon the chapter with little hesitation. The scene was heavy on talking, showcasing the playful nature of Allegro's personality.

As they fell toward the rocky terrain below, Allegro bemoaned the loss of such a fine rocket, all the while showing no concern for their plight.

In the middle of writing their plunge, he realized a glaring omission in the previous chapter. He had reworked the scene so Allegro had not revealed Teardrop to be the children's mother, but what was keeping them from recognizing her? His solution, the villainess would wear a mask that tapered down from her ornate and jagged headdress. Satisfied with his cover-up, he returned to the new chapter.

Back to the story's thrilling nose-dive, he played up how casual Allegro was taking their situation. Irving and Tyler were begging him to stop jabbering and help them figure something out. He tried to keep it quick as they couldn't fall forever.

As the rocks grew closer, Irving tried to wish for a parachute. The jacket offered no help. This served as a reminder to the reader that he could only use wishes that had been retrieved by the jacket. Having used the gills wish already, his jacket was empty.

With not a second to spare, Allegro whisked them out of harm's way. He conjured up a dimensional portal underneath them and fell through it. They landed with a gentle thump in a meadow thick with giant spongy mushrooms. After bouncing off several toadstools, the threesome came back together. Tyler launched into Allegro, pointing out that if he could just escape by making rips in reality, why hadn't he done that in the first place? The alien confessed to loving high drama and had selected the rocket grab because it was more daring.

The chapter closed with Tyler's anger subsiding as she realized that while she had been scolding Allegro, they had been slowly surrounded by a tribe of aliens whose resemblance to their rescuer was uncanny. Only their attitudes were far less chummy. Each antlered assailant scowled at the threesome as the mob flew into a berserker rage.

* * *

I felt attacked from all sides. Bad enough, I had been knocked to the ground by a winged creature, but my mind reeled from the dangerous events my author was firing into my head. It was overwhelming. As I contended with the cliffhanger my creator had painted for me, I also had to deal with this new slap in the face.

Before I could break free of my attacker, it flew up and away from me. I felt around my eyes for any injury from its claws. Finding none, I set my attention to my assailant. It looped around, presumably in preparation to launch another strafing attack.

It wasn't a bird. As it zoomed closer, I again noticed the leathery wings. I had a hunch who it was. I kept my hands up, ready to knock it away if my attacker tried to grab hold of me again. The bat swooped down and made to land a few steps above me. Before its feet touched the ground, it transformed, shifting into the shape of my classmate, Roon. My hunch had been right.

"What the devil was that about?" I shouted.

She glared at me. "You and Raggleswamp messed up my investigation. What were you thinking, revealing yourself to the dean?"

"That wasn't my idea. Raggleswamp did that," I said with a sour tone. "Besides, we managed to keep you out of it. It's not like he caught you."

Roon considered this for a moment. She spun around, checking to see if her book bag was secure, then waltzed down to where I was standing. "I'll give you that. You did manage to do that right."

Sensing that was the closest to an apology I was going to get, I changed the subject. "I didn't see you in Snitpick's class."

"Oh, I was there. Sheesh, Irving, is there any class you're not going to be front and center in?" She punched my upper arm.

Before I could answer, she grabbed my wrist or the general area of that particular fuzzy joint and dragged me into the flow of students navigating the main stone walkway. "C'mon, let's go get a bite to eat. I'm starving."

I resisted. My author had given me a basic knowledge of vampires. I knew my sister would know more because he had written her to be a bit of a nerd about otherworldly beings. I knew just enough to make things dangerous for myself.

She stopped and looked at me expectantly. "What?"

Even though she couldn't see my eyes, I avoided looking into hers. "When you say bite, . . ." I trailed off, uncertain how to continue.

She playfully thumped me across the chest, then exposed her fangs to me. She gnashed them together as she spoke. "What? You think I want a nibble of you?"

"Uh, well, I . . ."

She squeezed my wrist. "Silly, I can eat regular food. I don't need to drink blood." She paused. "At least not today." Her dark lips curled upward as she yanked me along.

As she weaved in and out of the throng of students, I allowed a chuckle to escape.

This, of course, was immediately detected by Roon. "What's there to be cheery about, Irving? You're making a royal mess of things here."

"I'm just happy to see you not so gloomy," I replied.

She ignored my observation and settled into a specific line of inquiry. "Heard you had to see the Dean again. Bet that went splendid."

"It went," I said, not willing to elaborate.

Roon said, "You actually did pretty well against Snitpick. I think he liked what he saw from you." She stopped, allowing a herd of mushroom-helmeted elves to cross in front of us. "Gared, however, you're not getting on his best side."

"Oh, he has one of those?" I asked as I watched the last elf pat Roon's toes and whisper a thank you to her.

She accelerated our pace.

We arrived at the food court located on the second floor of the administration building that housed the Office of Fine Aunts with what little of our conversation we could fit in devoted to trading insults about the Golden Knight.

"You're not upset about the party thing? You believe me about Gared kidnapping me?" I said.

She nodded. "I did some rooting around and your story checked out. Cornered a misery mite named Singe who blabbed all about seeing you. Were you really tied upside down to a rafter?" She took me to the relative center of the food court where a three-sided kiosk displayed the various menus of the different food stations.

"It's true. I still have some rope burns if you want to see." I held up my hands. Realizing the injuries were hidden by my smudged appearance, I shrugged and withdrew them. "Oh, yeah, not that you could see anything."

"Don't worry, there's enough evidence to support what you said." She gestured to the menu. "See anything you want?"

I scanned the menus, all the while slightly disturbed by her comments. She didn't trust my word but believed my story only because it checked out with somebody else. I chalked it up to her writer giving her a detective's observational personality that eclipsed everything else about her. I had to admit she was quite good at snooping about.

"That thing, the misery mite, it's kind of creepy," I said.

"Tell me about it." She tapped on a menu for a sandwich shop, and glanced at me for approval.

I nodded. "What kind of creature was it anyway?"

She again grabbed my wrist and pulled me to the food station we had agreed upon. "A misery mite, it's a dopey little dragon thing. They fly around in herds usually. Be glad you didn't run into more than one of them."

Roon ordered a simple turkey sandwich with a side of chips. I ordered a ham and cheese and opted for two helpings of apple sauce. We slid our cards through the scanner and thanked the large bubble-blowing shark at the checkout before finding our seats at a tiny table wedged between two dwarf palms in large pots.

"Why? What's so nasty about them?" I took a large bite of my sandwich.

"They feed on negative emotions. They're drainers. You feel angry, fearful or hateful and they slurp it up. They drain the victim."

"Does it kill you?" I said.

"Oh, no, not quite that bad. You only spent a little time with one of them. It probably didn't get much off you. Besides, it's not permanent. Your feelings, or the degree to which you feel, it returns pretty quickly." She tore into her sandwich, trying to cover her mouth to shield her fangs from any passerby.

"So a whole bunch of them is bad?" I emptied one apple sauce cup and descended on the other.

"Terrible. My brother and I, we had to face down over twenty of them," she confessed.

"Where? Here, at the Academy? When did that happen?"

She frowned. "No, not here. In our story. They were the first trouble our author set on us. Did a real number on my brother." She bit her lip and looked away.

"Wait, the misery mites are from your book?"

"Yeah." She returned to eating, crunching away at chip after chip.

"You interrogated Singe to see if my story was all true?"

She nodded, her mouth full.

"But it's a character from your story!" My voice quickened.

She shrugged.

"We can't associate with characters from our cast. Doctor Ringle said that much at Orientation. Didn't you break the rules?"

"It's only breaking them if you get caught. I know ways to keep my comings and goings largely unnoticed, unlike some heroes I know." Roon darted her eyes at me.

"I wanted to talk to you about something," I said, changing the subject.

"Okay." Roon leaned in.

"It's about Revising."

Her eyes narrowed, and her hands gripped the table edge. She shifted back. "Sort of a touchy subject with me right now."

I took a deep breath, then let the words rush out. "My author revised my mom. He was writing about revealing who she was in the story."

"And who is she?" Her interest returned.

My voice wavered. "At the beginning of my story, my mom isn't there." I hesitated. "In the most recent chapter, there's this alien who helps me and my sister. He spills the beans that my mom is my villainess. She's Teardrop!"

171

"Whoa, talk about a dramatic punch!" She pursed her lips as if to whistle.

"Only he took it back," I mumbled.

"What do you mean?"

"The next time he wrote, my author decided not to reveal to us that Teardrop is really our mom. He revised it from the chapter."

"Well, that's not bad."

I said, "But I still know the info. I know he's going to reveal her identity later in our story. It's weird how it all gets in our head. Some of it is from what he writes and some is like I can read his thoughts. Does that make sense?"

She looked to the side, avoiding eye contact. Not that she had anything to worry about with that from me. Still, she avoided looking at me. "Sort of. Fleshing out our stories and our traits is tough. It's like you have to constantly be receiving messages and updates about yourself while still trying to go about your day. Your revision is nothing too alarming."

I didn't like her reaction. I thought she would be sympathetic to my revision. Realizing that her own changes might have hit her much harder, I abandoned the focus on my own problems.

"Your brother is still not back from Revision Ravine?" I lowered my tone.

Her jaw clenched. "It's not exactly a place where they let you come and go."

"What's stopping you from going to see him?" I knew I was treading on thin ice, but I also knew she needed to open up. "I mean, is it far from the Academy?"

"It's against the rules. There are huge consequences if I get caught," she offered.

"But didn't you break the rules when you talked to Singe?"

"That's a tiny transgression. Sneaking into the ravine is a major no-no."

From her response I could tell she had thought of the very same notion before. "But wouldn't the punishment be spread out a bit if two people broke the rules?"

Her eyes softened. "You're already in a lot of trouble."

"What's a little more?" I leaned back in my chair, attempting to be cool and collected.

"You'd do that?" Her voice rose with excitement.

"Absolutely. Maybe if I work with such a master sleuth some of your sneakiness might wear off on me, and I might not draw as much of the dean's attention," I said. "Let's go today, after my Soul Searching class. Can we be there and back before it gets dark?"

"If we're quick."

"Then it's a plan." I tucked the remains of my sandwich in its wrapper and stood to take my tray to the nearest trashcan.

I stuffed the trash in the receptacle and placed my tray on top. As I returned to our table, a girl with long red hair and glasses walked in front of me. She tilted her head in my direction, and I knew instantly who she was.

She smiled and waved, "Hi, Irving. Nice lunch date you picked for yourself." She looked at Roon and nodded approval. "Maybe she'll help you stay out of trouble. Somehow, I doubt it."

I stood there, knowing this was a moment where all color in my face should wash away. I wondered what that would look like to an outsider. Would my smudged features reflect my emotional turmoil?

I didn't have to wait long to find out.

Roon rushed past the girl and grabbed me by my left shoulder. She nudged me in concern. "Irving, you okay? Your face, it went from a normal color to bleach white. Your writer didn't turn you into a vampire, did he?"

I looked at Roon at the same time as I watched the reason for my mood change walk away and take a seat with a small group of other teenage girls. "You said I had a face, but I don't. It's all smudged still, isn't it?"

Roon whispered, "Just because your author hasn't seen fit to clear you up doesn't stop you from showing others who you really are. You have a face, Irving, and it's a good one. Don't be ashamed."

Roon darted forward and kissed my cheek. She inspected my cloudy features, then said, "Ah, there the color's coming back."

I smiled, knowing that Roon might not see it, but certain she could sense it. "Thanks."

"Who was that? A fan of your escapades here at the Academy?" Roon again dragged me toward the exit.

"No, she's family. That was my sister, Tyler."

Roon shouted at my sister, "Nice meeting you, Tyler! Wish we could stay and talk, but Irving really can't risk being seen with you. Hanging out with his cast, even if it is family, is just not allowed. See you around."

Tyler waved, rolled her eyes, and turned her back to me.

No longer feeling alone, I left the dining hall with Roon. Only thing was, I wasn't sure who to thank for that warm feeling—Roon or my sister.

Chapter 44
ON A WING AND A GLARE

He would try to write chapter ten Saturday night. Tonight, he had read over the chapters, looking at the flow of the story so far and catching minor editing mistakes he had missed.

During the course of putting a book together, he found it helped his focus to read what he had so far every couple chapters. In doing so, he probably ended up reading the book a dozen times before it was completed. The read-throughs allowed him to see the plot points develop and alerted him to where he had gone off track.

For example, this reading made him aware that he had not shared a complete physical description of Irving. The reader had no idea of his eye color, hair color, or whether his jaw was weak or finely chiseled. He thought ahead to the upcoming chapters, and it made sense to feature a descriptive passage outlining Irving's looks through the eyes of his mother. It would be a sequence where Teardrop was spying on her children. It would reveal that she had a connection to them and a very intense interest. This would make her conflicted. Irving and Tyler were obstacles to achieving her goals, but they were also her family. He made a few notes about the scene. He would have to play it carefully. He wanted the reader to suspect Teardrop's family ties, but not come out and state it. That reveal would have to be for when the characters came face to face.

He again pored over chapter nine. Allegro's people and their reasons for attacking Irving and his sister had not come to him yet. Was he creating a scene of jeopardy just to plop them into another tantalizing danger or did the scene serve another purpose? Was Allegro's race important to the story? Did they have a grudge against Wish Haven? Were they servants to the wish agents? They had to have some connection.

He closed the binder holding the chapters and placed it on his nightstand. He'd let his mind drift over the rest of the week. He had an uncanny knack for sniffing out proper motivations for his scenes when he took time to get away from them. By Saturday, he'd have a good reason. He clicked off the light and went to bed. His mind settled into sleep quickly.

* * *

I was noticing a trend. Everyone I was getting to know at the Academy, at least the girls at any rate, they all had wings. Roon could become a bat and Sarya had her delicate fairy wings. This observation came to me as Roon and I left the dining hall and ran into Sarya standing outside the exit. Her arms were crossed, and she looked at me with equal parts pity and anger.

She glared at me for a very long time.

I knew before she spoke why her demeanor was so sour. "Oh no, Sarya. I'm sorry. I got your note and was really going to meet you for lunch—"

She waved at me dismissively. "Stop, you don't need to explain. I've been waiting out here for a while, Irving. I saw it all. You just found yourself a better lunch companion."

"I forgot. My meeting with Harmstrike had me all turned around, and then I went to Snitpick's class. He didn't exactly put me at ease. Then I ran into Roon and we needed to talk about something." I didn't want to tell Sarya about my trouble under the library. Something told me she didn't need to hear Roon had been down there too. "It slipped my mind."

"You mean I slipped your mind." Her wings fluttered as she turned to walk away.

I didn't know what to say. My writer had not prepared me in how to deal with female relationships outside of my sister.

Roon stepped in to save me. "It's my fault, Sarya. I sort of pushed him into having lunch with me."

Sarya stopped but did not turn around. Her wings fell open and did not close.

"If it's worth anything, he talks about you all the time," Roon added.

Sarya turned to look back over her shoulder. "If he talked about me with you at lunch today, how come that didn't jog his memory enough to remember we had a date?"

A date? What was she thinking? I had agreed to meet her for lunch. Was that considered a date?

Roon kept control of the conversation with ease. "Not today. No, but all the other times I see him, he's talking about what a good friend you are and how happy he is to get to know you." She looked at me, nodding for me to take over.

I said, "Yeah, you've really helped me out so much. I've gotten the closest to you of anyone here." I winced, wondering if my gushing comment would hurt Roon's feelings.

Roon ignored me and gestured for Sarya to come closer. "C'mon, he's kind of hard to stay mad at, isn't he?" She smiled, being careful not to show her fangs.

Sarya's wings blurred as she took flight in our direction. She hovered off the ground, her smile and energy once again overflowing. "We can try again another time. It's not a problem, Irving."

"Yeah, sure," I said, risking a glance at Roon to see if her feelings were hurt. She was still smiling at Sarya, clearly not thinking about any of my awkward comments. I found her reaction pleasing. I had not hurt our friendship.

Sarya squeezed my hand. "Well, I gotta go get something to nibble on before my next class. I'll catch up with you after Soul Searching, okay?"

She flew past me, but not before tossing an observation Roon's way. "Thanks for watching out for him. He's such a newbie. Glad to see you're nothing like the rumors. You're not heartless at all."

Roon squinted and smiled in response. "Later."

I waited for Sarya to disappear into the dining hall before talking to Roon. "Thanks. I didn't expect such a strong reaction from her."

"She's getting quite attached to you. That's what supporting characters do. Since she can't be close to her own hero, she's picked you to glom onto. She needs that connection. Watch yourself with her. Don't get too close."

"Why is that?" I asked.

Roon's face tightened. "Because nothing's permanent here. Nothing lasts. We all have to leave and go out into the published world." She paused. "If we're lucky."

"So that's an excuse not to reach out to others?" I asked.

She looked down. "It can be."

I didn't know what to say.

Roon changed the subject. "You promised Sarya you'd get with her after your next class. Does that mean you aren't going with me to Revision Ravine?"

"Tomorrow's Saturday, right?"

She nodded.

"Let's go early, at the crack of dawn. Meet me here at 7:00, okay?" I suggested.

"Good thing my writer didn't give me any problems with being out in the daylight like most vampires. That's a touch odd, isn't it?"

"It is, but let's tackle one mystery at a time. Worry about that later," I said.

"Thanks, Irving," she said awkwardly. I sensed she was not used to assistance from anyone other than her absent brother. She nudged my shoulder before changing again into her bat form.

She flew off, leaving me to seek out my next class. I retrieved the campus map from my backpack and searched the key. Soul Searching was in a building I had never been to before. I double-checked its location on my map and trekked uphill. It was in a remote building next to the Menagerie. If I was lucky, I'd arrive with a few minutes to spare.

Chapter 45
THE NOODLEMEN CONSPIRACY

Chapter ten began with Allegro trying to sweet talk his people out of taking swords and spears to Irving and his sister.

He paused. Over the past week, he had tried to think of a motivation for the angry mob, but nothing had bubbled to the surface. He had started the chapter with Allegro, hoping he could nurse out the purpose through his playful ramblings.

As the boisterous alien chatted with his aggravated fellows, their involvement in the story fell into place. Through the give and take of his pleading and the overbearing anger of the crowd, the scene clawed its way toward purpose. Allegro's people had been squires to the whim wranglers of Whimville, assisting in rounding up wispy half-wishes. They had been front and center at the destruction of Whimville. Through the back and forth, Irving became aware that Wish Haven was not held in high regard by all. From their accusations, it was clear Allegro's people, the Nowrii, felt used by a council whose purpose was murky at best. With Whimville in ruins, they blamed the wish agents.

Allegro pointed to Irving being of use. With his second button missing, he could draw on the wishes he gathered. He could be used against the Wellwishers.

Right when it seemed Allegro had changed the outlook of the crowd, a dimensional gateway opened above the scene. Out charged a dozen wish agents. The chapter closed with them surrounding Irving and pressing back at the crowd with long, menacing lances.

What little trust Allegro had won evaporated as quickly as the dimensional gate above Irving's head.

He liked Allegro's grandstanding and the cliffhanger that again presented itself. He wondered if the agents would resort to violence. He'd have to think about how to approach the next chapter. He wanted the agents to be purposeful and a bit blind to the big picture. He wanted Irving and Tyler to question everything and everyone around them.

Right now, they didn't know who to trust besides each other. The author liked that just fine.

* * *

Professor Warhinder was stunning.

I had arrived at the classroom with plenty of time to find a seat. It was not in a large lecture hall like my other two classes, but in a smaller classroom. There were about a dozen folding chairs set up in a semicircle around the teacher's desk. The professor sat on her desk, scanning several note cards. We were the only people in the room.

She smiled and waved for me to pick a seat.

I tried not to look at her, but it was hard. She was breathtaking and not at all human. Her orange skin shimmered. Her large eyes framed by thick blue eyelashes were warm and inviting. She wore a headband to keep her curls galore in check. Only a few spiraled down, framing her high cheekbones perfectly. Her lips were rich and full. One other aspect distinguished her from human: the small rows of bone horns that served as her eyebrows. They were understated and took nothing away from her beauty.

Other students filtered in, and I fought the urge to steal more glances at her. Raggleswamp strutted in, seating himself between a scarab-headed baby with small feathered wings and a knight decked out in bubble armor. The villain nodded at me.

A king complete with a gem-encrusted crown and a long gray beard sat next to me on my left. Even astride a folding chair, he sat regally. A goblin carrying oversized knitting needles, which he waved about as if engaging in swordplay, sat two chairs to my right. Two teenage girls arrived. I thought they might have been the same girls my sister had been having lunch with, but I was uncertain. They sat to my right, on the two seats closest to the teacher's desk. A very tiny winged creature, his body clearly made of stone, flew in. He buzzed over to the scarab-headed baby and whispered something in the general area of where a set of ears should be. The bug boy looked agitated, but moved two seats away, freeing up the chair next to Raggleswamp. The new arrival took the seat and starting elbowing Raggleswamp. The two were clearly close friends.

Warhinder hopped off her desk and sighed. She surveyed the class. "Gideon won't be coming anymore. He got published." She closed her eyes briefly and stuck out her bottom lip. "The big lug will be missed."

She must have been referring to Gideon Thump. I recalled the book that had been on Harmstrike's desk at my morning meeting with the dean. I noticed the two girls looked particularly saddened. Had they been friends of the hero?

Warhinder nodded at each of us as she took attendance. When she finished counting, her face revealed frustration. It was clear not everyone was present. She started counting a second time, but was interrupted by the arrival of her late student. He charged into the room, arms and head flailing about. The bird clinging to his shoulder squawked at the turbulent treatment as the student settled into the seat next to me.

His head appeared to be an oversized noodle with eyes and a mouth stretched across it. I recognized him as the boy who had barged into Dean Harmstrike's office on my first visit. Small goggles perched atop his forehead, making me wonder if they would even fit over his bulbous eyes. His head wiggled about, clearly reflecting his antsy demeanor.

"So sorry I'm late again, Professor. Had a bit of trouble with a pair of gorgonsquids in the aquaria. Fenwick Noodlemen present and accounted for."

The two girls pantomimed the appearance of goggles on their own foreheads. He noticed and slipped off his aquatic gear and stored it in a satchel dangling by his side. As he did this, he paid little heed to the bird on his shoulder. His forearm brushed against its beak. This set the bird off. It began squawking with abandon.

Warhinder walked over. Based on my experience with the faculty so far, I fully expected her to toss the bird out the window and scold the boy for bringing a pet. Instead, she placed a hand atop the bird's purple crest and began stroking it. "There, there, Mrs. Noodlemen. Your son didn't mean to treat you so rudely. It's okay." Her voice combined with her stroking soothed the bird.

The bird cooed briefly then fell silent. The professor placed her hands on the boy's shoulders and kneeled to be at his eye level. "Fenwick, I don't mind if you arrive late. I'd rather you get here in one piece and consider the safety of your mother perched there." She glanced at the bird. "No more rough rides for her, okay?"

Fenwick blushed. It was clear he had a mild crush on his teacher. "Yes, Professor Warhinder."

The professor stood up and slid over to stand in front of me. "While we did lose Gideon, we gained a new hero." She looked at me and motioned me to stand up. "This is Irving Wishbutton. Another hero is among us. That's always cause for celebration, isn't it?"

As I stood, she put one arm around me and squeezed me tight.

"Nice to be here," I said meekly.

Raggleswamp gave me a sour look.

Warhinder released me and returned to sit on her desk. "We also have Lord Raggleswamp in attendance for the first time today. He has all the delicious potential to be quite the dastardly scoundrel."

She ushered in a round of clapping for the villain who stood on his chair and pumped his fists.

"Everyone at the academy has been so gracious. I'm looking forward to broadening my knowledge and getting to know more of the faculty and students here. I'm especially curious to see what Soul Searching has to offer. I've heard only good things about your tutelage, Madame Professor." Raggleswamp bowed toward Warhinder before sitting down.

She nodded at the villain and smiled. "Irving and Raggleswamp, you've arrived in midsession. We've already met about a half dozen times. You'll both need to make sure you pick up these review packets I prepared." She patted two blue folders stacked high with papers. "They'll help get you up to speed on what we've covered so far. We have a mid-term exam in two weeks, and I expect you both to be prepared."

Raggleswamp rubbed his hands together and saluted Warhinder. I wagged a thumbs up, but the signal was lost in my cloudy hands.

Warhinder stood and walked around inside the circle of chairs. The class pulled out slender notebooks. I followed suit, noticing that Raggleswamp didn't fetch anything with which to take notes on. She began, "We've been talking about playing our parts. Last class, your discussion of free will was very telling. I especially liked what King Druukus added to the conversation. Very good insights, your majesty." She curtsied toward the king.

The bearded royal next to me smiled. I liked how she made each of us feel worthy.

"Today, let's talk about what your role is. Why are you here? Why is the Academy here?" Warhinder said.

Wow, she was asking the very questions I wanted answered. Was this the class where I would finally get some answers?

Professor Warhinder continued, "Before we begin talking as a group, let's pair up and dialog about those very questions. Take five minutes, and then we'll share as a whole class." She waved for us to select partners.

King Druukus winked at me. "Young Wishbutton, I would love to chew your ear off. I've heard so much about you already, but I promised the Scarab Cherub over there I'd partner with him at the next opportunity." He pointed at the bug boy who was already scampering toward the king.

"No problem, your majesty." I bowed slightly.

Fenwick Noodlemen tapped my shoulder. "Hey, Wishbutton? Let's you and I shoot the breeze. What do you say?"

I shifted to face the noodle boy and his avian parent. "Uh, sure. Will your mom be joining in?"

"Nah, don't mind her. She's more of a listener." Fenwick arched his eyebrows and smiled.

His mother snapped at his noodle head in protest, irked at his dismissive comment.

I wanted to keep our discussion on track, so I restated the first question, "What role do you two play?"

Fenwick pointed his thumbs proudly at his chest. "I'm a hero. I'm on a quest. Bet you can guess what my quest is. It's pretty obvious." His eyes darted toward his mother and back as he comically shrugged his eyebrows.

"Your mom, she's trapped in a bird's body and you have to get her back?"

"Right you are. Not only that, but this noodle isn't my real noodle. I'm a normal boy, but the curse that was cast on my family gave my mom her feathery figure and me this silly flexible noggin." He wagged his head about. It jiggled.

"I thought we couldn't associate with others from our cast?" I said.

"True. That is an important edict, but my author cursed my mom and me to be stuck with each other until we fix our predicament. So, in our case, it's allowed." Fenwick beamed with pride.

Realizing we needed to move on, I said, "I'm a hero. My mom's going to be my villain, I think. Then again, I might actually be working for the bad guys. They're called the Wellwishers. My author's a little vague about their true motives."

"That sounds deep," said Fenwick. He licked his lips, then leaned in. He lowered his voice, but not his excitement. "I work at the Menagerie, you know."

I nodded hesitantly. Where was he going with this? We were supposed to be discussing why we were here and why the Academy existed. Not that I thought he had much to add. His responses so far painted him as a very simple hero.

"I got in trouble for those emberhounds of yours escaping," he said, his voice barely a whisper now.

"Sorry about that. I wish . . ."

"No, no, not your fault. Not anyone's fault." Fenwick paused. He reached over and slid his hand under my vague chin. He directed my head upwards so as to be sure I was looking at him when he spoke next. "Actually, I think it is somebody's fault. Somebody real high up here at the Academy. Nothing's ever escaped the Menagerie. Too many magical spells in place. It just doesn't happen."

"So why did it happen?"

"Meet me at the Menagerie tonight, and I'll tell you. Meet me at midnight. That's when my shift ends. I'll give you a little tour and tell you what I know." Fenwick glanced at Professor Warhinder.

"You don't want to tell me now because of her?" I asked.

"No, no, she's cool. Warhinder's the nicest teacher here. I don't think she's a part of it at all." He looked at his classmates. "But the others in here, they could be reporting back to him. I can't take the chance, all right?"

"Okay," I said.

Professor Warhinder clapped her hands three times. The buzz of discussion stopped. "Time's up. Let's share some of your insights, okay?" She skipped across the room and snagged Raggleswamp. "In fact, let's hear from our two newest first."

Fenwick nudged me and muttered, "Get up there and spill what we talked about, but not what we really talked about, okay?"

Noodlemen's mother squawked at her son to be quiet. He shrunk back into his seat as I stood and moved to the center of the room.

Once again, all eyes were on me. I looked over at Raggleswamp. He projected anticipation, the opposite of what I was feeling.

He seized the spotlight and began.

Chapter 46
MIND ALIGNED

During the fight sequence with the wish agents and the Nowrii, Irving was going to find another wish. He wouldn't use it, but the process of retrieving the wish would be looked at more closely. Irving would stumble across how to determine the wish's nature through his jacket.

As he set upon trimming the overgrown shrubs in the garden bed, his mind whirled with ideas for the next chapter. He would have to write the chapter on Sunday afternoon. His wife was taking the kids to a clay place to make special gifts for the grandparents.

Irving would hesitate in taking sides, allowing the wish agents to plow through the Nowrii without interference. His sister, she wouldn't play it safe. While Irving remained indecisive about the Nowrii's story of how the wish agents couldn't be trusted, Tyler didn't hang back in taking sides. She joined Allegro in the battle. In the process, she would be injured. Nothing lethal, but severe enough to force Irving to agree to return to Wish Haven where she could be helped.

The battle would end with Allegro and his people beaten back, their view of the wish agents driven more toward mistrust.

The writer liked the direction the story was heading. He needed the characters to see that there was true threat and jeopardy in this world of wishes. This book, it was important that the stakes be real and have consequence. He felt his earlier works, while all ages, had been lacking in action and peril. Irving's story would still be true to writing for a wide audience, would still be centered on strong character moments and relationships, but conflict and danger would also be constants.

He focused on the thorny hedge in front of him. He would figure out the wish Irving had obtained over the next few days and write the chapter on Sunday.

* * *

Raggleswamp went on and on about himself and his story. He went into great detail about the elaborate background his author had created for him. There was extensive talk of his family tree. He paraded out a multitude of titles and aliases for himself. He shared way too many particulars about his base of operations and previous schemes.

I noticed one little fact he left out: his motivation for being a bad guy. I decided not to call attention to this.

On the topics of why he was here and why the academy was here, he had little to offer, giving pat answers clearly designed to please the teacher.

At the end of his brief praise of the academy and the faculty, he turned to look at Warhinder, expecting to receive a nod of approval for his obvious kissing up. Warhinder smiled briefly and nodded. I could tell from Raggleswamp's reaction, he was displeased with her dismissive response.

She turned to me. "Let's hear from Irving. Tell us what you're thinking

"I'm Irving Wishbutton. I'm a hero who might be working for the bad guys." I looked at Raggleswamp for a reaction. He didn't disappoint.

"Oh, trying your hand in my playground, are you? Sounds like you might find a dark path ahead of you," he commented.

I knew he did this to rattle me. He had no desire to have me join him as a comrade in evil. He just wanted to tear at my heroic leanings. "No, I think I'm still a hero. It's the people I'm supposed to take orders from who might be doing bad things. I think my writer is going to have me uncover what's truly going on and fix it."

Warhinder said, "There are many heroes in quest stories who find the villains are the very same would-be saints who send them out on their adventures. It's a common theme of the one against the establishment. It plays on our fear of institutions we grew up with being riddled with decay and falling apart from an evil born within." While she delivered such heavy notions, she still held fast to her free-spirited nature. She smiled again, this time with noticeable warmth. "Continue, Irving."

I liked how she drew my name out, like it was a cherished word she didn't want to leave her lips. "I don't think all the wish agents are evil. I think it's just the Wellwishers. They're my inner circle."

I paused. My author was working on ideas for me. He wasn't writing them down, but his thoughts were still shaping my narrative. The event he was planning hit me hard. I shut my eyes and rubbed my forehead.

King Druukus appeared at my side and placed an arm under my left elbow to lend support.

I leaned against him.

"Young Wishbutton, are you all right? Something inward strikes at you?" he said.

"My writer is working on me. He was just thinking about the battle sequence he was about to write." I let the King guide me to my seat. My legs felt like rubber bands.

Professor Warhinder patted my shoulder and leaned down to console me. "Your writer, is he writing a chapter now?"

"No, he's thinking about writing. He's just playing with ideas," I said.

Warhinder looked at her students. Her voice contained a trace of amazement. "This is rare, class. Most of us are only in contact with our writers when they set pen to paper or type our stories on a keyboard." She looked back at me. "Irving, are you saying you can sense your author's brainstorming? He's not writing on paper or typing it out?"

"Yes, why? Isn't that how it's supposed to happen? When he writes about me, I can feel it. It's like he's moving furniture around in my head, placing ideas and motives where he wants them and switching out elements of my life that he doesn't want. When he brainstorms, it feels the same way."

Warhinder stood and looked down at me not with pity, but with a bit of awe. "Very few of us are that connected. We only get updated when our writers are actively writing. The connection you have to your author is rare."

"What does that mean?" Raggleswamp said. He eyed me with suspicion.

"It means the author is very attuned to his story. It means that Irving is likely to become one of the greats." Warhinder walked back to her desk and sat, drawing her feet up away from the floor.

"I don't understand," I said.

Warhinder's earrings swayed about as she grew more animated. "It means your author is very invested in you. That he is truly living and breathing you alongside his real life. From that kind of inspiration, truly great literary figures have come into being. This academy has been host to only about a dozen that I know of."

"Are there any others like me here?" I asked.

"Only one, currently," she said.

Raggleswamp interrupted. "This is preposterous! He's a smudge! His writer hasn't even figured out what face he presents to the world. How can he be of such importance? He's lying! He just doesn't want to talk in front of the class. I know him. He's just trying to hide a queasy stomach from us. He's weak in the knees because he doesn't like being front and center, that's all."

King Druukus joined in, "Still your tongue, mudspawn! Irving is a hero. I sense he is speaking true. I for one am thrilled to be attending class with someone of such potential nobility." He bowed his head at me.

Warhinder made her way over to Raggleswamp and put an arm around him. Because of his short stature, she had to go to one knee to comfort him. "Lord Raggleswamp, we are all special. Irving has his connection to his author, and you have such an ornate family background. And your secret lair, it's quite sophisticated."

"And it does have the latest in high-tech science and magic weaponry alongside comfortable seating for when I convene my malicious meetings with my underlings," Raggleswamp added.

She slapped his back playfully. "See, you have underlings. You forgot to tell us that." She looked out at the class. "Who here has underlings? I mean, really, that's quite a lot you have going for you." She nodded vigorously.

Everyone in class nodded, following the Professor's lead. The villain's self-importance swelled once again.

Warhinder clapped her hands together and rubbed them in anticipation. "Let's refocus our discussion as to how and why this academy is here. Anyone have any theories?"

King Druukus led the discussion as all offered theories, even a refreshed Raggleswamp. I was the only one who retreated from the conversation. My mind was reeling at what my author was contemplating. His thoughts had struck me hard. Before, being a part of his brainstorming had felt like simple nudging and prodding as he played with my memories.

His decision to harm my sister is what had caused me to lose it.

I didn't know what would happen to her character here at the academy. Would she also receive the same injury? If so, should I warn her before our author took pen in hand and delivered the blow?

Professor Warhinder saw I was not engaged in the discussion and made her way over to me. She whispered, "I can tell you need someone to talk to about what just happened. Please stay after class. I would be happy to listen to what burdens you bear."

I smiled weakly and tried my best to listen.

Chapter 47

CONFESSION SESSION

Someone had wished for the ability to switch their bodies with someone else. That was the wish Irving would find in the battle.

He put down the papers he had been grading and thought more about the wish. With what he had planned to happen to Irving's sister later in the story, was it too coincidental to have the wish focus on body hopping? He decided it was too good of a wish to not use and made a note to make sure the solution to Tyler's impending predicament would not be so easily solved by the wish. He knew he was treading on the stereotypical notion of wishes backfiring on the maker, but he trusted he could produce a scene that would be unique and heighten the tension.

He again thought of the scene where Tyler would be abducted. He needed to get them home for the abduction to have real world consequences. His next few scenes would be in Wish Haven, but he'd have to get them back to their father so Tyler could be whisked away by Teardrop.

He shuffled the graded papers on his lap. Looking at the time, he decided the last four or five factual reports could be looked over tomorrow night. He stuffed them in his backpack and grabbed Echo's leash. The family dog needed a quick walk before he went up to bed.

So many ideas were swimming about in his head. He was thankful that the project was proving so easy to write. He found himself eagerly looking forward to the concentrated writing time he would have on Sunday afternoon.

After nudging the back storm door open, he escorted their golden retriever out into a starless night. No chance to wish upon a star. The only wishing happening tonight would be intertwined in the brainstorming in his head as he fell asleep.

* * *

Eventually, I found myself drawn back into the class conversation. Much of the credit was due to King Druukus. I found his questions were my own. Warhinder encouraged us to answer our own questions with theories. She rarely stepped in to prove or disprove the theories tossed into the mix.

After class, I did stay behind. Professor Warhinder pulled up a chair in front of me and sat backwards on it. She leaned in, coiling and uncoiling a long curl on her index finger. "What did you think of our class today?"

"It was good. King Druukus is quite the talker."

"He is. Did you find answers that made sense to you?"

I paused. Why was she taking such an interest in me? Was she about to humiliate me like Ringle and Snitpick had? If so, she didn't want an audience. I found that odd.

Her next observation made me wonder if she could see right through me. "Your eyes betray you. You don't know why I'm here, why I'm cornering you." She leaned closer. "I can understand why you would think I'm positioning myself to pounce on you. All your other instructors have done so, lining you up to take a fall."

I nodded, knowing she didn't need my acknowledgement of her reading.

Her eyes crinkled playfully at the edges when she smiled. "I'm not out to get you, Irving. This is Soul Searching. I want you to find answers. I want you to find out who you are."

"And you want us to find out what this Academy is?" I regretted the mistrust my question contained.

"More so than others on staff, I assure you. I believe you need to know your surroundings if you hope to know yourself."

For the first time, I detected an undertone of frustration. "But why bother with this? Why have a school for characters who will go on to be trapped in books?"

She frowned. "Is that what you believe? That we are locked into a life with only one outcome? That all of our paths have been written for us?"

"Well, we are characters. Somebody is writing what we did and will do. Once we get published, we'll only exist on the printed page." With my last sentence, my voice trailed off.

"We are so much more than just characters on a page acting out tasks assigned to us. You overlook a major factor."

"What?"

Her eyes danced. "The reader's imagination. Each person that will open your book, Irving, will bring all of their experiences, all their hopes, dreams and nightmares along with them as they navigate through your adventure. Each time you are read, your life is reborn. New aspects are created. You're never read the same way twice. Do you understand what a gift you are?"

"I guess." My shoulders slumped. What she said made sense, but it didn't alter my mood.

"In class today, when you felt faint, something hit you hard. What was your author planning?" She put a hand on my shoulder. "And please only share with me if you want to."

I didn't feel like sharing, but she had been so sincere and upfront with me. I sighed and confessed, "My writer was working on a scene with me and my sister. It was a battle we were in. He wants her to be hurt. When he sits down to write my next chapter, she's going to be injured."

She tucked her lower lip inside her mouth. "Not a lethal blow?"

"No, she gets hurt bad enough that I agree to go back to Wish Haven where they can provide the right care." I felt my eyes welling up. If I cried, would tears fall from my smudged face?

"Irving, I'm sorry."

"Do I tell her? Should she know? Is she going to be hurt here?" I clenched my fists.

Warhinder said, "When he writes the chapter, the wounds will appear on her. She will report to the infirmary and get help. It will be okay."

"Won't it hurt her?" I asked, already knowing the answer.

"Yes, but she'll heal." Warhinder lowered her voice. "You said he's not planning on ending her life."

"I should warn her." I stood up suddenly.

She fell back, startled. "No, Irving. You aren't to have contact with others in your cast. You can't afford to break any more rules." Her eyes pleaded. "Let me alert the infirmary. They can send someone to watch over her at a distance. Then, when she is struck, they can be there to help her. They will lessen the pain as much as possible."

I ranted, "I should be there at her side. I'm her brother. That's a stupid rule. How come Fenwick gets to drag around his mother and Roon gets to be with her brother? Why are they so special?"

She replied, keeping her voice calm, "Fenwick and his mother are cursed to be together. They have special permission. As to your friend, I don't know her, but I would suspect she also has some sticky plot point that makes it so she has to have her brother at her side."

"Not anymore," I said. My mind still whirled around the image of my sister's impending injury.

"What do you mean?"

I wasn't sure I should share what was happening with Roon. It felt like I was betraying her confidence. I looked at Warhinder. She projected trust and compassion. I took a chance and spilled. "Roon's brother was revised. He was with her and now he's gone. Their writer decided it would be better if she ran her little detective quest solo."

She rubbed her knees. "Irving, revision happens. I am sorry it happened to your friend. In the end, it will be better for her."

I yelled, "But what about her brother? He had to go away. Now he's in some forsaken place called Revision Ravine!"

"Your friend, Roon, she told you of the ravine?" Warhinder's eyes widened. "Did she say she wants to mount a rescue?"

I nodded.

"It's a dangerous place, Irving. It lies at the edge of the Academy. It is not a place you visit willingly." As if suspecting my intent, she added, "You should not go there."

What I did next didn't surprise me. After all, my writer had been quite particular about my flaw. I fibbed. "I would never go there."

She paused, unconvinced. "Don't go. You can't bring someone back to the Academy unless the author decides."

"So it's like being dead?"

"Not completely. It's a limbo of sorts. The writer may bring your friend's brother back later in the story or redesign him for another story."

"Or never work on him again. In that case, he's stuck in Revision Ravine?"

She nodded. "You need to help Roon. She needs the support of a friend to help her move on. Don't even think of going there with her. It's not a nice place."

I was silent.

Sensing she had not totally convinced me, she said, "Don't go, Irving. There are other ways you can help her. Don't trip over yourself to be the hero. You're not ready for that yet." She stepped closer and held her gaze. "I was a smudge like you when I arrived."

I knew she was changing the subject and I was glad. I didn't want her to hound me anymore about Roon and her brother. "How'd that go for you?"

"Not easy, but it helped me to see things more clearly. It helped me to see what others go through."

It was my turn to change the subject. I didn't want her sympathy. Being a smudge, I was getting used to it. I targeted something she had brought up in class. "The teachers are characters, right?"

"Yes, everyone here is a character," she said.

"Then do teachers come and go quite a bit? They get published just as much as the students do, right?"

A nervous twinge played across her face. "Well, some do get published, but many of the faculty are simply, for lack of a better word, stuck here."

"That doesn't sound good."

Warhinder explained, "It's not bad. I guess that came out wrong. See, when a writer abandons a project or never finds a publisher, their character doesn't leave the Academy. It's only natural that Harmstrike select instructors who will stay for a while."

"So do you resent your students for moving on?" I asked.

"I don't. Me, not at all." She walked back to her desk and stowed away a stack of notebooks in her bag.

I knew from her answer that she only spoke for herself. That could mean other instructors did not think so kindly of their classes. It made a wicked sense.

"I'm glad you're here. You've answered more of my questions than anyone else." I added, "You can't tell, but I have a big smile on my face."

"Glad to be of service, Irving." She winked. "Smudged face or not, I can read you just fine."

I grabbed my book bag and headed to the door. "Thanks for a great class, Professor."

I looked back to catch her smile.

She said, "It's you who makes the class. You sure there're no other questions rattling around in that murky noggin of yours?"

I held the door open, leaning against it to keep it from closing. "Just one. You said there's another like me. Another person here who can sense when their author brainstorms without writing their ideas on paper."

"Yes."

"Who is it?"

She hopped off her desk and retrieved a sweater from a wall hook. Gliding across the room toward me, she offered, "I think that's something you already know. After all, you've already met them and made quite an impression."

She exited past me, playfully nudging me in the ribs. "See you next week. Don't do anything dangerous on your first weekend here, okay?"

I lied again, "Okay."

Chapter 48
STAND UP GUY

He had left school on time, a feat that didn't happen too often. Getting home before 5:00 gave him some time to spare before fixing dinner. He glanced over at his daughter and son. They were busy working on their spelling and math homework. He slid a yogurt cup next to each and squeezed their shoulders. He told them he was going up to write for half an hour and they could call him down if they needed his help. His son gave a playful salute, and his daughter nodded. He dashed upstairs and changed into his pajamas while the computer booted up.

He scrolled down to the newest chapter and began to write. He at least wanted to get to the point in the battle where Tyler would be hurt before stopping. The thrill of writing the action sequence took over, and his fingers feverishly zipped across the keys.

He remembered to have Irving distracted as the action heated up. He was caught up in feeling out the new wish he had acquired. This would prevent him from giving the fight his full attention. He liked the idea that Irving's guilt would double when his sister would get injured because of his inattentiveness. It also highlighted that Irving was a thinker first and less of a doer, while his sister could juggle both. He plowed through the battle, filling it with slashing, clashing, and numerous near misses.

Of course, one of those near misses would not be such a miss after all. The stakes needed to be raised.

* * *

I found Sarya waiting for me outside of class. In fact, she hovered a few feet above the double doors to the building, chatting with a flying dinosaur that barely held aloft an oversized golden shield.

She drifted downward upon seeing me exit the building. "Irving, up here." She waved goodbye to the dinosaur who fluttered higher, the shield he carried skimming the tops of the trees he flew over.

Her wings sparkled in the sunlight. I smiled, knowing I had to make up for our missed lunch. "Thanks for waiting for me. Who was that pterodactyl guy?"

"That's Harangus, one of The Golden Knight's good buddies."

"I thought we didn't like that guy. What are you doing talking to one of his minions?" I started walking.

Sarya winged past me and grounded herself, blocking my path. "I can't stand Gared. He's no good, but Harangus can't help but do what he says. Remember, the silver tongue makes all monsters do his bidding?" She knocked an open palm against the side of her head. "Clear your head, Irving. When they're not around Gared, he doesn't have any control over them. They revert back to their normal selves."

"He's still a monster, Sarya. Doesn't that make him bad by himself?"

She frowned. "You're a smudge. Some would say that makes you not worth the time of day. What do you say to that?"

"I'm sorry. So Harangus is a good guy?"

Sarya smiled. "Oh, no, he's a minion through and through. He's one of those inept henchmen who intends to do bad, but always ends up helping the hero because he so thoroughly messes up his master's plans."

"What was he doing with the shield? Is that Gared's?" We resumed walking, no destination in mind.

She said, "He thinks so. He's not sure why he has it. He recalls Gared telling him to take it somewhere, but once he flew out of range of his control, he lost track of his mission."

"Wow, how does Gared get them to do anything for him?"

"I would imagine he has to keep close tabs on anything he wants to be sure gets done. Maybe the shield wasn't that important to him."

Or maybe he was still upset at someone for upstaging him in Snitpick's class and he had forgotten the unreliability of his ability. "So where's Harangus taking it?"

"I told him I thought it looked beautiful, and he offered to let me have it. He's taking it to my dorm. It'll be my first decoration until I get to the school store to buy some more furnishings." She blushed. "He's kind of sweet on me."

I muttered, "Let's hope you hold more sway over him than Gared, or it'll never make it to your wall."

She laughed then circled me twice. One of her wing tips brushed my cheek. It didn't sting but felt soft and smelled of honeysuckle.

"It's a little early for dinner, but would you want to get something to drink?" Sarya's nose wiggled pleasantly.

"Sure." Wanting to make further amends, I said, "I'm really sorry about lunch."

"It's okay. You're making up for it now." She flew slightly ahead, playfully dive-bombing an unsuspecting dwarf. She called back to me, "How'd Soul Searching go? Did you like Warhinder?"

I accelerated to catch up, nearly colliding with a swarm of warriors astride oversized bees who had chosen that moment to cross in front of me. "I liked it."

"Really found out some things about yourself?"

"Definitely. Warhinder's different than the other teachers." I gained enough ground to find myself alongside of her. It didn't last. Her conversation quickened as did her pace.

"She is. She cares about her students. Most of the others don't get involved enough. Of course, I'm not an expert. I've only been attending class two days longer than you."

"Could you slow down?" I stumbled over a raised slab of the walkway, nearly falling to one knee.

"Oh, sure. Flying is still a little new to me, and I tend to forget how fast I'm going." Her feet dipped to the ground, and she abandoned her wings to walk alongside me.

"When do you feel your writer working on you? Is it when he's actually writing the chapters?"

"Of course, how else would it be?" She pointed to a building off to our left and veered in its direction.

"I can detect my writer when he's just thinking of ideas. Warhinder said that was rare," I said.

"Wow, I hadn't heard of that. You mean, you know when he's just thinking about you and your story?"

"Yeah," I said. "Warhinder said there's another here at the school who has the same talent. Someone I've already met. I thought it might be you."

Sarya blushed and took my hand, tugging me toward the entrance to the building. The sign outside indicated our destination of The Drink Station was on the first floor. "That's sweet. You wanted to find something we had in common."

I didn't know how to respond and I didn't have the chance to anyway.

As in Professor Warhinder's class, my mind came under attack. My author was hard at work on my story. Worse, he wasn't just brainstorming, he was writing.

I pitched forward, my left knee crashing against the uppermost step. Sarya kneeled to assist. "Irving, what's wrong?"

"My author's working on the next chapter!" I shouted.

"Well, that's good, right? Why does it hurt you so?"

I stood, taking two steps back from the entrance. A crowd had started to loiter around us, whispering to each other. "He's writing a horrible scene. It hurts."

"Then let's take you inside and sit you down. Maybe a cool drink is just what you need. You look a little pale. At least, I think you do." She peered closer at my smudged complexion.

"No, I need to find my sister. She's in danger!" I swept her to the side.

She scowled. "What's gotten into you?"

I wanted to run off and hunt down my sister. I fought that urge. Sarya deserved an explanation. "My creator's about to write a scene where my sister gets badly hurt. Warhinder told me not to worry, but I have to do something. Where do you think she is?"

"Are you serious? You can't seek her out! It's against the rules." Sarya looked distressed. "You've broken enough rules."

"I don't care. I need to find her. Quick, there isn't much time. Where would she be right now?"

A purple-skinned goblin stepped between us. He wagged a long bony finger at me. "That's enough out of you. Mind your manners when around a damsel."

"What? Who?" I stammered.

He turned and took Sarya's hand, gently landing a kiss on the back of it. "My apologies, fair lady. Your young hero knows not what precious a gift he is treating so roughly."

Sarya said, "Oh, it's alright. I—"

I snapped. I directed my outcry to the crowd. "Somebody has to know where my sister is. She's new. Her name is Tyler Holland. Long red hair. Wearing sort of librarian glasses. Tell me if you've seen her!"

No one from the crowd offered me aid.

"You're Irving Wishbutton?" the goblin asked. He lowered Sarya's hand and spun to face me. He scanned me up and down. "You're what everyone's all in a tizzy about?"

"I-I—"

He held up a hand to silence me. His eyelids shut as he rattled off a response. "Can't say much about how you treated this lady, but it sounds to me, what little I overheard of your conversation, you're a bit determined to get to your sister." The goblin let his statement linger between a declaration and a question. "I saw her sitting on the steps of the library not more than five minutes ago."

I shook his hand. "Thank you." I turned to face Sarya. "I'm so sorry. I'll make this up to you. I have to go!"

She nodded. "Go, I understand."

The crowd parted, allowing me through. I set off, my in-focus boots almost as much of a blur as my hands and face. My thoughts dwelled not on the fact that I had stood up Sarya yet again, but on my sister.

I was already around the corner and almost out of earshot when the goblin confided to Sarya, "She wasn't alone. She was in the company of the Golden Knight."

Chapter 49
SPITE THE KNIGHT

For a third time, he read what he had so far.

One of the wish agents had grabbed a spear thrust at him by a Nowrii. Yanking it out of the attacker's hand, his momentum had swung him around. Not knowing that Irving's sister was behind him, the agent had plunged the weapon into her torso.

Irving saw the tragedy from across the village square turned battlefield. The scene unfolded in slow motion from Irving's perspective. His scream cut through the air but did not cause the fighting around him to grind to a halt. It was only when the Nowrii retreated that the agents fell back, and Irving was able to make it over to his sister.

The leader of the squad approached Irving and indicated his sister could receive proper medical attention back at Wish Haven. He didn't respond, numb to anything other than the pain in his sister's eyes.

The author paused. He had to snap Irving out of his daze and get him to agree to be taken back to Wish Haven. He also wanted to show his devastated emotional state.

His daughter chose that moment to pop into the studio and announce her stomach was empty. Her pleading eyes opened wide to build sympathy for her starving state of mind.

He saved the file and left the document open. Maybe after bedtime and before he started grading papers, he could finish the emotionally draining scene. Right now, he had two adorable and vocal mouths to feed.

* * *

I arrived at the library steps too late.

Not caring how much my lungs protested, I scaled the steps three at a time to be by my sister's side. Except, I wasn't the only one there offering aid.

Tyler lay crumpled on the ground. Her legs draped over several steps while her upper body was supported by the person who had beaten me to the rescue. Her light blue t-shirt was stained with blood from the spear wound.

"Why are you here? Get away from my sister!" I snapped at the Golden Knight.

He didn't answer. He removed one of his gauntlets and pressed his bare hand against Tyler's cheek. "She fell forward as she was walking up the steps," Gared said. "I didn't get to her in time. She hit her head."

I glanced at her forehead. An ugly bruise was already forming. "I need to get her to the infirmary."

"I know where that is," Gared replied. His eyes played over Tyler's body, halting at her wounded torso. "How did she get that? She just fell on the steps."

Despite my mistreatment by Gared thus far, I recognized his genuine concern. His writer had apparently not shed all of his noble intent. Whether that was enough to make a hero out of him in the end remained to be seen.

"My writer did it. She gets speared in a battle. I wasn't able to stop it in the book or . . . here." I kneeled at her feet, wanting to examine the severity of the injury by lifting her shirt. My lack of medical wherewithal and my respect for her privacy kept me frozen. "I knew it was about to happen. I wanted to get here to help her. I don't know what to do!"

Gared seized the moment. "You don't need to know. Be at her side. I will summon transport."

We switched positions. He transferred her head gently into my lap, supporting her with much more gentleness than I would think anyone with such heavy armor could do.

"She's unconscious!" My voice rang with panic.

Gared flipped a stray hair away from her head injury. "The blow knocked her out, but she's breathing, Wishbutton."

He barked at a large lizard walking past us. The creature was at least two feet taller than the Golden Knight and radiated evil intent. A ridge of razor sharp spikes descended from the back of his head and down along his spine. They looked coated in poison. His dark eyes went blank when Gared addressed him.

"Caldera Cutthroat, to my side!" Gared's silver tongue snapped the monster into rigid attention. The beast looked at his master with muted hatred. "Transform into your dragon form and take us to the infirmary!"

The monster swelled twice his size, sprouting leathery wings that threw half the steps into late afternoon shadow. "I will do your bidding, miscreant! Know the weak magic you use to hold me under your sway will mark you forever more as my enemy."

"Enough with the dramatic threats. Take the three of us to the infirmary!" Gared shouted.

The dragon slid a clawed hand under Tyler. Despite his vile demeanor toward Gared's control, he was careful not to jostle her, thankfully.

Caldera glared at Gared and me. "I can only carry one of you in my other hand." His eyes darted to the spikes along his back. "Unless one of you wants to take your chances clinging to my quills. The poisons dripping from them aren't that toxic." He chuckled in disdain, nodding at Gared to be the volunteer to ride bareback.

Gared looked at me. "Be at your sister's side. You should go."

The dragon moved his free hand toward me. Each clawed digit was as thick as my waist. I waved him off. "No, not me. You need to take your bossman."

Gared looked perturbed. "Far be it from me to tell you how to be a hero, but your sister needs you, Irving."

I resisted the urge to ask him when he had ever held back from telling me what and what not to do. "No, it's safer if you go. If that dragon flies out of the range of your power, it might decide to drop her."

"How did you know my—" Gared stopped, not wanting to draw any more of the crowd's attention to his limitations.

"You take the full ride with her and be sure she gets the help she needs at the infirmary. I'll find my way there on my own," I said.

Gared, wishing to recast his image as being in control, issued a series of harsh orders at Caldera, "Take hold of me, beast, and take us to the infirmary at a safe speed. No fancy flying and no playing with your cargo, especially our injured maiden."

As Caldera Cutthroat launched into the air, Gared shot me a menacing look. While he only had sympathetic eyes for my sister, the look he reserved for me was again filled with hate. Perhaps calling attention to the limits of his abilities in such a public place had not been wise. The Golden Knight bore me another grudge.

I shook it off and raced after them, attempting to keep the airborne trio in my sights.

Chapter 50
VISITING HOURS

He closed down the computer. It had been a long night, and time had escaped him. Bedtime had not gone smoothly. His children had been too wound up. Both he and his wife had lost their tempers several times with how often they had snuck out of their rooms to play with each other. On one hand, it was endearing to see how close they were as brother and sister. On the other, they and their parents needed their sleep.

He didn't have the energy to finish up the chapter. It would have to wait until Sunday.

As the computer powered down, he thought about where he was leaving his characters. Tyler was unconscious, and Irving was paralyzed by indecision. It felt appropriate to let the scene linger. It would allow him a chance to step back from it. He wanted it to pack an emotional punch. A few days away from writing would allow him to approach it fresh.

He wanted their emotional ties to feel real. He had no better example of the unique sibling bond his characters shared than to look at his own children. They fought, they pushed back at each other, but in the end, they needed each other. It would be the longest relationship they would ever have.

He stuck his head in each of their rooms one last time, blowing each of them a kiss. His son playfully caught it and tossed the invisible pucker across the room, his eyes tracking the nonexistent path of a smooch ricocheting about only in his imagination.

His daughter snagged her kiss and coaxed it into hiding under her pillow for safe-keeping.

He returned to the living room, hoping they would finally be settled in for the night.

* * *

Dean Harmstrike greeted me at the infirmary entrance with arms crossed. He didn't wait for me to mount the handful of steps that led to the doors of the building. He dashed down them, squaring off with me at the bottom step.

"Once again, news of your misdeeds has spread quickly. I'm here to stop you from making matters worse." He planted himself between me and the infirmary.

"My sister's in there, hurt. I need to be there," I pleaded.

"I'm fully apprised of your situation. You had quite a revelation in Professor Warhinder's class today, didn't you?" He smirked. "I hear you're very in touch with your creator."

I wondered who had told him but didn't want to waste any brain power speculating. "Please let me by, sir."

He scratched at his chin, his eyes drifted upward as he contemplated my request. "No one is to interact with a member of their own cast. I understand what you are feeling, but you cannot visit your sister."

I turned away from him. Why was he so concerned about me? I didn't see him devoting such attention to any other students. Why me?

As if sensing my line of thinking, Harmstrike offered, "You are special, Irving. That can be a good or bad thing for this Academy. Your time here is critical to your development. What you put into this school, you will get back a thousandfold. Think of the Academy as a living thing. It grows and achieves as the individuals it contains evolve. When you excel, the school obtains so much from your successes." His tone darkened. "At the same time, when you err on the side of destruction and chaos, it has a magnified effect on my institution. I will not allow that."

I was getting nowhere. I lashed out. "But why even have such a place? Why is there a school for us? We're just characters."

He slapped me hard. Even with my smudged features, his blow was solid and stung.

He shouted, "We offer hope, relief, and knowledge of how to conduct oneself in the pages of one's book. That is potent magic. You would deny others this?"

My jaw tingled. I wanted to respond but still reeled from his attack.

"You will not see your sister! She is safe. Gared delivered her into capable hands. My medical staff are seeing to her every need. They know what to expect of these types of situations. If her fate is transcribed for her to survive, she will heal."

"I don't see the harm in letting me see her," I said.

"But I do and I know the chaos that results from cast members getting too close here." He inflated his chest. "You will not set foot in the infirmary. You will return to Smudge Hall and muster up the strength to make it through your first weekend here."

Before I could protest, our mutually assured tension was interrupted by Gared. The Golden Knight raced down the steps to stand, oddly enough, by my side. "Sir, may I speak?"

Harmstrike nodded his consent.

"I think Wishbutton would be less likely to go against your orders if he knew of his sister's condition. I just came from her side and could fill him in on what's going on. It would probably defuse the situation." Gared smiled, making a noticeable effort to keep his silver tongue hidden.

Dean Harmstrike considered his request for a long time. Finally, he grunted and said, "Very well, escort Wishbutton back to his housing and tell him what you deem appropriate. I have an appointment I'm late for, anyway."

The dean brushed past me, another mission wedged in his head.

He walked down a side path and veered left. I lost sight of him as he entered a row of sheltering trees that ran along the perimeter of the library.

I looked over at Gared. A joyful smile competed for attention with his natural tendency to smirk. "So, let's get a move on. I have a lot to tell you."

I glanced at him, puzzled. "You're actually going to do what you said?"

"Of course. I mean, it's in my best interest to keep you informed."

"I bet. You've got a lot of nerve, making this about yourself! You don't care a fig about me or my sister."

'You got that half right, Irving," he said.

Chapter 51
SWITCHEROO HULABALOO

He was home from school today. His son had a fever and was very bleary eyed. He had not thrown up yet but looked close to it. He set his son up on the couch with a TV marathon of his favorite alien-shifting teenager. He watched two episodes with him and then brought the laptop down from the studio. He retrieved from his bedroom the binder of the printed book thus far. He kept it by his bedside in case of a fire. It was a silly notion, but he drew comfort that it was so close by his side at night and could be rescued without risk.

Situated at the kitchen table so he could keep one eye on his son, he resumed work on the emotional scene.

He had Irving agreeing to let the wish agents take them back to Wish Haven.

What about Allegro? Should he run off with his fellow Nowrii or should he slip away to pop up later in the story? He thought it wiser if Allegro be free. In fact, it might be good to have the next time they encountered him be on Earth. He jotted the idea in the margin of the last page of the printed manuscript.

He wrapped up the chapter with Irving stressed over the decision to return to Wish Haven. A portal was opened and he and his sister were taken back.

His son coughed. He checked to see if he needed to use the bathroom. His son shook his head. He decided to start the next chapter. He wanted to have Tyler taken to a healer and really play up the use of magic.

Along with the healer's presence, several but not all of the Wellwishers would be on hand as they brought Tyler back from the brink. He wanted Irving to feel obligated to the overseers of Wish Haven, to be tied to a duty he was uncertain should be performed.

The next chapter's title slipped into his head: Saved by The Spell.

* * *

Gared gave me a detailed report on Tyler's condition. It sounded quite serious. I was happy to hear the bleeding had stopped thanks to the quick work of the infirmary staff. I knew my author intended to heal Tyler in the next chapter but didn't offer up that information to Gared. I found myself frustrated by his expressed concern for my sister. Why was he being so genuine? This had my suspicions raised. What did he get out of this? Even though he was distressed over my sister, his animosity toward me still intruded on our conversation.

"She's been unconscious the whole time?" I asked.

"Yes, and it's shameful your author would strike at her over you. Why prey on such a kind and gentle creature?"

"You don't know her. You haven't even talked to her before today." I tried not to sound defensive but failed.

"Actually, I sat with her in my Lending Support group. She was rather quiet, but something about her caught my eye. I had no idea she was your sister becuase she never offered her name."

"Is that a class? Why don't I have that?" We were almost back to Smudge Hall, and I still found I wanted his company. No, correct that. Not his particular company. I needed to be with someone who was connected to my sister's plight.

"It's a support group. It's only for supporting characters, except for me. I run the group. We meet twice a week and talk about the role we play."

"Why would you be a part of that? What's in it for you?" I didn't want him to talk about himself, but I found what he was saying infuriating. How dare he run a group that listens to my sister's worries and woes.

"The Academy is a place to find out about yourself and others. I'm simply taking advantage of every opportunity."

"So you can get close to Tyler, and I can't. That's just wrong in so many ways." I stopped and waved an indistinct finger at him.

His mood darkened. "My grudge with you does not involve your sister. I'm only talking with you because it would be something she'd expect me to do."

And there it was. I didn't know how. I didn't know why, but a dastardly plot had developed without the aid of either of our writers.

Gared had feelings for my sister.

I felt even more isolated. My enemy here at the Academy was falling for someone I could have no contact with. She needed to know what a foul person he was.

Gared tried to sound consoling, but it came off as conceited. "If you want, I can go back to the infirmary after I escort you home and be by her side when she awakens. I have a feeling it'll be soon."

Based on my writer, I did, too. He was working on her healing chapter as we wasted time talking. I wanted to be the one she opened her eyes to see, not this monstrous blowhard.

He was rubbing it in, his ability to get close to my sister.

"I know you wish you can be by her side, but you can't mess up anymore, Irving. You really can't risk another clash with Harmstrike." He patted my back dismissively. "Leave it to me. I'll see your sister through this hardship."

That's when inspiration struck. I knew what I had to do. I couldn't set foot in the infirmary, but Gared practically had an open invite. I targeted the last wish I had gathered. It would allow me to change my circumstances. It would allow me to switch bodies.

I took a step away from the Golden Knight and barked, "Thanks for the idea. It's perfect. I know just what to do."

My confidence sounded shaky, but Gared's surprised look told me he didn't detect my unease. I had not used a wish from my jacket here at the Academy. I wasn't altogether sure it would even work here. I had triggered the jacket with no success when the emberhounds had attacked me. Back then, it hadn't contained any stored wishes. Now it had two. I had no idea of the limits of the wish. I didn't have time to worry if it was permanent. I had to act.

I inspected my wishbutton. I lifted my left hand to hover over it.

"What are you babbling about? What are you doing?" Gared looked rattled.

I thumped the red button on my jacket, landing two fingers soundly on it. The button depressed easily enough, producing a sharp click.

Then my world went black.

Chapter 52
BEDSIDE MANNER

The healing sequence had just enough razzle dazzle to leave Irving and the reader in a true sense of wonderment.

He had orchestrated the scene so that Irving's distrust of the Wellwishers would be put on the backburner. He hinted at his main character's desire to have a little magic in his life. After seeing a very gentle wish agent repair the damage done by the spear in such a dramatic fashion, Irving felt pressured to become part of the wish agents. The scene ended with him greeting his sister as she regains consciousness. Having not seen the magical medicinal act she had just received, she was still unimpressed and wary of the Wellwishers. Irving tried to describe the miracle he witnessed, but stumbled through it.

He had Irving argue that anyone who can perform such feats can't be all bad. The scene closed with his sister unconvinced and to some extent Irving still having doubts. Only he had pushed those doubts deeper, burying them under his giddy enthusiasm, a consequence of his exposure to magic.

He reviewed what he had written. Almost two solid hours of work.

The morning had been a bit rough. His son had gotten sick, barely making it to the bathroom to empty his stomach. He had helped him through it, rubbing his tummy when his son returned to nest on the couch. He had quickly fallen asleep. For two hours, his son had rested. His breathing had been steady, and he hadn't stirred despite several rough coughing bouts.

He printed the chapter and pulled out a pen. As much as he edited on the screen, it was no substitute for holding the script in his hands and marking it up proper. He always felt more concrete about his corrections when they were made in the physical world and not just the electronic.

He checked on his son before scooping up the five pages from the printer tray. He'd try to read over it twice before moving on to fixing lunch. He doubted his son could hold down anything more than a few crackers and he, himself, didn't have much of an appetite.

* * *

As I marched up the steps of the infirmary, I thought of what had happened in the last half hour.

I had returned to the waking world, my perspective altered. I soon found it was more than my point of view that had changed. The wish had been a success. I now occupied Gared's body. It had felt strange, being taller and burdened with the bulky armor the knight chose to wear.

Gared, in my body, had started screaming and ranting. He had kept touching his face and remarking about the tragedy of becoming a smudge.

I hadn't thought my wish through. Sure, I now had the means to infiltrate the infirmary and visit my sister, but I had not counted on having to deal with a hysterical Gared lodged in my own body.

Luckily, two many-horned monsters had chosen that moment to lurch past us. I had used Gared's silver tongue to force them to tie up and gag Gared. Manipulating them had made me feel unclean. I had not liked forcing someone else to do my bidding. They had secured him in the battered shed located in the backyard of Smudge Hall. No one had been around to see my vile plan executed. I had to admit to feeling a little shame at what I was doing, but I quickly buried the feeling.

I had no idea how long I would remain in Gared's body but was reasonably sure it would not last very long. My writer's thoughts on the wish had led me to believe it would only work for an hour or two.

I had told Gared I would return to free him.

As I pushed open the doors to the infirmary, I decided I would make it a quick visit. I didn't want us switching back while I was still visiting Tyler. Then I'd be trapped in the shed. I doubted Gared would be in any such mood to seek me out and untie me if that was the case. I would have to get back to him before our minds realigned with our bodies.

The three nurses who greeted me at the front desk reminded me vaguely of the aunts from the Office of Fine Aunts. Their brightly frosted hair and sweet demeanors announced they were further along in the family tree. They wore name tags, and I quickly discerned they were not aunts. Meema, Nanna, and Gran Gran Gil clearly established them as grandmothers. It made perfect sense to have these nurturing characters take on such bedside roles.

The grandmother named Meema approached me, smiling warmly. "Visited twice in one day by a knight in shining armor, it must be our lucky day, right, girls?"

"Can I see her again?" I asked.

Nanna, the shortest and plumpest of the three, said, "Oh, can't get enough of her, can you?" She directed her next comment to Gran Gran Gil. "Didn't I tell you, Gil? I sensed some chemistry between those two. See, he's back for more."

Gil remarked, "Oh, yes, of course, you detected the romantic stirrings between this brute and our comatose patient. How could I miss the sparks flying between them earlier?"

"Don't be so dry, Gil. My word, you always have to bring down the room. Can't a girl spy a little romance here and there now and then?"

Gil shrugged as if recognizing she faced a losing battle with the pluckier grandmother. She went behind the desk and began shuffling patient files.

Nanna grabbed me by the arm. "Go right in. Sit down with your sweetheart. She hasn't woken up yet, but I'm guessing you'll do the trick." She whispered in my ear, "And pay Gil no heed. That's what comes from being a widow twice over. Bitter as all get out."

"I'm not Tyler's boyfriend," I stated firmly.

She heard what she wanted to hear. "Oh, now look at you. Gone not more than a few minutes and you've already figured out your lady love's name. Did you raid enrollment? Gotta say, those aunts run a tight ship. You couldn't have snuck past them. I bet you sweet talked them into tellin' you her name, didn't you?"

Sensing I would get to my sister's side faster if I resisted objecting and just went along with Nanna's take on me, I said, "Absolutely. I walked right in and charmed it out of them." I added, "I just want to peek in on her before heading back to my housing for the evening. One last glance at her beautiful face will help me sleep tonight."

"Oh, how exquisite! Well, come, come, let's get you reunited with your long lost love. When did you say you met her?" Nanna dragged me down a long hall. She was surprisingly strong.

"Two days ago in a support group." It pained me that I was making Gared look good to these grandmothers. Couldn't anyone sense how evil he was? Then I remembered who was current captain of this body. Maybe they were reacting to me. After all, I was only the Golden Knight on the outside.

"Sounds cozy," she said. She stopped at a door to our left. Grabbing the knob, she pushed it open and gestured for me to enter. "After you, sweetie. Maybe your presence can rouse our princess from her slumber."

I entered to see Tyler sitting up in bed talking with Dean Harmstrike.

He sat on the edge of her bed, rubbing her left hand in his cupped hands with equal parts reassurance and control. He stopped playing the comforting role when I marched in.

Nanna stated, "Oh, look. Our illustrious leader has gotten her to pay a visit with the waking world. Good evening, fair lady. You had us a wee bit worried." She curtsied, stumbling a bit as she misjudged how low she could execute a proper bow.

"Tyler, you're awake!" I blurted out.

"That's stating the obvious, tall, dark, and heavily armored." She withdrew her hand from Harmstrike's. "How is it you know my name?"

Realizing whose body I occupied, I stammered, "W-why in our support group. I found it on the roster."

She gave me a questioning look. "You sure? I never signed up in advance for that. And I'm positive I didn't volunteer my name. I just sat back and listened to everyone else. I thought the whole point of the group was we could stay anonymous if we wanted to."

I was trapped. I suddenly noticed how clammy this body was in parts where I never normally sweated. Gared was clearly older than me and more prone to his body perspiring in tight situations.

Dean Harmstrike looked at me funny. "You feeling all right, Gared? You don't look at all yourself today."

If he only knew the half of it. "I'm fine. Just a bit stressed over this fair maiden I rescued. You're feeling better, are you?" I tried to deliver a line that would sound suitably Gared, concerned, but also indulgent and prideful.

Ignoring my apprehension, Tyler steered the conversation back to my misstep. "So how is it my name rolls off your tongue with such familiarity?"

I took a wild stab. My answer sputtered out, very unconvincing. "It was another in the group. I asked about you after class, and they were more than happy to give me your name."

She took a moment to weigh my answer. "It was that ditzy gorgon, wasn't it? She knows me from Ringle's class. Not much of a looker, but a real talker, apparently."

"Apparently," I said softly, willing a change in topic.

Tyler still appeared on guard.

The dean came to my rescue. Harmstrike clamped his hands down on my shoulders. Even through my armor, his grip was strong. He steered me back to the door. "A word, please, Gared?"

"Certainly, sir." I noticed Nanna still waited outside the door. Gran Gran Gil had joined her and was prodding Nanna. Her furtive glances at Harmstrike made it clear her intent was to address the dean with a matter most pressing. Nanna struggled to keep her at bay.

Harmstrike, unaware of how in demand he was out in the hall, said, "You know I have high hopes for you, son. I really do. I know you're going through a tough time right now. Your creator is still sorting out whether it's you or your brother who turns bad, right?"

I nodded. I was surprised by the level of concern the dean was heaping on my adversary.

"I'm rooting for you to wind up on the side of good, Gared. There's something about you, something I can't quite put my finger on, but it really shined through today. You weren't your normal prideful self, all concerned with appearances and ramming your accomplishments down any spectators' throats." He looked into my eyes. "Like right now, you radiate such purity of purpose. That's got to mean you're heading down the right path."

"I certainly hope so," I said.

Harmstrike advised, "Then visit with her but stow away the smugness. Be yourself. I suspect this girl has a way of bringing out the best in others. At least, from the little time I spent with her, that's my impression."

I smiled inside; proud Harmstrike was so impressed with my sister. It also made me wonder why he held me in such low regard. Perhaps she had not made a wreck of the Office of Fine Aunts or trespassed in a forbidden section of the library.

He clapped me on the back and nodded at Tyler. "Miss Holland, I will be by tomorrow to check on you. I suspect you'll be feeling more yourself then. Sometimes, creators get their favorites on the mend quite quickly. I can't imagine he'll let you languish in such a subdued state for long."

"Thank you, sir," she said.

Harmstrike slid past Nanna. I heard Gran Gran Gil stop him in the hall and mutter something about a noodle-headed boy causing a disturbance up in the waiting room. I didn't have time to think anything more of their conversation because Tyler was ready for a second round.

"So you're nosing around, digging up info on me. What's that all about?" she said.

"I just wanted to know your name." I suddenly wished Gared's suggestive silver tongue worked on more than just monsters.

"Well, Harmstrike's right. You are different today. When I met you in that group, you really were all about you. You were insufferable. I couldn't wait for that group to be over."

I didn't want her to continue. I didn't want her to think Gared had changed when it was me in his body making her think differently. What she said next threw me even more.

"But when we were carried by that dragon, I woke up in hysterics. And you, you didn't make it about yourself. You talked me down. You were kind and caring." Her eyes softened.

This was not at all what I expected. Gared wasn't supposed to be a good guy. He was evil.

"And you're different now. You walk around with a lighter step, with less concern for how much space you take up in a room. You're suddenly not as large."

That's because I'm not Gared, I wanted to scream. *I'm your brother, risking the dean's wrath to see you.* I wanted to say something to make her hate him. I wanted to make him look bad. "It's a small room," I observed.

"And then you know my name. I've been very tight-lipped about that because frankly this place creeps me out," Tyler confided.

"It does," I agreed.

"I lied about the group. There was no gorgon. But you didn't know that because you weren't really there." She cocked her head.

"Of course I was there. Are you saying it was some other golden armored knight?"

She ignored my question. "And there's the warm feeling I got when you entered the room." She paused and allowed a pleasant shiver to overtake her.

"I'm sure they just keep this place toasty for the patients," I said.

"No, I only got this feeling once before." She pushed the sheet down to her ankles, revealing the tightly wound bandages around her torso. I could see no blood. She dropped her bomb. "When I snuck in to see *our* father."

"What?" I gasped.

Tyler leaned closer. "Our father. You haven't seen him, have you? You're not the only one who can break the rules, *Irving*. I'm just better at not getting caught," she admitted.

And for what I imagined probably the first time, The Golden Knight's silver tongue was thoroughly tied.

"You're not Gared, are you? I don't know how, but it's you, Irving. Tell me I'm right!" She strained to rise to her knees as I fell to mine.

Chapter 53
SISTER SEES ALL

He woke early on Saturday, clear-headed and wanting to write. He snuck out of bed. Sparing a glance at the clock, he saw it was 5:45. He could get an hour of writing in before his kids tilted out of their beds and into immediate action.

As the hour flew past, he poured fanciful description into the healing sequence. It had to bewitch Irving. The grandness of the magic on display had to sway him into pushing aside the injustice and uncertainty he had been shown of the Wellwishers' methods. He needed Irving to crave the magic, to want to have it in his life. He had Irving lie to himself, justifying his station as a wish agent could help him in finding his missing mother. He made sure both the reader and Irving knew it was a conveniently noble excuse, but enough for all to live with. He portrayed one of the Wellwishers as slightly less arrogant and more benevolent. This would make Irving feel a little better about his decision.

The chapter closed with a distinct focus on Tyler, newly mended in body, but still torn about the wish agents and their purpose. He thought about Irving's sister. She was a trusting soul as long as the person had earned her trust. Newcomers into her life had to prove themselves to her. Magic had its place for her, in the books she read. Outside of that, her suspicions were raised.

He read over the last half, correcting a few punctuation marks and adding two sentences of elaboration on Tyler's guarded persona. He saved the file and went downstairs to walk their dog. The rest of the house was silent, but that would not last for long.

* * *

"I know how you did it, too," she gloated. Tyler sat on the edge of the bed, attempting to pull me to my feet. "Help me out. I'm a little

218

wounded here. You're not at all light in that getup." She rapped her small knuckles on my chest plate.

"You're delirious," I replied.

"Oh, stop it, Irving. I busted you fair and square. You're not the only one who knows what's happening with our author. When he writes our chapters, I find out stuff, too. Like the last wish you acquired. It switches bodies. You traded your body with blowhard Gared here and walked right in under the dean's nose."

"That's—"

"You knew you couldn't get in trouble with Harmstrike another time. Pretty ingenious. Tell me I'm right," she said, opening her eyes wider, expectantly.

I whispered, "Okay, everything you said is true. It's me."

Even though I knew my sister from our story, this was the first time we had been physically together. I found I didn't know how to act. I waved at her meekly.

Tyler had no such hindrances. She catapulted out of the bed and wrapped her arms around me. "It's my little brother!"

I lightly patted her back. "Hey, you're still injured. Take it easy."

She squeezed tighter. "Not true. At least not anymore. Our author wrote my healing scene just now."

As she said this, I knew it to be true.

She pulled up her shirt and grabbed hold of her bandages. She unwound them slowly, but, as she got closer to the end, she sped up, anxious to reveal what we both knew lay underneath.

As the last layer of wrap fell to her lap, tender pink skin greeted us. There wasn't even a scar.

"Whoa! That's amazing! It's like brand new!" I exclaimed.

"I could feel it happening. When Harmstrike came in to see me, it was healing."

"No pain?"

"Not anymore. It tingled a little as it was happening." She pressed at her torso, testing it. "I'm kind of glad the bandages were over top of it. Not sure I would really want to see it mend itself."

I added, "Well, in our story, you sleep through it. I get to see the magic they use. It's pretty spectacular."

Her mouth drooped. "I know. It's what clouds your head into thinking being a wish agent could be a good thing."

I started feeling uncomfortable about our topic. Discussing what we were going to do in our story felt off. Maybe that was why Harmstrike wanted cast members to stay away from each other.

"You've seen Dad?" I said.

"Yeah. Snuck in. Kept it low key. Unlike what you've been doing. I can't go anywhere without hearing about your latest snafu. You've got to rein it in, Irving." She nodded in approval. "That's why I'm happy to see you gussied up in Gared's body. Shows you're finally thinking smart."

"Yeah, well, I can't stay long. I have to go before the wish switches us back. I'm pretty sure there's a time limit."

"Well, then let's make this visit quick." She slipped out of bed and retrieved her shoes from the chair situated next to the window.

While she was occupied with tying her shoes, I inspected her appearance. Our writer had chosen to fully describe her early on. The result: all her features were carefully catalogued in my head. She was definitely not a smudge. Her red hair was tightly curled. Her rectangular librarian glasses hung atop her nose with knowing poise. The sharp chin and lean jaw matched perfectly with her no nonsense demeanor. Every aspect of her radiated confidence and a willful spirit. I was secretly glad she couldn't see me in my smudged appearance. It was bad enough she knew of my wishy-washy personality and nitpicky flaws our author had heaped on me.

"How is he?" I searched her eyes for comfort. Here was my sister, and yet I felt strangely disconnected from her. It was as if our memories were only sketched out, incomplete. I knew she sensed it, too.

"He's handling it well. Odd thing is he's worried all about our villain. Keeps claiming he hasn't seen Teardrop anywhere on campus. He's a little obsessed about tracking her down. That seem healthy to you?" She apparently didn't remember our author's original plan of making Teardrop our mother. Our author had written the shocker then taken it away to be revealed later. Why did I still remember it and she didn't? I decided not to ask.

I confessed, "You're talking to the guy who switched bodies to touch base with his sister. Not sure I'm thinking straight myself."

She laughed. It was deep and comforting. "True. So what do you think of this place?"

"I'm not sure what to make of it," I said. "Most of my professors are jerks. Warhinder's the only decent one so far."

She looked out the window. I watched her gaze target the administrative building. More specifically, it fell on the top floor, Harmstrike's office. "Yeah, she's cool. Little bit of a hippie with all the feelings and free spirit stuff, but I get what you mean about her. Ringle's a flake and Snitpick, well, I'm glad I don't have him. I heard he's a bit on the dramatic side."

"You could say that." I sat on her bed. The frame groaned in protest. Realizing it was from the weight of my armor, I stood up.

"Not used to being so cumbersome, are you?"

"Really not a fan of having to use *this* body."

"Gared's not all bad."

"Oh, no. Please don't tell me you think he's some sort of sweet hero type just because he commandeered a dragon to rescue you. If I know him, he has his reasons."

"Maybe so, but we all have our flaws." Tyler didn't take her eyes off Harmstrike's office window. "I'm glad you came. You probably need to go soon."

I shrugged. "I sort of do."

She turned, keeping one knee on the chair. She held out her arms, gesturing for another round of affection. "I know it's not really your body, but it still feels like you when we hug."

I approached her slowly. She again wrapped her arms around me and squeezed tight. I did more than just pat her back. I returned the embrace, being careful not to grind any part of Gared's armor into her.

She whispered, "I've done a little snooping. I can tell you this, Harmstrike's rotten. I don't know what he's up to, but I have a bad feeling about him." What she said next came out in a rushed exhale. "And he's got it in for you, Irving. You specifically over anybody else."

I dropped my head, allowing Gared's strong chin to nuzzle against her curls. "I know."

She started to cry. She burrowed closer to me, hoping to drown out her sobs.

"Tyler, I'll be okay."

She pushed me off of her, wiping away her tears on her forearms with broad movements. My sister turned away and looked out the window again. "Be careful and don't try to see me again."

"Tyler, I—"

"Go. I don't want Gared to zip back into his body and see me like this, all right?" She snuffled.

I exited her room, permitting a tear to fall and stream down the Golden Knight's chest plate.

Chapter 54
CAW OF DUTY

When the opportunity presented itself, he had to take advantage of it. He was getting more writing time this week than he had expected. Here it was Saturday afternoon and his wife had taken the kids to meet up with their cousins at the park. She told him to stay and do what he wanted. He could've tinkered away the hour on the Internet, but five minutes in, he had already visited his favorite sites and was itching to write.

It was a perfect time to pen an interlude chapter featuring Teardrop. He needed to lay the groundwork for Tyler's abduction by having the villain ponder her scheme as she admired the creature she would send to snatch Irving's sister.

He looked back at his notes, searching for the beast he had slotted for the task. It had been some sort of hybrid of a rhino and jellyfish, hadn't it?

He almost missed it. The sketch of the creature was on a small post-it note stuck to the back of an early list of chapter titles. He inspected his handiwork. He had doodled a triceratops head atop a jellyfish body. Scribbled underneath with an arrow pointing into the tangle of wispy tentacles was a reminder that there was a jelly sac up inside the beast where Tyler would be stored away.

He did a quick web search of the Portuguese Man-of-War to see what the appendages looked like. The curled randomness of the tentacles worked well. He added two primary tentacles that terminated in large fins that would propel the aquatic creature through its environs. He stumbled across the name medusoid and found he liked that classification. He did an additional search of Triceratops and began a larger sketch of the beast, fusing the tri-horned head of the dinosaur with the distinctive gelatinous body of the man-of-war. Dubbing it the Triceramedusoid, he took the completed sketch and taped it on the wall above his monitor.

He grabbed a soda and some crackers before launching into the chapter with a heavy emphasis on frightening description. He wanted a sense of dread to be established for the reader.

It only took forty minutes to write the dark and disturbing scene. He printed it to read over later that day. Being a chapter ahead of schedule, he earmarked tomorrow to finish a revision that had been long overdue: inserting a proper description of his hero's good looks in an earlier chapter.

With eerie precision, the rumble of the garage door opening dovetailed with the completion of the chapter. He smiled at the convenient harmony and made his way downstairs, hoping to beat his daughter to the door before she started her knocking assault.

* * *

I left my sister's room and retraced my steps to the infirmary lobby. I was surprised to see Harmstrike still there. He was talking to Fenwick Noodlemen. They were quite animated in their discussion.

As I walked by, they did little to hide their topic of discussion.

"I don't care how you feel about it. It must be done!" Harmstrike said as Fenwick shrank back from the dean.

"But it's so underhanded. I won't do it," Fenwick declared half-heartedly. "It goes against my nature."

The dean leaned even closer, his nose only inches from Fenwick's flimsy brow. "You will. Need I remind you of my little leverage being escorted and caged in my office as we speak? You will do what I say, period!" Harmstrike's voice cracked.

"Hello, Fenwick," I said. I slid past them as quickly as I could, but not before catching my mistake.

Fenwick looked at me, confused. He stumbled through his reply. "Um, hello."

I felt his eyes stare at the back of my head as I raced past the nurses, managing to avoid being pestered by any of the grandmothers as to the romantic particulars of my visit.

I grimaced. Why had I said anything? It was clear from Fenwick's reaction that he had never spoken with Gared before. What had compelled me to blurt out his name? I hoped my little slip-up would go unnoticed by the dean, but I had little time to think about it as I felt a tingling inside my head. I broke into a run, certain that what I was experiencing was the beginning of switching back. I needed to get my body untied and out of the shed before the process was complete.

Despite the Golden Knight's armor, I kicked my manic marathon into overdrive.

One question rattled around in my head as I sprinted across campus: Where was Fenwick's mom?

Chapter 55

BODY SWAP

He had made sure to have one of Teardrop's minions sneak in and cast a spell on the beast without her knowledge. He kept the saboteur's identity and loyalties hidden. He wanted the reader to infer the shadowy figure worked for the Wellwishers, but he didn't want to make it too obvious.

He had thought Sunday would start with major work on Irving's description but found he needed to add a mischievous chapter with one of Teardrop's minions casting a deliberate spell on the Triceramedusoid. He left the reader unclear of the spell's purpose and even more in the dark as to the new mysterious player's allegiances.

He had three more hours of writing time. He really wanted to nail down Irving's appearance, insert it in the most appropriate chapter and even try to start work on the new chapter. He cued up a playlist of songs on his computer and charged into the fray.

* * *

The sensation in my head was no longer a minor tingle. A full blown tug of war was underway, as if some unseen hand were pulling at my mind, attempting to yank it from Gared's skull. The closer I got to my real body's hiding place, the more the tugging increased.

As I sprinted down the side yard of Smudge Hall, it grew unbearable, causing my legs to fail. I stumbled to the ground, rolling twice. Luckily, my tumbling covered enough ground to put me within arm's reach of the shed's door handle. One quick pull, and I could let go and see my mind to its proper return.

Laying on the dusty ground, only inches from freedom, the pain subsided. I sensed my reprieve was only temporary and the next bout would pack even more of a wallop. I took several gasping breaths, attempted to get my bearings and then hesitated. I had a firm grip on the handle but was frozen in place. Had I just heard casual conversation issuing from the rundown shed? A girl's voice, throaty yet smooth? Even a gentle laugh, sounding much like my own, in fact?

I willed Gared's thick arm to fling open the door. Not aware of the strength the Golden Knight possessed, I wrenched the door nearly off its hinges.

There, exposed to the late afternoon sun, sat my body atop a tipped over cabinet. At my feet, the rope I had bound Gared in lay cut. Sitting across from my possessed body was Sarya. She was astride a rusty riding mower that clearly had been let out to pasture. She playfully turned the steering to and fro as she chatted with Gared.

"Look who's finally back!" Gared announced. "And not a moment too soon. Bad enough my face is in such disarray, but if I had to spend one moment more in this cramped skull, I might have lost it."

Sarya said, "About time you got back, Irving. I didn't know how much longer I could keep Gared here. He wanted to go after you. I convinced him he really didn't want to strut about campus as a smudge. He agreed, and we've been waiting for you ever since."

Her smudge insult hurt, but I ignored it.

"You know that's Gared in there?" I pointed at my body as I rose to my knees.

"Yeah, but not at first," she admitted.

"How'd he get out of the ropes?" I asked.

Sarya sunk her head between her shoulders and raised her hand half-heartedly. "That would be me. After you ran off to find your sister, I figured my best bet of meeting up with you was at Smudge Hall. I knew they wouldn't let you into the infirmary, so there was no sense catching up with you there."

"And it's a good thing she came, too," Gared spouted. He stood up and scratched at the back of his, my, head.

"Yeah, I was waiting for you on the porch when I heard a lot of racket coming from the shed," Sarya said. "It took a little doing, but I got that nasty door open and found you tied up."

"But why did you untie him?" I said. I knew Sarya did not have a high opinion of Gared and was wondering why she was suddenly so cheery around him. Had he worked his excessive charm on her as he had apparently done on my sister?

"I thought he was you. I mean, here I find you tied up in a shed, what am I going to do? Of course, I got you, him, free." She looked at the knight fondly. "He filled me in on what you did, and I convinced him to wait here for your return."

Why was she so friendly with him?

Gared stepped closer to me. "Let's get this over with. I want everything back in its proper place. The tugging has returned." He tried to rub his forehead, but grew frustrated at how his hand could not locate anything remotely stable on his smudged face.

I felt it, too. The wish was at its end. I closed my eyes.

Gared had time to spit out a threat before the wish dissipated and flung us back into our bodies. "You better not have damaged any part of my fine physique, Wishbutton."

This time, I felt more of the switch. I was swept out of Gared's body and plopped back into mine. While it was not a physical feat, it still reminded me of being buffeted about by a determined wind. I felt like a genie being stuffed back into its bottle.

Free of the entanglements of Gared's armor, my body felt lighter. I spun my arms about and wiggled my legs, happy to be back in my sound body. I immediately felt rather deep friction burns from the rope I had tied around my own wrists.

Gared caught me rubbing at the approximate location of my wrists. He chuckled. "Odd that your hands are so indistinct and yet the skin can be rubbed raw by someone determined to leave their sweet little mark. Enjoy, you earned it and so much more."

Gared lurched at me, swinging his fist high. I ducked and felt him graze the outer edge of my smudged head.

He twisted back around, preparing a second attack when Sarya squeezed her tiny fairy figure between us. I retreated, afraid her wings might be damaged in the tussle.

"Enough! To your corners, children!" She pointed at opposite sides of the shed.

I moved back first.

Gared glared at me as he patted himself down, checking to see if his own body was in order. "No damage here. Of course, I'm pretty tough. I wouldn't expect you to know how to inflict any pain on the likes of me."

"That's it, Gared. We talked about this. You promised me you wouldn't lash out at Irving or report what he did to Harmstrike." She looked at him with her wide eyes.

Gared shrugged. "Fine. I did pledge an oath. A foolish one, but I will honor it."

Sarya said, "Well, that's refreshing. Twice in one day, you've acted like a hero."

Gared positioned a sly grin on his face. "Must be damsels who bring it out in me. First Wishbutton's sister, now you."

I sighed. Again, he touted his accomplishments. Performing a few good deeds here and there didn't make somebody a hero. "You stay away from Tyler. She doesn't need you mucking about in her life."

Gared exited the shed, kicking the door off its last remaining hinge. He didn't look back as he spoke. "Oh, I don't think so. I never promised anything of the sort. Your sister is fair game. I intend to—what's the word I'm looking for? Oh, yes,—woo. I intend to woo her for all it's worth. And I'd love to see you stop me!"

My mind was empty. I didn't have a comeback. Gared said nothing more. I watched him disappear around the corner before stepping out of the shed. Meekly, I went to retrieve the door.

As I attempted to secure it back to the door frame, Sarya said, "Don't bother. Remember, Smudge Hall is cursed. Leave it. Tomorrow, the shed will be put back together, restored to its normal ramshackle charm."

"I guess I disappointed you again, huh?" I said, propping the useless door to the side.

She took my hand and began walking toward the back entrance to Smudge Hall. "No, you'd be surprised by my opinion of you right now."

"But I stood you up again."

She wheeled around and vigorously shook a finger at me. "You did what is expected of a hero. You took action. I'm not going to fault any brother who rushes to be by his sister's side, not caring of the consequences." She paused and then winked. "Besides, the body switching spell, that was genius. You'll have to tell me all about how you did that."

"Um, . . ." I hesitated.

Sarya snapped, "Must you be so thick? It's over. We've made nice. You keep dragging out your insecurities enough, you might start convincing me they're true. Let's just go inside and get a snack. You can also tell me about your visit with Tyler, okay?"

I smiled and I knew, smudged face or not, Sarya read my happiness.

Chapter 56
FACE TIME

There it was. Finally, a description of what Irving looked like. He was pleased with how it turned out. He had thought the description would've come first, but after wracking his brain for almost thirty minutes, he decided to find the scene where the description made the most sense. He reread the first few chapters and found the most natural place: the aftermath of the emberhound attack and Irving fetching his first wish down by the pond. Once he had the scene, he attempted to sync the description with the action.

He decided against having Irving look at his reflection in the water as too lazy. It was too convenient. He did have Irving slip on the water's edge. As he reached out for something to halt his misstep, he'd knock loose the seeds of the cattails infesting the pond. The seeds, embedded in their fluffy down, would get tangled up in his hair and he'd have to pluck them out of his curls. That would be a more natural way to showcase Irving's tangled mop of a head. From there, the description flowed outward. He somehow managed to include details about his hero's brow and jaw line without bogging down the text.

Upon completing the description, he eyed the clock. He had less than half an hour before his family returned. He decided to begin the new chapter.

He started in on the scene. It was a critical one, depicting Irving coming to an agreement with a wish agent assigned to be his mentor. He was working out the mentor's personality when the phone rang. He picked it up. His wife offered to pick up Chinese. He placed his order and closed down the writing. They would be home in under twenty minutes. He decided to look over the printouts of what he had written over the past three days, while doing a couple miles on the stationary bike. He set the belt to moderate tension and began pedaling.

* * *

Upon entering Smudge Hall, the first thing I noticed was Val's absence in the kitchen. A quick check of the first level revealed he was nowhere to be found. I wondered if the robot-armed do-gooder had checked out. Maybe he had gotten himself fully described. I was disappointed at the notion. Val had been a constant at the house, and his absence made the place incomplete.

Sarya retrieved the ingredients to make sandwiches and placed them on a tray. She received a scolding from the winged fairies who still resided in the kitchen. They seemed irritable, which could've been a result of Val taking his leave. I didn't feel like upsetting them more by asking, so we took our food stash to my room. My roommate was not there either.

"Where is Val?" I asked.

She dropped the tray on my bed and scooped up the large butter knife. "I noticed that, too. He's always lurked around the kitchen." She slathered mustard on two of the slices.

"Should we check his room?" I moved toward the door.

She waved the mustard-coated knife at me. "Don't bother. He didn't have much in there except his books and, if he had class today, he might have all of them with him. He likes to be prepared for anything."

"I like having him here," I stated.

"I did too. There's something about him that makes you feel looked after," Sarya said. She handed me two slices as she finished stacking the meat and cheese on her own sandwich. "Go ahead and make yours."

"Thanks." I ignored the mustard, smearing my bread with mayo and a brownish cheese spread that I remembered was Val's favorite. I tucked a layer of lettuce under my ham and roofed the sandwich with a somewhat mangled slice of bread.

"So you snuck in to see your sister?" She took healthy bites. Her tiny cheeks playfully puffed outward as she chewed.

Yeah." I compacted my sandwich, desiring a flat target for my appetite.

"That was really smart of you to use Gared's body. How'd you do that?"

"It was a wish stored in my jacket. Because I'm missing the other button, I can use the wish." I licked some fugitive cheese spread from my thumb.

"I don't get that. You're not supposed to use the wishes?" Sarya tilted her head.

"Well, my author decided most agents have two buttons. The second one is like a lock. It keeps the agent from using the wish. We're supposed to just fetch wayward wishes and bring them back to Wish Haven. A couple jackets are out there without the second button. Those agents can use the wishes they gather up."

"So you're a criminal?"""

"I don't think I am. In fact, I think who I work for is using the wishes for something evil. I don't know what yet. They definitely want to be the only ones with access to the wishes." I managed to take a few bites between my responses. "I think I'm supposed to find out what they're up to."

Sarya finished her sandwich. "So you had a body switching wish in there?" She tugged at the fabric where my sleeve met my shoulder, almost tickling me in the process.

"Yes. I wasn't sure it would work here, but I guess it does. The wish wasn't permanent, though. I wonder if that's because it's supposed to stay in my jacket until I use it in my real story."

"So you think you can use it again?" She sat on the bed, patting an open spot on the blanket and gesturing for me to sit beside her.

"I'm not sure. I would say probably not."

"Oh." She looked disappointed. "Because a wish like that could come in handy."

I sat on my bed, keeping ample space between us.

"You have any other captured wishes?"

"Just one more. It'll let me breathe underwater. I'm not real keen on using that one, because it kind of backfired in my story." I held off telling her the exact chain of events and hoped she wouldn't ask. My actions had been clumsy and foolish.

"How do you know you can still use it here if you already used it in your story?" She coyly brushed a wing against me.

I couldn't tell if it had been deliberate or accidental. "Just a sense I get. I don't know." I wanted to change the subject. "I thought you were asking about my sister."

Sarya's cheeks reddened. Her eyes darted away from me. "Oh, you're right. That's very insensitive of me. I'm sorry." She placed her hand on my shoulder, holding it there for longer than necessary. "How is she?"

"Her wound is healed. Our author wrote the chapter where she gets fixed up," I said.

"That's quick. Good thing he didn't take time off between those two scenes."

"He's working quite a bit on our story. Things are happening awful fast. Too fast. It's a bit overwhelming."

"It can be a lot to keep track of, especially for you main characters," she said with a hint of envy.

"Sarya, there's something off about the whole thing, though," I said.

"What do you mean?" she asked, leaning closer to hear my impending confession.

"I think there's a time difference between the real world and here. Sometimes the time between writing sessions with my author is long, but here it's only a few minutes or hours."

"Oh, that." She waved a dismissive hand at me. "Doctor Ringle explained it in an earlier class. Time here and in the real world doesn't always match up. What might be weeks here is only days there and vice versa. Don't worry about that. In the end, it matches up. Two years here is roughly two years for your author."

"But that's a little odd, don't you think?"

"It is, but you can't do anything about it." She stood up. "There'll be weeks that go by here when it's only a few hours for your writer. At least, that's what they say to expect."

She occupied herself by scooting our plates back on the tray and placing it out in the hall. "I'll take it down to the kitchen later." She turned and walked over to my window. "Don't you think we should plan for another official lunch out? This little picnic doesn't make up for you standing me up twice."

"Hey!" I protested. I knew she was being playful. "You said you understood about the second time."

"I'm just giving you a hard—" She turned to look at me and shock registered on her face. Her wings stopped fluttering.

"What's wrong?"

"Your face, it's there." She leaped onto the bed next to me and started tugging at my cheeks.

I started to put up my hand in protest but stopped. She was indeed grabbing hold of my flesh.

Having no mirror in the room, I asked, "Is it all there? I mean, do I have two eyes, a nose, and a mouth?"

"Yeah, that's all there and you've got one massive head of hair." I felt her root around under my new do. "And there's two ears hidden in that mess. Guess you're all complete."

"Even my hands," I said, holding them up to reveal slender fingers that I flexed several times in awe.

"Yeah, kind of weird that he left your hands undescribed for so long. Guess you didn't grab hold of much early on in your story." Her excitement caused her to bounce up and down on my bed.

I explained, "I have a watch. Look." I offered up my left wrist. Secured by a simple leather band, the watch face depicted a large squirrel monster chasing a fleeing nut. "I think this is my favorite cartoon. It's called Senor Squirrelly."

"I don't know what a cartoon is." Sarya looked saddened.

"Oh, it's like a show that is beamed into your house. It's a silly play that's acted out for you in a box called a television."

"Oh. We don't have television in my world."

That made sense. She was from a fantasy world. They probably relied on magic more than technology.

"Your eyes are very handsome. They're green like the upper leaves of the jikpul tree with little flecks of golden brown." She peered closer at my features.

"Uh, thanks," I said, feeling a bit like a bug under a magnifying glass.

She rocked back, clearly startled by something on my face. "Oh, a tiny scar just appeared in the crease of your right eye. It points back to your ear." She stroked the injury.

I searched for an explanation. "Yeah, he just said that in the story. I fell pretty hard on the corner of a table when I was little. It left a small gash, but not one big enough to need stitches. Does it look bad?" I felt around for it. My hand enshrouded her tiny fingers briefly.

"No, not at all. It's nice," she said.

"Well, I guess I know what this means." I looked around at my empty room. I was struck by how much comfort I drew from my simple lodging. "I've got to say goodbye to all this."

Sarya grabbed my hand and pulled me out of the room. Was she that eager to have me leave?

"C'mon, it's time for you to go to the special room."

"What do you mean?" I asked.

She practically flung me down the stairs. "You remember the room off of the kitchen that Raggleswamp got to go in when he was fully formed? Now it's your turn. It'll help you deal with no longer being a smudge."

She weaved us through the hole-ridden hallway and led me into the kitchen. Val snooped around in the fridge.

He waved his robotic arm at us. "Hello, Irving, Sarya. Nice to see you two together."

I tipped my head at him, noticing he was still a smudge. Good, he hadn't left yet.

Sarya blurted out, "Irving's not a smudge anymore. I know it's a little late to cook up a proper farewell dinner for him, but maybe we could do a bon voyage dessert?"

Val sized up my new appearance. "Gotta say I liked him better all mussed up." He chuckled to himself. "I'll whip up a proper treat for the few here tonight."

Sarya sent her signature warm smile at the cyborg. "I'm ushering Irving to 'the room.' Can we do the dessert after he comes out?"

"No problem. Take your time, Irving."

Before I could say anything more, Sarya had opened the door to the mysterious room and shoved me in. My left boot tripped over the edge of a thick rug, and I fell forward. She shut the door behind me, leaving me in complete darkness.

Okay, what next?

Chapter 57
ROOM WITH A VIEW

He couldn't resist working on the next chapter. When he stopped work midway through a chapter, it was a good motivator to work on it on a weeknight rather than waiting until the next weekend. He was taking a half hour while his wife played a board game with the kids. He wanted to nail down the mentor wish agent. He immediately wanted the mentor to have a past with Irving's father, but not spill the beans about it just yet. Did he want the mentor to be crotchety or calm and peaceful? Both approaches felt too obvious. No tall bearded guides or short grouchy gurus would share the stage with Irving. What if the mentor was noticeably younger than Irving? That would cause some tension. His mind stumbled onto the word "seedling." Would it make sense to have the mentor be a young plant creature? He liked that idea. A little sprout that would spout worldly wisdom.

The scene fell into place. He was careful to completely describe the plant wish agent and Irving's reaction to how young it was. Yorn Greatseek was his name, and the exchange with Irving had a certain antagonistic charm to it. Irving tried to keep his frustration at having a younger mentor under the surface, but Yorn's spunky personality kept causing Irving to reveal his bias.

As he wrapped up the scene, he had Tyler enter and be very dismissive. She urged Irving to take her home, and he complied. They left Wish Haven, but with the understanding that Yorn would come to them soon to begin Irving's training.

* * *

I made my way forward on my hands and knees. The room had gone dark after Sarya had closed the door, but my eyes had soon adjusted, and I spied a faint green glow coming from something hanging on the far wall. Crawling was the best way to cover ground as I was fearful of knocking into the three or four low-hanging chandeliers revealed by the glow, the green light reflecting in their dazzling crystal festoons. I went around two highback chairs tipped onto their sides. The fabric had large gashes as if some clawed animal had worked it over.

As I drew closer, more details of the room came to light. In addition to the two fallen highback chairs, there was an armless statue along the wall to my left and in the center of the right wall, a fireplace whose mantle was decorated with two squat candles.

If I had to guess the room's purpose, I would've said a ballroom of some sorts. Otherwise, why so many chandeliers? Plus, it was large. It felt longer than Smudge Hall. I didn't know how; it may have been the act of crawling was causing me to misjudge the distance I had traveled.

All interest in dissecting the rest of the room fell to the wayside when I centered my attention on the source of the green light. An arm's length away from me stood the largest wall mirror I had ever seen. The light came from its frame, which was braided lengths of golden waves, looking as if the artisan responsible for the mirror had weaved the tides together. Each corner was decorated with a seahorse alongside a large sea shell. I had no thoughts on why such an aquatic-themed piece should reside in Smudge Hall. I turned my concentration on what lay revealed in the mirror.

Sarya had been right in her description of my hair. It was a tangled mess. Luckily, my bangs, while riddled with corkscrew loops, didn't extend over my brow. I felt the scar along the side crease of my right eye. It didn't look new. My hands worked over my nose, prodding and tugging at it like it was putty. It wasn't large, but it was hooked, making it a bit like an eagle's beak. How had my author described it? Aquiline had been the word he used. It seemed appropriate.

I licked my lips, then pulled them back to examine my teeth. I was almost fearful they wouldn't be there. White, presentable teeth stared back at me. They looked relatively straight. I knew my author had described them as almost to the point of needing braces, but I saw no such imperfections. I chomped down several times, pleased at the impact.

I scratched at my chin, baby soft and bare. I would not need a razor for at least a few years. I searched for the tiny scar my author had mentioned existed between my chin and Adam's apple. In the dark light, it didn't present itself. I had apparently been awarded that scar when I was eight and had foolishly tried to use my father's shaving kit.

Two tiny freckles and a mole, all on my neck, were the only blemishes to my skin. I couldn't tell my skin tone in the garish green light, and my author had not gone into detail as to whether it was finely tanned or pale and prone to sunburn. Probably not a detail that worked itself into crucial character description. If I had to guess, I had some skin tone but was a far cry from anything remotely bronze.

My face and hands had arrived.

I inspected my clothes once more. With my wishjacket, pants, and boots, I was all present and accounted for. I was no longer a smudge, which meant I had to leave Smudge Hall.

This was my author's idea of Irving Wishbutton, the hero. My appearance now realized; it was time to enter out into the world, to live among fellow heroes.

I should have felt relieved.

I should have felt complete.

Instead, what looked back at me in the mirror was a stranger. Memories poured into my head didn't change how I still felt. If anything, they made me feel conspicuous, like I was a fake.

In my mind, I was still a smudge.

And as I made my way back across the room to the door, I knew I wasn't ready to leave.

Farewell dessert or not, I needed to stay at Smudge Hall.

I wondered how Harmstrike would take the news.

Chapter 58
STAYING POWER

Massive destruction was on the weekend agenda. He was so excited by the next chapter he had already decided to write a sizeable chunk of it on Friday night instead of waiting for Sunday. It was Wednesday, and he was brainstorming on the back of an envelope as he watched his kids play video games.

Tyler and Irving would return home to their father a wreck at them being gone for several hours. Oddly enough, Tyler would notice that he had not called the police. It would be good to have her pull Irving aside and point out how their dad acted like he knew more than he was letting on.

Right when they were going to confront their dad, it made sense to have Teardrop's Triceramedusoid roof-ripping attack. He made a note to research roof structures so he could use the correct terms. He had still not figured out what Teardrop's henchman had done to the beast. It had cast a spell to alter it, but he didn't know what form the magical sabotage would take. Should it happen as soon as Tyler was captured or when the beast floated back to its home dimension? He opted for later as he wanted the drama of Tyler being taken to be the primary focus of the cliffhanger. What the spell did would make a perfect ending to the next chapter.

He stopped writing to settle an argument between his children. Sometimes, the stress of playing a video game caused them to be short-fused. His daughter was complaining about not needing to hear advice on her game play. She wanted to play through the level without her brother's commentary. He weighed in on the conflict and helped steer his son into playing a quieter role.

* * *

Emerging into the kitchen from the mirror room, I was surprised at how drained I felt. I had no idea how long I had been gone. Val and his winged assistants were nowhere to be found. I heard Sarya's voice coming from the dining room. I slipped through the kitchen and entered the room in question.

My farewell was not as well attended as Raggleswamp's had been. Val and Sarya sat together on one side of the table, while a large hooded red serpent of some sort lounged along the other. Despite the snake thing's body being coiled, it took up the entire floor on its side.

Sarya nervously introduced the serpentine guest. "This is Salreedus. He's some sort of primeval netherlord." She looked at the creature. I noticed she placed her attention on his chest rather than what lurked under his hood.

The creature nodded and emitted a series of clicks. I found I understood him just fine. "Arch Netherlord of Primeva, soft one. The young fairy is wise not to look directly at me for my scribe has determined my features can melt the very sanity from your soul."

I surveyed the creature. Everything was clearly defined. I whispered to Sarya, "So, if he has a terrifying face, how is he a smudge exactly?"

"His face is a smudge. His author didn't go into enough detail as to how horrific he is. I'm playing it safe and not looking at him just the same." She patted at a chair, inviting me to sit next to her.

"He's a bit overdone, don't you think?" I said.

Val served each of us a slice of pie. It appeared to be cherry. "He's quite the unruly, I'll give you that. Been spouting horrendous dialogue since he got here around lunch time."

Salreedus clicked at us again. "A feast of entrails and hidden parts is more suitable for a celebration. What is this muck?" A disgustingly long yellow tongue decked out in grey blemishes probed at the Netherlord's slice.

"It's customary to serve food native to the person leaving us. Irving is from Earth, modern day, and cherry pie ought to suit him fine, right?" Val said.

I nodded.

Taking my agreement as a sign to dig in, Val inhaled three bites before I even had my fork in hand.

The snake beast reared, snapping his tongue back into his mouth. "This academy will quake at my presence. All around will fear my gravity."

What was he talking about? He wasn't making any sense. I could tell he wanted his threats to sound dark and ominous, but they came out plain silly.

Sarya sensed my confusion and offered, "He's probably a dud. That's what Val thinks. I'll tell you later what that means. Don't want to say too much in front of tall, dark, and slithery because I could upset him and end up getting a taste of his gravity." She let slip a snicker. "It's best to play along and not rile him up too much."

Val remarked, "Well, I, for one, will be sad to see you go, Wishbutton."

"Thanks. I appreciate that. This place grew on me." I finished my pie and looked at Sarya.

She smiled and offered me a second piece. I declined.

"Vile tidings are in store for any who cross my path," chimed in Salreedus.

"Yes, we'll do our best to not get in your way," Val chided.

Sarya giggled.

"You'll stay the night and seek out Hero Row tomorrow, yes?" asked Val.

"I claim the Eldritch Blade for my clan. Do any here stand in opposition?" Salreedus spoke as if rehearsing a pivotal scene in a play. None of us responded.

"I'll stay the night. Actually, I wanted to ask about that." I stood up. "You think we could discuss this in a place a little more private, away from the evil rabble-rouser?"

Sarya and Val filed out of the dining room and retreated to the kitchen. I spared a glance at the snake creature. He was staring at his lower half. Even though I couldn't see his face, I would've sworn he was admiring himself.

In the kitchen, I spoke softly, paranoid someone other than Val and Sarya would hear me. "I definitely want to stay tonight."

"Good, this house needs your brightness of character, especially tonight." Val glanced back at the dining room entrance.

"Well, actually, I want to make it longer than that," I said.

Sarya's eyes bulged. "What?"

"I want to stay here. I think I'm supposed to," I offered.

"But you'd be breaking the rules! Harmstrike's deal is that smudges must leave once they find themselves." With every word, she grew more unhinged. "You went into the room. You saw for yourself. You're no longer a mystery. You finally have a face."

Val said nothing. Instead he sized me up.

"Look, I may no longer be a smudge on the outside, but I'm all twisted and confused inside. That sort of counts as being in an uncertain state."

Sarya inhaled, puffing up her torso in preparation of her response. "Irving, everyone here feels that way to some degree. None of us know ourselves. That's for our writer to figure out. You can't do this. Harmstrike will do something horrible to you. He'll see this as you mounting a rebellion." Sarya's wings were fluttering at a breakneck speed.

"How is it a rebellion when I'm only one person going against his wishes?"

"That's how they start," Val said. "I've seen my share. Been at the heart of some rather nasty uprisings." Val sat up on the counter, kicking his boots together with playful intent.

"Smudge Hall is where I need to stay. I think I can do some good here. My roommate, I don't know if he'd find me if I go." I sent Sarya a meaningful look. "And I don't think he's the type to hunt me down."

"Oh, here we go with the imaginary roommate. Nice. At least, if you want to stay, don't blame it on something made up. Have some backbone, Wishbutton." Val shook his head.

I ignored Val. "This academy is here to help characters know themselves, prepare us for our story challenges. I know our free will is limited, but this feels right. I don't think me rooming with a bunch of other heroes is going to get me where I need to be. Besides, smudges have been treated like dirt for too long. Maybe me staying here will change how people treat us." I huffed, putting several of my curls on my forehead into tailspins.

"Argh! Just when I think you're doing things right, you do something reckless. I don't want to hear any more of this." Sarya shot out of the kitchen, heading toward the front door.

Val laughed. He cleared his throat, casting his voice deeper. "This is where you chase after her. Go! Git!"

I sped after Sarya, hoping I could catch up to her before she took to the open air.

Chapter 59
SHEDDING LIGHT

Oddly enough, he found himself working on a chapter about Allegro. The Nowrii alien needed a chapter back at his village where he would petition his people to let him seek out Irving.

He had thought this weekend would bring the Triceramedusoid crashing down through Irving's house to whisk away Tyler, but that would have to wait until next time. Allegro and his people's plight were weaving themselves into the story with much more importance than he had originally imagined.

He visualized Allegro called to task by a council of Nowrii on the outskirts of their decimated village. Allegro's playful nature would be set aside to showcase his serious side. He would agree to some pretty harsh conditions laid out by his people if his faith in Irving backfired yet another time. Having Irving recognize the degree to which Allegro honors a pledge might help him to see his own words needed to mean something, and it would serve as a contrast to how careless Irving was with the truth. He would need to see just what a shallow mask a lie is, and having him exposed to a culture that takes their oaths very seriously would help him along his path.

He began work on a chapter where oaths undertaken portrayed strength and honor.

* * *

I burst onto the porch not to see Sarya fleeing into the air, but sitting at the bottom of the steps. I sensed she had not expected me to chase after her as she was surprised by my appearance.

It was night. Apparently, I had been in the viewing room longer than I originally thought. I didn't think it was too late as there were still many students roving about on campus.

I stood at the top of the steps, uncertain of my next move.

Sarya vigorously rubbed both palms in her eyes, attempting to wipe away her tears. "I don't want to talk to you."

I took a step toward her. "Well, you don't have to but please listen to what I have to say. I want to explain."

She opened her mouth to respond but clamped it shut, remembering what she had said. Her silence was my punishment.

"I didn't like Smudge Hall when I got here. I hated how I was treated as a smudge. Back then, I would've leaped at the chance to call Hero Row my home. But after being here longer and seeing just what type of heroes I'd be living with, I'm not in any hurry to leave."

She looked unconvinced.

I settled on the step next to her, keeping her at arm's length. I didn't want her to take flight because I got too close. "There's something off about the Academy. I don't get a good feeling from Harmstrike. Plus, you heard what my roommate said. Something's up, and I think staying at Smudge Hall will help me to figure it out." I shrugged. "I know this sounds silly, but this place makes me feel shielded. So far, I've only run into trouble everywhere else on this campus. Here, it's like something is protecting me. Does that make sense?"

"I guess," Sarya said.

I shared an immediate thought. "And Harmstrike, I can't explain why, but, I think he can't get at me if I stay here. Like he can't step foot in the house." I blinked, losing confidence in my theory. "That sounds dumb. How can that be true?"

I was about to take back my weak theory when a booming voice intruded, "Your instincts are correct, Master Wishbutton."

Both Sarya and I looked up to see a stunning sight. Standing in the scraggly grass of the front lawn was a tall lamppost. It was green with its arch looping over to hold secure a light source more than twenty feet off the ground.

"Who are you?" Sarya said.

It tottered closer. "I helped Irving find his way home one night. Poor fellow was headed into Villain Way, and I set him back on course. Looks like I'll have to do more of the same tonight."

"I'm not lost," I said.

"Well, now, be honest, everyone here's a little lost. That's the whole point isn't it? Some of us are just better at hiding our cluelessness."

The lamppost bowed, sweeping its light within a few feet of us. The warmth radiating from its bulb was welcome.

"Why are you here? How can you move about?" I said.

"Look at you. Aren't you cute? You're completely accepting of me talking, but when I pull up out of the ground and take a stroll, you're chock full of disbelief. That's really quite sweet."

Sarya giggled. She directed a smile at the lamp.

"I was coming to see you, Master Wishbutton, on urgent business. Good thing you're out here. I really don't have the flexibility needed to ring the doorbell. That porch roof is rather low and not altogether sound." It paused and projected its light onto the porch's ceiling. "Yes, well something I can't help but do is listen in on others. You try standing around all day and night and not wind up an earnest eavesdropper. Can't be done, sir and madam."

Sarya and I waited for it to continue. The fairy had softened with the arrival of the chatty light pole.

The lamppost reared up, girding itself for its next proclamation. "Irving's right. Smudge Hall is the only place Harmstrike can't enter. Your instincts are very good, young hero."

"Why is that? That doesn't make sense." Sarya frowned.

"Oh, the whys and why nots are not so important right now. What matters is the decision Irving has made. You are choosing to stay, yes?"

"Y-yes," I stammered.

The lamppost swiveled, positioning itself a few feet from Sarya's wings, causing them to shimmer. "And he needs you to understand. You are important to his success."

If the light was expecting agreement, he sorely misunderstood my fairy friend. Sarya snarled, "Why should he cause himself more grief? The dean is going to freak out about this. Why does everybody talk to Irving like he holds some sort of secret, some hidden plan to making things right? Is the Academy that wrong?"

"Not the school proper, young fairy. Evil cannot reside in a place. It can only issue from someone with intent." The lamppost continued. "It's important that you show Irving your support. After all, it's what you were written to do."

Sarya nodded. A look of dissatisfaction at her role flashed across her face and then was gone. "I can do that, but I don't have to like it."

"Dear, we want to keep Irving safe. We both want the same thing," the lamppost said.

Sarya said, "Between you and Irving's roommate, it's like everything non-living has his best interest at heart. Next you're going to tell me the sidewalk is watching out for him."

"I can't speak for common concrete, but, yes, Irving's roommate and I are working toward a common goal." The lamppost straightened itself, reminding me of a person stretching out the kinks in their back.

"You know my roommate?" I asked.

"We have dealings here and there." The light from the lamp flared. "Now, I love a good back and forth as much as anyone else, but I really did just come to relay a warning to Irving."

Sarya held her tongue.

I nodded at the lamppost to continue.

"As you know, loose lips happen quite freely around me. I'm very discreet with who I talk to so most students see me as a simple lamppost, a stalwart sentinel in the night." He beamed with pride then brought himself back to the topic. "I overheard a very confused boy with a head made of pasta rambling about his plight as he walked by."

"Did he have a bird on his shoulder?" I asked. It had to be talking about Fenwick, the person I had a meeting with later tonight.

"I didn't see any such despicable beast perched there. Let's not pollute this conversation talking about such depraved winged creatures." The lamppost shone a spotlight on Sarya. "No insult intended to the fairy folk, my dear. I just can't stomach the common feathered fiends that leave their mark on me."

She waved him off. "No offense taken."

"Where was I? Oh, yes, Irving, this noodle fellow is planning no good. He's very torn about what to do, but one thing's clear from his ramblings."

"What's that?" I asked.

"Don't meet up with him at the Menagerie. He doesn't wish to cause you harm, but he feels painted into a corner. I believe those were his exact words." The lamppost stopped, taking time to organize his thoughts. "Yes, he's clearly regretful about it, but the end result is still not looking good for you, Master Wishbutton. If you go to meet with him tonight, you place yourself in grave danger."

Sarya widened her eyes at me as I shrank back on the porch. Even with the encroaching darkness of the night, thanks to our lamppost visitor, my midnight rendezvous had been brought to light.

Once again, Sarya did not look happy.

Chapter 60
B AND E AT THE MENAGERIE

Bringing down the roof proved easier than expected. Teardrop's beast crashed through the rafters, sending wood splintering and its tentacles probing. It latched onto Tyler and hoisted her up into its underbelly sac. Irving and his father watched it happen as the neighbors came charging out to see the grotesque spectacle.

The author leaned back in the chair. The authorities would be called, and he'd have to deal with the aftermath of the abduction in a future chapter. He was committed to having the real world fully aware of the magic intruding upon it, and there would be repercussions for Irving's family when they tried to return to normal—if that was even possible.

He revisited the paragraph describing the destruction and added more description of the setting. He paid particular attention to several telling objects in Tyler's room and what happened to them when her room collapsed. Irving's room was on the first floor and was only minimally affected.

In a stroke of inspiration, the father's room was equally tossed into chaos. Among the wreckage, Irving unearths a strange rod that his father gets all tongue-tied about. The staff would be a tool from his day as a whim wrangler. The next chapter would have the father reveal his past with Wish Haven and what exactly happened to cause Whimville's destruction. The staff would even be critical in their eventual pursuit of Tyler.

The chapter closes with the beast taking Tyler away through a dimensional gate while Irving and his father look on.

After four hours of writing, he had a very dynamic chapter. He saved the document and went downstairs to find out what his wife was doing with their children. There was still a few hours left of the weekend, and he hoped they would want to do a craft or play a board game.

* * *

It took all of my persuasive talents and quite a few winning comments from my lamppost guardian to convince Sarya I would not go to the Menagerie. After a very long time, we had her persuaded I wasn't going.

She said a reluctant goodbye to me and left at the same time as the lamppost departed. I went back inside to my room. I waited there for several hours, hoping my roommate would return to give me advice or at the very least another cryptic clue. What was his connection to the lamppost? Why did they see me as some sort of savior? What exactly was so wrong with the Academy that it needed saving?

The lamppost had revealed that it was more a case of someone or several someones whose intent was not for the greater good. I was positive Harmstrike was involved, but I didn't see how. So far, his actions were about punishing rule breakers and running the school. He didn't seem evil on the surface.

I really wished I had Roon there to aid me. Her detective talents would've helped me see something I had missed. I didn't feel right heaping this on top of her, what with her brother's disappearance. I still intended to help her seek him out at the Ravine, but tomorrow was a long way away. My next order of business was my midnight meeting. Despite assuring Sarya I wasn't going to the Menagerie, I saw no other way around it. Going meant finding out answers. It also meant I might catch a glimpse of the horrible beast that had abducted my sister in my story. A chill ran down my spine at the thought.

As I snuck out of my window a little past 11:30, I felt shame over breaking my promise to Sarya. Especially after knowing the amount of effort my author had put into Allegro's chapter about the honor of seeing your promises through to the end. I was still flawed. The ends justified the means right now. I had to lie for the greater good, I told myself. Later, when my writer gave me more of a conflicted conscience, I might act differently. Right now, lying was necessary. I didn't feel good about it, but there it was.

I made my way across campus. Very few students were out and about, and I was surprised the campus had no security to speak of. It seemed like Harmstrike would've seen the value of keeping tabs on those who were frequently out of their housing at night. Probably because so few broke the rules, he didn't feel the need.

Hiding behind a row of bushes, I scrutinized the Menagerie. It didn't match the appearance of the other buildings on campus.

It was blocky and made of stark concrete. It looked to be three or four stories tall. Tiny vertical slits spaced very far apart on the sides of the structure were the only evidence that outside light could find its way in. The front had the most ornamentation, with two columns framing the double doors. Above the entrance, a slithering dragon's body had been carved. Chiseled below his menacing talons was the name of the building. It was oppressively large, stretching twice the length of any other building on campus. That made sense, considering it held the habitats for all the bestial creatures populating our stories. I hoped I would not encounter the emberhounds again.

While I had seen several students on my way across campus, there was a noticeable absence of people on the grounds around my destination. A sense that the coast was clear only because no one wanted to be caught near this place took hold of me. For a place that supposedly housed a large number of animals, there was an eerie silence. I was not reassured.

I dashed up to the front entrance and eyed the four doors before me. The first three were locked, but the last swept open. *Fenwick's doing, maybe?*

I looked all around, fearing someone like Gared would spot me and rat me out. When no one appeared, I stepped inside and immediately froze, thinking that an alarm would sound from my intrusion. After almost ten seconds of absolute silence, I tamped down my jitters and moved deeper into the building.

Chapter 61
NIGHT AT THE MENAGERIE

The staff would open dimensional doors. He thought of having Irving steal his father's staff and use it to go after Tyler, but he decided to keep it a family affair and have the father go along with him.

He plugged away at the scene, mindful that he needed to have Allegro meet up with the would-be rescuers before they left the earthly plane.

He was ecstatic about his progress. He was getting two chapters done a week. His teaching workload was not too heavy yet, so he had time to work two nights a week on a chapter in addition to the weekend chapter he completed.

Irving's father would not know of the Nowrii. Allegro would still be big and bold, but there would be a more dire urgency to his motives. He needed Irving to see the light. The three would agree to go rescue Tyler. It would be a challenge; he wanted Allegro to be the lively smart mouth, while at the same time the one who kept Irving focused on uncovering the Wellwishers true plans.

He looked at the clock. He had a half hour before he would need to fix dinner. He could get the bulk of the scene written tonight and finish the rest on Thursday.

He started in, liking the notion of keeping the viewpoint of the chapter very much from Allegro's perspective. It was time to get inside the alien's head and really magnify the importance his race gave to keeping their word.

* * *

I had no idea where Fenwick would be. I had hoped the caretaker would've met me in the foyer, but the noodle boy had been a no show. I tugged open the large grey door before me.

I called out as I took several steps into the curved hall that sloped downward. "Fenwick, are you there?"

As the door behind me closed, the bright lights from the foyer no longer illuminated my path. The hallway was dimly lit with uplighting stationed every few yards at waist height. The ceiling lights were off.

As I progressed forward, the air grew more humid and musty. I could hear faint animal cries and calls somewhere ahead. There were no doors on either side of the hall. As I got closer to the source of the animal noises, several signs posted on the walls caught my eye.

Caretakers Only Beyond Red Doors!

Hazard Alarms Located in Yellow Panic Boxes Along Path!

Day Bombs Stashed at Entry Point for Use with Nocturnal Predators Only!

Up ahead was the red door the first sign had mentioned. I was relieved to spy Fenwick standing off to the side, fishing around in a storage box mounted on the wall. He stashed several orange globes in his jacket pockets. His mother was not on his shoulder.

"Where's your mom?" I remembered Fenwick's conversation with Harmstrike at the infirmary. The dean was holding his mother hostage. What did Harmstrike expect Fenwick to do for him? I knew not to ask; I didn't want to explain how I knew about his meeting with Harmstrike because I had been in Gared's borrowed body.

Fenwick chuckled nervously. "Oh, she's back at my dorm. Managed to give her the slip. Just as well. She doesn't like going into the habitat where I'm taking you."

He's lying. I began to wonder if his deal with Harmstrike might somehow involve me. Of course, he had asked me to meet him at the Menagerie before his run-in with the dean. Maybe the two incidents weren't connected. "You told me in class to meet you here. Why this late and why here?"

He stepped closer and invasively pressed his finger to my lips. It was then he noticed my new condition. "Oh, hey, you're no longer a smudge. Good for you." He whispered, "Keep it down. I'm taking you somewhere we can talk and not be heard."

His answer made me more nervous. "I'm taking a big risk being here. Why do we have to go any further? What's so important and secretive you can't just tell me?"

"Look, let's just take a quick tour, and I'll tell you a few things I think you need to know, okay?" He tugged at my arm, pulling me toward the red door. At the same time, he slipped one of the orange spheres into my hand. He patted it affectionately. "It's a day bomb. Only toss it at a predator if they take a run at you, okay?"

I held the device tight, afraid to drop and trigger it. "What's it do? Why do I need this? Aren't the animals kept locked up?"

He nodded as he punched in a code on a small keypad mounted to the left of the massive door. "Most are locked up. Once in a while, some prove more resourceful, and we have to drive them back with what I handed you. It douses the area in blinding light. It's required when visiting the Menagerie at night." He added, "If you do throw one, cover your eyes and yell out a warning. I've been blinded enough times by my own self and don't care to see spots tonight."

I had enough time to read the sign above the door: **Jungle Habitat D**.

The door opened with a whoosh, and thick, moist air assaulted us as the environs of the room spilled out into the hall.

I entered the habitat to sights and sounds of unearthly origin.

Chapter 62
IT'S A JUNGLE IN HERE

It was nearing the weekend, and he had finished the chapter with Allegro joining up with Irving and his father. Tonight he was having a hard time falling asleep and had decided to curl up on the couch and brainstorm events for the next scene. He'd only stay up fifteen minutes or so. His mind was racing, and he found if he did something creative before going upstairs, it settled him down and he fell asleep faster than if he went up with his mind all atwitter.

Irving's father would use the staff to take them to Whimville, indicating it was the safest place as they would be immediately detected if they crossed directly into Wish Haven. Irving would get to see the devastation firsthand. More history of Whimville would be recounted, and his father would take him to a small group of rebels who opposed the Wellwishers.

While his father would not be familiar with Allegro's people, another of the Whimville rebels they meet up with would have had dealings with the Nowrii. He decided to have the rebel incredibly in awe of the Nowrii, adding further substance to the argument that the Wellwishers are not on the up and up. Irving would begin to regret his decision; if such a proud and honorable race held the Wellwishers in such low regard, why was he scampering back to them?

He would voice his apprehension, and his father would put forth the idea that Irving go along with the Wellwishers so he could infiltrate the organization and maybe bring it down from within.

He paused. He needed to make sure there was a bit more structure to their plan. He shelved the brainstorming pad by the mail counter and went upstairs. Maybe on Saturday, he'd have a spare moment or two to do more brainstorming.

He slipped into bed, the fervent storm in his head dying down for now.

* * *

The plant life wasn't too different from what I would see in a rainforest. There was an upper canopy, thick with drooping vines, along with a plethora of ferns and creeping plants on the forest floor. One noticeable difference: while many of the plants were green, a large number were orange and purple. Our path wound through the thickest section of the jungle, lit by red lights at regular intervals. The ceiling was one long stretch of a sun roof, a feature I hadn't noticed when looking at the Menagerie from the outside.

A flock of fat birds with ears twice as long as their wings veered away from us as we began our trek down the path.

Several molelike creatures nibbled on the underbelly of a patch of upturned mushrooms, their long hairless tails glowing green, providing light for their fungus feast.

"Glojubs," said Fenwick. "Native to Fenris Fortune's story. He's part of a bounty hunter duo that's rather famous in their fantasy world. Good fellow. You might see him around during your stay. Just give his partner some distance. Quite a hothead and a troublemaker, he is."

"You know all the animals and which characters they go with?" I asked.

"Have to. That's part of my job as a caretaker. Of course, I'm only responsible for two habitats. This one and the one I'm taking you to."

"How many habitats are in here? This place seems a whole lot bigger than what it looks like from the outside." I swept my hands upward and out.

"As many as are needed. We've got all types: desert, swamp, open plains, rocky crags, and quite a few aquatic sections. The building's size never changes on the outside. When a new habitat is needed, a new door appears inside, and we can access it."

"How's that possible? Doesn't someone have to build the new habitats?" I looked back. We had proceeded far enough that the red door we had entered through was no longer visible. I pushed several yellow fern fronds out of my path.

"That's how all buildings happen on campus. They appear overnight. Harmstrike attributes it to the magic in this place." Fenwick stopped and tapped on a yellow box mounted on a pole. "By the way, these are panic boxes. Flick open the front panel, pull the switch, and the habitat goes into lockdown."

"What's that?" Lockdown sounded a bit harsh.

"Time freezes in the habitat and only caretakers can move around in the place. I've only had to use it once." Fenwick moved on.

"Are my emberhounds in this jungle?" I asked.

"Oh, no way. They're off by themselves because of the ruckus they caused you at Administration." He motioned for me to pick up the pace.

To our left, a waterfall spilled out, sending bright green water onto a cluster of rocks below. Hovering above the waterfall was what appeared to be a dragon, its tail twice as long as its body and terminating in a nest of spikes. Despite it being night, the glow from the water and many of the surrounding plants gave off enough light for us to see everything in the habitat. "Is that dragon going to bother us?"

Fenwick looked over at the creature. The dragon, sensing our interest, drifted closer to us. It didn't flap its wings to do this, which I found odd.

"Nope, not unless you plan on disturbing her nest. That's a Waterfall Walloper. That nasty tail of hers can utterly pulverize her prey. It's actually from my story." He kept his eyes on the dragon as he moved a hand into his pocket, grabbing hold of one of his day bombs. "Something you should know, Irving. We can be harmed here at the Academy. It's very rare, but it can happen. You want to know how?"

I nodded and leaned in closer.

"Characters from other stories can't really do more than bruise us up, but if it's somebody or something from your own book, it can not only hurt you, it can cause your death." Arriving at a fork in the trail, Fenwick moved us deeper into the jungle, choosing the path leading us away from the waterfall.

"So that dragon could do you in?"

"She could, but I'm no fool. I wouldn't dare tussle with her." I noticed he kept a hand in his pocket, still cupping a day bomb in his tight grip. He was rattled about the dragon more than he was letting on. Or was it something else?

"So I was in real danger with my emberhounds?" I said. Ahead, I could see the path ended at another red door. This one had a sign overhead that read Aquaria 3.

"Yes, you were, and that's what I need to talk to you about." He pointed to the Aquaria entrance. "We can talk safely in there. Come on."

As we exited one habitat and entered another, we shifted our gaze in the direction of the dragon who made one last caterwaul.

The red door closed behind us with a faint hiss.

It was only then that I saw Fenwick slide his hand out of his jacket, no longer needing the reassurance of having his day bomb at the ready.

For some reason, a sense of danger washed over me. I wrapped my fingers around *my* day bomb even tighter.

Chapter 63
WATERY GRAVE

He couldn't believe it. He had written the Whimville chapter in less than an hour, managing to embellish their plan so that it had weight and made sense. He was particularly pleased with the bond Allegro was forming with Irving's father. Because Irving's father would be too easily detected in Wish Haven, it had been decided that Irving go to Wish Haven alone using his father's staff. Allegro and Irving's father would attempt a rescue of Tyler. Oddly enough, Irving's father confessed to knowing where Tyler has been taken. Irving doesn't question this, but it was becoming clearer that his father had encountered Teardrop before.

He liked how the scene closed with the reader being given more clues about the father's connection to Teardrop than Irving. Giving the reader more info than the characters made them feel more tuned into the story and more invested in what would happen next. It gave them a sense of power and control over the narrative.

He checked with his wife to see if she needed him to stop writing. She was making cookies with the kids and waved him off.

He grabbed a soda from the fridge and dashed back up the stairs. If the next chapter really came out as fast as the last, he would get twice the work done this weekend. He eyed the word count on the screen: 24,678 words was a good length. If everything went smoothly, he'd be adding another thousand words or so to the mix before his time was up.

He jumped into the chapter concerning Tyler's imprisonment with his mind sharp and determined.

* * *

The Aquaria was twice as large as the jungle habitat we had just left. It was one giant ocean of a swimming pool; the only way across for air breathers was the infinite number of catwalks that crisscrossed a good twenty feet above the rolling waters. We stood on a large metal platform located only feet above the water. The floor was a series of metal grills that allowed us to see what swam below. Fenwick marched up a set of metal stairs off to our left.

As we made our way onto the catwalks, I saw my first assumption was wrong. The habitat was not one large tank. The Aquaria was divided into smaller tanks by nearly two-feet-thick plexiglass partitions. From above, it was obvious the color of each section's water differed. We were crossing over a brownish-yellow tankful when Fenwick spoke.

"Pretty noisy in here, isn't it?" he said.

It was. The habitat's acoustics magnified the rollicking waves. While the sounds of the jungle had been largely made by animals, it was the water that produced a thunderous tone in this habitat.

"It is loud!" I shouted.

"Well, it's still not loud enough. There's one tank where it's even noisier. That's where we need to go." Fenwick glanced down. A school of fish with vicious teeth and membranous fins large enough to be wings were jumping up at the catwalk we were on. A few looked close to landing on the walkway.

"Those don't look so nice." I hopped forward. Several of the fish targeted me, slamming their teeth into the underside of the catwalk. The sound of the teeth scraping against the metal was alarming.

"Fear Fish. The more emotion you show, the stronger they get. You stay over this tank much longer, and your whimpering is gonna make them strong enough to jump up here." Fenwick pushed a green button on a control panel that hung from above. A series of clicks sounded, and a panel on the ceiling to our left opened. A cascade of small crescent-shaped crabs fell into the fear fish tank.

The school of fear fish stopped jumping at us and swam away from the crabs. A few slower ones met up with the shelled invaders. Blue arcs of electricity flew from the crab's claws toward the fish, sending them into spasms.

Fenwick smiled. "Shellshockers. Very useful for calming down the aquatic predators. Every tank has them overhead."

"But the fear fish aren't from my story. You said they couldn't hurt me."

"Oh, now, not quite. They just can't do long-term damage. Their bites will still hurt, trust me." Fenwick proceeded right, along a catwalk that was twice as wide as the others. "C'mon, time's awastin'."

We moved along the main walkway without further attacks. I saw a wide variety of marine life. There were turtles with coral stacked on their shells like termite mounds. One tank had several creatures that were see-through. Fenwick called them phantom eels and gave them a cautious eye. Another had a forest of anemones as tall as trees that swayed hypnotically.

I knew we were rapidly approaching the tank where we could talk because the noise level increased. As we stepped onto the section of the walkway over the tank in question, I saw why it was so loud. The red water below was constantly churning, resembling a pot of boiling water.

"That's not blood, is it?" I asked.

"No, not at all. Apparently, the creature housed here must come from a crimson sea. It's a new arrival. Rather big. Came in a little before dinner today. I helped escort it to its housing. Not a fun task. It came in very agitated." Fenwick waved at the churning waters.

"So, this is it? We can talk now?"

Fenwick flashed a nervous smile. He fidgeted with the drop-down control panel for the tank. It ran on a track and could be pulled up and down and to some extent a few feet left and to the right. Strangely, he situated the panel between us. It was the same size as a shield and reminded me of such. From my vantage point, I couldn't see the buttons.

The water underneath rolled as if the creature below us was agitated by our presence. I still saw no sign of it.

"I brought you here tonight to tell you what's wrong with the Academy. I really wanted to help you." Fenwick's voice sounded strained, but not because he was trying to talk over the din of the water, more like he dreaded what he would say or do next.

"Okay, so what is it? You can tell me." I took two steps back, unnerved by his tone.

"When I talked to you in class, this meeting was set up for that reason. You have to believe that's why I called you here." He looked around, still nervous he would be overheard.

"Okay, so spill," I said.

"I'm still going to tell you. I owe you that much." He hesitated.

I waited for him to continue, sparing a glance below. Not knowing what was down there had me spooked.

"Harmstrike's bad. He's doing all sorts of things that are wrong. I thought you might be the one who could stop him. People are saying you could be the one to do it." His eyes were pleading as if asking me for forgiveness. I didn't know why.

Fenwick said, "That's why I brought you here, to tell you about Harmstrike, so you could maybe stop him."

"Okay, I hear you, but what is it that he's doing? What's so wrong?" I moved closer, hoping to peek at the control panel.

Fenwick gripped the edges of the device even tighter. He seemed to be fighting with himself. "Only he took my mother."

He was talking about Harmstrike, of this I was certain. "That's why your mom wasn't with you at the infirmary."

"How'd you know I was at the infirmary?" Fenwick looked further unhinged.

I ignored him, not wanting to open that can of worms and hoping he wouldn't press the issue. The less I had to talk about being in Gared's body, the better. "What does he want you to do?" I swallowed.

"I'm sorry. I have to do this. He'll let me have her back if I do it." Fenwick pulled the panel closer.

"Do what? What's he making you do?"

"I'm sorry, Irving, but it's my mom. She's all I have." He bit down hard on his lower lip and shoved the control panel at me. It wasn't the buttons I had to fear him pushing; it was the bulk of the apparatus itself.

It swept toward me, slamming into my shoulder. The force of the blow sent me flying over the rails of the walkway. As I plummeted, I reached out, managing to grab hold of the floor panel. It sagged but held my weight.

Fenwick was rattled. He roared, "You have to go! You have to go! She's all I have, don't you see?"

I said, "No!"

His boot came down hard on my fingers, grinding them into the metal. I let go and fell into the churning waters.

I fought to rise to the surface but was grabbed from below and pulled under. Wrapped around my body, pinning my right arm to my side, was a large spotted tentacle. A constant stream of bubbles spilled all around, the creature's movements growing more agitated now that it had caught me.

The water cleared momentarily, and I saw what had me in its clutches.

It was the creature that had abducted my sister. I looked deep into its black eyes and all I saw was rage.

All I could think of as I was whisked through the water was what Fenwick had said: *Something from your story can do you harm, even kill you.*

Chapter 64
GILL PREPARED

He finally had it figured out. He knew what the henchman's spell would do. The sabotage the lackey performed would be misdirected. He had thought Teardrop's creature was sent to fetch Irving and his spell was designed to take Irving out of commission. Now that the Triceramedusoid was back at Teardrop's lair, safe in its aquatic pen, the spell would be set in motion.

It was a stroke of genius. Scratch that. That seemed too lofty for a plot point that was good, but not overwhelmingly so. It was more a dab of cleverness, what the spell would do. It would create a problem to be fixed as well as reveal that Teardrop cared about what happened to Tyler.

He crafted the scene, making sure to keep Teardrop's guard up. He wanted the villainess to be cautious, but hint at her connection to Tyler and Irving. It would be apparent to the reader she was their mom, but the characters would be too flustered to connect the dots.

He was writing the scene where Teardrop uncovered what had been done to Tyler and the Tricermedusoid. Downstairs, he heard his kids arguing about who could play with a toy. He stopped to solve the dispute.

When they were reading at bedtime, he would sneak over to the computer and try to finish the chapter.

* * *

Here I was, with a creature from my story. Unlike the attack by the emberhounds, this felt different. For one, I knew that someone wanted to harm me. I briefly flashed on the notion that Harmstrike might've been responsible for setting the emberhounds on me but quickly pushed the idea aside; I had more pressing matters.

The Triceramedusoid pulled me toward its mouth. Unlike my sister, which it had stored in a sac underneath, its intention with me was different.

I thought about what my author had written about the beast. It was used to abduct my sister, but I also knew it was under some mysterious spell by a renegade servant of Teardrop. As to what the spell did, I found it hard to sift through the ideas my writer had on the subject, partly because of my panicked state of mind and partly because my author was still in the middle of firming up the scene.

Overtaking any further analysis of the creature was my immediate concern with the burning sensation in my lungs. I was running out of air. Would I drown before becoming its next meal? Was that a more comfortable demise? I shook off my despair and in doing so, remembered I had one wish still in my jacket. I allowed myself a brief moment of joy, realizing how perfect the wish given the circumstances.

Ignoring the tightness in my chest, I summoned the wish. Luckily, it took effect almost immediately.

My lungs tingled and shifted about. At the same time, several slits along the sides of my neck appeared. It was not altogether comfortable, but there was no bleeding. In a matter of seconds, I felt emboldened enough to try out my new form of respiration. The newly formed gills drew in the water and whatever had been done to my lungs, extracted the oxygen from the water.

It was awkward at first, but I had only seconds to get it down. After several attempts, the tightness in my chest disappeared, and I was breathing underwater.

I didn't have any time to celebrate my victory. I was only feet away from the creature's now open mouth. Rows of needle-sharp teeth swelled into view. The creature's long tongue snaked out to guide me into its maw.

I had no more wishes to exploit, but I was not weaponless. With my free hand, I retrieved the day bomb from my jacket, activated it with my thumb and hurled it at the creature's eyes.

The bomb, exploded.

The Triceramedusoid screamed, releasing its grip on me in an effort to cover its eyes from the blinding light. I wish I had been so prepared. I closed my eyes a bit too late. The world around me disappeared.

Even blinded, I had the sense to swim away from the thrashing behemoth. I felt one of its tentacles sweep past me as I kicked furiously to the surface.

I reached the surface and blasted out of the water. I still could not see but could hear screaming and shouting coming from the catwalks above the tank.

Fenwick was arguing with someone. I didn't have time to figure out the identity of the other person because my gills were on fire. I clutched at my chest in agony. I could no longer breathe the air. I submerged, catching my breath under the rolling waves.

As I did so, I rubbed my eyes, willing my sight to return. I opened them underwater to hazy images. My sight was returning, but a bit slowly.

The large dark shape of the Triceramedusoid still thrashed about and tore at its own eyes. My only hope was that it being a dweller in the deep made it more sensitive to sunlight. Would the time it took to recover from the light be enough for my gills to wear off? I couldn't leave the tank in my current state. I was trapped here until my wish dissipated. I had to hope it wouldn't last as long as the body-switching wish I had used earlier. If it did, I was dead in the water.

I treaded water for several minutes, keeping my head submerged to ease my new method of breathing. I took my eyes off the creature every once in a while to look up at who argued with Fenwick.

My eyesight was not fully recovered. I recognized the silhouette of the noodle boy. Whoever he was talking to was not on the catwalk. They were flying about. The shape of the wings helped me to identify Fenwick's attacker. It was Sarya. She must've snuck in to see if I'd kept my word.

I stole glances at their confrontation. Because I was underwater, I could only make out snatches of words. I watched as Sarya dove at Fenwick, knocking him into the tank.

Fenwick's arrival in the tank drew the monster's attention. It swung itself around, trying to pinpoint the new arrival. I could tell by its movements that its vision was not back to normal but was improving. It swam toward Fenwick and away from me.

My own vision had cleared, and I could see the look of terror on Fenwick's face.

He flopped about in the water, attempting to move away from the beast. His thrashing only helped it to zero in on Fenwick. I saw its two main tentacles snake out toward him.

What I did next was foolish, but I couldn't watch him get gobbled up. It didn't matter that I was in this predicament because of him.

I had no weapons at my disposal, but I knew Sarya might be able to help. The question was: would she? Clearly, she had followed me, seen Fenwick's underhanded deed, and lashed out at him. Could I get her to calm down enough to do what was right?

I felt for my gills, knowing they were still there. I pushed myself out of the water. As I bobbed upward, I shouted, "Push the green button, Sarya!" I fell back in, reveling in the warm rush of water over my gills.

I surfaced again. "It'll drop down something that might scare off the big baddie!"

As I went back under, I saw her expression. She was confused and distressed.

I emerged one last time. My gills ached, and I knew I risked damaging my current method of breathing beyond repair. "Do it! Fenwick doesn't deserve to die!"

Sarya snapped out of her inaction. She slammed down on the button. As I fell back into the water, uncertain if my gills would work, I watched a shower of Shellshockers splash into the water between Fenwick and myself.

They needed to chase away the Triceramedusoid. Instead, I watched in horror as the tiny electrically-charged beasts shot through the water, aiming at the two smallest prey in the tank: Fenwick and myself.

I managed to bat away two of them before the sting of their electricity stabbed at my body repeatedly.

As I lost consciousness, my only thought was that Sarya not do anything foolish like enter the tank to save me. I felt the water erupting all around me as everything went dark.

Chapter 65
A TENTACLED REPRIEVE

There it was. The spell had been executed. The traitor's booby trap had been sprung. He had thought writing the scene would be very straightforward, but it had turned out to be a little more challenging. Now he had Tyler in a much different set of circumstances and definitely out of her comfort zone in addition to out of her body. He reread to make sure it was clear what had happened between Tyler and the beast.

When Irving's father and Allegro arrived for their brave rescue, this would definitely throw them for a loop.

He saved the file and went downstairs to read. He had a good half hour before his wife came down, and they watched television. He flopped on the couch and tore into his book.

* * *

I was being shaken. I woke up to find myself once again held tight by the Triceramedusoid. Only this time, the creature held me out of the water. I felt my neck. My gills were gone. What had happened? I looked down to see the creature pulling Fenwick out of the water. He too was unconscious.

My captor's head emerged from the water. It kept its eyes on me as it moved me toward the catwalk where Sarya was screaming at it to let me go. My eyes never left its impressive horns.

The beast placed me gently onto the catwalk. A few seconds later, it deposited Fenwick as well. Sarya rushed to my side. I didn't take my gaze off the immense creature. It floated in the tank, looking at me expectantly, the rage gone from its eyes.

As my mind became clearer, my author's recent writings filled my head. I suddenly knew why the creature had helped me, why it was looking at me with its now big saucer eyes.

I allowed Sarya to hug me.

"Irving, you're all right!" she sputtered. "I thought that horrible thing was going to eat you."

"But it didn't," I said. My eyes locked with the creature; I knew its secret.

"It was pulling you to its mouth when it just stopped. Then, it lifted you out of the water." Sarya pulled away.

"It sensed when my gills went away. It got me out of the water at the right time," I said, expecting a nod from the beast for my answer, but none came. It still looked at me with great expectation.

"Why would it do that? One minute, it was all set to eat you. The next, it's saving you and making eyes at you." Sarya had apparently noticed the way it was looking at me.

I waved at the Triceramedusoid. It wagged several tentacles in response.

"Why is it all friendly now?" Sarya said.

"Because it knows me."

"Well, I figured that much. I heard your conversation with that vile little noodle-headed boy. He set you up. He knew that creature was from your story. I heard him tell you how it could do you in. That's nasty. He wanted to hurt you."

"No, he didn't. He wanted to save his mom. Harmstrike wanted to do away with me." I put my hands on the rail and leaned out over the water. The creature inched closer to me so its mouth was only a few feet away.

This frightened Sarya. "You sure you should be that close? What if it reconsiders? You're pretty much within chomping distance."

"It won't hurt me, Sarya, because it's not in its right mind."

"Wait, you used your body-switching spell to put somebody else's mind in that nightmare?" She wrinkled her nose in disgust.

The Triceramedusoid thrashed at the water near her, spraying the fairy's wings at the insult.

"Careful what you say. She's temperamental under the circumstances." I smiled.

"So you switched a girl's brain into that?" Sarya said.

"No, I didn't do it. My wish won't work again. My writer did it. In my story, that beast was sent to kidnap someone and bring that person back to Teardrop. She's my alleged villain."

"Okay, got it, but how does that result in the monster not being itself?" She moved closer to me.

"There's a traitor in Teardrop's crew. It cast a spell on the beast to switch minds with the person it captured," I explained.

"So who did it capture?"

"My sister, Tyler."

"What? Your sister's in there? How is that possible? Why would he do that? That's a horrible plot twist." Sarya's voice wavered.

"I know, and I can't do anything. She's trapped in there until he switches her back." I stared at my sister, feeling helpless. She looked back at me with wounded eyes.

"She saved you and now she's stuck," Sarya said, breathlessly.

"I know.".

Sarya realized the other horrible truth. "But what about her? What will the beast's mind do in her body? Will it go berserk?"

I looked at her. Fear seeped into my voice. "I have no idea."

Once again, I was about to rush across campus to my sister's side. Only this time, I really wanted Harmstrike to try and stop me.

Chapter 66
IN HARMSTRIKE'S WAY

A fit of brainstorming was his reward for taking the extra time to shave with a straight razor. As he swept his cheeks clean of the shaving cream, his mind was on fire.

He needed to go back to an earlier chapter and add some clarification about the wishes. His mind had wandered to a very low-key wish; Irving would gather up a pretty useless one. The wish would clearly be from someone very young. After all, not many adults would wish for more pockets. Only a child with his hands full would invest time in such. This made him think more about why the wishes lingered. Why were some given high regard while others were labeled whims? Clearly, a wish for an increase in pocket population would be more of a whim.

As he thought about the different degrees of wishes, his mind seized on how Irving's mother would end up a villain. She would have been a wish agent, but like her son, her jacket would be one that had only one button. Her husband would still be a whim wrangler. He would get in some life-threatening trouble, and she'd have to use the several wishes she'd accumulated to rescue him. The last wish she would use would be a huge sacrifice. That last wish was twisted. It had been one she'd gathered with great reluctance. After all, who in their right mind would wish to be a villain?

To save her husband, she became Teardrop. By becoming the villainess, she didn't lose the memories of her family, but she could no longer be with them, not with her mind now fouled with nefarious motivations. In that instant, he had the logical motivation for why she had left.

At the same time, he realized that Irving's father would need to really resent the Wellwishers and the power of having a one-button wishjacket. It would change his reaction to his son's new wardrobe. He'd have to work back through the book and change the scenes with the father to reflect this development.

He frowned. Next weekend would not produce a new chapter because of the amount of retooling he would have to do. His sadness was temporary. After all, he had a fine plot twist that would really amp up the tension in the story.

He finished shaving, pushing his used razor deep into the trash, away from the curious hands of his son who was fascinated by the idea of shaving his own pristine cheeks. He knew he was being a tad overprotective, but that's what parents did. He dwelled briefly on the parallels to his recent thoughts of Irving's parents before exiting the bathroom to start his Monday morning.

* * *

I carried the unconscious Fenwick out and deposited him on the steps to the Menagerie. Luckily, we had no further encounters with any predators in the water habitat or in the jungle environs we backtracked through. I tore off down the steps, heading toward the center of campus.

Sarya flew alongside. "You know where you're going?"

The tails of my wishjacket flapped in the wind. "No idea."

Sarya took charge. "Well, I do. Your sister's a supporting character. She'd be in my dorm. We need to go there."

I stopped, bending over and clutching at my knees as I caught my breath. I was more winded from what had happened in the Menagerie than from my aimless midnight run. "Can you get me there?"

She smiled. "I can. Follow me."

Sarya took the lead, shunting us down a path to our left. She kept the pace brisk, but not mad dash.

"You followed me," I said.

She looked back at me, biting her lower lip. "You're not mad, are you?"

"I generally don't get upset at people who swoop in and save my hide." I scanned the campus. It was well past midnight, and we were the only ones outside. The windows of each building we passed were dark. "I knew something was off about Fenwick tonight. I just didn't know it would be so potentially lethal."

Sarya veered right, ducking below a low hanging branch and turning sideways to pass safely between a light post and a water fountain. "I heard most of what he said. Harmstrike is really up to no good?"

I nodded. She took us through a miniature forest that eventually spilled out into the mall. She landed and pointed at a six-story building. Unlike the other buildings we passed, many lights were on near the building's west wing. A small crowd gathered at the entrance, all of them female. As we approached, I could see the crowd was made up of dorm residents. They mulled about in their pajamas, some clutching pillows and stuffed animals. They looked put out and a bit concerned. A few kept glancing at the entrance to their dorm, expectantly.

As we stepped through the crowd, a few recognized Sarya and nervously waved. Oddly enough, several of the onlookers pointed at me, displaying looks of distaste and even shock. They knew me, but I had no clue who they were.

A large woman with orange skin and long purple hair cornered Sarya. Even in pajamas, it was apparent she was a warrior and used to dealing deathblows more than pillow talk. She too had wings, but unlike Sarya's wings, hers were scaly. Her large eyes stared at me as she talked to my fairy escort. "Sarya, where have you been all night? You've missed all the ruckus."

Sarya bowed slightly. "Lady Laroque, my apologies for not telling you of my whereabouts. I was engaged in a rescue." She nodded at me. "Irving, this fine warrior princess is my roommate."

Sensing I needed to be formal, I managed an awkward bow.

Lady Laroque sized me up. "This little one detained you? He's the Wishbutton fellow, isn't he? He's the reason our domicile is in turmoil."

"What do you mean? Is it his sister?" Sarya strained to look around her roommate.

Lady Laroque said, "Yes, she's filled with madness. She is why we are out here right now. Luckily, Harmstrike responded quickly and is dealing with her."

I tried to go around the warrior princess. She stopped me with an outthrust hand. Her grip on my upper arm was vise tight.

I protested, "Hey, I need to get to her. She's not in her right mind."

Lady Laroque said, "I'll say. She is in a berserker's rage! Clawing at any who get too close, flinging anything on hand at those who approach her."

Before I could inquire further, we were distracted by screaming and growling coming from the entrance. Exiting the dorm, held in check in a floating magic bubble, was my sister. She was in a fit of rage, snapping her jaw at the two wizards that flanked her and who generated the magic that held her captive. Behind them, Harmstrike strolled down the steps. His eyes were on me and not my sister.

I raced toward Tyler. One of the wizards used his free hand to fling a bolt of magic at me. I sidestepped it and kept coming. It was then that Harmstrike intervened. He grabbed hold of my wrists with a speed that defied his age.

"She can no longer hurt herself or others right now, Irving. Let my wizards take her somewhere safe, while you tell me what happened," he said as he guided me off to the side away from the crowd.

Sarya moved to follow, but Harmstrike waved her way. She complied.

"It's not really Tyler in there," I said, not taking my eyes off my sister.

Harmstrike released me. "Yes, I gathered as much. From what I know of your sister, savagery is not one of her traits. I was called here because she attacked her dormmates in the middle of the night."

"My writer switched her with one of my monsters, the Triceramedusoid. It's in her head right now." I puffed out my chest.

"And you saw this happen or was it just your link to your writer that informed you of this gamechanger?" Harmstrike didn't turn around to watch the wizards cart off my sister. I got the feeling he already knew where they were taking her.

"You know where I was. Don't pretend you don't," I snarled.

"Whatever do you mean?" Harmstrike's eyes widened, and he cast an innocent look across his face.

"I was at the Menagerie with Fenwick, your little stooge. You'll be happy to know he did exactly as you wanted him to. He walked me right up to my beast and flung me in the water with it. If my author hadn't done the switch, I would've been gobbled up." I clenched my fists.

He put his hands on my shoulders. "Irving, slow down. What are you talking about?"

"You blackmailed Fenwick so he would get rid of me!" I snapped.

Harmstrike played his reactions perfectly. To anyone listening to us, it would appear I was the irrational one, the one who was making up lies. He kept his tone even, discreet. "I understand your nerves are frazzled. There's no reason to toss out such hurtful accusations. I would never seek to harm any of my students, no matter how trying they are to my school."

I shrugged my shoulders to ward off his consoling hands. "Fenwick told me all of it! You took his mom away from him. I don't blame him. He only tried to hurt me because he wanted her back. He was only doing your dirty work." I looked over at Sarya who waved a fist of support at me.

"Young, misguided Fenwick told you this? That I stole away his mother and forced him to try and kill you? Do you realize how crazy that sounds?" Harmstrike steepled his hands in front of his chin and rolled his eyes upward.

"You've had it in for me since the beginning. Don't try to deny it!" I shouted, playing my unhinged part a bit too well. Several girls looked at me with mistrust.

"Irving, settle down. You don't want to do this. You're putting too much stock in what Fenwick said. He's a very troubled boy. I did take his mother away from him today, but not for the reason he gave you."

I waited for him to explain. I knew what he would say next would be a lie. After all, he didn't know I had overheard his threat to Fenwick at the Infirmary. How could he? I had been in Gared's body at the time.

"He attacked his mother quite viciously. It's the new nature of the curse they are under. Apparently, their writer added another layer to their predicament. Can't say it sits well with me to have such an ill-mannered young man here, but I do what I must. I removed her from him for the next day or so until this particular part of their curse cycles through. Some nonsense about being driven mad every fifth day. Quite random, but I guess it will all make sense once Fenwick's book is done."

He was very convincing. His answer sounded rehearsed, almost as if he expected to have to tell me this from the start of his conspiracy.

"Whatever Fenwick did to you at the Menagerie, which I might add is off limits to you, he did with his own agenda. I have no idea why he would try to harm you. I'm only glad that his attempt failed." He paused. "This new development with your sister, I know it's wearing on you. I will forgive your little trespassing foray in the Menagerie if you agree to get yourself over to Hero Row tomorrow morning and get situated. I'm so pleased to see you're no longer a smudge." Harmstrike smiled, holding his grin for far too long.

I didn't know how to respond. I knew he was lying, but I saw no advantage to calling him out on it. I hated that I had to go along with his plan for now, but with Tyler being under his care, I couldn't risk being too bold.

"Okay, but please keep me informed about my sister. Don't hurt her," I said.

"With your close relationship with your author, I suspect you'll know of her recovery before I do." He turned to walk away, but hesitated. He swiveled back around and wagged a finger at me. "Tell you what, I know it's against the rules to allow this, but I do think you've been through an awful lot. How would you like to have your father visit you tomorrow over at your new place in Hero Row?"

I nodded. Sarya approached me as she saw the dean leave.

"Splendid, I'll make the arrangements," he piped as he quickened his step to catch up to the wizards removing my sister from the building.

Once Harmstrike was out of earshot, Sarya said, "I heard the whole thing, Irving. Harmstrike is lying."

"I know," I said, watching the dean finally catch up with my sister and her magical entourage.

The dean looked back at me and waved.

I didn't return the wave.

"He told you to get settled in Hero Row. Are you?" Sarya asked.

"No, Smudge Hall is my base of operations now. He can't get to me there."

"Good, I was hoping you'd say that. As long as you're there, he can't do anything to you. I'm not even sure if you should risk going to class right now."

I looked at Sarya. "Oh, I'll set up shop at Smudge Hall, but I'm not going to hide myself away. I have somewhere special to go tomorrow. I promised a friend that much. I'm not going to let Harmstrike get in my way now that I know his intentions."

I turned away and started walking in the direction of Smudge Hall. I needed to get a little rest before the morning. I hoped it would be enough. Roon's mission to Revision Ravine filled my head. I certainly didn't want to give any more thought to the mess with Harmstrike and my sister. It hurt too much.

"What does that mean, Irving? What are you planning to do?" she pleaded. "Irving, answer me!"

I kept walking. Better to have her mad at me than to drag her any closer to the danger that swarmed around me.

Chapter 67
CONVERSATIONAL SPARK

He had to rework a total of six scenes to incorporate the father's different take on the wishjacket. He was pleased with how the father came off as still supportive, but was wary of allowing Irving to fully sign on to the Wellwishers. It was becoming clear that he thought the idea of Wish Haven was good, but that the Wellwishers had corrupted their original mission. This trepidation had been picked up by Irving, but even more by Tyler. Her role emerged more in the rewritten scenes, giving her a stronger personality and contrasting her logic with Irving's emotional nature.

He printed out the revised chapters and added them to his binder. Next weekend, he'd begin work on the Teardrop chapter. With the new back story, he was really looking forward to what would happen next.

* * *

I was plagued with questions on my return trek to Smudge Hall. It was becoming difficult to keep events at the school straight from what my author was revealing about my written story. With Tyler becoming more a part of my life at the Academy, I was starting to understand the dean's edict against letting cast members associate with each other. It certainly complicated matters. Couple that with how I was treating Sarya, and I felt thoroughly miserable. Why was I keeping her at a distance? Sure, I was telling her some things, but leaving her out of others. How I had walked away from her just now didn't feel right. And why was I not telling her about what Roon and I had planned? Wouldn't that infuriate her to find me gone tomorrow?

As I trudged up the steps of Smudge Hall, I noticed light coming from my window. Had Simon returned? I rushed inside and upstairs.

I entered my room. Sitting on the desk was my roommate. I tried to do more than frown but failed. I shuffled over to my bed and collapsed into a ball.

Simon floated over to me, reaching out an ashen tentacle to nudge me. "What's with the sour face?"

I rolled over to face my roommate. His tentacle retreated. "Everything is getting messed up."

He said, "Sounds like you have a story to tell. Why don't you spill it? I like when others tell me tales."

"I'm surprised you don't know about it all already. Between you and Harmstrike, you both know things way before anyone else," I said, sounding resentful.

"Well, I do try to keep up on current events, especially the happenings around you. Let's just say I missed some stuff, that I was indisposed for a while." Simon slipped over to his bed and coalesced into a pile.

It was rather comical to see him. I don't know how, and maybe I was reading too much into it, but my roommate, a pile of ash, looked altogether expectant.

I told him about all the events with Tyler and her injury. When I spoke of using my wishjacket to switch bodies with Gared to sneak into see her, he soaked it in with keen intent. I told him about my resolution to stay at Smudge Hall, even though I was no longer a smudge. With that, he nodded in approval. I shared how Fenwick had been forced to try and kill me at the Menagerie. How he had originally called me there to speak ill of Harmstrike. He was especially interested in how my author's actions influenced my rescue from the Triceramedusoid. I concluded with the lies Harmstrike spread outside of my sister's dorm and my helpless feeling at seeing her being taken away still in a berserker's rage thanks to her mind not being her own.

"Every time I make contact with my sister, something bad happens. Harmstrike's rule of keeping us apart is starting to make sense," I said, exhausted at finishing my summary.

"Nonsense. You have to forge ahead, Irving. It's your actions that are critical here. You must see that Harmstrike will do anything to prevent you from finishing what you have started."

"That's just it, what have I started? You keep telling me that I'm to do something important, that Harmstrike is evil, and I have to get rid of him. Why? Doesn't this place need someone to run it? Why is he not the right person?" I clamped my hands down on either side of my skull, rubbing at my scalp with intensity. "I can't think straight. There's too much bearing down on me. Between the events happening here and what my author throws at me, it's too much!" I weakly thumped a fist into my pillow.

Simon returned to the air, hovering slightly above me. "If it were too much, you wouldn't be here talking to me. You wouldn't be planning to stay at Smudge Hall despite your rightful home now being touted as Hero Row." He hesitated. "Most important of all, you wouldn't be contemplating the next step."

"Which is?"

"Accompanying your vampire friend to Revision Ravine," he stated.

"How'd you know? I never told you that. Where did you find that out?"

The ash floated away. "I can't tell you everything all at once. I must dole it out so you can move forward with purpose. If I told you everything, it might just freeze you into inaction, and we can't have that."

I whined, "I don't understand. You tell me you can't say too much because I can't handle it, then you turn around and tell me to handle all the other stuff thrown at me. Which is it? Why is everything so delicate? Why is this all falling on me?"

"Because, Irving, this place needs a wishtaker, not a wishmaker."

What he said made little sense. "This wish business alone is so confusing. What my author does only makes things worse."

"Does he? From what you related to me, it was only through the tools he fashioned for you that you were able to aid your sister, uncover Harmstrike's lies, and save your own hide. I would think you're not looking at your author in the right light." The ash maintained his calm air.

"But it doesn't seem fair. Why does he make all the decisions? Why does what he says go?"

"Free will is there if you look for it, just as enslavement can be seen if you give it regard. You interpret what's in front of you, Irving. You have a say while here at the Academy." Simon started to curl in on himself, preparing to warp away once again. "Go with Roon. She needs you. Your quest will show you where to go next. Remember, your author will bring you strength, not weakness."

He disappeared, and I was alone. The walls closed in on me.

I shook my head, attempting to clear it. I pondered what he had said. He spoke in riddles. I had no idea what he really wanted of me. I forced a different thought into my head. I looked past my room. I looked beyond the unsettled night. I dwelled on Sarya, the fairy who had supported me through all my endeavors. I focused on Roon, the vampire who would never admit she needed my help. I even considered Gared and Raggleswamp, displaced characters who I had written off as villains. Everyone was evolving, changing into something more because of their author and themselves.

Then and there, for the first time since arriving at the Questing Academy, I realized I was strong, that I was more than someone else's thoughts put to paper. I realized I was not alone, that through those around me, I was something more.

I was a hero with a cast, a rather odd batch of characters but mine while I stayed here at the academy. And right now, one of them needed me.

I turned out the light, anticipating for the first time what tomorrow would reveal about me and my quest. It felt good to have a clear mission in mind.

To Be Continued in Book Two: Revision Ravine

Acknowledgments

Extreme thanks to Keith Robinson for all the amazing back-and-forth. Special thanks to my fifth grade class of 2018. I read this to them, and we found some fixes to make to the original that greatly improve this edition.